This edition of *The Book of Bunk* is limited to
400 numbered copies and 15 lettered copies.

This is copy

80

THE BOOK OF BUNK

A Fairy Tale of the Federal Writers' Project

by

Glen Hirshberg

THE BOOK OF BUNK

A Fairy Tale of the Federal Writers' Project

by

Glen Hirshberg

Earthling Publications – 2010

First edition, first printing
December 2010

ISBN-13: 978-0-9795054-9-2
ISBN: 0-9795054-9-6

EARTHLING PUBLICATIONS
P.O. Box 413
Northborough, MA 01532 USA
Email: earthlingpub@yahoo.com
Website: www.earthlingpub.com

Author's website: http://www.glenhirshberg.com/

Printed in the U.S.A.

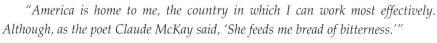

"America is home to me, the country in which I can work most effectively. Although, as the poet Claude McKay said, 'She feeds me bread of bitterness.'"
— Robert Hayden in *World Order 10, no. 2,* Winter 1975-76

For Meir Ribalow, Earl Ganz, Michael Seidel, Bryan Di Salvatore, and Bharati Mukherjee, who took me more seriously than I deserved, inspired me more than they realized, and taught me more than even I will ever know.

And for Kim, Sid and Kate, with storytelling.

April 1938, Erie, Pennsylvania

I didn't hear the knocks over the thunder. For the better part of an hour, I'd been sitting on the plywood slab that served as my bed, watching lightning shoot up the cracks in the walls. The soreness in my shoulders and legs and back felt almost sweet, but the ache from the wound in my side was stronger at night. I had my hand over it, and I was humming that song I learned from Grace Lowie on the day I met her, when another barrage of knocks rattled my door on its rusted hinges.

"Dent!" came my landlord's snarl. "You in there? You drunk?"

"I'm here," I said.

"Phone call."

I stared at the door. "What?"

"Calls himself the Senator."

"Son of a bitch." I stood up too fast, and the scar along my ribs stretched. I couldn't get used to the sensation.

The bald, hunched old man who owned the boarding house was already halfway back down the stairs to his bourbon. Along the corridor below, several of my cohabitants lingered in their doorways, smoking and looking out the front window at the rain. Most of them worked the docks with me. Their eyes followed me lazily as I made my way down to the hall phone, picked up the receiver off the top of the box, and turned toward the wall.

"How'd you find me?" I asked.

"Mrs. Duarte was delighted to help," said Lewis. "Erie, Pennsylvania. Interesting choice, Paul. What are you doing there?"

"Dockwork."

"No kidding? Dad would be proud. Are your lungs holding up?"

"Most of the time."

"I told you it was all in your head."

"Can I go now?"

"I'm calling to let you know you're about to get a congressional subpoena."

I put my hand against the wall and felt the drum of rain and imagined the soft scurrying of termites eating this house to its rotting foundations.

"You're out of your mind," I said.

"It wasn't my idea. You never were one for reading the papers, but you must have heard that most of the Works projects—and the Writers' Project in particular—aren't exactly at their peak of popularity. There are new hearings every day. Everyone's got their eyes open for swindles or Communists, and the knives are out."

"We didn't swindle anyone, and you know it."

"Well then, come on down to our nation's capital and tell my new colleagues just that. With any luck, your hearing will get lost among the many. They're just digging around, right now. They don't know what they're looking for."

"Lewis. If you make me do this, I'm going tell them about you."

He was silent for a moment. Then he said, "No. I don't think you will—assuming you want this to go away quickly. Plus, Grace's fame is so new. It wouldn't take much to destroy her reputation, and I know you don't want to do that…"

"You really are a son of a bitch. You always were."

"That's *Senator* Son of a Bitch to you, little brother."

"*Senator.* What's your new name again, now that you've ditched ours? I keep forgetting." I injected as much disdain into the question as I could muster.

"I am currently Senator L. Bertram Asbury. The L stands for Lewis. I kept that. You might want to write the rest down."

"Is Scott being subpoenaed?"

"Perhaps, although he didn't play all that key a role in what happened. And inviting him would turn the whole thing into even more of a circus than it already promises to be. I don't think my colleagues have the nerve. Not yet, anyway."

A flash of lightning played over the wall in front of me.

"When?" I asked eventually.

"Soon, Paul. I'll see you soon."

I hung up the phone, and the whole thing started playing out in my head yet again. There was no way to stop it. I stumbled back to my room and let it come.

PART ONE

The Old World

"These were his dying words, and the dying words, it seemed to me, of generations of storytellers, for how could this snowy and trumped-up pass, with its trio of travelers, hope to celebrate a world that lies spread out around us like a bewildering and stupendous dream?"
— John Cheever
from "A Miscellany of Characters That Will Not Appear"

1 – March 1936, Blackcreek, Oklahoma

Both of us had our hands on our father when he died. My brother Lewis was pressing his palms with surprising tenderness into the V of Dad's nightshirt. My own much smaller hands were palms-down on the bed, and I was leaning over my father's face. I put two fingers on his throat. It felt like a little bird had flown in there by mistake and was beating around frantically trying to find a way out.

The moment it was over, Lewis left the room and went downstairs. For a few minutes, I heard only prairie wind, freezing whatever grass there was outside and pushing at the warping walls of our tottering wood-frame house. At least there was no dust left for it to fling. Eventually, I heard murmuring as old, blind Lamplighter Johnson, who'd lost each of his eyes in separate incidents at the rail yard, recommenced his usual chatter, then a clang as Lewis banged a pan down on the stove. I started for the door, then stopped and looked back. My father didn't look any more peaceful dead than he had alive. More than anything—with his mouth open, his chest flat, one empty hand palm-upward on the sheet—he looked hungry.

When I entered the kitchen, Lamplighter was hunched in the shadows over the kitchen table, his blind gaze aimed somewhere to Lewis's right, babbling about trains. He was still wearing his old railroad uniform, though it hung even more absurdly off his skeletal shoulders, as if the uniform itself were consuming him.

At the stove, Lewis was still banging things. It made me nervous.

"Thanks for sending the telegram about Dad," I said to Lamplighter, moving toward the table, though there was only the one chair there.

"Yeah," Lewis muttered flatly. "Otherwise, we'd never have known."

"Shut up, Lewis," I said. He turned. His grin, as usual, alarmed me.

"Aw, now, of course I sent it." Lamplighter swung his head in my direction. Unlike other blind people I'd seen, he seemed unable to locate the face of the person speaking to him. Or maybe he'd just learned to look askance, stay deferential. "He asked me to. And your father, he never asked no one for nothing."

"And there it is," Lewis said. "The epitaph Dad always dreamed of. Let's go scratch that in the dirt out there, huh, Paul?"

Lewis had moved the only working bulb from the lamp in the front room to the one on the kitchen counter. The light made his hair look surprisingly bright, almost golden, like sloppily stacked hay.

"Shit, Lewis," I said abruptly. "We've got to bury him."

"Now, young Paul," Lamplighter started, "you make it sound—"

"Like a chore," said Lewis, turning straight to Lamplighter, and the old man went quiet. If he'd had a gaze, it would have been aimed at his knees. "Like something I guess we should up and goddamn do."

Shutting off the stove, Lewis strode out of the room and back upstairs. Lamplighter just sat, deflated, like a scarecrow with the stuffing pulled out.

By the time I got to the bedroom, Lewis had already wrapped our father's body in the sheets.

"What are you so mad about?" I asked.

"Mad?"

"You ought to be decent to Lamplighter. He was the closest thing to a friend Dad had. He took care of him when we left."

"I haven't punched him or thrown him out, have I? I'm treating him exactly the way Dad did."

"Right. You're humiliating him. You do realize that Lamplighter thinks he's taking care of us?"

"Well, that would make him just plain stupid. Oh, wait, he is stupid."

The long walk we'd had to get here—and the rides from Stillwater I'd hitched before that, and the thirty-six hours of watching our father kick and claw toward death without ever once waking up—dropped down on me. I leaned my hip against the splintering post of the bed.

"Do you think Dad actually wanted to see us?" I asked.

"Hmm," said Lewis. "Good question. Tell you what, I'll give you the choice. Head or feet?"

After that, we didn't talk. We hoisted our father between us. He was lighter than I thought he'd be. We carried him outside and down the little grade to where the creek used to be before the dust choked it. Lamplighter followed with a shovel, which he handed to me.

Lewis let me take the first couple of chops at the hard, frozen earth. But as soon as I started coughing, he laughed, grabbed the shovel, and pushed me aside. Our breaths streamed in icy, sparkling clouds. Around us, the bare maples leaned or hunched in what was left of the grass. A few hundred yards away, the scatter of buildings that constituted our town lay utterly silent, looking even more abandoned than they actually were. Lamplighter crouched by the body, and once I saw him stretch out his hand toward my father's chest, but he didn't touch him.

When the digging was done, Lewis and I laid our father in the ground, and I stood by the hole, staring down. It was only when my brother offered me the first scoop of covering earth that I felt a lone, shooting spark in my chest.

"You're thinking maybe you should say something," Lamplighter said. To my amazement, he put his hand on my shoulder. Lamplighter always kept everything but his babble to himself. His fingers felt pitifully cold, devoid of skin, like a crow's talons.

I waited for Lewis to laugh or swear or push Lamplighter away. But he just stood there. And when I glanced at the old man, I saw the ridiculous patches over his eyes, with the pennies our father had drawn there. As a cruel joke, I'd always thought. Dead-man's eyes, though Lamplighter thought it was funny.

Old Lamp's always going to get his two cents in," my father would say.

"Adios, Dad," I said, my voice flat. "You weren't the worst dad in the world."

"Or even in Blackcreek," Lewis added. I didn't think he was joking, though Lamplighter probably suspected he was.

"I hope the air goes down easier in heaven." I dumped the spadeful of earth into the hole. It made a hard, thunking sound.

"Amen," said Lamplighter.

"Hope there's someone up there to fight," Lewis murmured.

Hope the memory of your boys makes you happier than your boys did, I thought.

Lewis finished filling the grave in a matter of minutes. We turned for the house, but Lamplighter moved away, starting around the side toward the dirt road out front.

"Hey, Lamplighter," I called. "Don't you want some food? We'll make you some."

The old man swung around, his penny eyes aimed in the general direction of the grave. He smiled slowly. "Don't worry, young Paul. I done ate any food your daddy had in the house a long time ago."

Lewis's laugh came out as icy as his breath. "I like that," he said. "Good man."

I stayed alone just a few seconds longer in the night wind. Ten years or so before, when I was a grade-school boy and the ground stayed put and the grass grew high, the wind made sound as it ripped through here. Now, it was just a constant, relentless pressure.

Inside, Lewis had located eggs somehow, and he was whistling a tune as he cracked them into a frying pan. They smelled so good that I thought I might faint. Settling myself in the kitchen's lone wooden chair, I propped my elbows on the slab of pine that Dad had salvaged from the rail yard to use as a table.

Lewis chiseled around the eggs with a fork, then turned with the pan in his hands and shoveled one perfect, sunny-side egg onto each of the chipped plates he'd found in the cupboard. He offered the first plate to me, and I noticed his knuckles, fat from boxing. The burns on the insides of his arms formed purple and black furrows all the way past his elbows. Lewis saw me looking and held them up.

"Stars and stripes," he said.

I ate slowly, out of long habit. I wanted the egg to last. My brother sucked up his in two dripping forkfuls, then glanced around the kitchen as though considering ordering another. Through the window, in the moonlight, I could see the empty Gunderson house with its roof caving in under the weight of accumulated ice.

Twirling a cigarette out of his shirt pocket, Lewis popped it in his mouth, felt his pants for a match, and stopped when he saw me glaring. He stood up. "Forgot. Dad's lungs live on in you." He patted me on the back as he went toward the front room.

"Where are you going?"

"Town Couch," Lewis said, shrugging into the heavy work shirt that passed for his coat. "It's still there, isn't it?" Then he spread his hands. "It's all there is to do, little brother. Come announce, like you did that one time."

"I was making fun of you."

Lewis nodded. "It was good."

For the first time in ages, I thought of our mother, who'd slipped off one night when we were very young to go back East to her family and never sent one word, ever.

"You going back to that school?" Lewis asked abruptly.

I shook my head.

"Why not?"

"Didn't feel right."

"Guess we'll have to figure out something else to do with you."

"Not your problem."

"I have no problems, Soft-Paul. None at all."

The wind poured in when he opened the door, and swept him out.

June 1938, Washington DC

All three senators entered the chamber together, and the flags on the wall behind them rippled with their passing. The trembling in my hands, which had plagued me throughout the administering of the oath, had ceased. On the far left-hand edge of the dais, a garishly thin brunette in a white dress looked up from the nails she'd been filing ever since she'd led me through the hallways of the Capitol, down two towering staircases, and through the double doors at the back of this room. Standing, smoothing her dress, the woman waited until the senators had each found places behind their nameplates at the long table up on the dais, then slipped into her seat, her hands on the keys of her typewriter. Behind me, the little knot of reporters in white shirts and dark ties stopped chattering and leaned back in their hard wooden chairs.

I sat at the desk they'd provided me and tried not to look up. I didn't want to see Lewis's face, and I didn't want to give him the pleasure of my reaction.

"Mr...." boomed a voice, and my eyes lifted into a cloud of gray smoke billowing off the podium. Flags had been mounted on the wood-paneled wall at perfect forty-five-degree angles like the wings of some gloriously plumaged bird.

"Dent, is it?" the voice said, while the first tendril of smoke slipped down my asthmatic lungs and curled there like a snake. I started coughing. My eyes began to water. Senator Archibald Froad leaned forward, and I got my first good glimpse of him through tears and smoke.

His cheeks puffed out in fat, warty rolls. The skin cancer that would eventually kill him had already left crusty black spots across his nose and forehead and the rim of his upper lip. But on this day, he didn't appear so much diseased as amphibious.

I raised one hand, and Lewis spoke for the first time. "Mr. Dent suffers from a severe and at times debilitating respiratory condition." He was talking as if he had that information in the notes on the table in front of him. Perhaps he did. "So I'm afraid that your delicious cigar—which I and all the proud people of South Carolina are delighted to see you're enjoying, by the way—will have to be put out."

Finally, I swung my head in my brother's direction. There it was: that relentless, ruthless smile, the voice that had hounded me since the day I was born, instantly recognizable despite the new, exaggerated accent—all Bradford pears and lemonade—layered over our flat prairie cadence. He wore a cream-colored suit and yellow tie that matched his thatched hair. His outsized, perennially swollen hands lay neatly folded before him. There was a last moment of quiet, and Lewis's gaze met mine for the first time since the night Bunk County burned. He was searching my face, tilting his head. If I hadn't known better, I'd have mistaken his expression for empathy.

Senator Froad ground his cigar into a silver plate and glared at me. If he'd noticed anything that had passed between Lewis and me, he didn't say so.

"Froad, Goddamnit," said Senator Norman Cain on Froad's left, his fuzzy red mustache curling on his upper lip like a foxtail. He slammed a pencil on the tabletop, and the noise echoed around the hall. "I don't know what favors you called in to get yourself appointed head of this committee, but you're not going to stall your way out of doing your job anymore. Not one more day. Martin Dies isn't playing, and neither are the rest of us."

"Representative Martin Dies is a loudmouth, a political opportunist, a coward, and a traitor to the hungry, jobless, determined people who make up his own constituency," said Froad.

"Representative Martin Dies is a rare Democrat these days. He's honest and intelligent and brave enough to recognize when an absurd experiment has gone not just sour but dangerously wrong. The WPA, this so-called 'New Deal' which he initially supported, like so many other well-meaning crusaders blinded by the demagogue we call our President—has proven not only to be the most colossal waste of public money in the history of this nation, but a threat to everything we hold dear. To democracy, and to freedom itself. Martin Dies is protecting the nation. He may even be saving it."

Yawning, Senator Froad turned to my brother. "Ready, Senator Asbury? I think I'm almost ready. Anyone need coffee first?"

"Even Roosevelt knows the jig is up, Froad," said the senator with the mustache. "Even he has barely said a word against these hearings. So come on. Face the truth, like the great man I know you are. Let's see today's boondoggle, shall we?"

"Ah, yes, Norman," said Senator Froad, stretching in his chair and flipping open a file folder in front of him. "Your daily boondoggle. Surely if you and the Republican party and Representative Dies and the rest of his carefully unbalanced team on the...wait, let me get the name just right...House Un-American Activities Committee...keep pointing at everything you see, someone will finally stand up and confess. You want the hearings to begin? All right, let's begin.

"Mr. Dent, this is an exploratory committee only. We are here neither to aid nor to challenge the work of the House Un-American Activities Committee, which will hold hearings later this summer and try to identify and root out the fascists and radicals they are convinced have commandeered the Works Progress Administration. Instead, we are conducting our own investigation into the nature of the work being done in the WPA's name. We hope this will provide a more...*accurate* picture than the one we fear our colleagues on the House Committee may already be drawing."

"Froad," growled Senator Cain.

"Mr. Dent," said Senator Froad, "are you a Nazi?"

My hands froze on the desktop. "What?"

"No? A Communist, then? How about a Socialist? Do you have Marxist leanings and a desire to foment a revolution that will overthrow this cruel, unjust, government of the rich by the rich for the rich once and for all? No again? Good. We've got that out of the way. Too bad, because 'Communist' is Norman here's favorite word. After 'boondoggle'."

Senator Cain sighed. "Please, Froad. Enough with the grandstanding. It just isn't going to work anymore. Not for you, not for Harry Hopkins and the rest of the WPA apologists. We have the business of the country to conduct. A dictator to contain."

"By which I know you mean Hitler or Mussolini," Senator Froad said, his mood brightening.

"You know who I mean."

"Well, now." For the first time, Senator Froad's voice went quiet. Even my brother straightened in his chair.

My gaze fixed on the warty man's mouth.

"Mr. Dent, this passionate person with the remarkably exuberant facial hair is Senator Norman Cain of Missouri. He doesn't think much of our Mr. Roosevelt, believes the WPA has long since run its dubious course, and— correct me if I misrepresent you, Norman—harbors a particular disdain for the radicals and freeboaters he believes make up the entirety of the Federal

Writers' Project."

Senator Cain inclined his head toward me. In my lungs, the coil of smoke twitched, and I coughed hard again. Senator Cain continued scowling.

"And this nattily dressed young fellow here," said Senator Froad, gesturing to his right, "is our recently elected junior member from the great Palmetto state of South Carolina, Senator L. Bertram Asbury. He is, I am fairly certain, a clever young wolf in our orchard of state. I have no idea what he thinks of you, or me either, for that matter. I suggest you remain wary when he speaks, as I have already learned to be."

"Froad, *please*," murmured Senator Cain.

"And I am Senator Archibald Froad of Virginia. Froad, to my friends. Senator to you, or Sir. I am a close personal companion of the President's, and when he gives his fireside chats, I am generally listening from beside his chair. I was one of the architects of the Federal Writers' Project, and may be its principal remaining defender. I believe in it profoundly. And that leaves me at something of a loss about what to make of you and your…band of vandals? Too harsh, do you think? Co-conspirators, perhaps?"

I had no answer.

"Right. Well. Before my esteemed friend from Missouri launches himself clean out of that mustache he's worked so hard to cultivate, what do you say we leap right in? You have been subpoenaed and brought here, young man, because of your established connection with the so-called Scott Set, who do indeed appear to have grievously abused the trust placed in them by this government, and in so doing called into question the validity of everything so many other writers and administrators and elected officials have worked so hard to achieve. Your group also may or may not have directly or indirectly caused the devastating conflagration referred to in at least three places in the just-withdrawn preliminary manuscript of the *WPA Guide to the Old North State* as the 'Great Ashton Fire of 1936.'"

On the dais, my brother shifted his whole body away from me. Senator Froad leaned back and folded his arms. When he spoke again, his voice was quieter and infinitely more threatening.

"We're waiting, Mr. Dent."

"I…" I started, faltered. Even *my* voice echoed in that room. "I don't quite know where to begin. Sir."

Senator Cain grunted. "A writer, and no mistake, eh, Froad? Remind me, Mr. Dent, though I'm sure I've got it here somewhere. Where are you from, originally?"

"Oklahoma. Blackcreek, Oklahoma." I almost told them about Lewis—unmasked him—right there.

"Practically adjacent to North Carolina, right, Froad? Might as well be a sister state. Which makes our young Mr. Dent here yet another talent expertly introducing the entire New Dependent—oh, sorry, New Deal—nation to terrain he knows like the back of his spotless hand." Tobacco thwacked from under Senator Cain's mustache into a silver plate on the table.

Senator Froad sighed. "Just begin at the beginning, Mr. Dent. Blackcreek, I believe you said?"

2 – March 1936

Halfway up the ridge at the eastern edge of town, I dropped my pack on the ground and sat. After the dimness of my father's house, I couldn't seem to get my eyes adjusted to the moonlight, and my hands were freezing in their tattered work gloves. I took long, slow breaths as the wind's knife edge slit the sealed-up places in my lungs like a letter opener. Every time I exhaled, I made the wheezing noise that amused Lewis no end.

"Bird lungs," he'd say happily. "Tweet tweet tweet."

Down below, where he was, the remaining structures of Blackcreek lay in the dead grass like lifeboats roped together. Everywhere, roofs sagged and window holes gaped. The petrol station that had lasted all of three years was marked only by bits of pump sticking sideways out of the ground like the last, forgotten stakes from the great Sooner land run, when 50,000 desperate settlers had hurtled off at the crack of a gun into two million acres of newly opened Indian land in hope of throwing down claims.

By now, Lewis would have reached Town Couch, which had been the Gunderson's couch before old man Gunderson dragged it down to the market square on the day that he took his girls and fled. Perched on an arm rest, oblivious to the cold, Lewis would be whistling a tune as he waited for the CCC boys so he could beat someone bloody. Then, somehow, they'd all be buying him beers at the town's only surviving pub and hanging around him the whole night without ever knowing quite why.

The train whistle, sounding far away and as high and wild as a coyote howl, brought me to my feet. I was staring through the flecks of spring snow or ice-coated dust or whatever it was flicking around in the air. At this distance, all I could see was a black hump nosing through the dead, white grass.

I hadn't thought I'd actually leave until right then. My brother always took more chances than I did. Many more. But his were planned.

I moved fast through the copses of redbud trees at the top of the ridge. Newly bloomed leaves twitched like butterfly wings. They'd opened too soon. The cold would kill them. Off the other side of the ridge, I could see the uniform wooden cabins built by the Civilian Conservation Corps when they first arrived here with their government mandate to plant trees and build facilities and a road for two state parks in the dead prairie grass.

Ginny Gunderson and I had once snuck into one of those cabins while the Corps members were in town getting beaten up by Lewis. She told me I was the only boy in Blackcreek she liked because I never hurt anybody. I told her that was only because I couldn't, and she said it didn't matter. Then she sat down on a bunk and removed the floppy hat she always wore. I sat down next to her. It was even colder in there than it was outside. She kissed me, and I touched her breast through her sweater. It wasn't the first time, but she wasn't paying much attention.

"Dust cow," she said.

"Protect us," I finished. It was our oldest shared joke, the only one we had left. A few days after that, she and her family fled Blackcreek for good.

The train reached town more quickly than I expected. I watched it thunder through what had been our station without so much as a whistle. Its frozen wheels shrieked. I scrambled down the far side of the grassy, root-riddled slope toward the grove of redbuds clustered at the edge of the tracks. This was the invisible boundary of Blackcreek. Soon the town itself would be invisible, too.

For Lewis, hopping a boxcar was like wading a river. He just lifted his foot, and the movement took him. It wasn't so difficult for me, either. But the penalties for failure were greater. More than once, I'd been slammed into the dirt on my back, then lain there with my lungs paralyzed and my ribs wide open, powerless to catch or cradle the air as it roared through me.

But this night—almost as if it knew—the train rumbled to within a few hundred yards of me and, inexplicably, began to slow. The big, black engine shuddered, its stacks spitting steam. The hundred or so cars chained to it clattered in their couplings like herded cattle. By the time the first gondola passed my hiding place, they were moving no more than fifteen miles an hour and still slowing down. I moved to the edge of the trees, and counted at least twelve wooden boxcars. The fourth one had a suspended steel stepladder, and also a half-open door juddering brokenly on its runners. I stepped from the shadows and led with my legs. The train's momentum lifted me momentarily off the ground, and I felt the great chugging wheels beating through the cold steel under my feet.

A voice from the dimness of the boxcar said, "Nope."

Suddenly, I was ripped from the rungs, flying backwards. I hit the ground hard on my back, and breath sailed out of me.

Lewis waited until he saw my chest move before kicking me. He kicked my legs, not my gut, but he did it five, six, eight times. The stony toe of his boot pummeled my thighs and my kneecaps. He made no sound. I curled up and waited for him to finish.

Finally, he flopped down in a swatch of snow and sighed, then patted my back as if we'd just finished pitching a tent together.

"Big moon," he said.

I winced and opened my eyes. The moon was enormous, floating low over the prairie like an airship. My breaths came short but steady. No wheeze. I sat up.

Lewis had crossed his knees and was squeezing fistfuls of snow and grass. Stray strands of hair stuck out sideways all over his scalp. Under the ragged wool of his white sweater, I could see his shoulders heaving, and I realized he'd been running.

"How'd you know I was going?" I asked.

He shrugged. "You managed to find me after you got Lamplighter's telegram, didn't you?"

"You leave a trail, Lewis."

He smiled, stared at the moon, and I glanced down the tracks. While my brother had been kicking me, the train I'd tried to jump had eased to a complete stop. Not fifty feet from where I'd fallen, I could see the boxcar with the broken door.

"What happened to the CCC boys you were going to fight?"

"They're certainly not at Town Couch," Lewis said, and pulled me to my feet as he stood up. Hands in his pockets, he took a few desultory steps down the tracks. "That train's practically sending a carriage for you, Soft-Paul. Better hurry."

"You're letting me go?"

"Like I could ever stop you."

I glanced down at the imprint my body had crushed into the sopping grass. "You gave it a good shot."

"Didn't say I wouldn't make you pay."

"You're actually angry that I'm leaving?"

Lewis's laugh came out cruel, as usual. "I just wanted to make sure you had something to remember me by, little brother."

We set off together down the line. Thirty feet from the boxcar, Lewis stopped. "You sure you don't want to go back to that school? Sometimes I think you belong there."

I shook my head. "It wasn't for me."

"So where is for you?"

"How should I know? What about you?"

He threw his arms out wide to either side, and I got one more glimpse of the burns inside his wrists where his sleeves hung slack. "Everywhere's for me. Can I give you some advice?"

"You're giving me advice, now?"

"What you're looking for isn't out there, Paul. You're not going to just hop a train and find someplace, or somebody. If you want a home, you'll have to make one." He patted me on the shoulder. I nearly punched him.

"How would you know what I want, Lewis?"

"Don't claim to. I just think maybe you should try dealing with what's in front of you for once, instead of dreaming up somewhere else all the time."

"How about I give you some advice?" I snapped. "Try talking to people instead of ripping them off trains and beating them up. They might listen."

"I do talk to people," Lewis said. "They do listen."

The train gave a great, gaseous sigh, and I knew I had to go if I was going. Fifteen feet or so from the boxcar with the open door, I remembered the voice I'd heard just as Lewis had wrenched me loose from the ladder. Right *before*, actually. From inside the boxcar, saying, "Nope."

My brother was already sliding silently away, as though he'd been uncoupled and shunted onto a siding. I couldn't help thinking about the Hooverville where I'd found him the night before. The way he'd apparently been living before I brought him home.

"Hey," I called. Lewis didn't stop, but glanced back. When he didn't say anything, I added, "I'll write you."

The smile that bloomed on my brother's face was stunning, wide open, almost sad. "You'll write me where?"

After that, we just watched each other. Eventually, I dropped my gaze to the frozen grass, and when I looked up, Lewis was no longer there. I eyed the ridge, peered into the shadows of the redbud trees. Leaves lifted and sank in the river of moonlight like a thousand little canoes pushing inland.

The train was rumbling but still hadn't moved when I reached the boxcar for the second time. I put my hands on the ladder, glancing up and down the line for railroad bulls. I couldn't see anyone. Stepping onto the first rung, I checked inside the car but couldn't make out anything in the gloom. I was on the second rung when I heard a woman's sigh.

"Listen," I called, not wanting to get kicked. "Can I come up?"

"Careful," the voice said. "Don't wake the Patrol."

The air smelled of must and, more faintly, of urine. My feet were off the ground. We hadn't even moved, and already, for one of the first times in my life, no part of me was touching Oklahoma.

Careful, the way she'd suggested, I climbed in.

The boxcar was all but empty. A few trunks and sagging cardboard boxes lay against the walls. My legs ached where Lewis had kicked them, and the air felt heavy. I sat down. Except for a scattering of wheat chaff, the wood floor was bare. A bundle that might have been a dog or a half-rolled sleeping bag or just an old covering was bunched in the back right corner.

"Gently," murmured the woman against the wall to my left, and I stopped trying to find a warm spot and held still. Despite the rotting slats that made up the boxcar walls, only slivers of moonlight squeezed through. All I could really see were the woman's boots crossed at the ankles under a heavy, knee-length gray skirt. Then her hair, red even in that light, under a wool cap pulled down below her ears. The redness made her head look warm, though nothing else about her did. Her arms were crossed tightly across her chest. I couldn't see her face at all.

"Maybe everyone's shoveling snow," I said. "I didn't see any patrol."

"You will."

After that, we just sat. The woman had a wicker basket propped beside her and a book on her lap. Eventually, I was able to make out the gold-leaf lettering on the spine, which read *Galsworthy*. The wooden floor seemed much colder than the snow-laden ground I'd been lying on a little while earlier. In addition to the bruises all over my legs, I could feel more rising along my spine and tailbone. I shifted, and the woman hissed, "Shush," then gazed out the half-open door, as though she'd picked this spot to picnic and there was no one else around for miles.

I started to shiver. "Does that door stay open even when we're moving?"

"I know, can you believe the service on this line?"

More silence. "I'm Paul," I tried.

A chorus of owls hooted from the redbud trees, followed by the yipping of coyotes up on the ridge. The moonlight caught the woman's face: high, hard cheekbones, a sharp beak of a nose, eyes so dark that they seemed to soak up the shadows. Only her hair looked soft. "Paul, right? I'm bored, Paul."

"I'm cold," I said, and noticed the apple in her hand.

She saw me looking, reached into the wicker basket and tossed me another.

"You'll get colder. Trust me, the boredom's worse. Where are we?"

"Oklahoma."

"Obviously. Be more specific."

"Blackcreek. Just outside Blackcreek."

Biting into her apple—cringing at the sound—the woman leaned back against the wall, and the darkness dropped over her face again. "Good. Tell me about Blackcreek."

The apple she'd thrown me felt flinty, cold, dry against my teeth. But it had a taste to it, or I imagined it did. Wind-and-apple. Traveling-apple. Apple-from-elsewhere.

"Well, see, my dad—" I started, and the train lurched forward, toppling me sideways onto my bruised ribs. I just lay there, trying to hold on to my breath. But the juddering made it even harder, and I pushed upright.

My companion sat impassively against the wall, legs still crossed at the ankles, apple poised near her mouth, as if she were preparing to take dictation. Slowly, then not so slowly, the train gathered momentum. Freezing air whistled through the boxcar's half-open door. It smelled metallic, like the blade on a new axe, and hurt my lungs.

"You didn't tell me your name," I said.

"You didn't technically ask." Her smile flashed and disappeared like light glinting on glass.

"Can I ask now?"

"Will you get on with your story if I answer?"

"What story?" I asked.

"The one you got half a sentence into before you fell over."

I nodded, but her face stayed expressionless.

"Grace," she said.

The wind chattered and slapped against the outside of the boxcar, and the beat of the train wheels tapped at my bones like fingers on a telegrapher's key.

"My dad was dying. I mean, he's dead, now. He was dying yesterday."

Grace sighed. Not in sympathy, I didn't think.

"Anyway. He'd sent word to find my brother and come home. I didn't bother sending a reply. I knew my father would just be waiting in his bedroom, drinking and sitting at the window. He used to say staring at all the abandoned houses made him feel like a king, because he owned our place outright. King of the dust."

"What was he dying of?"

"Pneumonia."

"The real kind or the dust kind?"

I shrugged. "His lungs were bad. They filled up."

Grace rubbed the uneaten side of her apple softly against her skirt.

"My brother Lewis left us four years ago. He's older than I am, almost three years, and he and my dad were getting into fist fights. I mean, they always got into fist fights, but Lewis was starting to win. Then one day he just up and left.

"My brother never came back home, but I saw him in town occasionally, and I heard about him a fair bit. He took up on some ranch, got fired. Worked in the wheat fields back when wheat grew in them. He would come to Blackcreek on Saturday nights and box the CCC boys bare-knuckled." I looked up. "The Civilian Conservation Corps."

"I know who they are," Grace murmured.

"I used to go watch him fight sometimes. He really was…is…he's like a magician."

"Sounds like a block-headed ass."

"I don't mean because of the fighting. Well, that, too. I never saw anyone but my dad whip him, and not my dad, either, any time recently. But the way those boys clustered around him afterward…blood pouring down their faces, him yanking them out of the dirt, them putting their arms around him. All standing there laughing and yelling. Everyone else left in town screaming out the windows for them to shut up. I think my brother liked when I was there to see it. Right at the end, he'd give me a glance. Maybe wave a bloody hand.

"All of that's to say he wasn't exactly hard to find. Wherever Lewis went, people talked about him. All around Blackcreek, there are these sorts of…camps that have popped up. You know, for people who have nowhere else to go. Or no way to get there."

"Hoovervilles," said Grace.

I nodded. Such a cruel, sardonic name for a place.

"He wasn't in the first camp I tried. Or the second. At the second place they told me about a bigger one, seven or eight miles out on the prairie, right by the railroad tracks."

Grace leaned forward, her dark eyes locked on mine. She looked like an eagle zeroing in. "Seven or eight miles?" she repeated.

"Huh," she said.

"What? You know the place?"

"Not really."

I waited, but she didn't offer any more, and I couldn't think what to ask. So I just went on. "They told me that this big camp...this Hooverville... was nowhere you wanted to be. 'Pretty rough and tumble,' one guy said. 'Real mean. Low crowd.' Kind of funny coming from a man living with a bunch of shoes and pans in a covered wagon with three wheels and only half a cover."

"Not really so funny," Grace said.

I shrugged. I'd seen plenty of people without wagons *or* shoes. "Took me until dark to get out there. It was freezing, there was this *big* wind, and I was starving. The weird thing was, the closer I got to it, the more excited I was. I knew I'd find my brother there. But that wasn't even it. It was just...so many people have disappeared from our town these last few years. Maybe three-quarters of the human beings I've spoken to in my entire life. Coming up that last rise, I had this crazy, charged-up feeling that I was about to see them all. Not that I even liked most of them, but...as soon as I got to the top of the ridge, I could see it was in this sort of hollow. The Indians used to run buffalo into it off the cliffs on the other side. But now it's just a mess."

"Yeah," Grace said.

"All around the perimeter, there were broken-down cars pointed head-to-head. Like they were getting ready to butt each other. People's stuff was all over the place, but there was a kind of order to it. Some of them had arranged everything into little squares, like dollhouse rooms with no walls or roofs. This one family had recreated their whole house that way. They had a kid's-room square, with corn-shuck dolls and some flags, and a kitchen square with some pans and plates stacked together on an old blanket, and a living-room square with a ratty blue rug and a coffee table. The whole family was kneeling around the table when I walked by, sipping something steaming out of metal cups. They didn't look at me; they just kind of sidled closer together, like they thought I might break in.

"I was walking this sort of crooked path through the camp. It really was big; there had to be three hundred people living there. More, maybe. Way up ahead, I could see a bonfire, and I figured it must be the central gathering place, so I made for it."

Around and beneath us, the train picked up speed. It rocked and rattled, and the wind rasped like a saw over my arms. There wasn't really anywhere to get away from it. Grace stayed huddled under her sweater. Her mouth was tucked into her collar. To keep my mind off the chill, I started up again.

"The closer I got to the bonfire, the fewer people I saw. The piles of junk on either side began looking less like dollhouses and more like piles of junk.

Kids were watching me from under wagons or beside cars. One old guy in a rocking chair yipped at me, coyote-style. I guess my little leap was pretty satisfying for him. He laughed a really long time. He had on a short-sleeve shirt and no shoes, even though it had started to snow. And I think he was holding the butt of a rifle. Just the butt, no gun.

"I could see figures by the fire. Young guys, from their silhouettes. I couldn't see my brother yet, but I knew either he'd be there or these guys would know where he was. I passed a bunch of women roughly my age just standing there smoking. One of them was Chinese, maybe, but another, older one was colored, I mean really dark colored, and…"

Abruptly, I noticed that Grace's eyes were wide open.

"It…made an impression on me, you know?" I said. "She wasn't the first colored person I'd seen. We had some working on the railroad, and some Chinese, too, when the trains still stopped in Blackcreek. But the way she stood. Mostly staring at the ground, but also pushing the other girls away when they got too close, and they all kept trying to huddle around her. Then she looked up, right at me. I swear, if she'd had a gun, I think she might have shot me dead."

"And then?" Grace said into her sweater, her eyes on the bundle in the corner of the car.

"Then my brother appeared. Right at my elbow. He threw an arm around my shoulder and winked at the women. 'You go easy on my brother Paul, here,' he said, as if he'd known I was coming and was meeting me at the station. 'He's not ready for you.'

"'Your brother,' the colored woman said, and there was something so hard in her voice.

"The Chinese woman dropped her cigarette and stamped on it and laughed this mean little laugh. But the colored girl went still and started to turn away. Then a really weird thing happened. My brother Lewis stepped forward and grabbed her shoulders. I'm not sure what he was trying to do. The rest of the women scattered like crows, and he…I don't know. The two of them just stood there a while, until one of the guys by the bonfire began yelling, 'Lewis, we're not waiting,' and the rest of them joined in. Eventually, he glanced in the direction of the fire, and they all shut up.

"'Be there directly,' he said.

"But he wouldn't let go of the colored woman, and I could see that she was crying. Then he whispered something to her. I have no idea what, and he wouldn't explain any of it later. The two of them glared at each other.

"'You give 'em hell, Lewis,' the Chinese woman said, staring at the bonfire.

"And the colored woman…she spit on the ground, and said, 'Or take 'em there.'

"'Okay,' Lewis told her. 'Wait right here.'

"As soon as he left her, she half-stalked, half-staggered down the nearest path and vanished in the dark."

I hadn't meant to go quiet. But I could still feel the heat from that bonfire on my face, the same way I could feel my father's pulse in my fingers.

"What time do you think it is?" I asked Grace.

"Night time," she said.

The train had been chugging at a steady clip for God knew how long. I shoved to my feet, wincing at the pins and needles jabbing under my skin, and peeked around the edge of the door. The country outside had flattened. There were no hills and no trees, just scrubby bushes and an occasional farmhouse. The wind seemed warmer, or maybe I'd gone numb.

"I didn't mean to talk so long. You can sleep if you want." I was shivering in the wind-blast.

"I'd rather hear more," she said.

I returned almost to the same spot where I'd been sitting, thinking the floorboards would still be warm. They weren't. I stretched out my legs and leaned back on my hands.

"Lewis looked really thin. I mean, he's always been thin, but not like that. And his arms were huge, with these big ripples in them. As if he'd seeded them, straight up to his shoulders, you know? He turned me right around and steered me toward this one really big guy with black hair hanging in his face who kept bobbing up and down next to the fire, real slow, like an oil derrick. I couldn't even see his eyes or his mouth for the shadows, but I could tell he was furious. He started to say something, and Lewis pushed me forward and said, 'Jay. Meet Paul.'

"My brother pointed to the second kid and said, 'That's Fred.' I kind of recognized him. I'd seen him around Blackcreek. At Town Couch, maybe. I thought maybe he'd run off from the CCC, although most of those boys stayed put, no matter how much shit they got from whatever townspeople they ran into wherever they went. Maybe I would have stayed, too, if I'd had one of those jobs."

"What jobs are they doing way out here, anyway?"

"They were building some giant prairie park. So that fifty years from now, people can come back and see where we lived, maybe? New Deal stuff. Make-work, my dad calls it. Or fake-work. The kind that keeps you dependent instead of setting you free."

"Yeah," Grace murmured into the muff of her sweater, and crossed her arms.

"The third kid was named P.D. That surprised me, because we'd had a P.D. in our town, too. I reminded Lewis, and he said, 'There's always a P.D. around,' and tossed a stick into the fire. As soon as I got a good look at this kid, I knew what Lewis meant. He was a lot like the guy I remembered. Short and buck-toothed and permanently annoyed-looking. Our P.D. used to scavenge food from our lunches at school because he never had enough in his own, and he picked all kinds of fights he couldn't win. He was little and noisy and hard to catch. Hence, P.D. Prairie Dog.

"'You playing?' the big, black-haired kid—Jay—asked me.

"Lewis still hadn't taken his arm off my shoulder. 'Paul's my brother,' he said, as if that answered the question.

"'You really *live* here? By choice?' I blurted, shrugging halfway free so I could look back at the group of women and the piles of junk humped up like buffalo skeletons for a mile or more in all directions.

"'When I lose, Paul,' Lewis said. 'Only when I lose.'

"Jay just spat, and after that we stood around watching the fire, surrounded by this sort of dirt moat maybe eight feet in diameter. From what I could tell, they were burning wagon wheels, maybe some chair legs. I got this sick feeling, and not just from the smoke stinking up my lungs. I had this idea where they may have gotten their timber. I was thinking of that family who'd laid out their belongings in little room-shaped squares.

"I was just about to mouth off when I remembered why I'd come. I hadn't seen my dad yet, but I had a feeling there wasn't much time left, or he wouldn't have bothered sending word. Also, just being near Lewis again was like…I don't know. Like holding a pillow down on my own face. I literally could not breathe right. So I shouldered him aside and caught the big guy's eye and said, 'I'm in.'

"That's when my brother socked a fist so deep in my gut, I thought he was going to pull me inside out. I dropped to one knee and got right back up, but I couldn't straighten. I didn't gasp. I can tell you from experience there's no point. Breath comes back when it comes. Gasping doesn't help.

"Meanwhile, Lewis…he just watched. He does this head-cock thing when he looks at me sometimes. I don't know what it means, but he only does it to me. Then he stepped in, real close, and said, 'Not what you're here for.' After that, he half-pushed, half-eased me down so I was sitting on the grass, and left me there.

"'Who did you say this was?' the new P.D. asked. I guess Jay was kind of inspired by what Lewis had just done to me, because he knocked the little guy out of his way.

"'Let's ante up.'

"'Go ahead,' my brother said.

"'You first, for one Goddamn time. You always hold back till you see what we have. I think most nights you don't offer half of what you've got.' He was at least six inches taller than my brother, and looked scared to death. Up on the cliffs, the coyotes were going wild. You ever hear coyotes hunt, Grace?"

Grace didn't answer or even lift her head. But her expression reminded me disconcertingly of Lewis when he did the cocked-head thing.

"Anyway, Jay told my brother to ante up again, and my brother just stared at him until—"

"Shit!" Grace snapped, tumbling out of the tucked position she'd held for the last hour or so, and banged her elbows against the back of the car as the train rocked sideways.

The car lurched once more, and I bounced along the floor a little, pitching forward. Out the vibrating, broken door, I could see blue-orange light pouring down the hillsides of tall, stick-thin pines like lava flow. The light looked warm, even though the air wasn't. Glancing back at Grace, I realized she was banging her elbows against the wall on purpose.

Also, the bundle of cloth against the far wall was twitching.

Alarmed, I scrambled backward. The bundle twitched again, stilled itself, then split like the skin of a cocoon. Out popped a little colored boy, maybe four years old.

"Time's up," Grace murmured, squeezing her eyes shut. "Meet the Patrol."

Coiling into herself like a hedgehog, she eyed the newly awakened boy the way people watch rattlesnakes. When it was clear that she wasn't going to say anything and the kid wasn't turning around, at least not yet, I whispered, "Is he yours?" Grace shushed me with a violent sweep of her hand.

The kid kept his back to us. One of his hands strayed absently between his legs, and the other balled into a fist and rubbed at his eyes.

A few seconds later, when nothing whatsoever had changed, I said,

"What?"

Grace sighed, closing her eyes. "Just listen, Paul."

All I heard was wind coursing through the door and through the grooves in the splintering floor like a river down a riverbed. Outside, the orange light had grown harsher, though the grass looked greener and wetter than the grass I'd grown used to.

"What am I listening for?" I finally asked.

She stood up. "I'm going outside."

Before I could react, she was past me and gone. Gaping, I scrambled to my feet, stumbled to the door and stuck out my head. I expected to see her tumbling down the grassy incline into the pines, already yards behind me.

Instead, I found her perched on the top rung of the outside ladder, fingers wound through the frozen door handle. Her hair was flying and her mouth distended as the wind pushed through it. Slowly, her lips flattened, as if she were about to smile. Then I realized she was singing. Almost shouting.

"When my blood runs chilly and cold. I got to go. I got to go. I got to go."

"You'll freeze!" I yelled, inching my head out a little farther, and the wind leapt on my back, clawing like a cat in a frenzy. Ducking inside, I shivered hard. From the far wall came a flurry of movement. I watched as the child patted a hand through his blankets and came up with a green metal canteen. Two quick, knifing coughs reminded me that it had been at least twelve hours since I'd drunk anything.

The kid in the corner, taking absolutely no notice of me, unscrewed the top of the canteen, tipped it back and drank. He was wearing green pajama pants with horseshoes stitched into the seams and a white sweater that looked warmer than anything I'd ever owned and earmuffs the color of dust, or maybe just coated with it.

When he finished drinking, he capped the canteen, laid it back in the blankets, and patted around again. This time he came up with a crust of bread. The kid stuck the bread in his mouth and bit. I could hear the crunch even over the wheels and the wind. Outside, Grace was still singing, though the words had folded themselves into the roar. In one unfolding movement, as though someone had inflated him, the kid stood up.

For a moment, he tottered, reaching out his hands, leaning forward, brushing the wall closest to him with his fingers and then tilting. His head turned halfway toward me.

The kid's eyes were shot through with yellowish veins and arteries. Even the irises looked yellow-gray. There were no pupils whatsoever.

"I'm right here, kid," I said, stretching out my arms. "My name is Paul."

The kid took his hands off the wall. Turning sideways, he edged vaguely toward me, stopping when the wind from the open door smacked him in the face. He looked impossibly small with his pajamas flapping around him and his hands waving, like a balloon that had blown into the car and would soon get sucked out again. Shuffling out of the airstream, the kid retreated, in profile to me. Then he opened his mouth, and I started toward him again. I was three steps away, reaching out to touch his shoulder, when he let loose.

The most amazing thing was that the kid never seemed to breathe. He didn't stretch onto his tiptoes or squeeze his eyelids shut or throw his head back. His lips just parted and sound shot through them like water from a pressure hose. And it kept coming. It didn't change pitch, wasn't aimed in any direction. Every time I thought it couldn't possibly get any louder, it did.

I guess you could call it a scream, though there was also grunting and wailing involved. Even with my hands squashed against my temples, it was like having a hot needle jabbed down my ear canals.

"Jesus Christ," I said, staggering sideways because I couldn't go forward. Finally, I got myself turned around and managed to keep my eyes open long enough to stumble toward the door. Somehow, over the wind and the shrieking kid, I heard Grace. She was screaming, too. At least her scream had a tune, and something specific to communicate. I even caught the words.

"Do, Lord. Do, Lord. Do remember me."

As soon as I pushed my head through the door, the wind whipped my hair against my ears. Grace looked pinned to the side of the car by the flying edges of her skirt. Beyond her, the countryside—tranquil, springtime green—stretched to the horizon.

"Grace!" I yelled.

She shut her eyes and sang louder.

"Please. Goddamnit, what do I..." Swinging back inside, I plugged my ears again with my fingers. It didn't help. Several long minutes passed before I realized that the only thing worse than listening to that sound might be making it. I turned around. The kid was facing the back wall, nearly crumpling every time the car rocked.

"Hey," I yelled. Maybe murmuring soothingly would have been better, but I didn't think he'd hear me. "Little boy. I'm...."

The kid lurched away, screaming and spinning and banging against the boards. I sidled forward and penned him in along the wall where Grace had been sitting. He knew I was there, because every time he touched one of my arms he'd hurl himself backward and slam his spine against the wood. His whole body was shuddering under his sweater. He didn't stop screaming or wriggling even when I grabbed him.

The pajamas turned out to be thinner than they looked, and they were unraveling everywhere. The shirt collar was hanging halfway off his shoulders and down his chest like the sagging mouth of a burlap bag. When I tried to turn him toward me, he raked my arm with fingers curled into claws. I let go, and the kid kicked into a spin and whirled away, his scream shredding the air like a circular saw.

"Little boy. Wait. Please. It's all right."

"He can't hear you," Grace called from the door.

She'd slid just far enough inside to get out of the wind and was gazing at the top of her right index finger, which was glowing reddish-blue, like the wick of a lantern. Behind her, on a post, a wooden sign flew by. I thought it might have said *Arkansas*.

"Frostbite," I said, gesturing at her finger.

"Not yet," said Grace, wincing as the kid tumbled past and howled yet again. She pushed the afflicted finger into her palm with her other hand, made a fist, and slid the fist under her sweater. Then she turned her head so I could see her earlobes. "What about my ears?"

I surprised us both by laughing.

"Well?" Grace said.

"They're red."

Grace rubbed them, then looked at her fingers again. The blasts of frigid air were too much for me, and I stepped sideways. She stayed where she was. When the kid roared by, she didn't even look up.

"He's blind," I said. "Obviously."

"Also deaf. Obviously."

Sliding to a crouch, I put a hand on the floor and felt the hammering of the wheels for a while. Grace folded down next to me with a sigh. She clapped her hands over her ears. A few seconds later, I heard her say, "Ow" as sensation returned to her extremities. Her ears had gone even redder, and were now the same color as her hair.

We watched the kid through tearing, squinted eyes, trying to block out the sound. He was rolling back and forth along the far wall, shuddering to the rhythm of the train, still screaming.

"God," I said. "It's like…spray from a skunk."

Grace shrugged. "Maybe he's just saying hello."

Without thinking, I took one of her frozen hands and started chafing it between both of mine. It was like rubbing a brick of ice.

Just then, the rhythm of the train wheels hitched and started to slow. I dropped her hand and peered around the door into what was now full daylight. I saw hills, and a grain elevator planted in the grass like an anchor we'd dropped. We slowed to a crawl, and I caught some shouting from outside, then hard laughter.

"We should hide. Right?"

Grace swept her gaze over the virtually empty car, her kicked-over apple basket, the kid's ball of blankets. "Okay, Paul," she said. "I'll count to ten."

We rolled halfway up a hump, and the train stopped.

The moment the train ceased moving, the kid stopped screaming and dropped to his hands and knees. He felt his way along the floor to his blankets, sat, then stuck his thumb in his mouth like a plug. Instantly, Grace was up, stepping across the car, and sitting next to him. She touched his wrist, then his elbow. He turned toward her and leaned forward as she slid an arm around him.

In broad daylight, in the absence of wind and screaming, the boxcar barely even felt like a structure. Light poured through the crumbling slats, illuminating the floorboards. Tucked against the unbroken section of door, I felt the morning sun, almost warm, stippling my back. Outside, metal scraped together as connecting bars swung loose and clanged to the tracks and cars came uncoupled. When I glanced at Grace, she was almost smiling.

"Like those first glorious minutes out of jail, huh?" she said.

Her red hair was pressed so tightly down on her head that it looked plastered there. The wind had pasted individual strands of it across both cheeks, where they resembled half a dozen needle scratches. Even so, her eyes remained utterly alert.

"You've been to jail?" I asked.

"It's just how I imagine it. Have you?"

"Only to pick up my brother a couple of times."

The voices outside got nearer. One of them was chattering in what sounded to my untrained ears like Chinese. The other, cutting over it, kept saying, "Shut your flappy mouth, hear? Shut it now."

"Won't they be loading this car or something? Grace, really, they're bound to find us."

She was watching the door, not me. Her hand slid absently back and forth across the kid's back. "And what is it you think will happen then?"

Once, less than a month before the Blackcreek rail yard closed for good, on my father's last working Christmas Eve when absolutely everyone had been drinking, he and his work pals had pulled a swearing German man with a scar across his Adam's apple out of a coal pile on a late night freighter. They gave him a five-minute head start, then tracked him across the prairie onto Dust Cow ridge and pumped both of his legs full of buckshot. Afterward, my father—who claimed to have done only a little of the shooting, said he liked the chasing better—got Mr. Gunderson's truck and drove me and the German man all the way to the hospital in Stillwater. On our way home, I asked if the guy was going to be all right, and my father looked as if he might punch me. Then he said, "He'll get a hell of a lot better Christmas dinner than you or me, that's for sure." My brother didn't come home until the next day, and he was furious because no one had told him about the hobo hunt. My father just rubbed his hungover head and said, "Goddamn, Lewis. Goddamn."

Grace was singing softly, rubbing the little boy's back. I thought the tune might be a lullaby, then remembered that it wouldn't do any good.

"Tell me about the kid," I said.

The boxcar nudged forward, settled again. The kid moved his head around and shook off Grace's arm but left his thumb in his mouth. I held my breath, and Grace stayed absolutely still. After a few seconds, the kid relaxed against her.

Exhaling, I shook out the hands I hadn't realized were clenched. "He's the Patrol, right? That's what you call him?"

"That's what he is," Grace said. "Not who he is."

"Ain't this cozy," said a new voice, right beside me.

I jumped to my feet as an enormous man in work overalls climbed into the car. He had an orange, curly beard that rolled all the way up his cheeks into his hair and tangled over his ears. In one hand, he held a giant wrench, dulled a dingy rust color, which made it look like a leg bone he'd yanked from something living, and not too long ago, either.

"Oh, goodie," Grace said. "Look, Patrol. It's Paul Bunyan."

The bearded man smiled. Ugly smile. "Hungry, little lady?"

He reached into his pockets and withdrew a crusty sandwich and some carrots bundled together with a rubber band. Kneeling, he reached for the kid's hands, which trembled when he touched them. Gently, the man passed the food to the child. The child buried it in his blankets.

For a moment longer, the bearded man crouched, hand tugging at the bottom of his beard as though working a well-pump. He lifted his other hand as though he might pet the kid or slap Grace, then put it down. He looked at me and stood up. The wrench tapped twice against his immense thigh.

"You hungry?" he said.

"You kidding?" I answered.

He took another half-sandwich out of his pocket and looked at it. Then he said, "Been riding long?" and tossed it at me.

The second the sandwich hit my hands, a huge bite of it was in my mouth. Peanut butter and railroad grit.

"Share it with her over there if you want to," the bearded man said. "Just make sure she doesn't steal one crumb from the little nigger. Got it? Latrine's right out the door on the left."

He hopped down from the car and disappeared. Grace gazed at the open space in the door, her mouth turned down.

"I've got to stop doing that," she said slowly. "Really bad habit."

"What?"

"Baiting people." She gestured at the rest of the sandwich in my hand. "You sharing?"

I'd already devoured all but the crust. Embarrassed, I extended what was left to Grace. My head was whirling with hunger and the echoes of the scream. I climbed out of the car to use the latrine, which I could smell ten feet away. When I got back, both Grace and the kid were asleep. I curled up against the warm, broken door and closed my eyes.

*****

When I awoke, we were moving again. The Patrol lay hidden in his blankets. But Grace had propped herself up exactly where she'd been the night before. On her raised knees, she cradled some leathery, flappy thing. I thought at first it was an upside down hat. Then she drew a pencil from behind her ear, and I realized it was some sort of writing case.

Standing, I went to the door and stared down the long, empty stretches between railroad towns. We rolled across trestle bridges, along the rims of gorges and over creek beds, through miles-deep clusters of trees whose new leaves winked like running water in the wind we made. All day, the air warmed and kept warming. By late afternoon, I could see thunderclouds drifting in the distance like dirigibles, though they never came closer and didn't burst.

In all that time, Grace talked to me only in short, occasional outbreaks. I learned that she'd once broken both arms climbing a maple tree in the Prospect Park neighborhood of Brooklyn, New York, but she "couldn't go back there," and that she'd spent two months one frigid autumn driving a horse-drawn book wagon through rural counties in New England before abandoning the last of the books in a rowboat and setting them adrift down the icy Batten Kill river, wrapped in blankets. "Like Moses," she told me.

She ate very little, drank even less, and must have filled fifteen pages in her flappy leather case by day's end.

"What are you writing?" I asked.

But she only pursed her mouth, shrugged her shoulders, and murmured, "Nothing, as far as I can tell."

Sometime in the mid-afternoon, the kid woke up, ate what Paul Bunyan had given him, howled a while, then sat back down. For dinner, all three of us had the wormless segments of half an apple each, plus a swig from a canteen I hadn't known Grace was carrying. The water had flakes of dust or rust or metal in it, and reminded me of the Gunderson girls and home.

"One time," I said around the last, grainy bits of apple, "this dust tornado swooped down on my town. Blackcreek."

Grace had been leaning forward, pencil in hand, but now she stopped and looked up. In the evening dimness, I couldn't tell if she was annoyed. She didn't interrupt, though, so I went on.

"It blew down some sheds and broke some windows and filled whole cars with dust. It felt like a blizzard with ten times the wind. The Gundersons, our neighbors, had a couple of their cows out grazing, and the wind just picked up one of them right off the ground. Ginny Gunderson swears that she saw it kind of lean sideways, and then *fwwwp*, disappear. A couple of days later, we were walking, Ginny and me. There was wrecked stuff everywhere. It was even worse than the year before, when the Blackleg came."

"I don't know what that is," Grace said.

"Me either. But it comes out of the ground and gives the cattle lots of crackly sores, then kills them."

"Nice."

"We'd walked, I don't know, two or three miles. A long time. And then we came to this grassy hollow, and there was the cow. The one that blew off. Just standing there, chewing dead grass. It had pink scars on its ears from the Blackleg, so there was no mistaking it. Ginny took one look, then raced home and came back with her dad. Her dad just walked around it. He couldn't believe his eyes. Finally, he took a jar out of his pocket, squatted down beside her and milked her. When the jar was full, Mr. Gunderson kind of swirled the liquid around and stared at it. As if it was a crystal ball or something. And then he drank some. And he made us drink some. For luck, he said. So Ginny and I invented this stupid little chant."

But I didn't tell Grace the Dust Cow chant. She just watched me a while, then went back to her writing.

At dusk, the train began climbing through dense pines that seemed to prop up the sky like tent posts. The breeze pouring through the door was chilly, but nowhere near as brutal as the previous night's. There were so many birds that we could hear them sometimes even over the chug of the wheels, though we never saw a single one.

Well past the point when it seemed too dark to see, Grace folded up the flaps of her writing case and laid it beside her. When she caught me watching, she tilted her chin and held my gaze. Her hair looked darker, almost black, and the moonlight reflected off her pale face. She was prettier than I'd noticed, and I was increasingly interested in her in a way I hadn't remotely expected to be.

"Could you tell me about the kid?" I mumbled. "Please?"

"Have to pee first," she said. She went to the door and stuck her ass in a downwind direction, while I stared between my legs at the floor.

"Fucking cold," she said when she was done.

"Not as cold as last night."

"Thanks, Pauliana." After that, she was silent so long that I thought she was asleep. I was nearly asleep myself when I heard her say, "The night it happened—the night the Devil came back, and the deal got made—was positively steamy. Dead summer North Carolina heat. You've experienced nothing like it, Prairie Paul. But if you follow this line to the end, you will.

"Low mist hanging. Hovering on the grass, understand? Any wetness that appears there, the heat sucks it right up into the air. Even at night. So picture it now. Lots of perfectly mown, beautiful green grass, frosted with mist. Crumbling but freshly painted white plantation home just there, on the hillside. The South Roanoke School for the Negro Blind Deaf. First and only institution of its kind. Survived on donations from colored churches for a thousand miles around, from Okefenokee to the Great Dismal, the Piedmont to the Panhandle. Almost survived, anyway. Survived until this day.

"The three matriarchs of the place—Mrs. Richardson, Mrs. Duarte, and Mrs. Jones, in their seventies, all colored except for Mrs. Jones—had done their pleading. Written letters to their congressmen and preachers, newspaperman and local associations. Now they were trying to disperse the children for a few weeks to sharecropper farms and a few town families in the vicinity, just in case some last-second donor turned up. After that, if none did…well. They were packing kids' bags and making a dozen sack dinners and staring each other down anytime one of them got close to crying. Then came the knock they'd all been dreading.

"It was Mrs. Richardson who answered the door. She'd always been the bravest of the three. As a little girl, she was lynched by her masters on the morning they fled the Union soldiers, and survived when the wet, rotten rope she was dangling from fell apart. She'd had to confront the bald man three other times, and she faced him now.

"He didn't have to say anything, and he knew it. He was a businessman. A powerful white one. He just stood on the porch with his hat in his hand, his tie tight at his throat, his scalp steaming. They looked at each other a while. Both were used to giving orders, and it was a point of pride for each of them. Finally, Mrs. Duarte and Mrs. Jones unpacked the children's bags and led them back to the only safe rooms those kids would ever know."

I felt as though I were being rushed downriver, anticipating the inevitable smash against some boulder. Grace didn't say anything more for a long while. I couldn't read the series of expressions ghosting across her face; most of them were shadows, anyway.

"In the end," she said, her voice barely audible above the churning wheels, "they picked five. Four orphans, and one high-yellow little boy who'd been found on the front porch in a diaper and socks. Only five children, and only one at a time, once a month. Such a small price to pay, really, for the permanent funding the bald man provided for the school. Once a month, the man would come at dusk and stand, sweating, on the front porch. He was never asked inside. Only Mrs. Richardson would come to the door, leading one of the chosen. She'd hand over the child, along with satchel, canteens, loaded food sacks, and any small items the child had shown an attachment to, for whatever reason. The bald man would give the child a hard candy and sign a register. Kind of like checking out a library book. And *voila*. One Patrol, bound for the station."

"I don't understand," I said.

"You see, Paul, for the Wilmington & Western Railroad, the primary problem posed by tramps is that they're *dirty*. They leave a stink, even when they don't piss or shit in the cars, and most of them do. They vomit.

They leave moldy crumbs from whatever food they've scavenged, and the crumbs attract insects and rats and even larger rodents. Also, they're like flies. The tramps, I mean. Stop swatting them even for a day, and they multiply. Then you never get rid of them. But you can't just chuck 'em off, not just anywhere. Not anymore. It doesn't look good. Hits too many people the wrong way these days. Wouldn't want a picture in the newspapers."

"Grace," I interrupted, unfolding my legs, opening my whole body to the wind. It was nowhere near warm. "This isn't really true. It can't be."

We eyed each other. After a few seconds, she said, "Why not?"

"You're saying…you mean, he uses the kids? As…watchdogs, or something? To keep tramps off the trains by screaming bloody murder? Wouldn't just hiring some guards be cheaper? And saner?"

An unreadable expression clamped down over her face. "Ah. But Paul, you must understand. The bald man considers it the greatest good he will ever do in this world. And maybe it is. Just think. Thanks solely and utterly to his largess, an institution like no other, which serves perhaps the most pathetic segment of the whole, desperate population of our country, remains open indefinitely. Not just open, but richly supplied with food, medicine, doctors, everything the children need or want. In exchange, he takes just one child, plants him in a boxcar, and asks only that the child do what he does naturally: scream. The bald man even sends surrogates along to watch over them, and arranges for food and drink and clean underwear and bathroom breaks at every station. Handpicked employees like Mr. Bunyan are paid extra to check on them, and even give them kind pats. All the children have to do is stay on board for one whole round trip and make the noise they make. And the blind deaf all seem to make that noise whenever they're moving. It is unique, isn't it?"

I just stared. Grace shrugged.

"Genius, really. And it's working, too. The word has spread. Hop the Wilmington & Western, and you'll go mad. That's what they're saying. The whole line is haunted. At least sometimes. And now you see, don't you? No one gets arrested. No one gets hurt, unless you count the child, and who's to say he's being hurt, anyway?"

Grace looked down at her fingers, then touched the tips of them with her tongue.

"But Grace, why would…I mean, how would this guy—the bald, white guy—even find such a place, let alone dream up a plan like that?" I saw her wince. "You really might be frostbitten."

"The bald man has personal knowledge. An afflicted son of his own."

"A colored son?"

Very slowly, Grace lifted her head, and her black eyes bore into me. Then she lowered her hands, spread her skirt with them, and opened her flappy book. "He *could* have a Negro son," she said. "It's not impossible. Though it is hard to imagine, I'll admit, at least the way I've got it set up."

Instantly, I was up on my knees, furious and a little astonished. "You mean it isn't true? None of it? You just made—"

"Oh, it's true. Some of it. More than half, depending on how you measure. There really is a South Roanoke School for the Negro Blind Deaf, and that really is where this boy is heading once I—"

"Why the hell would you make up a story like that?"

"Just…amusing myself. Trying to amuse you, too. Seeing how much you'd believe. Me, I wouldn't find something like that so very unbelievable, at this moment in our history. I've seen worse. I bet you have, too."

For a long minute, I couldn't speak. I glanced at the crumple of blankets in the corner. Even in the fast-deepening dark, if I looked very closely, I could see them twitching. I turned back to Grace.

"There's another flaw in your story. What would stop someone from just chucking the kid off?"

Grace leaned forward over her writing case with a sigh. "That's no flaw. I never said that couldn't happen."

She said nothing more the whole night. A few hours later, she was still hunched against the wall, tipping her writing case toward whatever light there was, her pencil scratching at the paper like a claw.

*****

Another shift in rhythm woke me at dawn. Pushing awkwardly off the floor, I tasted dust and my dry tongue and whatever the wind had whipped over me in the night. I looked around for a canteen, though I knew we had little water left, and saw Grace sprawled asleep. Her writing case lay beside her, flaps open like the wings of a dead bat. I sidled close enough to pull the case onto my lap.

And so I got a glimpse of Grace Lowie's greatest achievement before pretty much anyone else. He was already the character you know, already Roth, readily discernible through the prickly hedge of cross-outs and scribbles from which Grace was creating him. That first time, I didn't read any complete scenes except one when Roth flees home and winds up crouching in a stolen winter coat in the snow in New York's Washington Square Park with his smallpox stare and polio limp. There was another bit that didn't end up in the book about Roth seducing a Polish girl who spoke no English using only his grin, two balloons, and his "deadman whistle." It didn't work, but there was something painful, even sweet about it. I think it was that sequence, more than anything else, that gave me a clue about who Grace was, or at least what she was capable of, even before I knew what I was actually reading.

In any event, I didn't hear Grace awaken, and I had no idea how long she'd been watching me.

"Interesting move," she said.

Jerking, I glanced up, and the writing case stirred on my lap as if she had summoned it. I'd read most of the pages still attached by a clip to the warped, stained blotter. But the leather pouches inside the case were stuffed to overflowing.

"I just—"

"I'll take it back now, if you're quite done. Don't let me rush you."

Closing the case and tucking its dog-eared flaps together, I pushed the whole thing back to Grace. She laid it beside her, then stayed still, looking at the floor.

"I'm sorry," I said.

A few minutes later, the Patrol awoke, launched immediately into his shriek, and Grace went outside. He kept at it almost the entire morning.

Right around noon, somewhere in the Mississippi swampland, the kid's voice gave way in mid-wail like a bridge buckling in a flood, and tumbled us into silence. He was half-facing me, and for a moment, he looked surprised, straddling his blankets and swaying with the slow, steady movement of the train. Then he smiled and sat down. His front teeth were crooked, leaning against his gums like sleds in a barn.

Immediately, Grace was back inside the car. She went to the Patrol, knelt beside him, and began stroking the matted, curly hair.

"Alright, Doak. Home soon," she said.

She hadn't even looked at me. I knelt, too. "That's his name? Doak?"

"One of his names." She went on stroking his hair. "Nickname."

"Which he'll never know."

The kid turned fully toward me. His eyes were impenetrable. No way in or out.

I folded my legs beneath me and sat down. Only then did Grace look my way. Her expression hadn't exactly softened.

"Where's he from?" I asked.

"Originally? No idea. Out West. He belongs to a friend of mine. Kind of."

"So…he doesn't even live at that deaf school?"

"Not yet," Grace said, her voice dropping deeper. A while later, I looked up again and found her gazing openly at me, the way you might stare at a cloud before giving its shape a name.

Very carefully, I touched the Patrol on his protruding shoulder bone with my fingertips. When he neither squirmed nor screamed, I lay my palm against his back and felt his heart hammering in there. One of Grace's hands was still on his head. Eventually, he shook free of both of us and lay on top of his covers.

"Think he's getting used to us?"

"What, because of our comforting reek?" Grace said.

Exhaustion overcame me. I edged away, propped myself against one shuddering wall, and closed my eyes. When I opened them, it was evening, deliciously spring and almost warm. I went to the door. Some of the deep, mossy green outside seemed to have seeped into the puffy clouds overhead like a stain. I'd never seen ground or sky that color. The Delta spread out before me.

"I'm sorry I looked in your writing case," I said to Grace. "I don't know anything about you, except that you write a lot. I was just…curious."

She'd been sitting with her case in her lap. "Maybe you should finish that story about your brother," she said.

"I don't want to."

"Sure you do."

I felt the wind, nearly warm, on the back of my neck, and tried hard to find words I could rub together to conjure Lewis's firelight. Never before had my brother seemed so far from me. Not even when I'd had no idea where he was. Then, just like that, he seemed to materialize right behind me, practically whispering in my ear.

"So when the big kid—Jay—told my brother to ante up, Lewis gave him this really ugly grin and pulled out four crisply folded dollar bills and said, 'Ante enough?'

"'God*damn*, Lewis,' said P.D., the little guy, shuffling up to study the money. 'Fucking magician. You really are.'

"Lewis said, 'Why thanks, P.D.' The firelight was weird on his face. It was like watching a big, invisible dog lick him.

"P.D. stood around and whistled every couple of seconds. Jay came over to take the dollars, but Lewis stuffed them into my hands.

"I was sure the rest of them were going to jump me. But Jay shrugged, so everyone else pulled out what they'd brought. P.D. gave me the rusted shell of a pocket watch with no watch and no workings. The others put in coins and a few wrinkled apples that looked like those shrunken heads in medicine shows. You ever seen those?"

Grace tapped her fingers impatiently on the floor of the boxcar. The Patrol rolled over.

"It didn't seem like the antes were exactly even. And I said so.

"'Never are, are they boys?' Lewis said. 'Anyone mind if I go ahead and finish this quickly tonight? My brother's here, after all, and I have some things on my mind.' He glanced once over his shoulder in the direction of the women. Then he threw himself into the fire."

Through the gathering shadows, I thought I saw one of Grace's eyebrows rise up. It was strangely satisfying.

"Actually, *threw* isn't the right word. It was kind of graceful. He just lifted himself off the ground, like an owl or something. And there he was floating in his wretched work boots with his arms stuck straight out, flames flying all around him like a hundred hands trying to grab him. He sailed over the hottest, longest part, landed on the other edge, dropped to the ground, and rolled away. Then he stood up.

"The rest of them went silent. Except for P.D., who was still whistling. I'd kind of clenched my fists when Lewis jumped, so everything in my hands had gotten crushed into these two pathetic lumps. I stared down at them. I was furious at my brother.

"'How much you got there, Paul-O?' Lewis called. He sounded like he did standing over some bloodied CCC-boy at Town Couch, right before he invited everyone into the pub to buy him drinks."

For one of the few times I could remember during the entire trip, Grace interrupted me. "I just want to be clear on the game. These boys go out hunting whatever they can rustle up. No rules about how they do it, I assume."

I shrugged. I didn't know.

"Whatever they find can be used to buy their way into the evening's contest, right? Which amounts to who can take the most idiotic, life-threatening leap across a bonfire? Winner gets the day's take? Have I got that right?"

"I guess." I felt my throat close up.

"Go on," she said.

I swallowed, kept going. "Lewis came dancing around the fire. It was like the rest of them weren't even there. He was only talking to me. 'Got to be six, seven dollars' worth, yeah? Come on, Paul. I need to go find my friend, and we'll walk you home. Steaks on me, if we can find any.'

"I was just kind of swaying, listening to him. I hadn't really noticed until Lewis reached my side, but P.D.'s whistling had started up again. The other boys, Jay and Fred, had walked away as soon as Lewis had landed. They were standing a good ways away from the fire. None of them were talking.

"'Lewis,' I murmured, and he gave me one of his looks. Not the nasty one, he was still feeling too good. Then he looked at P.D. and unfolded his arms. First time I noticed the burns.

"'Something on your mind?' my brother said to the kid. 'Little Dog?'

"But P.D. was just looking at my hands. His watch-casing was right on top, and he was staring at it. Into it. I told him, 'Don't.' I thought he was going to grab it all and make a run for it. Instead, he jumped into the fire.

"At first, I thought he'd miscalculated. But he'd hit exactly the spot he was aiming for, which was pretty much the spitting, pumping heart of the fire. Right dead center. And when he hit, he didn't jump again, either. He planted his boots in the ashes and…stood there.

"I mean, for longer than you can believe, too. For forever. His arms were kind of half-spread, his mouth open. He was kind of humming, but not screaming. He looked like a phoenix, except he never rose. Finally, he started yelling, then screeching, and in the end he just strode out.

"The second he was clear, Lewis drove him straight into the ground. To put out the flames, not to hurt him. When Lewis moved, the rest followed. Jay dropped himself on P.D.'s legs, and Fred grabbed a handful of snow and smashed it into the kid's face.

"The only person who did nothing was me. It was all so…I don't know. I mean, that morning I'd been at college. At Stillwater. Not that Stillwater felt real either, but this was like some completely other planet. My brother's planet.

"Then I had an idea. As far as I could tell, P.D. wasn't actually *alight* anymore, at least. The rest of the gang had slid off him. God, you could hear his skin sizzling and popping in his shirt. But the worst thing? He was smiling. Skin blistering already, some of it flapping off his cheeks, and this kid was just lying there grinning. His eyebrows were gone. His forehead had this row of red blisters puffing up like volcanoes.

"Well, something about it inspired me, if that's the right word. I shifted all the loot into the crook of one arm and fished around in my pockets for an ante of my own. Or, tribute, maybe. I don't know. I had a quarter, a dime, some straw from a wagon I'd hitched a ride on, and two fountain pens. I took out everything but one of the pens and added it to the collection.

"'You're insane', Jay said to P.D., and spat near his head. 'Stupid little bastard.'

"'Insane,' Lewis agreed. I couldn't read his tone at all. 'Dumb, dumb, dumb.'

"P.D. just grinned wider, then cried out. He told us, 'Soaked myself in snow. While none of you looked. Figured...' He tried licking his lips, but that made him scream. A while later, he said, 'Figured I had...a few seconds.'

"By now, I was standing over him, and I caught his eye. He went quiet, and I held my hands out straight, real ceremonial, like I was presenting him with a crown or something. I positioned my hands by his head so everything would land near him. Then, real slow, I just rained it all down. Fruit, coins, watch-casing. The last thing I did was kneel and tuck Lewis's dollars under one of the apples in the snow. The whole time, P.D.'s eyes never left me. He just lay there with this horrible glow, grinning like a jack-o'-lantern.

"My brother said, 'Shit.'

"Eventually, Lewis pulled me away. He didn't say another word to any of them. He just kept his arm around my shoulders, steering me back toward the little gaggle of women, and I finally remembered what I'd come for.

"'Dad's dying,' I told him.

"He took his arm off me. 'How soon?'

"'Might have happened already. I haven't seen him. Lamplighter wrote and said Dad wanted me to bring you home. So here I am.'

"'Perfect,' Lewis said. 'Just...stay there a second.'

"He hurried over to the women, then started down the path that snaked through all the miniature family encampments. 'Lewis,' I called. 'We've wasted enough time.'

"That stopped him, but he didn't turn around. He just gazed into the dark a while.

"'Lewis,' I said again. 'He sent for *you*, Goddamnit. It's the only reason he even got Lamplighter to write me.'

"'Shut up.' He turned to the Chinese woman and said, 'Go find her.'

"But she just laughed her mean little laugh.

"'I have to go home. That's my brother over there.'

"'Lucky you,' said the woman, and gave Lewis a look I will never forget. Eyebrows pinched in, mouth twisted up. Totally contemptuous. Also in love with him, I thought. They all were. The whole insane camp.

"Lewis clenched his fists, like he was going to deck her. But he just nodded. 'Yeah. You bet,' he said. Then he beckoned me forward, and we were off. I couldn't even catch up to him until we were well beyond the perimeter of the encampment. At first, I actually thought he was hurrying to see our father. But he was just angry. At the bottom of the ridge path, he stopped and waited.

"Away from the fire, I was freezing. I was having trouble getting my breath, and talking came hard. 'What happened back there?' I said.

"'What?'

"'With that woman.'

"He stared at me a few seconds, then stalked up the hill.

"'Lewis,' I panted after him.

"'You know what, Paul? I've been playing that game every night for the past three weeks. Every blessed night. That little freak P.D. never won a Goddamn thing.'

"'So? It's your stupid game. What are you so mad about?'

"That's when he gave me his first real Lewis look of the whole night. Like he was going to beat me up, or burst out laughing. Or both. 'I wanted the money, idiot. I wanted a steak. I wanted to treat you to one. And my friend back there, too. She damn well needs one, not that she'd eat it.' He glanced back, one more time, toward the light.

"After that, we just walked. The whole way to our father's house, he never took his arm off my shoulders.'"

"You didn't press him about the woman?" Grace said, so softly that I almost didn't hear her.

"I was too tired. And thinking about my dad, I guess."

Grace stayed quiet a long while. Outside, the sky had gone dark and cloudy over the Delta. The Patrol stirred again in his coverings. Hours passed. The moon had risen before Grace tapped her pencil twice on the floor and nodded to herself.

"Hey," I murmured as the train began to slow its glide through the soft spring evening like some landing migratory bird. The Raleigh, North Carolina, train station was probably less than a mile away. The Patrol had wandered over near the door, and for once—by the grace of God, or because he somehow sensed that our trip was about to end, or because the air felt as sweet on his cheeks as it did on mine—he was awake but silent. Now was likely our best chance to get off without him wailing. But Grace just continued rolling the kid's blankets, collecting the top of his long-empty canteen and tightening it thoughtfully, blowing on and brushing at the new pages in her writing case before closing the flaps and patting them.

"Hey, Grace," I said again, more urgently, as the wheels squealed against the tracks and the hydraulics hissed. "Shouldn't we be getting off?" The railroad men we'd met on our journey had been kind enough, mostly. But I'd been around too many railroad men in my life to be lulled into any sense of safety.

We'd been barely crawling for the better part of an hour, and now, without so much as a heralding gush of steam, we stopped. Grace tucked her writing case under her arm and handed me the roll she'd made of the Patrol's blanket and belongings. Without checking to see where we were or whether it was safe, she moved to the kid, stroked his shoulder softly for a few seconds, then scooped him off his feet in one gentle motion. He squirmed violently, twisted around as if he was going to hit her, and I covered my ears, glancing nervously toward the door.

But the Patrol didn't wail, and no one came to roust us. Grace leapt from the car and landed with a soft smack in the dirt. She and the kid were already walking fast toward the station house as I hurried after them, glancing around. Train tracks spoked away in all directions. The yard was far from deserted even at whatever late hour this was, but none of the railroad men seemed to notice us. Overhead, a fat, yellow moon nestled like a bird's egg in tufts of gray clouds. Across the tracks, away from the station, I saw oak trees. Lots of them.

I heard shouts and scuffling behind us. Whirling, ready to grab the Patrol's hand and run, I saw a shadow leap from a coal gondola a few cars behind our boxcar and dart through three startled railroad men into the trees.

More shadows stirred to our right. Huddled on one of the benches on the passenger platform, gazing blankly at us, I saw a father and son. Or man and boy, anyway. Even in the absence of light—the only illumination in the station house came from the bulb over the front entrance outside—the man's silver stubble looked painful, like pins stuck through his pallid skin. The boy wasn't sleeping, but he didn't lift his head from the man's lap.

"You know, Paul," Grace said. "I think I'm going to introduce you to Mother."

She had stopped outside the front entrance, a docile Patrol by her side. The change in her manner was alarming. Something about the way she'd pulled her hair back into a neat, red ball, or her determined stroll through the train yard and then through the station house. Maybe it was the disconcertingly clean white gloves that she'd slipped from some pocket in her long skirt and slipped over her pale, ink-stained hands. Whatever it was, Grace didn't look like the woman I'd been hobo-ing with on a train all the way from Oklahoma. She didn't look like she'd seen the inside of a boxcar in her life.

"Your mom lives here?"

"My mom? Oh," she said, smiling brightly. "*Mother.*"

"Is that what you're doing here?"

"Not that kind of mother," said Grace. "Come on."

When had I decided I was going with her? I wasn't sure, but it no longer mattered. It must have been midnight, maybe even later, and the streets of Raleigh felt like nowhere I'd ever been. A cluster of teenage girls who couldn't have been older than fifteen were sitting on the steps of a little white church, each with a pile of pebbles beside them. As the three of us passed, one of them called out, "Welcoming committee!" and they started throwing stones at our feet. I jumped off the sidewalk, but Grace just turned her gaze on them in a way that reminded me vaguely of my brother. The pelting stopped.

Further on, we saw two policemen escorting a staggering man with what appeared to be some kind of wagon wheel in his arms out of a grassy town square onto the sidewalk. The policemen gave us a long look until Grace said, "Fine night, gentlemen," in a brand new voice, at once civil and commanding. They nodded and returned to their quarry.

Eventually, we reached a long, commercial street called Fayetteville Road with the longest row of businesses I'd ever seen. The stores and restaurants were shuttered for the night, but the hotel windows blazed with life. Murmuring rivers of conversation could be heard amidst the quiet music and wafting tobacco smoke spilling out the open lobby doors. In the distance, I saw what I assumed to be the state Capitol, three stories tall, domed, lit up and glowing.

Abruptly, Grace turned onto a much narrower thoroughfare that cut north and east from the center of town. Here, the houses were dark, the carefully tended lawns nearly black in the shadows. Our footsteps rang on the sidewalks.

We walked a long time, the Patrol stumbling between us as Grace tugged him along. Soon, I heard pathetic bleating sounds rising from his throat, like the mew of a kitten in a sack.

"Grace," I said quietly, not wanting to wake the street or set the Patrol wailing, though of course I knew he couldn't hear me. "Slow down. The kid's exhausted."

"Well, pick him up."

The kid tripped on a raised paving stone and almost went down, and I caught him. He didn't squirm or scream when I handed his belongings to Grace and lifted him. He also didn't nestle against me; instead, he stayed absolutely rigid. Holding him was like carrying a fence post. Grace marched relentlessly farther from the center of town, and the houses to either side began dwindling in size, their lots squeezing together. At some point, as the kid hung heavier and heavier on my forearms, it occurred to me that this was the first child I'd ever held.

"What's his real name?" I asked.

Grace seemed surprised by the question, and a long time passed before she said, "I'm not sure she told me."

"She?"

"Not now, Paul, okay? I'm tired. Let's get where we're going."

Suddenly, the Patrol awoke, jabbed at my collarbone with his fingers, then bit my ear, and I dropped him.

"Ow!" I shouted, stumbled, then reached to keep the kid from falling backward. He'd landed on his feet, at least. "Sorry," I said when Grace motioned impatiently for me to pick him up again. Carefully, I knelt, slipped my hands around his shoulders, and held him a few seconds. When I was fairly sure he was too tired to fight me, I tried lifting him once more, and he let me.

Exhaustion had set in for me, too. The rhythm of walking—so strange after days on the train—beat in my bones. The night-shadows seemed to gain weight, settling on my shoulders as the kid's head drooped forward. I didn't even notice that Grace had stopped until I'd stumbled past her several steps.

She was standing in front of a squat, stone house tucked deep in the shadows of two dead trees on a lawn cropped almost bare. Behind the house was a long, black iron gate that separated the yard from what looked like a park on the other side.

"This is it," Grace said.

"This is what?" I lowered the Patrol. The kid wobbled but didn't fall.

"Go ring the bell, would you, while I straighten his clothes? He has to look presentable for Madame Duarte."

"What? Wait. There's a Madame Duarte? I thought you made that up."

"Not Madame Duarte," Grace said. "She's the matron of the Raleigh Institute for the Negro Blind."

I didn't even want to try and keep up with her. It was all I could do to stay standing. "It's got to be two o'clock in the morning."

"It doesn't matter. Come on."

Taking one of the Patrol's hands in her gloved one, she pulled him forward, and I dragged myself after them. Grace marched right up on the porch and banged the knocker. The sound went off like gunfire but triggered no immediate response. No lights sprang on. No rifle muzzles poked out of the neighboring windows. Indeed, I sensed no movement whatsoever before the door swung open.

In the entryway, holding a single candle in a brass holder, stood a tall colored woman in a green nightgown. Her curly, salt-and-pepper hair spilled loose and wild over her shoulders, and her black eyes flashed at me first, for some reason. Then she took in Grace, and finally dropped her gaze to the Patrol. She watched him for a long time before she said, "You actually found him."

I let out a breath and shook my head. This was too much to assimilate.

"I said I would," said Grace.

"You say a lot of things," said the woman in the doorway, and she dropped into a crouch before the Patrol. "Well, come on in, Sugar. What's your name?"

She stayed in that position several seconds. I waited for Grace to explain, then saw understanding spread across the colored woman's features. She stood, waving a finger. "Deaf, too?"

Grace nodded.

"He can't stay here, Miss Grace. He needs to go to South Roanoke. I expect you know the way."

Just like that, she started to shut the door, but Grace put her hand on it.

"Please," she said, and again, I found myself marveling at the confidence in her movements, her sure-handedness. "We've come a long way. He needs to sleep. He needs to be among people who can take care of him. Just give him a bed. Have someone take him to South Roanoke in the morning. I have to go home."

The colored woman and Grace stared at each other. Then the older woman shrugged. "What you need is a bath," she said. The woman took the

Patrol's hand, pulled him inside, and the door closed in our faces. Grace and I were alone on the porch.

Grace started past me out of the yard. I turned and called after her. "Grace, wait."

She looked back, and now her face wore the mask she'd mostly shown me on the train. "I'm tired, Paul. Let's go. I've done everything I can."

We went back a different way than we'd come, and when she slowed enough for me to walk beside her, she said, "See, Paul, that's the first key to useful dreaming. Like with the Patrol. You have to see what the relationship in front of you really is. Then you can start thinking about what it could be. But only then."

At a shambling, clapboard house not too far from Fayetteville Street, Grace turned off the sidewalk, strolled into a yard, and a stick-thin man with a brutally articulated jaw that stuck out like the edge of a spade stood up from the porch rocking chair where he'd been sleeping in his undershirt.

"Need a bed," Grace told him.

The man smirked. "Honeymoon suite's done booked."

"For him." Grace jerked a thumb at me.

"He got a dollar?"

"For the Project. I'm one of Mother's. You and I have actually met."

"Oh, yeah," he said.

Reaching into the pocket of her skirt, she pulled out a tiny roll of bills and handed one to him. "That gets him a bath, too, right?"

The guy shrugged and sat back down in his chair. Then Grace turned and put her palm against my cheek. "Get some sleep. Tomorrow, first thing, get cleaned up. She won't hire you unless you're clean."

"Hire me?" I mumbled. I almost reached up to take her hand, or hold it where it was. But I was too tired. And I was trying to see the relationship in front of me.

"Paul. Are you hearing me? Be out here in the morning, ready and clean, or you're on your own. This is your one shot, and I probably shouldn't be giving it to you. It could get me in trouble. Got it?"

"One shot."

Grace dropped her hand. I did reach for it, then, but she seemed surprised, and our fingers just bumped together. Blushing, I looked away.

"Sleep," Grace said, and left.

After a few more seconds of my standing there, the man in the chair grunted and gestured with his formidable chin. "The only bed that's left is all the way upstairs in the attic. Way back against the wall. Three other people are already sleeping up there. Don't wake 'em; they won't like it. Don't turn on lights. Anywhere."

I went in the house and up the stairs, which tilted dangerously. Whatever light there was fell away as I went up and up. I found the attic room, opened the door, but could barely make out the shapes of the three cots arrayed in a haphazard line across the room. A fourth, empty one was shoved against the back wall under the sloping eaves. The sleeper in the nearest cot stirred and grunted angrily. I shut the door and moved quickly to the vacant cot and sat down on it.

I waited for my eyes to adjust, but there was no light anywhere. Only blackness, the memory of train-rhythm, the echo of a blind and deaf kid's wail in my ears. Oklahoma was a made-up place some unimaginable distance from here. My father's last breath was no longer traceable. The only thing that suggested I was anywhere but in my grave was the occasional groaning of the faceless sleepers around me. In my filthy shirt and disintegrating shoes, I lay back on the pillowless slab of mattress and wept.

*****

Despite my exhaustion, I slept only fitfully, and slipped out of bed before dawn, catching barely a glimpse of the bearded hulks splayed like trolls across the other cots. There was no shower in the house, and the bathwater came out pond-colored, flecked with bits of bug and dirt. But I washed the best I could, shaved, and tried to brush off and straighten my only spare shirt. For the next few hours, I sat on the sidewalk as the day warmed. There was less dust in the air here and no train-grit, but each breath seemed to trickle down slow and taste too sweet, as though I were inhaling sap. The trolls lumbered out of the flophouse together, pushing one another and tugging at their beards. They took no notice of me. Grace showed up a little after nine in a blue-and-yellow-checked sundress and a floppy straw hat. Her hair seemed darker, almost wine-colored in the sunlight. All the way downtown, she reeled off instructions. I didn't understand a word of them.

I first saw the words *Federal Writers' Project* stenciled to the door of a cramped basement office in one of the relatively new state buildings near the Capitol. The words *Works Progress Administration*, in larger letters, had been printed across the top. I froze as Grace jiggled a key in the lock, cursed to herself, and finally pushed the door open.

"This is a WPA thing?" I said, still trying to get my mouth to move properly in this new, heavier air.

Grace fixed me with the stare I'd come to know well during our boxcar trip from Oklahoma.

"I don't take relief," I told her.

"Good," said Grace, "I'm not offering any." She moved through the door without checking to see whether I would follow.

The Raleigh bureau offices of the Federal Writers' Project amounted to two windowless rooms, some filing cabinets, stacks of paper piled everywhere, and a few desks with virtually no available surface. Grace put me in a chair, rummaged through the nearest cabinet, and came back with some forms and a pair of yellow pencils.

"Fill them in," she said.

"Grace, what am I doing?"

"You hungry? I'm hungry. She might have food; hold on."

Vanishing into the other room, Grace reemerged a short time later. "Would you believe, apples?" She tossed me one.

"This makes…what, eight meals in a row?"

"Finish those forms and do what I tell you, and you might be able to buy bread to go with 'em one day." She bit into her fruit, and I studied the forms she gave me. Pretty soon, I came to the section marked *Professional Experience*. The first box asked for a list of publications and/or educational work.

"Grace. This applications seems to be for…for writers, or something."

"Check."

"I'm not a writer."

Lowering her apple, Grace raised one eyebrow, then said, "How do you know?"

It was the way she looked at me as much as her voice that delivered the shock, as if I'd just been plugged into an electric socket. My spine went rigid, and my skin prickled. After a long time, I said, "What do you mean?"

"You think you know what a writer is?"

"Someone who writes things for a living?"

She broke into a grin and gestured around the room with her half-eaten apple. "A living? I guess I've been hanging around different writers than you have."

Just then the hallway door burst open, and the woman I would come to know as Henrietta Klein came roaring through it like a locomotive. Grace jumped up, grinning even wider, so I stood, too, feeling certain that I'd just been caught red-handed at something. The woman chuffed to a stop, her kinked hair coiling over her ears and across her eyes, bracelets jangling, her coal-black skin slick and glowing, her gauzy dress sweeping about her like steam. Her eyes flicked at me once, then at Grace.

"What's that?" she said.

"New recruit, boss."

"I don't remember asking you to recruit."

"'Helping the worthy in their time of greatest need.' Isn't that how you put it, Mother?"

Mother? My thoughts were already spinning too fast. Now they flew away from me altogether.

"So he's worthy?" Mother asked.

Grace looked over at me, then shrugged. "Needy, anyway."

"Those my apples? That my apple you're eating, Grace Lowie?"

Without waiting for an answer, Mother stomped into the other room, and Grace laughed. "Hurry up, Paul," she said, tapping the form I'd half-completed with her pale fingers. "You're going to miss your train."

"Miss my…Grace, I don't even know what to put down here. I can't fill in these boxes. What am I supposed to be doing?"

"I understand how you feel, young man," Mother's voice boomed from next door. "She makes me feel like that every day I see her."

Motioning me out of the chair, Grace grabbed one of the pencils and began writing on my form. When I leaned over the paper, she snatched it away, then stood up and waved me into Mother's office.

Mother seemed to have too many hands. Somehow, she had the receiver from a black phone, a pad of paper, various writing implements, and a dusty glass filled with amber-colored liquid all suspended in mid-air at the same time. After a few seconds of finishing four or five of the tasks she was doing simultaneously, she put down the glass and held out two fingers for the forms that Grace had just finished for me. She scanned them once, then lifted her disconcertingly sad brown eyes to me.

"This all accurate?"

At my side, my fingers quivered. "As far as I know."

Grace broke out laughing. "See, Mother? Smart. Quick. Promising. His name is Paul Dent. Paul, this is Henrietta Klein, also known as Mother. Mother, you should hear his stories about his bro—"

"I'm going to lose this, now," Mother said quietly, and slipped the form with my name on it into the largest pile within reach on her overflowing desk.

There was silence just long enough for me to feel the dust crawling down my lungs. I started to cough, and Mother studied me once more. "I don't care about his promise. Or his past. I care about his work. Is he going to work?"

"He'll work." There was no laughter in Grace's voice anymore.

"At what you tell him to? Wait, scratch that." Mother waved a hand before Grace could answer. "At what *I* tell him to?"

The women stared at each other. I coughed again. "Listen," I said, "I've got to go outside. The air in here—"

"I'm thinking Mountain Scenic," Grace said, ignoring me. "His specialty is smaller towns."

"He has a specialty?" Mother eyed Grace suspiciously.

While the two women went on with their stare-down or jousting or whatever it was they were doing, my breath started to rasp. I turned for the door. Grace moved to accompany me, and Mother called after her one more time.

"Eleven months, Grace, and I'm still less than sure that you understand the nature and purpose of this Project."

"More than a year as Bureau Director, Mother, and you're saying you do?"

Mother's voice dropped lower, and her eyes flicked back and forth between Grace and me. "I'm pretty certain none of us know what it is yet. Or what it could be. Go ahead, take him to the train."

Grace grabbed me hard by the wrist and pulled me out the door. She made me wait in the hallway while she pulled open drawers and gathered a stack of notebooks, some pencils, pens and a fistful of paper clips, eventually stuffing all of it into a stained, shredding canvas bag she found balled up on one of the chairs. She looked furious as she dragged me up the steps and back into the morning sunlight, but as soon as we were walking, her mood brightened again.

Meanwhile, once we were free of the office, my lungs relaxed, and I found myself adapting my walk to the weight of this thicker sunlight. The air dripped down my lungs. It tasted heavy in my mouth, and glowed a kind of dusty, fleck-filled yellow color. At one point, while waiting for the first traffic policeman I'd ever seen in my life to wave us through an intersection, I put out my hand and a tiny, yellow clump alighted on it, as though the atmosphere itself had crystallized on my skin.

"Well?" Grace said, and I realized she'd been talking to me for some time. I held out my hand to her, and she stared at it, then at my face. "Pollen?"

"That's what it is?"

"How do things grow out there in Blackcreek, Oklahoma?"

"Slowly," I said.

The cop waved us forward, and we walked a little faster now, under the stately rows of tended oak trees, along Fayetteville Street's shiny-clear shop windows, though even here, more than a few of the shops were abandoned.

Every time we encountered someone new, Grace would swivel her head and her eyes swallowed them. Every step she took seemed to energize her; I kept expecting her to break into a run. Only the sun slowed her down, burning through her pale skin like paper, and she took periodic advantage of any available shade. I wasn't in love with her, though in the sleepless buzz of that first North Carolina morning, I probably thought I was. I'd just never seen anyone react to the world this way, skittering over its surface like a water droplet across a heated pan.

"Listen, Grace," I said as the Raleigh train station appeared ahead of us. "What am I doing?"

Grace trained her formidable gaze on me. "You haven't been listening?"

An anger I hadn't expected flared in my chest. "You didn't ask me if I wanted to sign up for this. Whatever it is."

Grace shielded her eyes. She couldn't have slept much more than I had. "Sorry, Paul," she said. "I skipped the beginning, didn't I?"

After that, walking a little more slowly while bells tolled whatever mid-morning hour it was, she talked and I listened. The way Grace explained it, the Federal Writers' Project was a sort of grand, doomed compromise. "The bastard child of Frankenstein's bastard child," she said. An unwieldy, almost unimaginable offshoot of the WPA, itself spawned by bizarre creatures "hitherto unknown to history: bureaucrats with so much smarts and heart and power, all at the same time, that they'd actually started believing in the bureaucracies they'd created."

Essentially, my job was this: I was now a member of a nationwide team of teachers, researchers, scholars, editors, poll-takers, and writers employed by the federal government. Our work was to conduct interviews, check and calculate distances on maps, study local histories, observe and collect folklore and social customs and, in the end, produce guide books to every state in the Union that captured the distinguishing characteristics and most notable attractions of every single American town— not for study or historical import but to be used by traveling motor-tourists.

"You know," Grace continued, "*leisure* travelers. All those happy, lucky families with cars and extra gas and free time these days." We were inside the station now, and Grace had just handed me a train ticket and an envelope with several one-dollar bills in it.

"So you're sending me to some town to write about it," I said, when we'd sat down in the shade on the white, wooden benches beside the tracks.

"Right," said Grace.

"And I'm to…"

"Meet people. All kinds of people. Dig up stories. Find their P.D.s and Town Couches, their little fears and grand hopes. Learn what they do on Saturday nights if they actually have a dollar in their pockets and aren't too tired. Discover what they show out-of-towners who come to visit, and what they prefer to keep to themselves."

The morning warmed, and her words began to melt together as the sheer incomprehensibility of what I was about to do and how my life had changed overnight rattled around inside me. I watched the flight of fat insects, which bore no resemblance to the skeletal, frantic things I'd grown up swatting, while a white-uniformed colored man in white gloves stood on the platform at parade rest, sweating. He stirred only to lift the bags of a trio of older women in flowered hats who had lined up together like a cultivated hedge.

"Name everything," I heard Grace say. "Trees. Clocks. Houses. Places people seem to stop in the street. Use those observational skills I'm fairly certain you've got. Before I start writing about a place, I make damn sure I feel like I live there. It's a decent exercise, anyway. Harder than you think. But make no mistake." Abruptly, she swung to face me. The look in her eyes was hard. "This isn't writing, Paul. It's training, at best. But mostly, it's humiliation, plain and simple. It puts you in your place and makes you grateful. It's a handful of dimes and something to fill your time. And that's all it is, unless you make it something else. It's bought time, and dearly bought. So you better use it wisely."

I'd almost accustomed myself to the speed of her mood changes. But this one confounded me. I wasn't even sure exactly what she meant. For a while, though, the bitterness in her voice sounded disconcertingly like my father's. Eventually, I realized she expected some sort of response. "Thank you…" I stuttered. "I mean, the last few days have been so different than…"

Her smile came fast, and vanished just as quickly. She understood the expression on my face before I realized I had one. Her own softened.

"Well, we have shared something, haven't we? Here. After you've wandered around Trampleton for a while, go to this address." She produced a pad of paper and a pen and scribbled something down.

"Trampleton," I said. "What's that?"

Grace smiled again. "That's for you to tell me. It's where you'll be living for the next couple of months. It's the first place you're going to capture for me. Then we'll send you somewhere new."

She tore off the paper and handed it to me. "Go here. Introduce yourself to the proprietor. His name is not Robert, by the way. It's pronounced 'Row-bear-t.' Don't ask me why, and whatever you do, don't ask him. He's a good man—a friend—but proud. Easily annoyed. Quick to anger. And colored, did I mention colored?"

"Why am I going there?"

"Because you need a place to stay, and he owes me. Tell him I sent you, and don't aggravate him. If you listen and observe and pay attention like a good little Project member, he might just give you something worth writing about. Maybe he'll even help you find people to talk to. I don't think you'll be lonely for long."

It wasn't the first patronizing thing she'd said to me. Just the first that felt wrong. I hadn't said I was lonely, and I wasn't actually thinking about that right now. Even so, I didn't want to leave her side, though I suspected I might be at least as good at talking to strangers as she was. "So will I see you again?"

"Of course. I'm your field boss. And you better damn well have pages when I come, or Mother will have us both for breakfast."

Five minutes later, Grace put me on the train. On board, I moved to a bench against a window and looked out to wave. But Grace wasn't looking at me. She was watching the shadows under the overhang at the far corner of the station house. I glanced that way, too, and saw my brother Lewis step out of the shade into the North Carolina sunlight and head straight across the platform. I found myself standing, half-shouting her name, pounding on the window. The young couple across from me got so upset that they left the car to find other seats. The train lurched as it picked up speed, though the lurching did feel gentler in a passenger car than it had in a boxcar.

I put my head in my hands, then jerked up, convinced that I had imagined the whole thing. Pressing my face to the warm window glass, I tried to see back down the track. But the station house was no longer in sight. It didn't matter. I'd seen Lewis, all right. Filthy, wild-haired, grinning. Lifting a hand to introduce himself to Grace. Who'd lifted her hand, too. In greeting.

As if she knew him? My heart pounded against my ribs; my breath came in spasmodic gasps, the way it did during one of my spells. I'd never had someone talk to me the way she had, or offer me such an opportunity, which I'd believed was for and because of me, but now…

To my amazement, I realized I was smiling. I thought of the figure I'd seen leaping from the coal gondola the night before, and I knew that Lewis had followed me here. He'd never been more than a few cars behind me at any point. Sooner or later, in his own inscrutable time, he'd show up at the door of my new home. The thought was almost reassuring.

I settled back and watched the trees. The train stopped often, and the car filled around me.

A few hours out of Raleigh, I got to talking to a man named Cutter who'd lost a leg in the Great War. He said that he'd had a dream, not long after returning to his Carolina mountain home, about his blown-off limb stowing away aboard a freighter, wrapping itself in scraps of newspaper to keep warm, and hopping a grain car once it had reached the States. When it arrived at his cabin door—veined and muddy and still in its army-issue boot—it jumped up in the air and knocked.

The whites of Mr. Cutter's eyes had so much red in them they looked feral. Bristles clumped on his wrinkled chin and cheeks, as if he'd just been shoved face down in gray sand. His stained blue cotton suit hung limply across his shoulders. If not for what he'd told me about being a teenaged soldier, I might have taken him for seventy years old. He cut me a linty slice of cheese from a slab he'd been carrying in his suit-coat pocket with a jackknife. Sitting across from each other, we both ate as we looked out the window.

I'd never ridden in a passenger car before. I was surprised by how much softer the country looked in motion, through glass. The new, white blossoms on the Bradford pear trees sparkled like cake decorations. Fence posts and tree trunks stood prettily wrapped in the kudzu that the Civilian Conservation Corps had recently planted to control erosion. The CCC had tried kudzu in Oklahoma, but even that miraculous, omnivorous vine had found no purchase in the earth where we lived.

I opened the window to release the steadily intensifying heat, then closed it again as clouds of pollen poured down my lungs. Not long after noon, the grassy plains of the Piedmont gathered themselves into low, green hills, and the sun climbed all the way overhead.

I told Mr. Cutter about my new job. He asked how I'd gotten it, and I told him I didn't exactly know. Then I described the agency's office in North Carolina, and Grace Lowie, and Henrietta Klein.

Mr. Cutter edged forward on his seat. "Runs the whole thing, you say? The colored woman?" After that, his questions came in a torrent. "Who's this book for?"

I tried to shrink away from the intensity in his face. "For the rich motor...I mean, for motor tourists. I mean for everyone. For you."

"Who's publishing it?"

"We...the govern—"

"They want town stories? Real people's stories?"

"I think so."

"And they're sending people like you to gather them?"

I nodded, though I had no idea what that meant. I was profoundly relieved when he turned toward the window again.

A few minutes later, a gray-haired porter came down the aisle, his red uniform smartly pressed and his visor-cap pulled low over his eyes. "TrrrrAMpleton," he chirred as he passed by us. Mr. Cutter was scowling now.

Then I caught sight of the train station. Entry #1 for my new notebook. *The Trampleton depot has a slanted, slate roof of forest green. With its red doors and gleaming windows edged in red, it looks more like a gingerbread house than a traveler's stop.* I bent forward slightly so I could see more of it through the towering trees, and Mr. Cutter almost banged skulls with me.

"Your stop, too?" I asked hesitantly.

"Help me off."

I carried the man's beaten black satchel, then lifted him from the bottom step of the train onto the platform. He came away too easily, like a weed stem off its roots, and for a second I thought I'd pulled him from his peg-leg. But he got his good foot under him and shook off my hand.

"I think maybe I've got something for that book of yours," he said. "Fourth of July. You got plans?" His cough was an ugly, ripping thing.

"July? I just got here."

"Then meet me at the old Screwpine mill around midnight. Screwpine. Got it? You want a real story? You'll find it there."

From *The WPA Guide to the Old North State, Asheville*

"The definition of 'buncombe,' (spelled also bunkum *and contracted to* bunk), *as meaning anything said, written, or done for mere show, had its origin in a speech made in the Sixteenth Congress by Felix Walker, Representative from the district of which Buncombe County was a part. The address was a masterpiece of fence-sitting, and when a colleague asked the purpose of it, Walker replied, 'I merely speak for Buncombe.'*

(p.139)

June 1938, Washington, DC

All morning long, I told my tale while Senators Froad and Cain asked occasional questions but mostly listened. And all along, I was thinking that maybe I'd let Lewis think I wasn't going to unmask him, then turn at just the right moment in my testimony and ask him for clarification. *Do I have that right, Lewis? Is that how you remember it, brother?*

If only once over the course of that morning he had given me a pleading look, or even a defiant one, anything other than that unfazed, faintly amused, and, yes, senatorial gaze, I would have done it. But Lewis just sat and gazed at me keenly, as though he was really curious about what I would say. At times, he seemed to be the only interested person in the room.

With a grunt, Senator Froad straightened in his seat and held up a hand to stop my talking. He hadn't stirred in some time. "Mr. Dent, you'll allow me to interrupt here for a moment. You mentioned the Project Office in Raleigh. And you mentioned having the opportunity to meet Mother." Snapping a match to life in his hand, he drew his cigar off the tray in front of him, lit it, and puffed gray smoke into the air. Several seconds passed before he remembered, scowled at me and pinched out the cigar again. More smoke rose from his fingertips like residue from a failed spell.

Senator Cain, too, had stirred to wakefulness. "Mother. Yes. Henrietta Klein. An actual member of the Writers' Project at long last. The first in an entire morning's testimony that our distinguished guest has gotten around to mentioning. Other than the…*remarkable* Miss Lowie, I mean. I was beginning to despair."

"Mr. Dent, I'm afraid my good friend Norman has a particular disdain for Mrs. Henrietta Klein," said Senator Froad.

"And why would that be?" my brother asked. Under the table, he'd stretched out both legs and crossed them at his elegantly sheathed ankles. His voice seemed to have smoothed over even more.

Senator Froad lifted three stubby fingers and ticked off his points. "Colored. Woman. Writers' Project Regional Director."

"Only one of those things matters to me and you know it, you imperious bastard," murmured Senator Cain, his face reddening under his formidable mustache.

"Two."

The men looked at each other. Senator Froad was smiling.

"Two," said Senator Cain. When he smiled back, I decided I had no understanding whatsoever of the events going on in this room.

"If only you could tell us, Mr. Dent, that Mother was the brains behind the Scott Set's activities from the beginning, well, that would make my colleague from Wisconsin overwhelmingly happy. He'd be scampering over to his new protégé Representative Dies this very evening, telling him about the bright new target for his committee of vigilantes. My God, a Harvard-educated Negro woman using her position of trust to promote...what? Mingling of the races? Some sort of unionization? Maybe a few of those pesky labor demands about maximum hours and minimum wages? Artist's rights? I mean, we've yet to establish exactly what your little group was up to, Mr. Dent, but if you were to tell us that Mrs. Klein was even *aware* of your activities, Mr. Cain would consider the entire day a resounding success. A bellwether day, even. But you're not going to tell us that, are you?"

"Oh, skillfully done, Froad. The most effective *not*-asking of a crucial question I've seen all month."

Senator Froad chomped happily on his unlit cigar. "Mr. Dent, I want you to return with me now, for just a moment, to Mrs. Klein's offices. I want you to describe for us again—with the same care and thoroughness with which you traced the circuitous route you took to get there—exactly what you saw."

We seemed to have turned abruptly in some new direction. But I had no idea what that was. I glanced toward Lewis, hoping for a warning twitch of his lips or something. But he was gazing over my head at the bored handful of reporters still in the gallery. I hadn't dared a glance back there, but I was pretty sure one of them had been snoring for the better part of an hour.

"Mostly," I said, "I saw piles of paper."

"Paper. Excellent. Now, could you describe the papers? Anything you happened to see?"

"Well, as I told you, I wasn't there for long. There was the application form that Grace gave me. Lots of different notebooks and pads all over the place, with lots of different writing in them. I don't know what else to say, the place was just overflowing with people's work."

Senator Froad shifted with exaggerated casualness so that his gaze was half on me and half on Senator Cain. "Overflowing, you say. With people's work. I like that, Mr. Dent. I like that very much. Do you think it's just possible, Norman, that at the end of today's investigation, we're going to discover not only no evidence of overt—or even creeping—radical subversion in the North Carolina Federal Writers' Project, but none of your party's beloved shiftlessness of labor, either? Not even...dare we think it...a boondoggle?"

"Did you happen to notice any newspapers lying about?" Senator Cain interjected.

I tried to think back, but all that came to mind were dust motes, apples that tasted of desk drawer, and the morning sun through the high windows. "Not particularly, no. I mean, I don't remember any."

"Leaflets?" Senator Cain leaned forward. "This is important, sir. You're under oath. Anything at all, Mr. Dent. Maybe you didn't realize what you were seeing. This committee isn't looking for villains, we're not witch-hunting—"

"Not yet," Senator Froad murmured.

"But we need to know. For the good of the country. Hell, for the good of your blessed Project. Did you happen to see any publications with initials you didn't recognize? I.W.W., for instance, or—"

"All right, I think we've quite covered *this* subject," Senator Froad said, steepling his fingers below his chin. "Thank you, Norman. And thank you, Mr. Dent. You've got to admit, Norman. And Senator Asbury, I haven't forgotten you hovering over there as if you hadn't an opinion in the world. If there's one thing our young guest this morning has proven, it's that he does indeed have a certain fondness, if you will, for the told tale. His placement on the Project may not have been as entirely fraudulent as I must admit I'd initially feared."

"Did you doubt it?" Lewis said. "I didn't."

Did he actually wink at me?

"Fondness?" Senator Cain snapped. "If he gets any more fond, *we'll* have invaded Czechoslovakia by the end of the day."

Both Froad and my brother laughed out loud, but Lewis's laugh was not one I recognized.

"As for his not being fraudulent, you'll be so good as to yield the floor for just a bit longer, Froad. I have a few more questions for our Mr. Dent here."

"I believe you're missing my point, Norman," Senator Froad said in his ominously quiet voice.

This time, though, Senator Cain ignored it. "I'll need no more than five minutes. Thank you very much."

Senator Froad lowered his chin onto his fingers and left it hanging there like the head of a puppet on a peg.

"Now, then. Mr. Dent," said Senator Cain. "This is a straightforward, factual question, not an invitation to tell us additional picaresque details of your adventures. Could you please tell us—precisely and succinctly, please— just how long you were on government relief before Mrs. Klein and Miss Lowie invited you to become involved in the Project?"

Heat rushed into my cheeks, and I thought of my father. The answer to this question was one of the few I could give about anything I'd ever done that my dad would have cheered. My eyes flitted toward Lewis. This was also a gift-wrapped moment for exposure. But if Lewis felt any concern, none showed in his tanned, markless face.

"I've never taken relief," I said. Snarled, almost.

Senator Cain shoved back in his seat and nodded. "Very good." He thumped the table with a fist and folded his arms across his chest. "Very good indeed, Mr. Dent. The concept insults you, doesn't it? No free handouts for you, sir. No need to be ashamed of that, young man; I believe— I *know*—that's how most sturdy American men feel. That's what the terminally well-meaning architects of our New Beggar's Deal fail to understand. But in this particular case, it does raise one niggling little issue, doesn't it, Froad?"

Senator Froad's cigar twitched between his warty lips. Otherwise, he stayed still.

"Mr. Dent, at any time during the registration process, did either Miss Lowie or Mrs. Klein or anyone associated with the Writers' Project mention that you were all conspiring to defraud the federal government?"

"Oh, for Christ's sake," Senator Froad muttered.

"Did no one mention that the charter drawn up so thoughtfully and championed so manfully, in the face of so much common sense, as well as genuine need elsewhere, by the great man to my right, requires—"

"Qualifying for relief," I said. Senator Cain blinked in surprise as I went on. *"Before a writer becomes eligible for employment with the Federal Writers' Project, he will have proven, to the satisfaction of a qualified government agent, that he is pathetically and permanently incapable of taking care of himself. "* I wasn't just quoting Grace, but channeling her, it seemed. Even the barbed smile tugging at my lips felt like one of hers. *"To qualify for the Project, a writer must submit documentable proof of prolonged misery, shame, and embarrassment. Preferably two years or more. Don't mention any job you ever managed to get that devoured your time and kept you from writing but allowed you to eat, whatever you do. Don't even try supporting yourself. Otherwise, you can't possibly be a true writer or researcher, because you can't possibly be suffering enough, and therefore you do not merit assistance.* Yes," I finished. "Grace told me."

Senator Cain had sat up absolutely straight and seemed coiled to lunge at either Senator Froad or me. His grin was predatory. "Hmm," he said, "you're right, Froad. No creeping radicalism there. I wonder where our young Mr. Dent, son of a railroad man from Blackcreek, Oklahoma, might have come across such an attitude?" His hand flashed into the stack of papers in front of him and snatched out a yellow folder.

"And while we're on the subject of being a *true writer*. I'm so glad you mentioned that, Mr. Dent. Let's put aside that pesky relief provision which your Communist friends object to so prettily, shall we?"

"No one has been proven a Communist here this morning, Norman," said Senator Froad. "You're the only one who's even mentioned them."

Senator Cain barreled on. "After all, that provision was only meant to ensure that government help went to people who really needed it. In fact, let's grant Senator Froad's deepest wish and put aside the issue of traitors, Nazis, and Communists among us for the moment. Instead, Mr. Dent, let's see just how much of a *true writer* you are."

He made a great show of squinting, studying the pages in front of him, turning them this way and that as though they were blurred photographs. "I have here your complete publication record, Mr. Dent. I do hope you'll help us amend it after the session today if it isn't complete; it's so hard getting accurate records in these uncertain times. You've seen this information, haven't you, Froad?"

For a moment, I actually thought Senator Froad had fallen asleep. His breathing had steadied, and his eyelids were closed. After a long moment, they opened, and he gazed at me with his lizard-stare. "I've seen it. Doesn't matter."

"You're Goddamn right it doesn't matter. Because nothing can shake you, can it? In the face of all logic and hard evidence, in the face of billions of wasted dollars and an insidious threat to our democracy and a country staggering not out of the so-called Depression but into the even more devastating Roosevelt Recession under the weight of the millstone of permanent, crushing debt, you continue to cling to this naïve, namby-pamby, harmful notion that anyone claiming to be an artist must be possessed of some innate, unshakeable decency and integrity of purpose."

Senator Froad didn't even lift his head. "What I cling to," he said, "is the certainty that real artists sometimes inspire those qualities in me." He looked at Senator Cain. The Missouri man stared back in disbelief. To their right, my brother drummed his fingers on the table, then glanced my way. The smile that slipped over his face was his real one, which had terrified and drawn me all my life.

"Froad," said Senator Cain, "you understand this paper is completely blank. There's no proof that this boy ever wrote anything, let alone published it."

I was barely listening. I was looking at Lewis's hands. They were the only remaining giveaway, the one thing he'd been unable to transform into privileged South Carolinian, with their unmistakable crooked fingers and permanently swollen knuckles from all the years of brawling. As I watched, Lewis lifted one of those hands and gave me a little wave, nonchalant, carefree. Then he straightened his tie. His hair.

"Oh, all right," sighed Senator Cain. "In the scope of everything else we're dealing with, this level of fraud hardly matters. Barely even qualifies as a boondoggle. It's just your basic, everyday swindle." Settling back and gesturing wearily, Senator Cain yielded the floor back to Senator Froad, who popped upright like a jack-in-the-box.

"No, it's not all right. You've raised an actual point, Norman. I congratulate you. And I want to address it. So before we take our lunch adjournment, I'd like to ask Mr. Dent one more question. I'd like you to tell us, please, as clearly as you can, the first thing you noticed when you stepped out of that little train station and onto the main thoroughfare of Trampleton, North Carolina, for the very first time."

The about-faces in the questioning were becoming impossible to track. It took me several seconds to reorient myself.

"You mean Sherman Street?" I asked.

"Is that what I mean? I've never had the pleasure."

"For Christ's sake, Froad, stop wasting our Goddamn time," Senator Cain barked.

"That would have to be the elms," I said.

"Go on."

"The elm trees. I mean, maybe they have streets like that in other places in the country. But everyone in Trampleton has the same experience."

"Which is what, Mr. Dent?"

"There's something church-like about those trees. They make everyone quiet. They've grown in perfect columns on both sides of the street, and their branches arc over your head and make a sort of open cathedral of the whole town. Sometimes, it's all—"

"My point," Senator Froad almost hissed at Senator Cain, "is that this young man turns out to be more than capable—even exceptionally capable— of doing the job for which he was hired. And Grace Lowie recognized that. So she plucked a desperate young man with no prospects off a boxcar and through him, gave us Trampleton, North Carolina. There's your boondoggle, Norman."

"Froad, we haven't even scratched the surface of what your Grace Lowie might have done. This kid's capabilities are irrelevant."

"Wrong," said Senator Froad. "Not just wrong, tragic. The floor is no longer yours, Senator Cain. It's mine. And I think we'll just have some sandwiches sent up, rather than taking a lunch break. You, of course, Norman, are free to leave if you have other things to do. Now, then, Mr. Dent, if you please. Continue."

PART TWO

Colonization

"Your method should be to get the informant talking freely about himself…You should be able to 'talk the same language'; that is, converse on subjects and in terms familiar to him. Make him feel important as a collaborator."
— from *Supplementary Instructions to The American Guide Manual, Manual for Folklore Studies*

"I wish you'd get your mind off your precious self enough to write me a one act play about other people—what they say and how they behave.
　　　　With dearest love,
　　　　Your simply so-perfect too-too
　　　　Daddy"

— F. Scott Fitzgerald in a letter to his daughter from the Grove
　　　Park Inn, Asheville, North Carolina, Summer 1935

March 1936, Trampleton, North Carolina

Sucking hard at the syrupy air, I stepped onto Sherman Street and fell for the first time into the elms. Overhead, the branches fanned open, carving the sky into a thousand blue cross-hatched fragments. Giant bud-clusters hung up there like beehives suspended in the eaves, and from them came a deep and constant rustling.

I don't know how long I stood there. Awhile, though. Eventually, I became aware of bicycles drifting past. Lots of them, their riders mostly staring upward.

That first afternoon, I just walked and walked and walked. I forgot to eat. I don't remember sitting down. The air felt cooler and thinner than in Raleigh, and the tangy, resin scent of pine swept over me with each new breeze. For the first hour, maybe even more, I circled Sherman Street, mostly staring straight over my head. The majestic, intertwined branches seemed to recombine in endless configurations, reminding me of hundreds of conjoined hands or the letters of an unfathomable alphabet scrawled across the sky. Nowhere in Blackcreek had I seen a single tree as proud and deeply rooted and just plain healthy as the most diminutive of these elms.

Gradually, as the bicycles whirred by and the sounds of afternoon chatter mixed with the birdsong from the still-leafless canopy above, I became aware of the buildings I was passing. Stone and brick, mostly. Gray and red. During my seventh or eighth circuit of the few blocks that comprised the center of town, I came to a stop in front of the train station. The windows looked frosted in a vibrant red, and they gleamed. While I was standing there, two broad-shouldered men in matching blue suits stepped out of the entrance with sizable burlap bags slung over their backs. The men dispersed in opposite directions without speaking to one another. Several minutes passed before I figured out they were postmen.

The first establishment I actually entered was Riley's General Store, just to the right of the station. Built of weathered gray stone and pine, with no trace of red anywhere, it looked more like the train station's shadow than an actual place. Inside, the shop smelled—pleasantly—of raw meat and cut tobacco and shoe polish. I just stood by the doorway a while, watching the afternoon sun catch and glide along the hardwood floor, the rows of canned goods and stationery and dresses on racks and stacks of folded towels and jars of coffee and candy lining the glass counters. There was a whole wall of hammers, their handles polished to the same sheen as the floor.

The man behind the butcher counter—Riley himself—swung his gaze in my direction. He had tiny black eyes, and his flat, dark hair seemed embedded in his scalp rather than growing there.

"You need something?" he said, sounding neither kind nor welcoming. Then he added, "Stranger?" for good measure.

I shook my head and left.

Through the windows of the Sherman Street Tavern next door, I saw mostly smoke. The only people I could make out were a burly bartender wiping glasses with a rag and two solitary old men at either end of the bar. Both men had a plate of what looked like laundry but was probably boiled cabbage in front of them. A fourth man materialized, red-bearded, massive-shouldered, with a fiddle in his hands, streaming light behind him like a Greek god. It took me a long moment to realize that the light was pouring in from the tavern's back door, and the man had come in that way.

The bells in the tower of the Methodist church chimed five o'clock. Almost immediately, a clatter rose in the East and a locust cloud of working men on bicycles swept through town, the whir of their wheels and the whoop of their voices obliterating all other sound. I waited, watching, until they were mostly gone, and was about to cross the road when a second group seemed to pour down the street even more quickly than the first, the majority of them on foot. Every single one of them was colored. A few bicycles squeaked and rattled; otherwise, they made virtually no sound. Within minutes, they'd vanished up the side streets, leaving not a single person in sight.

My first impulse was to hide. I kept waiting for someone to ask what I was doing there, but no one paid me any mind. Finally, I slipped off down the block. At the petrol station next to the church, a filthy red truck with a bed as long as the building beside it had pulled up, and the chain-smoking, cap-wearing kid who served as gas attendant scrambled to fill it up.

"Warned you about smoking near the gas pumps, Danny-O," I heard the driver of the truck say as he swung down from his seat to stretch his legs.

The kid straightened, tugged the cigarette from his mouth, and dangled it near the truck's open tank. The trucker spat, shook his head, and wandered away, twisting his shoulders back and forth. The kid smiled to himself, then looked up and saw me.

"Want something?" he said.

"Not really."

The kid smiled again. It wasn't exactly a mean smile, but it wasn't an invitation, either. He went back to pumping, and I turned toward the center of town.

Not long afterward, I found myself standing for the fifth or sixth time against the blue, red, and white barbershop pole outside Mr. Gene's Nice and Clean, which was wedged between the tavern and some sort of real estate office. Only then did I remember that I was meant to be working.

I pulled out the notebook that Grace had given me and flipped to a blank page. Without taking my eyes from the window, I scrawled an instruction to myself: *Meet the blonde at Mr. Gene's.* I watched her a little while longer as she tidied a teenager's hair and snipped a few more strands off the top, her hands darting everywhere like frantic birds. She was a little plump, and red-faced from the work or the heat of all those bodies. Other boys were bumping around her chair and chattering. Some of them were close to my age, but most looked to be in high school. Mr. Gene kept glancing over at her, and so did the guy in Mr. Gene's barber chair as he puckered his lips to keep from sucking in dollops of shaving cream when he spoke. The whole time I stood there, alternately glancing around the street and sneaking glances into the shop, she never stopped smiling.

A good hour or so later, I realized I was cold. I opened the folded scrap of paper that Grace had given me right before she put me on the train. *Robert's Boarding House. 984 Lumberton.*

I'd seen Lumberton. It was one of the residential streets, just a few feet down the block from where I stood. I stared a few seconds down the long lane of boxy, two-story wooden houses, their tiny front yards framed by carefully painted white fences. A kid, maybe twelve years old, was toting three smaller kids in a wagon. Two women were standing in the shade of an oak tree, huddled over a newspaper. A few of the bicycling workmen curved around me and pedaled away down the macadam. I set off after them.

The houses on Lumberton seemed squeezed together, but as I walked, the lots slowly swelled in size, and garages or extra wings sprouted from the sides of the more imposing dwellings. The addresses proceeded in orderly fashion up to the 800s. The last house—a white, columned structure with porch swings swaying gently at either end of a veranda—dominated the end of the block, its yard rolling down a gentle slope into a dense, dark woods of pine and oak trees. The number on the black iron gate was 898. The pavement gave out at the edge of the property. Bewildered, I stood there awhile, wondering if Grace had given me the wrong address. Shivering, hands clenched and buried deep in my pockets, I walked all the way back to Sherman Street.

Most of the bicycles were either parked outside the tavern or gone. At the mouth of the alley next to the train station, I saw an old woman in a tattered raincoat slip into the shadows. The voices from the tavern sounded much more subdued, now, as if the exuberance I'd heard earlier was a fleeting thing, like the squawk a bird makes upon escaping its cage. I started inside, then stopped when I saw one of the curly-haired postmen emerging from Riley's General Store with a paper bag rolled under his arm. Another breeze blew straight down my exposed collarbone, and I hurried to intercept him.

"Excuse me," I called. The man didn't slow down; I had to cut directly into his path to get his attention. He looked up, startled.

"Huh? What?" he snapped.

"Sorry. I just—"

"Dropped something," he said, and I turned to see the scrap of paper with the boarding house address spinning away into the elms.

"Can you help me?" I said, turning back around. "I'm looking for an address. 984 Lumberton Street."

The postman started to point over his shoulder, then stopped. "You mean 894."

"I don't think so. At least, I was told 984."

For a long moment, he studied me. "What are you needing with the 9s, son?"

More wind. And I was so tired now. "Look. What's with your town? Never mind, don't answer. Can you just help me? Please?"

Finally, he shrugged. "Go straight down Lumberton, all the way to the end. Then keep going, through the woods."

"Through the woods?"

"Just follow the path." With that, he stepped nimbly around me and hurried away.

The conversation unnerved me some. But I couldn't think what else to do. So I returned to Lumberton, moving more quickly past the houses this time. Lights shone in many of the windows. I glimpsed families at dinner tables, figures moving behind curtains. Traversing the street didn't feel so much safer, or any more familiar, than walking up the rows of gathered debris and broken-down vehicles in the Hooverville where I'd found Lewis.

Reaching the edge of the pavement, I stood a moment in the shadow of the long, white house, listening to the porch swings stir on their chains in the stiff wind.

The woods proved warmer, or at least sheltered. And the path was easy to follow, despite the closeness of the pines on all sides. Wherever this led, I wasn't the first to come this way. Not even the first in the past hour. I saw cigarette butts among the pine needles and curled-up leaves, a gum wrapper, and part of a newspaper. From somewhere ahead, I heard sharp, irregular *thwacks*, as if someone were beating a pillow. After a short while, the trees fell back a bit, and strangely companionable shadows swirled over the ground. I came to the edge of the woods so abruptly that I had to stop a second, blinking in the new, bright moonlight. The thwacking ceased.

In front of me, circled together like a wagon train in the middle of a neatly swept dirt and gravel road, stood a group of maybe eight colored teenagers. Frozen in mid-throw, the one nearest me was holding a red India-rubber ball. We all stood there, watching each other. Then, as though someone had fired a starter's pistol, the boys dispersed into the small, white houses that lined the block or through the yards into neighboring blocks.

The tallest and widest house—and, even by moonlight, the most brightly painted—stood kitty-corner to me. It was two stories, with tidy steps up to a porch with a leaning railing. Hanging on the left-hand side of the porch was a swinging sign, hand-lettered:

ROBERT'S CLEAN ROOMS. FOOD FROM GOD.

The man I assumed was Robert himself was standing on the bottom step, with a long-handled broom propped business-end against his shoulder like a soldier at arms. Without moving, he watched me step cautiously onto the gravel road as I took in my first sights and smells of colored Trampleton. Up close, he looked even more intimidating. Under rolled sleeves, the muscles in his lower arms cut through his skin like girders. His eyes were dark, set above jutting cheekbones. The notch on the left side of his mouth where the lips met could have been a dimple or a knife-scar.

He considered me awhile. Then he shrugged. "Ain't buying."

I smiled tiredly and shook my head.

"No? Okay. How about...Sorry, haven't seen him." His mouth twitched. Then he sighed and rubbed his free hand across his forehead. "Well, I give up. What are you doing here?"

"Grace Lowie sent me," I told him. "You're Robert, right?"

Very slowly, the broom swung down off his shoulder and dropped to the ground. "Grace Lowie."

My smile melted under his stare. I couldn't remember ever being this exhausted, even on the train. "She said to say you owed her."

"Owed her. Goddamn it." For the second time, Robert pressed his forehead with his hand. But he kept his gaze locked on mine. "Row-Bear-Tuh," he said. "Got it?"

I thought I'd done it right the first time. But I repeated after him.

"No," he snapped. "Row as in Boat. Bear as in eat you for dinner. Tuh."

"I'm Paul," I said. "P-au-ll."

Robert looked me up and down, and eventually shook his head. "God knows what she's thinking. I sure as hell never do. But I guess you better come in."

*****

Every morning of my new Trampleton life, I came down to the common room at Robert's Boarding House to find the remains of other people's breakfasts scattered over what was at all other times an immaculate pinewood table. Coffee cups floated on their saucers in pools of grayish liquid, and cigarette butts crawled over the threadbare white tablecloth like flies. And yet, except for my host, I never saw or heard another living person there. Always, Robert left a place for me set at the end of the table farthest from the front windows. Within minutes of my appearance, he would appear, throw down a plate of scrambled eggs and one piece of toast, and return to his sweeping and cleaning.

The eggs were butter clouds that melted on my tongue, easily the best I'd ever had. Every morning, I'd try to compliment him, but he'd only nod or grunt. The instant I took my last forkful, he'd collect my plate and vanish until I was out of the house.

By the time I'd retreat upstairs for my notebooks and pens, the day's first smack of rubber ball against curb could be heard on the road out front. The game they played made no sense to me. It involved a lot of scrambling, some shoving each other face-first into the gravel, a sort of beehive formation where they all ducked their heads together and kicked at the ball in the middle, and—the big highlight, apparently, since it was always accompanied by explosive cheers and laughter—full-speed throws ricocheting off one another's foreheads.

The moment they realized I was watching from Robert's screen door, the kids would stop, edge away to the far curb, and wait. I tried nodding good morning to them, but they mostly lowered their heads. Finally, I'd head for the trees and make my way toward Trampleton proper for another day of wandering.

I spent the first six days trudging around town, clinging as closely as possible to the shade of the elms, which lowered the quickly elevating temperature but did nothing for the humidity. Now, one week to the night after my arrival, I was back on Sherman Street, standing in the slowly gathering dusk and staring through the barbershop's glass door. By this time, I'd come up with at least three excellent reasons for going in there.

First, the shop had fans whirring away on a shelf above the red barber chairs. As usual, I'd been walking all day, and I'd sweated clean through my shirt.

Second, I'd had remarkably little success convincing anyone in Trampleton to have a conversation with me. I wasn't nearly as good at doing this as I'd thought I would be. Locals hurtled by on their bikes or meandered past in prides of three and four, heads tilted toward each other or up at the trees. I never caught anyone by themselves in a reflective moment. Trampletonians spoke slowly, but they rarely stopped talking. At least not so I could actually learn anything about them. I couldn't seem to find any natural entry points into their conversations. Once, I stopped the postman who'd pointed me to Robert's on that first night and said, "Hi. I'm working for the Federal Writers' Project. I'm here to capture the essence of your town."

But the man just looked me up and down while running an ink-stained hand through his curly hair. Then he said, "You just missed it. It went thataway." And off he went, grinning to himself.

The closest I'd come to an actual chat was at the fruit market in the vacant lot on the far side of the gingerbread stationhouse. There, I'd handed over more than half the money that Grace and Henrietta Klein had advanced me, a dime at a time, to the three regular sellers. Two of them were middle-aged, sandy-haired women, possibly related, with mouths like tightly sewn stitches. The third was much younger, wore the same handmade, long-sleeved white blouse of too-heavy material every day, and bound her black hair in a tight, checked kerchief. The women barely spoke, even to each other; they just sat and smoked and stared at the baskets of unripe spring fruits and vegetables they'd stacked in their respective wagon beds. The conversation I managed to have with the younger woman occurred on the fourth day, and

I was so excited that I wrote it down verbatim in my notebook:

Me: "Any idea where I can find the old Screwpine mill?"

Woman, after a long pause: "You buy a lot of pears." (She has blue eyes, kind of icy and mean.)

Me, after several seconds of standing there: "They're good pears."

Woman, with a snort: "Might could use you in the Chestnut Garden. Good pears, my left eye."

Me: "Chestnut Garden?"

Woman goes even more silent than usual, if that's possible.

Me waiting. Woman silent.

Me: "How about that Screwpine mill? I'm supposed to meet someone there."

Woman: "Then you better be damn sure they like you."

It was almost shift-change now at the lumber mill, which meant the street would soon fill with bicyclists and the businesses with patrons. Overhead, woodpeckers and swallows stirred as the heat lifted like an iron off pressed fabric and set the town free to ripple and breathe again.

Finally, the third and best reason for going into the barbershop was busy as usual behind her chair. She looked as worn out as I felt, except that she still had that smile pasted to her face. Everyone in the place seemed to be tripping all over themselves to speak to her.

I almost opened the door right then. But even after a week, I still wasn't ready. So I continued to watch her through the glass. Behind me, rising from the ground like the nightly rattle of the cicadas, came the first whistling of bicycle wheels as dusk fell. I wandered past the real estate office, Riley's General Store, the diner and the tavern I'd sat alone in a couple of times, and continued down to the eastern end of Sherman Street. At the petrol station, I spotted the kid who manned the pumps. He was smoking, as usual, and this time had tucked his lit cigarette behind his ear while gassing up a truck. The cigarette glowed under the lip of his insignia-free baseball cap like a bullet hole in his temple. I crossed the street and moved toward him, palming the pear I'd been saving for dinner.

The kid leaned against the pump. He was tall, with long legs and small feet, which made him look hiked up on stilts.

"Doesn't that hurt?" I said, tapping my ear with my hand.

"If I twitch."

I thought about offering him some of my pear but decided I was too hungry. Any second now, the grasshopper cloud of bicycles would swoop down from the mill in earnest.

The kid snatched the cigarette off his ear so gracefully that I half-expected a curling burn-line to loop across his temple like a signature. He took a long drag and offered the butt to me.

I shook my head. "Bad lungs."

"Shame." He sucked down more smoke. The way his eyes shone made me think of a five-year-old with a lollipop.

"Sherman Street," I said. "That's a strange name for North Carolina, isn't it? Obviously, it's not for—"

"But it *is*," said the kid. "You're not from around here, are you?"

"I'm Paul."

"Danny."

Another truck pulled into the station, and the driver nodded curtly while Danny pumped, then gave him two dollars and two cigarettes. Neither of them said anything. After the truck had rumbled out of the lot, Danny returned to the precise spot where he'd been standing before and propped himself on his shadow like a scarecrow on a fence post.

"I don't get it," I said after a while.

Danny had sucked out almost the entire cigarette. He dropped the remainder and ground it out. The evening breeze kicked up, filling the air with the sweet smell of the elms.

"Sherman Street. Was this some kind of Union strong—"

"Oh, look, where the hell do you come from, anyway?" His laugh was a much older person's, and it wasn't friendly. "Listen. Paul, yeah? Let me tell you a story about Mr. General William Tecumseh Sherman. They say he rode in here on a big, black charger. Biggest, blackest horse you ever saw. Came straight down Main Street through the smoke, maybe an hour after burning every single building on it. That made him pretty much the tallest thing standing."

"Except for the trees."

Danny glanced up at the elms, and he nodded. "Not even Sherman messed with the trees."

"You tell the story like you were there."

"There were dead bodies in the street," Danny said. "Women crying. Children screaming. They say Sherman just smiled the whole time. He stopped where the railway station is now and said, "*That's* what I like to see, gentlemen. A good and trampled town."

"Trampled town." I stood stupidly for a few seconds. "*Trampleton*?"

"The survivors changed the name after Sherman left," Danny said.

I rubbed my palms over my cheeks. "I don't understand. Why would they do that?"

"Took me a while to figure it out, too. See, down here, they hold tight to their grudges. Keeps 'em…*fresh*. I like it." He'd been rolling the cigarettes that the trucker had given him back and forth between his fingers, and now he tucked one in his mouth, struck a match off the asphalt, and lit it.

They. So he wasn't from around here either.

Waving the smoke from my face, I asked, "What was the old name? Before the place got trampled?"

He blew a stream of black breath from his lips. There was something ferocious in the gesture. Danny shrugged, then grinned. "No idea. Never heard anyone mention it."

Down the block, I heard a distant clamor, then the whistling of bicycle wheels as the day-workers poured out of the mill. Moments later, they were on Sherman Street. I moved away from the pumps, and Danny did, too. Nodding at him, I hurried back toward Mr. Gene's. When I glanced once over my shoulder, I thought the kid was still looking at me. But he must have been looking past me, because he didn't acknowledge my wave.

By the time I reached the barbershop, I'd counted at least six men muscling into it, and the whole place had swelled with chatter and smoke. For a second, I thought she'd left, and that I'd let yet another day slip by. But then I spotted her, still hard at work over a customer in her chair at the back. She was too short and round to be beautiful, but she drew me all the same. Mostly, I think I'd never seen anyone smile so much.

Miss Melissa Flynn appeared on Sherman Street every day at precisely 10:45 a.m., ash-blond hair bobbing on her shoulders, gaze skittering over passing faces like a stone she was kicking. "Hey, now, Melissa Flynn," was the way virtually every single person greeted her, which was how I knew her name. "Well, hey," was what she answered. She'd throw open the door of MR. GENE'S NICE AND CLEAN and stride in to a chorus of "*Hey, now, Melissa Flynn.*" Mr. Gene himself—salt-and-pepper curls, boxer's smashed nose, jowly mouth—would look up from whomever's face he was lathering or head he was cropping and say, "Hey, now," and she'd say, "Green-Bean." Slung always over one or the other of her slightly stumpy shoulders was a long, black bag which I assumed held a flute or some other instrument.

I had an easy excuse—a professional mandate, even—to talk to her, but there was one major problem: she was never *not* in the midst of listening to somebody, and in the barbershop, her customers were mostly children aged sixteen and younger. As far as I could tell from my periodic peering through the open front window, all the adults went straight to Mr. Gene. The only thing he seemed to say during the whole procedure was, "There, so," except once, when I saw him swing his quivering jowls over a towel-wrapped older guy and murmur, "Whoops. Nick ya?"

So I'd been hoping to time my entrance just right. Mr. Gene needed to be occupied with a customer, and preferably have more customers waiting. And Melissa Flynn needed to be free of the gaggle of school kids that closed around her every time she took up her station like hummingbirds around a feeder.

A time like right this second.

The last of Melissa Flynn's daily charges had just hopped from her chair and was scurrying through the forest of trunk-like legs like a spooked squirrel. Melissa, meanwhile, had turned toward the wooden shelf where she kept her scissors and folded towels and that long, black bag. By the time she turned around again, I was in her chair, coughing.

I could feel her eyes on me, and not just hers. Hunching, I waited for a cruel joke from the mill workers or a "Whoops" from Mr. Gene, or for Melissa to say she was just leaving. Instead, she put her bag back on the shelf, where it clinked. Then her stubby hands were in my hair, pulling up strands, comparing lengths. As conversations broke out once more, she laughed and said, "My lord, who did this to you?" Then she reached for her scissors and said, "What's your name? You new around here?"

I managed to get some oxygen into my lungs and said, "Paul Dent. Good to meet you."

"Well, hey, Paul Dent. I'm—"

"Melissa Flynn," I said.

She held her scissors poised by my ears, her quick brown eyes alighting momentarily on my reflection in the mirror. I blushed. She smiled. Her smile reminded me of the kid's from the gas station; hers, too, looked borrowed from someone older.

"So where are you from, Paul Dent?"

"Far away. You?"

"Not too far. Not here, though."

Then I just blurted it out. "When you're done, would you like to—"

"Look at these," she said, breaking into a laugh as she tugged at my earlobes. "You borrow these from an elephant?"

After that, I forgot about luring her out of the shop. Around us, Mr.

Gene's customers were shouting to each other about Dizzy and Daffy Dean and some famous air-race show that might be coming somewhere nearby later this summer. The fans whirred, but whatever breeze they created got lost among all those overheated bodies.

I don't know why, but halfway through my haircut I started telling her the Dust Cow story. I began with the true events, but then I kept going down one of the paths that those events could have taken, if Ginny's family hadn't left, or if either of us had been surer of ourselves at the time or truly in love— or if we'd lived somewhere other than Blackcreek, in some less desperate, dusty decade.

I don't remember exactly what I said. Something about us being obsessed with the cow. Holding hands, going on timid dates into the pasture where her dad kept the animal so we could rub its flanks or inhale its breath, because to us, it was the last luck to be found in Blackcreek. I said something about Ginny whispering wishes with each tug of a teat but not telling me what she wished for.

"And then one day," I said, while Melissa put a finger to my temple and tilted me sideways, "she told me that she'd mostly been wishing about my brother."

"Uh-oh," said Melissa, still smiling, cutting away.

For some reason, I couldn't stop talking. It was like being on a tree-swing and feeling that gentle push at the small of my back.

"My brother…He was a couple of years older. Crazy."

"Was?"

I let that pass. A little implied tragedy could be just the thing to further her interest. "He liked to get mixed up with people. Fight them, hurt them, challenge them, make them fall in love with him, whatever. When our father died, it kind of drove him over the edge. He started doing all these desperate things. Jumping into bonfires. Getting his friends to stampede cattle, then sprinting straight through the center of the herd going the other way."

These weren't lies, of course. Lewis had really done those things, just not in the order I was inventing.

"Anyway, Ginny felt sorry for him. Also, he was a big, tough, handsome guy."

"Would you sit still?" said Melissa.

"Sorry." I could feel bits of hair sifting down my neck and every touch of Melissa's fingertips. Also, each breath I took dragged smoke into my lungs, and it prickled.

Over by the window, one of the mill men said, "Who you got there, Melissa?"

Her brown eyes stared down over mine. She actually winked. "I'm trying to figure that out myself."

"Not her usual sort of customer," observed Mr. Gene dryly from behind his chair as the body in it shifted in front of him.

"Jumps all over the chair like one of 'em, though," said the guy by the window, and everyone laughed. Even I managed half a smile, feeling ridiculous.

"This'll be over in a minute," Melissa murmured, startlingly close to my ear, and I thought I could feel the softest press of her body against my upper arm. No matter what else happened today, I knew I'd be waiting outside Mr. Gene's door, in the nearest elm-shadow I could find, until she came out.

"I don't know if Ginny actually loved my brother," I said. "Maybe she just wanted to save him. Either way, she should have known better. Maybe she could have saved herself. Maybe if I hadn't been so upset about what was happening, I could have saved them both."

"Or at least the cow," said the customer in Mr. Gene's chair, and I jerked around as if I'd just been cattle-prodded. Mr. Gene lifted the towel off my brother's freshly shaven face and began to mop his neck with it.

I hadn't forgotten, obviously, that Lewis was in the vicinity. But it had been a week, and Raleigh was a good day's train ride away. Of course, it made perfect sense that Lewis would pop up at precisely this moment. If I hadn't been so thoroughly flummoxed, I might have punched him.

"Done," said Melissa, sweeping the cloth off me. If she had noticed that my back had lifted halfway off the chair or that my legs had gone completely rigid, she didn't say anything. I felt sticky, hot with shame, and more than a little sick.

Lewis had been scraped so clean that his face sparkled. He didn't grin, and he sure as hell didn't wink. He just folded his ropy arms against his chest and checked his haystack of newly raked hair in the mirror.

"Little smoky in here for you, isn't it?" he said. He pulled a half-dollar coin from his pants pocket with a filthy hand and flipped it to Mr. Gene. "Keep it, friend."

Mr. Gene's jowls quivered, then spread apart into a wide smile. "Well, I thank you," he said.

But Lewis was already striding through the mill men, who nodded or patted his shoulder as he made his way outside.

"You know that guy?" Melissa asked.

I couldn't look at her, and instead fumbled in my pocket for money to pay her. I tipped her more than the price of the haircut.

"My brother," I mumbled.

"From Oklahoma? The one you couldn't save? The one who—"

"Yeah, I kind of…exaggerated some of that."

"Exaggerated?"

I glanced up long enough to see her staring at me, which was more than enough to drive me out of her chair.

"Well, well," I heard her say.

"There, so," said Mr. Gene.

I pushed out the door and found my brother standing next to Grace Lowie, waiting for me. Both of them were grinning.

For a few seconds, I stood utterly still in the cooling twilight. Overhead, thousands of new elm leaves trembled in the evening breeze.

"Hello, Paul," Grace said, meeting my gaze. Once again, she seemed different. Her whole body was crane-like: taller, thinner, her plain cotton dress lifting off her skeletal frame with the wind.

It was too much. I didn't want to think about what had apparently been going on between them.

"One week on his own, and look at him," Lewis said, hands tucked in his pants pockets, flannel sleeves rolled up. "Playing it up to the haircut girl. Telling towering tall tales. Who'd have thought?"

"Maybe being a writer has gone to his head," said Grace.

I started some furious, useless response, then noticed her hand nestled on my brother's arm, and gurgled to silence.

"Glad to know you've been thinking about me, too, little runt," Lewis said. "*Good* call, too, the whole doomed triangle bit. Positively inspired. If only I hadn't been there, I think it might have hit her just the way you intended."

"You were in the coal gondola," I said. "A few cars behind Grace and me the whole way."

He smiled.

"Why?"

"Call it a whim," he said. "You know how I get. Anyway, with you gone, there wouldn't have been anyone interesting left to play with in Blackcreek. So I thought I'd tag along."

"Come on, Paul," Grace said. "Show us your town." Her hand slid back down my brother's arm. She gathered his fingers in her own.

Even then, I realized that he and Grace shared something. A peculiar curiosity, perhaps. An instinctive detachment from other people, coupled with a hunger to provoke or at least interact.

Behind me, the barbershop door opened, and I turned to see Melissa Flynn. She slowed but didn't stop as she eyed my brother and Grace. "Hey," she said.

Grace inclined her head, Lewis grinned, and Melissa bobbed off down the block. But she surprised me by looking back. She wasn't smiling, but her gaze was on me.

"It was a good story," she said. "Too bad I didn't get to hear the ending."

I watched her walk up to Danny at the petrol station, kiss him on the cheek, draw the cigarette from behind his ear and take a drag, then carefully replace it. Even from forty feet away, I could hear her bag clink as it dropped to the ground.

"Dent," came a snarl from behind me, and I whirled around.

The red-bearded man with railroad ties for arms, whom I'd first glimpsed wielding a fiddle through the smoke in the Sherman Street Tavern, was glowering from the tavern's doorway. But not at me.

"Who's that?" Grace asked.

"Tom Reaveley,' I said.

"Mill foreman," said Lewis, freeing his hand from hers. "I'm maybe a week from taking his job. Back in a minute." His fighting smile unfurled across his face like a pirate flag.

"Lewis," Grace said softly, but he was already striding away.

The man seemed to rear up like a bear. Then he grunted as my brother threw an arm around his shoulders. "How's your little girl, Tom?" Lewis said, sweeping the man through the tavern door. They disappeared into the buzzing hive of banjo music.

"You're actually taking all this pretty well," Grace said. "I wanted to write and warn you, but your brother will have his little entertainments."

"I saw him with you at the Raleigh station as my train was pulling out," I said dully.

"Pretty fascinating character you created for me."

I felt woozy, a little nauseous. "I didn't lie, did I?"

"Not to me." She glanced toward the petrol station.

I looked that way, too, but could only see Danny. He waved. Melissa was gone.

Grace brushed away a thread of red hair that had dropped over her eyes.

Her gaze drifted up to the treetops, then down like a helicopter seed, slow and spinning, and alighted briefly on my face.

"You know," I said, "when I was telling you about him on the train? I think I wanted the fascinating character to be me."

That made her laugh. "You? You're too much like me."

Something ignited under my ribs. I wasn't ready for this conversation, so I changed the subject. "I've got something for the Guide."

"After almost a week? I damn well hope so. Let's have it."

"I know what the town's named for."

The tavern door banged open, and out strolled Lewis. His face was flushed, as though he'd been shouting or fighting or dancing. Whichever it had been, he was sauntering now, glancing casually up and down the street as if he'd already claimed it. Sherman himself couldn't have looked any prouder.

The three of us set off down the block and ended up in a booth at the back of the diner having scrambled eggs and syrup. Throughout the meal, Grace and Lewis kept finding excuses to touch each other, though not always gently. Once, Lewis scooped a dripping pool of syrup off a corner of Grace's plate into his mouth, and without any hint of a smile, Grace socked him. Lewis dumped his usual shovelful of sugar into his coffee, but when he got up to speak to another mill-worker who'd just come in to the restaurant, Grace switched mugs with him. Eventually, Lewis sat back down, took a hearty swig from his cup, swallowed the liquid without so much as a grimace, and asked me how it was sleeping "in colored-land." I was halfway through my answer when he elbowed Grace right under her breast.

"Ow," she said. "Hey."

"Where are *you* sleeping?" I shot at him. Watching the two of them together was even more agitating than my brother's untimely appearance.

He glanced sidelong at her, then away. "Greenlane. Two towns east. Near Grace."

"And you got a job at the Trampleton mill?"

"Best job in the region. Other than cushy government work, I mean." Lewis grinned.

I went quiet and tried not to watch them. But it was strange how, as the meal wore on, both Lewis and Grace got less playful. Each of them kept shifting around on the seat or stealing glances, as if they weren't quite sure what the other one wanted. It was weeks before I realized that was a huge part of their attraction.

Back on Sherman Street, Lewis paused a moment to stare up at the moon through the elms.

"Well now that I'm here, little brother, make sure you keep track of me, huh?"

"So you're staying," I murmured.

"I've got more reason to be here than you do."

"The hell you do," Grace said, with surprising force. She glowered at Lewis, then nodded at me.

He put his arm around her, gave me a little wave, and together, they headed in the direction of the train.

Somehow, I didn't envy either one of them.

*****

I let a few days pass after my self-inflicted humiliation in Mr. Gene's Nice and Clean, rehearsing my next encounter with Melissa. I wanted it to seem casual, an inevitable meeting between townsfolk at the end of a work day. Instead, the moment I saw her in the street, I jerked up my hand in what was meant as a wave but probably looked like I was slapping myself, and said, "Can I take you to dinner? Sometime?"

Stopping amid the flow of workers still pouring down the block, Melissa shifted her black bag on her shoulders. "Well, hey. It took you long enough."

"What do you mean?"

"What do I mean? You've been skulking around out here pretty much every evening."

"You noticed?" I couldn't tell if Melissa's laugh was gentle or encouraging. It was just so bright. "Does that mean yes?"

She shifted her bag again and studied the elms. "It means you can walk me up the Back sometime. Maybe Tuesday next." Then she dropped her voice to a whisper. "Better leave your brother at home, though. No telling what might happen between us." Grinning, she bounced off toward Danny and the petrol station, leaving me to drift over to Lumberton Street with my head buzzing and the pen in my right hand tapping uselessly off the blank top sheet of the notepad I'd been carrying around all day.

That night, it took me forever to fall asleep. When I awoke, it was still dark, nowhere near dawn, and there were voices downstairs. I sat up fast and listened.

Flipping back the covers, I shrugged into pants and a shirt, tiptoed to the top of the stairs, and crouched. From there, I could see two pairs of feet outstretched from the couch. One pair sported shiny black loafers that reflected the candlelight. The other wore only holey black socks. I pushed an ear between the railings but couldn't make out distinct words, just a steady murmur. I moved another step down, and everyone in the common room turned and looked at me.

All of them were colored. The guy with the holey socks seemed roughly my age and wore a silver engineer's cap cocked too far back on his head. The man wearing loafers was bald, broad-shouldered, and considerably older, and turned away as soon as he saw me. A third man lurked near the open front window, almost hidden in the makeshift curtains billowing around him. The candlelight barely reached him; all I could make out was his long, thin shadow.

Slowly, I settled into a sitting position right where I was. Something seemed to be sticking out from the side of the man with the loafers, but I didn't realize what it was until he curled his fingers around its neck and strummed. The kid in the engineer's cap stared at me, then turned his attention to his companion.

The guitar let loose a single, weeping sigh from note to not-quite-note. Then another. I watched loafer-man's long fingers glide down the frets as though stroking the chin of a cat. The sounds he made never became a tune or acquired a rhythm. But he kept making them, and sometimes he'd say, "Welly," or something that sounded like welly. Slide. "Welly." Longer slide. *Down* that well, with the draggin' hands." Or maybe "dragon hands."

The engineer kid laughed and leaned forward. Loafer-man picked and slid and strummed. This went on for a while, with both of them shaking their heads from time to time as if they were swirling dregs at the bottom of a coffee cup.

I have no idea how I fell back to sleep. One minute, I was gazing into the common room like a bird perched on a telegraph pole; the next, the engineer kid was stepping over me. The light through the windows had gone yellow and warm, and both the man with the guitar and the thin guy in the shadows had disappeared.

"Where are you going?" I mumbled.

"It's almost morning." He was past me now.

"I was listening."

"Also drooling, some." He gestured at my cheek, stepped into the room across the hall from mine and shut the door.

I sat on the stairs a bit longer, but there was nothing else to hear. Eventually, a door below banged open, and Robert appeared, first arranging the couch covering, then surveying the sitting room with his broom slung over his shoulder.

"Morning, Robert," I called.

Robert didn't even look up from his cleaning. "I'll get your breakfast," he grunted, and retreated through the swinging door into the kitchen.

Struggling to my feet, joints popping, I made my way downstairs. Moments later, he was back with my plate. The instant I'd finished, he stopped his housework and reached to clear all trace of me from the table.

"You get a lot of musicians here?" I asked.

"They're the only paying black folk traveling who ain't running." He kicked open the kitchen door and left again.

I was lingering in my chair when the kid in the engineer's cap reappeared with his guitar slung over his shoulder and a duffel bag in his hand, heading straight for the front door. Robert came out with a large, brown, steaming bowl cupped in his hands. "Forgetting something, Reggie?" He handed him the bowl without so much as glancing at me. The kid dropped his duffel and took the bowl. He started to sit in the chair opposite me, then seemed to remember I was there and stayed standing.

A smell filled the room, acrid and unpleasantly sweet, like kerosene.

"What's that?" I asked.

"You wouldn't like it," Robert said.

And right then, my frustration got to me. I couldn't seem to initiate a single decent conversation with anyone, let alone the coloreds; I seemed to be surrounded by stories no one would tell me; Lewis was here and making quite a name for himself at the mill, not to mention seeing Grace; and Robert obviously disliked my presence but didn't appear compelled to throw me out.

"How would you know?" I snapped, gripping the back of the chair as though I might fling it.

Robert stared. For a second, I thought he *would* finally order me out of the house.

Eventually, he shrugged. "Hold it right there, then."

He went back to the kitchen and returned with another brown bowl. "Home recipe." He settled the bowl in front of me. "I call it *Friend of the Working Man*." He glanced at Reggie. "This ought to be good."

The smell alone almost knocked me unconscious. I hadn't even tasted it, and already my tongue was curling into a tight ball against my back teeth.

"Thanks," I said.

Reggie burst out laughing. "You might want to wait on that. The man's kind of known for lighting fires, after all."

"Shut up," Robert said, and suddenly, I didn't think Reggie was kidding. I also had no idea what he was talking about.

Lifting the bowl, I took a slurp. For a second, I registered only heat. Then the taste began to ferret down my tongue, rooting terrified taste buds from their sockets and igniting them before plunging down my throat. It really was like gulping gasoline, except sweeter, maybe. Stronger. And on fire.

I tried to speak, but managed only a teary-eyed whimper. I kept my hands around the bowl, which shook but didn't tip. Slowly, slowly, I felt myself steady. "That's..." I started, expelling hot air from my mouth, and tried again. "Is that some kind of pepper in there?"

Robert just smirked.

"You know he slept on the stairs last night," Reggie said, sipping at his own bowl of *Friend*. "Listening so hard, you'd think he understood."

"He's awake now, ain't he?" said Robert, nodding to himself.

Reggie drained the rest of his bowl, handed it to Robert, and straightened the cap on his head.

"You be careful out there," Robert told him.

"You, too, Robert. We count on you being here." He collected his duffel on the floor. Almost as an afterthought, he nodded at me. Immediately, I nodded back, but he was already on his way out the door.

I was amazed to find my hands lifting the bowl to my lips again. "It seems I want more," I stuttered, the words slipping off my tongue before I had formed them. Then the second jolt hit me, and my whole mouth went numb.

Robert watched, his muscled arms crossed. "A few more sips, and even you'll be ready to work some."

"I've been working the whole time I've been here," I answered, when I could muster the words. "Trying to talk to you, and to other people who might occasionally respond. That's half my job."

"I guess working's the other half." He started sweeping last night's cigarette butts off the table, but he didn't march off into the kitchen this time. "So where're you from, anyway, Mr. Dent? You're not local, I know that."

"Paul," I said. "Oklahoma. Blackcreek."

He looked surprised. I waited for him to ask something else, but he just went on wiping crumbs.

"I came here with my brother Lewis. I mean, I didn't exactly come with him. He followed me. He works at the mill."

"Uh-huh. So explain this to me. You're Grace Lowie's office boy, or something? Some kind of storyteller?"

"What?"

"Why did she send you here? Seriously, what do you want, and how long do you think it'll take? You're making my regular clientele nervous."

"I don't know. I work for her. In a way. I work for her project."

"Oh, right." Robert had been standing uncharacteristically still, but now he shook himself out of it. "Federal Waste-of-Time Project."

I think my smile caught him off guard. "I'll add that to the list."

"What list?"

I sucked down the last mouthful of Friend of the Working Man before handing the bowl to Robert.

"I said you wouldn't like that," he said.

"Did I say I didn't like it?"

"It's making your cheeks all red. What list?"

"Well, let's see. You know Mr. Riley who owns the general store?"

Robert grunted. "I know him."

"When I introduced myself, he said, 'F.W.P. Federal What Project?'"

"Kind of clever for Riley," Robert said.

"Someone else, I forget who, called it the Forgot Why Project. Then there was Fellas Without Points, I kind of liked that one. And last but not least, Fishes-out-of-Water Project. Who were the other guys here last night?"

"Long Shorty. He plays the spoons."

"And the third guy?"

Robert didn't say anything.

"The really thin one by the window, who never sat down?"

Drumming the tabletop with his thumbs, Robert pursed his lips. Then he said, "Teddy Anklebones. The man can sing the needles off an evergreen tree. But you won't ever hear him." He swept the remaining ashes into his palm. "I'll bring you some lemonade. Cool that tongue."

"Okay. Thanks for giving me something to write about."

"Don't write about Teddy."

"Why not?"

"He wouldn't like it. Neither would I. Matter of fact, don't write about my guests or my house. They're mine."

He was halfway through the kitchen door when he glanced back. He seemed about to ask me something. Instead, he said, "W.P.A. White. Poor. Asses." He was nodding and humming to himself as the door swung shut behind him.

Later that day, at a checkers tournament in town, a truck driver from Cherry, North Carolina, told me that Teddy Anklebones was an escaped murderer from a road-building crew in Louisiana, that he'd killed a couple of prison guards, and that his guitar playing could lure trains off their tracks and drive full-grown truckers to their knees.

"You've heard him play?" I asked.

"Heard about it, kid. Just heard about it."

Later, at the boarding house, Robert corrected me.

"Alabama," he muttered. "Not Louisiana. And the first guy he killed tried to steal his guitar."

*****

So, for more than two months, I lived the WPA dream. Sometimes, it was sweet.

Robert made me breakfast in the mornings: butter-cloud eggs, yeast rolls with honey, and occasionally a heavy, cinnamon-soaked oatmeal. At the end of the meal, he'd bring me a bowl of Friend of the Working Man, which I eventually learned was brewed from coffee, molasses, orange rinds, peppers, nutmeg, and two spices he wouldn't reveal. Then he'd stand over me while I drank it. If I was capable of speaking in between sips, he generally replied.

"You ever play that game out there?" I asked one day. "The one the kids play in the street with the rubber ball?"

"It's called *Still Standing*," he answered as he cleared the rest of the table.

Gradually, our exchanges got longer, stretching up to three, even five minutes at a time by the fourth week or so.

Meanwhile, more slowly than Grace could believe, though she always seemed pleasantly surprised by the pages I gave her, I got to know the town. One Sunday, when I hadn't found anything in days to write about and couldn't think of anywhere else to go, I went to a service at the Methodist church on the east end of Main Street. It was the first time I'd been to church since I was maybe five years old. The pastor's name was Reverend Clarke Beagle. I learned later that he was almost defrocked for refusing to oppose teaching evolution in the Trampleton schools.

The service proved dry and disappointingly music-free, the sermon primarily concerned with the privilege of work in desperate times and the "creeping, socialist temptations" of unionization. I'd had vague notions of clapping hands and organs, maybe even a chicken lunch, but for a good hour afterward, I stood in the red-tinted light beneath the building's lone stained-glass window while Reverend Beagle shook hands and then lowered his bald head and rested his chin on steepled fingers as he listened to various members of his flock. Just as I was about to leave, he surprised me by meeting my gaze and saying, "You're that fellow from the Writers' Project, aren't you? If you can wait, I have an unusual someone I think you'll enjoy meeting. Oh, yes."

So, after everyone else had left, he walked me all the way through town to the Baptist church at the other end of Sherman Street. Trotting up the low stone steps, he turned abruptly and flashed a childlike, completely unexpected grin. "Mr. Dent, you're about to meet Mr. Norman Henry. I really think you're going to like him." Then he threw open the church door and barged through it like a little kid arriving home from school.

Where Reverend Beagle was pasty, Mr. Henry, the Baptist minister, had the sun-baked, ropy physique of a ranch hand. And though he, too, kept his voice carefully modulated, it had a rumble in it, like thunder coming closer. We'd exchanged all of five minutes worth of pleasantries, in which I'd told Mr. Henry what I was doing in town, when Reverend Beagle bobbed once on his sensibly soled heels, shot me that grin again and said, "Go ahead, Norman. Tell him about your mission."

Mr. Henry scowled, and the thunder in his voice rumbled just a little louder. "You mock, Reverend Beagle."

"Far from it, Norman. I enjoy."

"I won't be mocked."

"We both know you want to tell him. So tell him."

Way up north, Mr. Henry began, several hundred miles away near the Virginia state line, he'd recently discovered a "rare opportunity. A genu*ine* phenomenon. Right here on our very shores—in our *very state*—a whole community of Negras so confused in their sense of the Lord, yet so committed in their worship, that they actually believed themselves to be direct descendants of the Lost Tribe. *The* Lost Tribe. 'Black Jews,' they call themselves, can you believe it? *Black Jews*."

Reverend Beagle piped up again. "Mr. Henry believes it's his great calling, and the reason our Lord brought him to the cloth, to go among these people and bring them safely home to Christ." After that, we all sat down at the rectory table to a grilled trout and potato lunch that was easily the best meal I'd had outside of Robert's house since my arrival in North Carolina. For the rest of the afternoon, I joined them in playing poker for dried beans.

The following Saturday, having finagled a second fish meal out of Mr. Henry so I could learn more about the Black Jews, I stepped out of the Baptist church into my first utterly perfect North Carolina spring evening. The humidity had eased, the breeze had softened, and the daffodils and rhodo-dendrons had erupted everywhere. The air was flooded with scent and the gardens and roadside fields and copses with color. Instead of returning to town, I continued walking west and was surprised to discover what had to be a majority of Trampleton's young adults, grouped mostly in dancing pairs, milling around an unmown lawn hidden by an overgrown hedgerow. Set far back from the road was a shuttered shed with a cardboard sign staked in front of the door that read, *FULL MOON DOUBLE FEATURE. THIS SATURDAY, 8 P.M. BRING A SCREAMING PARTNER.*

The evening was still springtime-cool, but the girls wore thin, summery dresses, and the boys flitted around them, bumping into each other and laughing too loud, their smiles flashing like firefly light. Unexpectedly, I spotted Melissa and Danny near the front of what passed for a line, not far from the shed.

As soon as she noticed me, Melissa waved me over. I was only a few steps away, and she was already offering a "Well, hey," when Danny took her hand. She let him, but her smile flickered. Or maybe I just hoped it did.

"Where's your screaming partner?" she asked.

"Yeah," said Danny. "Didn't you read the sign?"

My eyes darted toward Melissa's face, then away. "I'm just here to watch. Doing my job."

"See?" Danny said to Melissa. Of course, I had no idea what he meant.

The shed door swung open, and in the dimness, I saw a short, balding man with round shoulders. "Well, come on," he said, and tried a smile that didn't look entirely comfortable on his face. His teeth were brown. "A quarter a piece. Hey, now, Melissa Flynn."

"Hey, Mr. Pierman," she said.

Two by two, everyone began filing past him. I only had three quarters left to last me through the weekend, but I was happy enough to give one to Mr. Pierman so I could follow Melissa inside. There were no chairs or benches, just a sawdust-strewn wood floor. In the center of the room, taking up nearly a quarter of the space, was a bulky table with a film projector set up on top of it. The first reel of film had already been threaded onto the spools. On the far wall, Mr. Pierman had tacked a tall, white sheet, stretched taut and flat.

The room could barely hold all of us, and I wound up squeezed against Melissa to the right of the projector table. Danny was on the other side of her, still clinging to her hand. She was talking to pretty much everyone except him. She didn't look at me particularly often, but she was generally smiling when she did.

The only light came from a single bulb fixture overhead. Once Mr. Pierman had collected everyone's quarters, he pulled the string and shut it off, then flicked two switches on the projector. A loud, mechanical rattle filled the room. All the talking ceased. And just as a square of white light material-ized on the sheet, the door to the shed slid open one more time.

The light sprang on abruptly, the projector choked off, and Mr. Pierman marched straight through the audience, paying no attention to the hands he almost crushed. He was jabbing both of his index fingers toward the figures in the doorway.

"Out. Out, goddamn you."

Half-crouched inside the door were two colored boys. They didn't bolt, though one of them stood up straight. He was lanky, mahogany-skinned, with a red cap in his hands. I knew him, or at least I saw him every day. He was always among the first Still Standing players to arrive, and the last to leave.

"We've got quarters," he said.

"I said *out*." From its leaning spot against the doorframe, Mr. Pierman grabbed a broom.

Someone a few rows behind me whistled, but whether at the coloreds or the situation in general, I couldn't tell.

"Mr. Pierman," said the boy with the cap.

Mr. Pierman flipped his broom bottom-side up and slammed the handle against the wall. Beside me, Melissa jumped, and everyone else in the shed went quiet.

The colored boys left without another word.

"Sorry about that," Mr. Pierman mumbled as he stalked back through the silent throng to the projecting table. He looked neither sorry nor satisfied. Moments later, the lights went out, and the first picture began.

The disturbance at the door had unsettled me. I kept thinking of the kid in the cap laughing as the rubber ball rocketed off his face. I thought about him backing carefully to the sidewalk whenever I came out of Robert's house.

But gradually, the pressure of Melissa's shoulders and thighs drew my attention back to her.

Both movies had thunderstorms in them, and hulking, dark houses with shutters that banged in the wind and lots of drafts because candles kept blowing out every time one of the characters walked down a hallway alone. In the first film, the killer was a vengeful aunt getting back at her nasty nieces and nephews who just wanted her money. In the second, the killer was a monkey escaped from a rundown circus. That one made Melissa laugh, and twice during it, she turned her face to mine. Both times, I wracked my brain for something clever to whisper but wound up grinning stupidly instead. My legs had fallen asleep ten minutes into the first feature, and every time I moved, little pinpricks shot through them. Also, the sawdust had gotten up my pants, and my skin itched. All around us, people were clinging to each other. Some of them were kissing.

At the end, Mr. Pierman shut down the projector, tugged the light cord, and promised a new double feature in two weeks.

"More scary ones," someone called out from the back corner.

"The only ones I show," said Mr. Pierman.

Outside, the full moon hung directly overhead like some great, leaning boulder, and the oak and pine trees had come alive in the night breeze. The crowd proved quiet and calm as they filed back up Sherman Street toward Trampleton. I'd expected more of a raucous, post-Town Couch fighting atmosphere. But the whole experience really did have a mirage-like quality: three consecutive unfettered hours in the flickering dark, dearly paid for, surrounded by people no one had to answer to.

"Coming for a Coke?" Melissa asked.

I turned toward her in time to see Danny blanch. Melissa, I noticed, had freed her hand.

"Go ahead. I'm going to…" I gestured behind me toward Mr. Pierman's shed.

"You're working," she said. Her apparent interest delighted me.

"I'll see you Tuesday," I told her.

"What's Tuesday?" said Danny.

Melissa laughed. She slid her elbow through his, and off they went. She looked back twice, though. The second time, she waved.

I stood at the edge of the lawn and watched owl shadows lift from the evergreens. The breeze blew cool. Twenty minutes later, Mr. Pierman emerged with the film canisters under his arms, locked the shed, and started across the grass. He looked surprised to see me.

"Forget something?" he asked.

"Can I ask you a few things, Mr. Pierman?"

"Who are you?"

"I'm Paul Dent, with the Federal Writers' Project. It's a government—"

"Yeah, yeah, I know."

"Really? No one else around here seems to know."

"Well, I'm from Chicago."

I wasn't sure what that meant. But he stopped, leaned the canisters in the grass against his leg, and seemed prepared to go on chatting. I was so unaccustomed to getting any response that it took me a few seconds to think what to say.

"What church do you go to?" I asked. It was one of the few questions all Trampletonians seemed prepared to answer.

Mr. Pierman laughed. "I'm Jewish," he said.

I stared. "Jewish?"

"I guess you're *not* from Chicago."

Blushing, fumbling in my pocket for my pad, I nodded. "Jewish. Sure." I didn't think I'd ever met a Jew before.

Mr. Pierman was about to scoop up his canisters and go when I said, "Chicago?"

With a sigh, he straightened and gazed past me toward town.

"I came south not long after the Crash," he said, "with my wife and a fair-sized bundle of bills I'd made calling the horses and was wise enough not to invest."

I couldn't quite get whether 'calling the horses' meant announcing races or betting on them, but I decided it was best not to ask.

"My plan was to open the area's first motion picture theater and retire. But my wife wound up preferring more regional attractions."

"Like what?"

"Well, mill workers, mostly. She liked their shoulders."

I'd been scratching notes on my pad, and now I stopped. My eyes stayed on the paper. Mr. Pierman's voice sounded completely flat, and gave no indication of how he felt or why he was telling me this.

"I'm sorry," I said.

"I'm not." Again, his inflection was unreadable. "I opened the theater anyway. Kind of. I can't seem to get my heart into it except maybe once or twice a month, and no one around here could afford to come more than that, anyway. It sure brings the young people, though, doesn't it?"

From the pocket of his coat, Mr. Pierman pulled out a tin of tobacco, carved himself a plug, and jammed it in his cheek. The tobacco smelled old and dirty, like something cut from the Sherman Street asphalt.

"So…how come you like horror films so much?"

"I don't," he said. He picked up the film canisters. Abruptly, he turned. "You're the guy staying at Robert's, correct?"

In my head, I could hear the crack of his broom handle against the wall as he chased the colored kids from his shed. Several times before this, I'd received advice suggesting I find more *appropriate* lodgings. *I'm there for work*, I'd respond. I didn't mention how much I'd begun to enjoy it there.

"You know Robert?"

"Shoot, son. Everyone within fifty miles knows Robert. Or knows about him."

The pad dropped to my side, and my mouth opened. I'd almost never heard anyone mention Robert by name. And I'd never once seen him cross through the woods into white Trampleton, as far as I knew. But it was true; everyone did seem to know him. Maybe that's why they were all so reluctant to speak to me.

"He keeps a good house," I blurted, not sure what I was trying to say.

Mr. Pierman spat a glob of tobacco into the grass. Not at me. Not even in my direction.

"He makes great eggs," I said.

"Happy to hear it."

"He's been pretty good to me."

"Well, he damn well better be, don't you think? I'll see you around, Mr. Dent." He turned not toward town but away to the west. I slipped the pad into my pocket and made my thoughtful way back to the boarding house through the empty streets.

*****

The first time I went to the Trampleton Sawmill, I walked the mile and a quarter from downtown in a steady, remorseless drizzle. I'd left Robert's before sunup, just after five a.m. I didn't pass a single bicyclist, so I was surprised to find roughly three dozen men lined up silently against the gate, heads down so the brims of their hats blocked their faces. Few of them even glanced my way until I started wandering toward what seemed the front of the line, near the spot where the gates would open. Then one of them grabbed me by the elbows and held me back.

"Where do you think you're going?" he asked. Under his open coat, he wore overalls with repair-patches sewn across the chest and one strap tied around a broken clasp at the shoulder. His eyes glowed a fierce, bloodshot red, though nothing on him smelled of alcohol. He looked fifty, maybe older, but later I learned he was barely thirty. He was also missing three fingers on his left hand.

"I'm just…looking for someone to talk to."

"Well, talk to me," he said, still not releasing my elbow. "I'm friendly."

His name was Rowlands, and most mornings, he was at this gate by 5:30 a.m., though this particular morning he'd "had to shoot my damn dog. It was old and sick and half-blind, and throwing up everything we fed it. Walking around whimpering, scaring the kids. My wife wouldn't let me leave until I buried it. Even though she knew good and goddamn well that I'd wind up farther back in the line, and might not get work today because of it."

I hadn't taken out my pad. But in my head, I was scribbling furiously.

His voice became rougher, more agitated. "What the hell are you doing here, anyway?" Two of his companions swung their heads around and eyed me from under their hats. The rain intensified, beating down on all those heads like hoofbeats.

I tried to explain, but he just kept glaring, and he wouldn't say anything else for a while. Eventually, three men in white shirts and matching gray ties and hats strolled up to the gates through the muck of the yard, between the giant, felled evergreen trunks and under the jaws of the overhead gantry crane. One of them unhinged the padlock with a rusty, bronze key. The other two stood on either side of him. Stupidly, I thought that the long, black sticks in their hands were tools. I'd never really seen a blackjack.

"Sixteen today, boys," he said. "Sorry."

Quietly, without much jostling, the sixteen men closest to the front slipped through. Each mechanically touched a finger to the brim of his hat or his bare forehead as he passed the men in white shirts.

"Goddamn that goddamn dog," the man who'd grabbed me muttered, but he'd miscounted. He made it in. I slipped through with him, but alerted the foreman who I was so that he could take another worker.

The one with the key looked me up and down, and the two with the blackjack moved closer.

"Government man," said the one with the key.

"Sort of. I just collect people's stories."

"You're not NRA."

Only belatedly did it occur to me that I'd put myself in harm's way. "I don't even know what that is," I said. When the three of them didn't react, I added, "I just wanted to see the mill." For proof—as if it would prove anything—I took out my notepad.

Then one of the blackjack men laughed. "It's all right, Joe. He's Lewis Dent's brother."

"Lewis Dent," Joe said, and took a startled step back. "Why didn't you say so?"

He let me pass.

I visited every day that week, though I'd pretty well sorted out the mill's ruthless, predictable routine by the middle of the first morning. The men who gathered at the gate—most of them well before dawn—weren't regular employees. Some of them were former employees laid off as demand declined and the mill cut back production. Some were bankrupt tobacco farmers or sharecroppers. Some had drifted in from other places where there was even less work. Most days, a foreman would emerge from the workhouse around five a.m. and pull in twenty to thirty additional hands for day labor. The bargain was simple: the mill paid for an ordinary, ten-hour day. But the morning workers put in the additional time until the regular shift commenced for free, in exchange for the privilege of having work. Not one of them complained about it.

Mostly, the mill reminded me of a louder, more bustling version of the Blackcreek train yard back in the days when there'd still been a Blackcreek train. All day long, the crane swung stacks of rough-hewn tree trunks onto platforms. Inside the barn-like building, two steam engines powered four immense blades rotating like seething dark suns as they shot sparks up the walls and all over the room. Steam from the engines rolled over the workers manning the belts and pulleys and moving carriages. The movements of dozens of men were timed to the precise, bumping, shrieking rhythms of the machines. The noise was overwhelming.

No one spoke to me. Even if they'd had the energy on their rare and minimal breaks, the so-called "stretch-outs" were in full effect, and supervisors appeared instantly behind any worker the moment he so much as paused to lift a filthy, sawdust-coated handkerchief to his mouth. The goal was to maximize every possible working second, and thereby employ fewer workers.

The white shirt I saw most belonged to my brother. I spotted him maybe fifteen minutes after my arrival on that first drizzly morning, sweeping past a line of men hustling around the loading platform. Not one of them so much as glanced around as Lewis clapped several on the back. Near the entrance to the main building, he stopped a moment next to Tom Reavely, the red-bearded foreman he'd supplanted. The two of them stared at each other, then Lewis grinned, and Tom Reaveley shook his head and stalked off to hound more workers.

That was the moment Lewis somehow sensed that I was near. Turning in my general direction, he saw me, grinned wider, and threw his arms out wide.

But only occasionally during my mill visits did he actually speak to me. Mostly, he bounded about the premises like a sheepdog, herding everyone he saw into their proper places with nudges or nods or gleeful yips. Amazingly, virtually everyone I spoke to seemed to like him.

"Fairest overseer they've ever had here," Rowlands told me. "Actually remembers who you are, too. Doesn't take no shit."

"The guy gets *production*," Joe, the gate-foreman, told me.

On the third day—with the sun blazing, so that the sawdust stuck to my skin and hot-itched everywhere, including my lungs—Tom Reaveley happened past the pile of shavings where I'd taken to eating my two-pear lunches.

"You're Paul Dent?" he asked, and when I nodded, he did, too. "Your brother is one scary son of a bitch." It was clearly a compliment, though not a happy one.

Barely ten minutes later, I heard shouting a ways across the yard, alerting me to a fight that had just broken out. Scrambling up, I reached the fast-forming ring of workers around the combatants just in time to see one grab a splintery two-by-four off a nearby stack.

That's when Lewis materialized over the man's shoulder, seemingly from out of the wood itself, and dropped him with a single, savage jab to the kidney. The guy went down hard, the two-by-four flying off as his face smashed into the woodpile. As though in one continuous motion, Lewis grabbed him by the neck, yanked him up, and dusted him off. The guy's mouth was gushing blood, and his eyes glazed. Lewis shook him once, patted him on the head. Then he shoved him toward the mill building, and blew once over the top of his own fist as though across the muzzle of a gun.

The fighter Lewis hadn't slugged was backing away with his hands raised. The watchers around me returned fast to their work. Several were shaking their heads. But several more were laughing.

At the end of that day, maybe fifteen minutes before the five o'clock whistle, I wandered out of the mill in desperate search of shade, circled a loading platform near the base of the gantry crane, and came across two men huddled in the shadows. Not foremen. They were leaning close, talking hard, and from their gestures, they seemed to be counting. Thanks to the racket all around and the intensity of their conversation, I got pretty close before they noticed me and scattered immediately in opposite directions.

I'd heard, or thought I'd heard, the word *union*.

Lewis materialized again. "Working hard?" he said.

"You really are like a genie," I told him.

"Damn right. I even grant wishes." He was gazing thoughtfully at the spot where the two men had been standing. It made me nervous, so I left him there.

In the evenings, almost every evening, I went to meetings. That seemed to be what everyone in Trampleton who wasn't too tired or too frantic with parenting duties or second jobs or drinking at the tavern did with their scant free time. The more people I met, the more invitations I received.

Reverend Beagle alerted me to the monthly gathering of the George Guess Society in his church basement. The Society was composed of local Cherokee from the nearby woods who spent most of the meeting reading the Bible to their blind or illiterate elders. According to Reverend Beagle, George Guess was an Indian who'd taught his whole tribe to read English a hundred years or so ago. Eventually, he'd gone west looking for some fabled lost Cherokee nation and disappeared.

Meetings of the Fine Trampleton School Board, on the other hand, were held in the backyard of the Baptist church. Those proved particularly well attended because Reverend Henry provided snacks: carrots, crackers, fresh lemonade. On the night I went, I was surprised to find a small group of coloreds in suits and dark ties standing quietly along the gates to the church's small, shadowed graveyard. The youngest of them, I realized about halfway through the proceedings, was the teenager in the red cap I'd first seen playing Still Standing, who'd tried to get into the movie at Mr. Pierman's shed. Robert told me his name was Mitchell Johns.

"The next Du Bois," Robert claimed. "Mark my words."

The coloreds didn't eat, and they didn't sit down, and not one of them spoke until the rest of the evening's business was concluded and the chair-woman with the gavel was about to close the discussion. She actually raised her gavel to do so, and then—as though the coloreds had just come in, or she'd only just realized they were there—she glanced toward the graveyard.

"Gentlemen? Did you need something?"

"Go on," I heard one of the older ones murmur, and Mitchell Johns took a step forward. He kept his head up, though he looked only at the chairwoman and not at any of the other teachers and parents and citizens seated on folding chairs in the grass.

"Well, ma'am," he said, his voice pitched low and carefully inflected, as if he were reciting rehearsed lines in a school play, "it seems we're short some desks over at South Pines."

"Again?" sighed a curly-haired, blond woman a few benches over from me. "What is it you all find to do with the ones we send you?"

There was a titter of laughter, but also a couple of scowls in the direction of the curly-haired woman. One of the scowls, I noted, came from the chairwoman herself.

"Thank you for letting me know, Mitchell," she said. Her voice remained completely unchanged, flat, professional. As if she were in the play, too. "I'm fairly certain we've got spares we can find you."

"Thank you, ma'am," he said, and his group faded into the shadows.

I saw the curly-haired blonde once more the following Saturday morning when I actually got to go through the iron gate and across the lawn of the great, columned house abutting the woods at the end of Lumberton Street. I wasn't invited inside, but I did spend the better part of half an hour rocking on one of the veranda's four porch swings in the company of ten ladies, thanks to the two older farming women who sold me my pears; they'd invited me along to their weekly session of W.A.R.: Women Against Roosevelt. The women represented a wide swath of Trampleton economic life: beside the farmers' wives and the curly-haired blonde, who turned out to be headmistress at the elementary school, there was Mrs. Riley, wife of the man who owned the general store, a couple of society ladies, both in elbow-length white gloves despite the heat, and Mrs. Taylor, the mill-owner's wife. It was her house.

To be honest, I can't remember much of what they talked about. There was some general complaining about "coddling" and "Washington meddling," and discussion of some kind of petition. I was too busy eating the flaky raspberry pastry laid out on doilies on the table beside the swings to care. Then one of the farmers' wives turned and said, "Wait a minute. Which paper did you say you wrote for?"

I flushed, started to put back the new pastry I'd just selected, then decided not to. "I work for the Federal Writers' Project," I said.

Mrs. Taylor replaced her teacup carefully in her saucer and gazed at me.

Her eyes were a stunning, metallic blue. "Young man," she said, "is that really how you want to be known? Is that really the best a capable, industrious person can contribute to helping this nation heal itself? Have some self-respect."

With a wave of two fingers, she excused me from her porch.

I did indeed get more industrious, if not more capable. Every time I saw a gathering of more than three people doing anything other than drinking, I devised some sort of reason to join them. Every time a passerby returned my gaze, I came up with a question for him. And every nugget of information I managed to uncover got transferred into my notebook and eventually delivered to Grace.

One thunderstorm-wracked Friday evening, I took shelter inside Mr. Gene's. I'd hoped to find Melissa, but she'd already gone, so I stood among the mill-workers and older men waiting for their shaves until the first lull in the downpour. Then I stepped out onto Sherman Street, intending to hurry for Robert's, and caught a glimpse of a line of filthy men with their hats yanked low over their faces slinking around the side of Reverend Henry's church. Curious, I bent my head into the sideways, slanting rain and made my way toward them. Every time I looked up, more men were ducking past the building, some stopping to turn and look around before slipping inside. Whenever that happened, I'd duck into the shadows and stay still. By the time I reached the church, the clouds had burst; I gave up being stealthy and scurried up the steps and through the front door.

Reverend Henry himself found me in the entrance way a few moments later. He looked startled, and then, after a pause, delighted.

"Mr. Dent," he said. "Good for you."

He led me through the church proper, and what seemed to be a vestry replete with clerical robes hung on a series of high wall racks, to a small mahogany antechamber at the back of the building. Inside the room, flickering candlelight reflected on the faces of maybe a dozen men.

What they were whispering about, mostly, was the UTW. Even I already knew what that was.

The United Textile Workers had triggered a massive strike throughout the region the day after Labor Day, 1934. The stories I'd heard mostly concerned a South Carolina town called Honea Path, where the striking workers—who'd already been permanently replaced by some of the desperate multitudes scouring the countryside for work—wound up trapped between the National Guard and a brigade of Pinkertons hired as factory guards. More than thirty of them were shot, most in the back while trying to flee the picket lines. The strike, and the UTW, collapsed within weeks.

"We're not looking to strike," I heard a forceful voice whisper from the front of the room. I couldn't see him from my spot next to the doorway, just out of sight, where Mr. Henry had stationed me. "We're looking to bargain."

"We've got nothing to bargain with," said someone else. "And I'm no fucking Commie."

"Neither am I," snapped the forceful voice. "That's got nothing to do with this. This is all us. *All us*. Local."

On it went.

Finally, half an hour or more into the debate, my curiosity got the better of me. Or maybe being designated recorder rather than participant had begun to wear on me. I stuck my head around the door.

In the scant seconds before he noticed my presence, I managed a long look at Tom Reaveley. His cheeks had flushed almost to the color of his beard with the force of his argument. He was using the bow from his open fiddle case to jab home points to the rest of the men in the room.

Abruptly, in mid-jab, his gaze lurched to me. "Jesus Christ," he said. "It's Dent's brother."

Half a dozen mill hands leapt to their feet and turned around. Reverend Henry, who'd been quietly observing from a standing position next to the wall, looked alarmed. Apparently, he was among the last men in Trampleton who didn't know who Lewis was. Or else he somehow hadn't connected the two of us.

"You've got it wrong," I started, backing away. "I would never—"

Then the church's back door burst open, and Lewis strolled right past me into the antechamber. The whole room went still. Only the candlelight twitched.

"Look here, Dent," Tom Reaveley finally said. But he wasn't wielding his bow, and his voice had a faint tremor in it. "This is an exploratory meeting. That's all. Peaceful and orderly. We're only—"

"You boys don't understand," said Lewis. He glanced back toward me. I knew that smile. "They don't understand, Paul. You don't need a union, gentlemen. You need me."

As the mill hands and Tom Reaveley dropped into their seats, Lewis detailed the plans he'd already begun discussing with mill management, who in turn, had already put in a bid with the Works Progress office and the county seat to build the region's long-promised minor league baseball park.

"It'll take all summer," Lewis told them. "Probably a lot longer. And once it's open, it'll lead to still more projects. Concession booths. Maybe a new tavern and a restaurant. There'll be plenty of work around here for some time to come. That means more pay. For all of us."

Within an hour, he'd led the entire group meekly into the rain and over to the tavern, where he bought us all beers.

*****

One blossom-scented, bee-swarmed evening in late May, Melissa finally agreed to meet me under the lacy shadows of the Sherman Street elms. She arrived in her work clothes: a plain cream skirt and yellow top, a pale blue ribbon tied in her ash-blond hair. She stood maybe a foot away with her arms crossed, pulling the loose-fitting top close against the curves of her body, and I imagined that I could feel her heat-slick skin on my arms, like a banked fire from across a room. Her eyes were brown and quick.

"Hey, now, Melissa Flynn," a mill man said, biking past and raising one soot-gloved arm.

"Well, hey," Melissa said.

"Where's your bag?" I asked.

She raised an eyebrow. "Want me to get it?"

"I want to know what's in it."

"You're a curious sort, aren't you?"

"That's my job." I grinned. "But that's not why I'm curious."

Melissa glanced down the street toward the gas station. I followed her eyes and spotted Danny on the sidewalk in front of the petrol pumps. He was staring back. I started to lift my hand but decided not to.

Melissa blew out her breath. "I think, tonight, let's just walk. Okay, Paul?"

She took me up the Back, a path that began at the southern edge of town where the sidewalk and gravel road gave way to overgrown grassy fields and foothills. Over the first mile or so, we met half a dozen people, some with dogs, most alone. One couple, colored, aged seventy or more, kept their eyes lowered and edged into the grass as we passed. They were the only ones who didn't say "Hey, now" to Melissa.

Then we were alone, tramping through cicada-buzz so intense that I kept checking the ground, half expecting to see downed power lines snaking through the dirt. Soon the grass dropped away, and we came into a dense stand of pines that pricked and brushed at us. It was cooler in there, less buggy. Melissa began whistling. I didn't recognize the tune and asked her the words. She said she didn't know them.

"They used to sing it back home."

"Who? Your parents?"

She smiled distantly, and we went on walking. When we cleared the trees, we were higher than I'd expected, way up on the tallest rise rimming Trampleton, in low brush already baked brown and brittle. The last daylight had bled away, and the moon had risen. I saw half a dozen owls perched like gargoyles in the trees.

Melissa sat down, breathing heavily, and I sat beside her, not too near. The skin under my shirt felt viscous, and my lungs kept clutching up, blocking air from getting in or out.

"Thank you for coming," I said, and looked over. Her cheeks had gone blotchy, and midges clung to her ears.

"I should have come sooner. I'm sorry. I have…people who need me to tend to them."

"Seems like you do a lot of that."

That distant smile ghosted over her face again, though this time she looked at me. "That's *my* job," she said.

She slapped at her forearms, and I whacked at something crawling under my knee and squashed it. In the trees, fireflies flickered like train windows passing.

"So, Paul," she said, after a short, pleasant silence. "About your brother…"

I winced. "What about him?"

"Well, I've got to admit, I'm curious."

"You and everyone else he's ever met."

"He just seems so…I don't know. He's sure a hot topic at Mr. Gene's."

"He'll get hotter if he stays. You never know what he's going to do next. I'll tell you a true story about him this time. My mother left us to go back East when I was barely two. Lewis says he remembers her oatmeal cookies, and that she sometimes hit our father with wooden spoons. But I don't remember her at all. We were born four years and eighteen hours apart, so we usually celebrated our birthdays on the same day. By celebrated, I mean our father would give us each a dollar and tell us to come home without it, and not before dark. Then he'd push us out the door.

"One year, when I was maybe ten or eleven, he announced he was throwing us a party. But his idea of a party was to put us on a caboose and get one of the drivers he worked with to push us two miles out of town on a hundred-eleven-degree, windless day. Lewis and I were supposed to jump out of the car and race back. First one home got cake. All of it. Loser got nothing. Well, my brother, he could have beaten me running backward. I can't breathe very well, so I'm not much of an athlete."

"What a bastard."

"Yeah…well, you'll see. When the caboose stopped moving, Lewis said he'd give me a head start. He waited until I was at the door of the caboose, then shoved me out onto the grass, jumped on my back, hopped off, and waited for me to roll over so he could make sure I saw him wave. He likes doing that when he's done something he's especially proud of. Particularly at me, for some reason. Then he took off.

"I didn't even bother running. The point is, I wouldn't have run anyway, and Lewis knew it. My father knew it, too. So I took my sweet time getting back. It was quiet out there except for the biting things. Kind of like here. But here's the complicated bit about my brother. The first thing I saw when I got home was a plate full of cake squashed on the road and Lewis standing on our stoop, laughing.

"'Saved you some,' he said. 'Happy birthday.'

"I started past him into the house. But he put a palm on my chest, reached behind him, and handed me a huge heaping plateful. A corner piece, smothered in icing. Chocolate, and really good, too. My dad actually made great icing. Lewis sat outside and watched me eat it. Then he clapped me on the back and went inside."

"Weird," Melissa said.

"Normal for him."

She was silent a while. The blotchy spots on her cheeks had faded. She still had that odd half-smile on her wide face. The last time I'd spent so long sitting with a girl, just talking like this, had been with Ginny Gunderson on Dust Cow Ridge. Half a decade ago. Eventually, Melissa said, "If he were my brother, I think I'd hate him. You must hate him."

"I used to think a lot of people must feel that way about Lewis," I said. "But you can't hate him."

"Anyone can hate anyone," Melissa said softly, and I realized I didn't understand her smile at all, and wondered if anyone in Trampleton did. "Easiest thing in the world."

Somewhere in the long silences and occasional chatter that made up the rest of our first evening together, my elbow brushed up against hers and stayed there. Her skin felt cool. She didn't move away.

"So who are all these people you tend to?" I asked.

"Just one person, mostly. Danny."

I didn't want to ask the next question, but I did anyway. "He's your boyfriend?"

The smile Melissa flashed then was closer to the one she used on Sherman Street. Quick and light. "Danny?" The smile vanished. "Danny is my leatherwing bat. My black-hearted magician. My closest friend. But he will never, *ever*, be my boyfriend. No matter how much he thinks he wants to be."

She went quiet again. The breeze drifting out of the pines had a furtiveness to it. By the time we began retracing our steps to the fields at the bottom of the mountain, the moon had filled the sky behind us. I'd been planning to take Melissa's hand, but didn't actually try to do it until the Sherman Street elms loomed overhead. Her fingers accepted mine but didn't squeeze around them. Above us, warblers chirred and trilled.

"Okay, Paul. Time for your personality test. I've had a lovely night. So I've decided to grant you one of two wishes. You can kiss me, or you can find out what's in my black bag."

We were standing in front of Mr. Gene's. For once, my eyes made no move toward the leafy canopy above.

"Is this a trick question?" I said. "I mean, is there a right answer?"

"Only your answer."

My mind raced. My strained lungs tickled, which made me want to cough, but I managed not to. "Does what I answer determine whether I get another night?"

Melissa rose onto her tiptoes, then settled back down. "No. But it might determine what kind of night the next one is."

"Get the bag," I said.

Melissa burst into a grin. At the shop door, she fished keys from the pocket of her dress, then disappeared inside. She came back holding the bag, which she dropped with a clank at her feet. Kneeling and tugging at the tie-straps, she reached in and withdrew a black leather sheath. From the sheath she pulled out a knife.

The blade alone must have been eight inches long. Melissa tipped the point at me, and I could see the icy, silver curve of the thing, like a scratch in the summer air. Then she turned it, trapping the moonlight in the blade's flat surface.

"You…spend a lot of time with that, don't you?" It wasn't just the shimmer of the blade, but the way the wooden handle nestled in her palm.

Wordlessly, she withdrew a second sheath, then a third before laying all the sheaths in the street and the blades along her thigh like a half-open fan. I glanced in both directions. The road was empty. We'd been up the Back a long time, I realized. It had to be midnight, maybe later.

"You might want to step back," Melissa said, untying the ribbon in her hair and then tying it tighter.

Gathering the knives into one palm, Melissa stood, rolled her head around her shoulders a few times, flexed her arms, and motioned me another foot or so away. "Hum something."

"Huh?"

"Something fast. I miss the music."

Miss it? The only fast thing that came to mind was the half-tune my father used to bray in the morning to get Lewis and me out of bed. I didn't mean to sing it so loud. I just couldn't imagine it any other way.

"Laying tie, laying tie. In the black October sky. No reason for to cry. There's stations by and by. We'll lie here 'til we die."

The second time I hit *reason for*, Melissa flicked her right wrist and launched all three knives into the air. I caught my breath but didn't dare stop singing for fear of disrupting her rhythm. Her hands flew up to snatch one handle, then another, release, snatch, darting forward and back, left and right while her body stayed ramrod-straight like the trunk of a tree whipping its branches in a twister. The knives sailed into the elm canopy, tipped over, somersaulted down between columns formed by the others as though performing a square dance up there, then plunged into some impossible springy place on Melissa's palms or sometimes her forearms or even her chest, and rebounded upward again. She started to move her feet, twirling and tilting, shredding the air around her into ribbons, and it was only at the end, as my singing edged toward panic and grew even louder and the knives flew higher and dove down harder, that I caught a glimpse of her face. Her smile looked wide enough to swallow the whole damn street.

Somehow, on the final toss, the knives went up together, reached an apex, leaned back in formation, and dove toward the earth in a sort of inverted V that looked like a falcon's spread talons before alighting lightly along Melissa's forearm as she dropped into a bow.

"Shit," she muttered. When she straightened and opened her palm, I could see that she'd closed her fist around the lower blade of the last knife to land. A thin thread of blood, much less than there should have been, was seeping from a tiny nick. But that ravenous smile still dominated her face.

I had my hands in her hair and my mouth against hers before the song had died on my lips. The knives dropped to the ground. I heard her grunt, felt our teeth clink together, and half-expected a knee to the groin or a rake of fingernails down my cheek. Instead, Melissa kissed me back for a short, sweet while.

"Don't step on the knives," she said into my breath.

We eased apart, and I looked down at the blades arrayed all around us.

"I said you had a choice." Her hands tightened in my hair.

"But I wanted both."

"Cheater."

Kneeling again, she swept the blades back into their sheaths and the sheaths into the bag in a practiced sequence of motions, then zipped the bag tight and slung it over her shoulder. She didn't kiss me again when she stood, but, having moved away, she turned. Her nod was different than her *Well, hey* nod. Then she glided down Sherman Street toward Danny's gas station.

*****

I was in Riley's General Store buying ink and five-cent licorice gum when I made my big mistake. Grace had been to see me the night before, and she'd not only paid me fifteen dollars but seemed almost satisfied with the pages I'd written about the movie hut and the trail up the Back. I'd kept Melissa and her knives to myself.

"This is the first time you've written something that might actually make it into the guide someday, you realize that?" Grace told me. "You've started discovering people and places that someone else might want to experience for themselves."

"How's Lewis?"

For one moment, it was as though the curtain that perpetually shrouded her face had parted; behind it, I glimpsed doubt, then worry, then an anxious, rueful smile. She lifted her hands, and the smile widened.

"Ask me something else."

But instead of waiting for another question, she suddenly bent forward and planted a quick, dry kiss on my cheek.

And that's what I was thinking when, halfway out of Riley's store, I turned back past the rows of carefully displayed foodstuffs and tobacco and stationery and toiletries, and rang the bell at the butcher's counter. Riley himself appeared in a heavy leather apron.

As usual, his hair shot off his scalp in a hundred directions and made him look like a puppy just shaking off a swim. The skin drooped under his raisin-sized eyes, and his expression was unfriendly.

"Fella without Purpose. Brother of Fella with a Whole Lotta Purpose, though I'm damned if I know what the purpose is."

"If you figure it out, let me know, okay?"

Riley waited.

"I need…meat, please."

"You don't say."

"The good kind." Not that he would've given me anything from the bottom bins, with the labels that said *Colored trimmings* and *Colored tips*. Except that I was fairly certain he knew where I was staying. Everyone seemed to. And I had to admit, it was part of the reason I kept staying there.

Still, Riley waited.

"Chops, please. Big ones. Enough to feed maybe three or four people?"

Riley folded several thick, bloody chunks of meat into white paper. The folds of the paper came out creased, perfect, like the ironed collar and pleats on a freshly laundered dress shirt.

"Fella with Pennies, for once," I said as he handed me the package.

"Yeah, but they're *my* pennies, that the government saw fit to take from me and hand out to you."

It was all I could do to resist telling him who would be eating the meat I'd just bought with his pennies. So I thanked him and sauntered out the door.

I'm not sure if I'd ever felt as good in my life as I did right then. I took my time wandering down Sherman Street, past the company houses, through the little woods toward my Trampleton home. If I showed up too early, Robert would harass me for not working hard enough—at least until he saw what we were having for dinner.

I found him sitting, cross-legged, on the front steps as I came out of the woods. The early evening sun lay heavy and hot on my shoulders, but Robert was wearing his long-sleeved work shirt, tucked in as always, with the sleeves rolled down. The lemonade glass beside him was all the way full, more prop than refresher.

I had to wait several minutes for a break in the Still Standing game, which looked faster and more dangerous at this hour. Mitchell Johns looked up once, having just taken a ball in the cheek, and nodded at me, which he'd taken to doing lately. Then another stringy teen caught a flung ball flush in the face and went down bleeding and laughing. That stopped the game long enough for me to scurry across the road.

"Robert," I said, and flopped down next to him. He made to get up. "Wait."

He studied me up and down. "Not sure I trust a man who looks the way you do."

"How do I look?"

Crossing his arms, he straightened, then shrugged. "*Satis*fied."

"Wrong." The grin I'd been restraining broke loose. "Hungry." Slipping Riley's white-paper package from behind my back, I tossed it to Robert, and he caught it with both hands.

He turned it upside down, rightside up, but didn't slit the folds. "I'm…supposed to make this for you," Robert said. "That right?"

"For us," I said.

"Us."

"You. Me. Everyone who's staying here tonight, there should be enough. It's from Riley's. The good meat. The stuff he won't sell to—"

As though pitching a penny, Robert flicked his wrist, and the package arched over my head, over the sidewalk, thwacked against the back of one of the kids in the street, and fell open in the dirt. Mitchell Johns stepped on the meat before he could stop himself, skidded, and sat down hard. The game stopped. The kids stared.

It was Mitchell who finally spoke. "Hey, Robert," he said, though his eyes remained fixed on the open package. "Dropped something."

"Ain't mine." Robert stood. Then he banged into the house.

I stood, too. The kids were all staring at me now. My cheeks burned, my legs went wobbly, and I almost tumbled into the throng. But I managed to stay upright.

"Not mine either," I said, and went inside. I banged the door, too, stalked up to my room, and didn't come down for dinner. Robert didn't call for me. In fact, I heard no sound down there for the rest of the night.

The next day, Robert served me breakfast as usual and brought me my bowl of the Friend, but he didn't keep me company. Nor did he speak to me the following day.

Then, in the middle of the third night, long after I'd dropped into a restless sleep, I was startled awake by hands on my shoulders and opened my eyes to find Robert's face staring down at me impassively.

"Get up," he said.

For a second, I thought he was going to punch me where I lay. He'd never once been in my room while I was in it. I'd never even seen him upstairs.

"Are you throwing me out?" My eyes adjusted, and I noticed his clothes.

White dress shirt, high collar. Some kind of dark tie, a dark jacket, cufflinks that flashed in the gloom.

"Get dressed."

"I don't have anything like *that* to wear."

"Damn right you don't. You won't need it. You won't be coming in."

I did as instructed, then followed him downstairs and into the night. Our footsteps sounded deafening on the wooden porch, especially Robert's, but no lights came on in the surrounding houses. Crickets and cicadas were clamoring around us as we set off down the road.

We walked maybe two-and-a-half miles in dead silence, out the other side of the colored part of town, cutting through some trees and eventually coming to the truck thoroughfare that dipped down onto the Piedmont on its way to Charlotte and the coast. Robert angled off onto a path that I hadn't even noticed in the roadside firs, and we walked another half mile or so, which brought us to an immaculately painted china-blue shingled house, hidden away in the woods like the hag's cabin in some children's story.

"This is your seat," Robert said, gesturing toward a copse of carefully manicured Bradford pear trees. He went on toward the house without me.

"Let me come in," I said, moving a step or two after him.

"Get back in those trees," he snapped, whirling around. "Don't make me regret this. You'd think a man in your position might be grateful."

"You'd think he might be curious, too."

Robert glanced toward the candlelit windows. There was no other light. "Let's stick to grateful." He straightened his tie and shot his cuffs in quick, efficient jerks, as though preparing his own undertaking. Then he looked at me, grunted, and continued inside. I cleared a dry spot in the dirt under a pear tree and sat.

And so I really did get to hear Teddy Anklebones sing. His voice was so high and reedy, at first I thought someone had a baby in there. Then it started threading itself into my skin. He sang about trains, and made me feel as though I'd never ridden one before. He sang about home as though it were holy, and also forbidden. *"Crow in the screwpine. Rats in the hay."* Half the time, I forgot even to notice the words; I was entranced, instead, by that *bend* to his voice: as though he were pressing a broken bottle to his vocal cords; as if he were dancing down a tightrope he knew was going to break. It was like being in the presence of the Patrol all over again, but grown up this time, with a voice stolen from a passing bird just so he could tell us exactly what being the Patrol was like.

After a long while, I slipped from the trees and crept across the lawn. I didn't dare go up on the porch, but I found a side window with the heavy, white curtains not quite closed, and got a glimpse of them all in the flickers of candlelight from at least a dozen candles. Twelve, maybe fifteen people, no more. The most startling thing was the dancing. It hadn't occurred to me until that moment that this was music you could dance to. Along the walls I saw a teenage kid bobbing his head hard. Behind him was a man tapping his hands on the kid's shoulders. Teddy Anklebones was standing in the shadows, out of the candlelight. Except for his hands, the only thing moving was one foot, lifting just slightly, tapping down. I didn't see Robert, and just then Teddy Anklebones started a new, much slower song, and his voice sailed out the window like a banshee's and sent me scurrying back to my hiding place.

By the time Robert came out, I was weeping. He watched my face a few seconds, then said, "Hmph. All right, then. Hurry up, before the rest of them see you."

*****

Grace generally came to see me on Saturday afternoons, and I was in the habit of waiting for her on the living room couch. She'd appear just after lunch and spend the first few minutes talking quietly to Robert in the yard. Today, she came straight in, wearing a long-sleeved sweater despite the scorching spring heat. The neckline had dropped and darkened with her sweat. Her plain blue skirt fell almost to her ankles.

"Aren't you hot?" I asked.

Grace shrugged and glanced around the house. She took a step toward the kitchen, then turned to me.

"Have you seen Robert?"

"This afternoon?" But even as I spoke, I realized I hadn't. Not since breakfast.

"Goddamnit. It's really too much. It's way past time he…" With a sigh,

Grace dropped down beside me and lifted the stack of carefully recopied notes I'd compiled for her.

"'Past time he' what?"

"Got his ass down there. You tell him I said so," Grace said, and started to read."

"Down where? What is it between you two?" I asked.

In the dusty sunlight, her eyes and the darker circles beneath them looked seared into her skin. "Never mind," she said, and her eyes returned to my pages.

Watching her read my writing always made me nervous. On impulse, I asked, "How's Lewis?"

For a moment, she looked exasperated. Then a mischievous, close-lipped grin slipped over her face. "I took him to a Party meeting. Just to rile him."

"What kind of party?" Then, somehow, I understood. "You're a Communist, Grace?"

The grin fell away, and she stopped reading long enough to gaze out the window. After a moment, she sighed. "Oh, Paul. God, I wish I was. I wish I believed that would make any difference. Now shut up. I'm reading, here."

She did that for quite some time before flipping up the covering on one of her own notebooks and copying an entire sentence I'd written.

"I gave you something useful?"

"This bit about Reverend Henry's Black Jews. Amazing."

Behind us, the screen door slapped open.

"Robert," said Grace, still scribbling notes, "where on Earth have you been?"

"Miss Grace," said a magisterial voice. I'd placed it even before I turned around. "I didn't expect to find *you* here."

In the doorway, her mound of curls carefully tucked up in a dark hat and her wide shoulders draped in a black velvet dress, stood Mrs. Duarte, the woman from the Raleigh Institute for the Negro Blind who'd taken the Patrol from us.

Grace stood, smoothing her own dress and smiling. "Madame Duarte. What on Earth brings you all the way—"

The kitchen door swung open, and Robert hurried into the room.

Had he been in there the whole time? Had he heard Grace calling and ignored her? He was past the couch, opening his arms for a hug, when he stopped. "Aunt Del? What is it? Why are you here?"

Aunt?

"Oh, no," Grace said. "It isn't the Patrol? Nothing's happened…"

Shifting the small parcel she'd been cradling in her arms, Madame Duarte reached into the pocket of her dress and withdrew a plain yellow envelope. Grace went still.

"What's that?" Robert said slowly.

"Read it and see," said Madame Duarte. On the night we saw her, she had seemed fierce, even ferocious in her force of will. But right now, she was seething. Even Robert looked intimidated.

"Come in, Aunt Del," he murmured, his head slightly lowered. "Please come sit."

"I'll stand, thank you. Read it." She held up the envelope.

"I know I should have come," said Robert. "I will come. I'll ride back with you today, if you like. It's just…been hard for me. The way she left. The way we left things. It's a bad old bruise. It still—"

"Read," said Madame Duarte.

Then Robert turned toward me. The emotion behind the expression on his face was clear enough: fear, plain and simple.

"You. Paul. You read it."

"What?"

"I'll read it," said Grace, reaching out her hand, and Robert stopped her. "No. Paul."

Dazed, I moved forward.

Madame Duarte scowled at her nephew. "A coward, to boot. "Maybe a coward all along."

That pricked him, anyway. His shoulders squared. "There ain't no colored person around—especially one from my own family—who has any right to call me a coward." They stared at each other, both coiled into themselves like boxers.

Carefully, I took the envelope, removed the single scrap of paper inside, and unfolded it. I could feel Grace and Robert watching me anxiously.

I looked it over and cleared my throat. "You better read this yourself," I said.

"For Christ's sake," Robert snarled, "read it."

The ink on the paper was blotchy and black, but the letters themselves were slanted and elegantly formed. "It says, 'Putting me out of your misery, now, big brother. You look out for my boy, you here? You make sure he's taken care of. Or I swear to God, I'll come back and haunt you right out of this world. Goodbye. Ruth.'"

"Oh, no," Grace said, and one hand floated over her mouth.

Robert went pale, and he sagged in place. The pleading edge in his voice made him sound like a child. "My sister's dead?"

"A package arrived this morning." Madame Duarte's tone hadn't softened. "It came with another note saying that Ruth wanted everything sent to me. You and your high and mighty pride. Lord forbid any sister of yours should make any mistakes. Because Lord knows, you don't make any."

"I can't hear this," Robert said, putting his hands to his ears. "I can't."

She shoved the parcel into Robert's chest. "Let's see, there's her tooth-brush, some ripped stockings, forty-five cents. Oh, and a note from whoever Ruth paid to send me this. Want to know what that one says?"

Robert just stood there.

"It says Ruth stabbed herself through the heart with the broken spoke of a wagon wheel. Goddamn you, she was my little girl. The closest thing I'll ever have to one."

Robert's teeth rattled together as though his aunt had punched him in the jaw. He grabbed the package out of her hands and clutched it to his chest. I felt Grace shudder next to me and make a whimpering sound.

"My God," she said. "I'm so sorry, Robert."

He stood with the package in his arms, crying openly.

"I liked her," said Grace.

Robert swayed. "Liked her? When did you even meet her?"

"In Oklahoma, idiot. Remember? Where you sent me, because you couldn't do it?"

"Or wouldn't," snapped Mrs. Duarte.

"Oklahoma?" I said stupidly.

"I really did like her." I'd never heard Grace speak so gently. "Obviously, I hardly knew her. But she was strong, all right. She reminded me of you." Then she turned to me. "The Patrol is Robert's nephew."

Robert's eyes had glazed over with tears, but they focused momentarily and swung in my direction. "You know my nephew?"

It wasn't a rhetorical question, and demanded an answer. But for just a moment, I couldn't speak. *I don't belong here*, I was thinking, and had to fight down a guilty urge to dive out the front door, and a simultaneous one to beg forgiveness. But what had I done? And why did I suddenly feel betrayed, and by whom?

I chose my words very carefully. "I met him on the train. In the boxcar.

With Grace. That's where I met Grace."

"You know my nephew," he said again. There was no mistaking the accusation in his voice.

"Better than you do, at this point," said Madame Duarte, and Robert flinched.

Grace moved a step in his direction. "You have to go see him, Robert. I'll come with you if you want. I can—"

"Get out of here, Grace," Robert said.

Madame Duarte threw her arms in the air. "Don't you blame her, now. You're done blaming everyone else, you hear? You're done with that, Robert, sure as I'm standing here."

There was another pause. "I really am sorry, Robert," Grace said. She collected her things and was at the door when he said, "You go too, Paul." His voice had lost all its tone, and the words were hard to hear. "Stay gone awhile."

Like a day? For good? Instead of asking, I followed Grace. She didn't speak until we were standing in the road.

"That poor girl," she murmured. "Oh, God."

"Why didn't you tell me the Patrol was Robert's nephew?"

"It didn't have anything to do with you. In case you haven't noticed, Robert likes his business private. But obviously, it's better that you know now."

She straightened her hat on her head.

"Just a minute," I said, and suddenly, I was furious. "You found the Patrol at the Hooverville. You already knew Lewis when he came up to you at the Raleigh train station. You knew him before you knew me. You knew all along. And you acted like—"

"I didn't know you were his brother. Not until you started waxing elegiac about bonfire jumping."

"But you let me babble on. And then you sent me out here for some weird reason."

"For the Project. Also because I thought your eyes could use some opening."

"So the colored woman I saw crying with Lewis. That was Robert's sister. Ruth."

"Yes," Grace said softly, and my anger evaporated. Now I just felt confused, and lonely, and a little dumb.

"Okay," I said.

"Listen, Paul. I wouldn't mention to Robert that Lewis knew Ruth, if I were you."

"Why not?"

"Because Robert is one proud, stubborn, whip-smart man. And your brother's your brother. If Robert ever meets him, he might leap to crazy conclusions. I told him I'd go get Doak—the Patrol—and the rest of this just happened. I didn't know I was going to meet you. Or your brother. Let's just…leave it at that for a while. Okay? God, that kid. That poor kid."

Tears were rolling down her cheeks. She slipped her hand into her pocket and pulled out a small silver watch on a chain. "Shoot. I've got to go, Paul. I have to be somewhere."

"With Lewis?"

"Sure. Maybe. Yeah, he'll be there. Look after Robert, okay? He's liable to drive himself insane with this."

Then she left me alone in colored Trampleton, wondering where to go. Melissa always reserved Saturday nights for Danny, because she thought that would make the adjustment to my presence in their lives easier. My writing notebook was inside, upstairs. Even the Still Standing players had disappeared. I sat on the steps, barely even thinking, and I stayed there all afternoon. Only once did I get up and creep onto the porch, because I hadn't heard the slightest sound from inside in what seemed like hours. Through the screen door, I saw Madame Duarte seated bolt upright on Robert's couch, and Robert coiled like a baby with his head in her lap.

*****

Melissa came up with the plan for Independence Day. It was a good plan, though it meant I'd have to spend the entire evening with Danny. "Trust me," she said as we huddled for a kiss in the alley behind Mr. Gene's during a rare work-break. There was thunder booming, but not too close, yet. "He's adjusting. Danny's not a fool. He's growing up."

The truth was, whatever misgivings I was having about being stuck with Danny for several hours, he had to be having more. He'd hardly spoken to me since the night I saw him with Melissa at the movie hut, and had sullenly repulsed the few overtures I'd made. He continued to blackmail Melissa into spending every single Saturday night with him, no matter what. So the thought of our night together causing him some anxiety didn't exactly displease me, and I wasn't ashamed to admit it. Still, I needed to get past this if I was ever going to make Melissa happy. She wanted the kid comforted. So that's what I'd have to do.

The holiday dawned dreary. Lead-gray summer clouds clamped down over the treetops at dawn, sealing in the heat instead of shading us from sunlight. Just stepping outside was like being loaded into a broiler with the lid locked shut. Worse, the mill had closed, despite the furious objections of most of the workers who couldn't afford the lost day's pay. In the tavern, where I'd gone to see what was happening—and also to stay out of Robert's hair, because he mostly wanted me out of the house—there'd been union talk again, and discussion of a slow-down. This time, when my brother showed up, he just sat and drank alongside Tom Reaveley and the rest of the millhands. Incredibly, none of them seemed to mind his being there.

"Aren't you management?" I asked him at one point, when he was on his way back from the bathroom.

He shrugged. "Not management enough to like not getting paid." There was no wink, no trace of his grin. And yet I still had the sense that he was playacting. Not spying or anything, just performing a role and relishing the performance. Maybe that was unfair. Maybe I'd known him too long. He patted my shoulder and continued drinking with his pals.

My original schedule for Independence Day involved hanging around wherever I could, just to see what Trampletonians did when they weren't working, because as far as I'd seen, they mostly worked. But I couldn't imagine anyone doing anything in this heat, and I certainly didn't feel like dragging myself around town. So I spent the afternoon on Robert's porch, carefully out of the way with a notepad on my lap, staring at the hills. Once, I heard a creak from inside the house and looked back to see Robert seated on his couch, gazing down at his hands as if he were reading his future there. When he noticed me watching, he stood and started back toward the kitchen.

"Robert, are you all right?" I called through the screen.

Without turning, he waved a hand in my direction. I had no idea what that meant, and then he was gone. I returned to my spot on the porch.

As the dreary day darkened toward evening, the heat actually intensified. I'd changed into my cleanest, lightest clothes, and headed for the woods. From the windows of the houses in colored Trampleton came the whirring of fans, an occasional clink of pitcher-against-glass, but no conversation. Even the leaves on the pear trees seemed to droop off their branches like the husks of cocoons. I didn't see another soul until the last block before Sherman Street, when a barrel-chested man who looked my father's age stepped out of his tiny house, dangling a silver and black rifle by its trigger guard. The man watched me, neither raising his rifle nor responding to my cautious wave. He was still watching when I turned the corner and escaped his sight.

The second person I saw was Mr. Riley standing at attention in front of his store. *His* shotgun was tucked in a tight diagonal across his chest like a sash.

More mill guys I recognized were congregating outside the tavern. One carried a bulky, black pistol that looked as if it had been chiseled off some Civil War statue. I heard a few low mumbles, but hardly anyone spoke. Two older farmers passed silently on the other side of the street, their rifles flipped barrel-up on their shoulders. They both wore church clothes, the collars starched, the jackets buttoned despite the heat.

Had the mill gone union overnight? If so…was it Lewis's idea? Was this his new version of Town Couch fighting on a grander, deadlier scale, to spice up an otherwise uneventful holiday? But Mr. Riley was no millhand. Neither were the farmers. Well and truly alarmed, now, I considered sprinting back the way I had come to warn Robert so he could tell the others.

And then I stopped and thought: I had to be wrong. Coloreds and whites didn't mix much in Trampleton, and they suspected each other plenty. But they got along. Or they kept to themselves, anyway. From what I'd seen, they all seemed to pride themselves on their uneasy peace.

I spotted Danny sitting on the edge of his gas pump island and moved toward him. His long legs were stretched and crossed on the asphalt, the brim of his baseball cap bent upward so I could see him staring back. A lit cigarette burned at his ear. His pistol was fat and black, with a spinning chamber someone had painted bright red. As soon as he saw me, he lifted the gun and sighted down the barrel, aiming straight at my stomach.

We'd been standing that way for several seconds—Danny with the pistol leveled at my gut, while I held absolutely still—when Tom Reaveley walked by, saw what was happening, and snapped, "You. Kid."

Danny glanced at him.

Reaveley gestured angrily at the gun. His red beard waggled. "The next time you get an itch for target practice, try your own ass. Understand?"

Danny flushed hard, but lowered the pistol into his lap. "It's a flare gun," he muttered.

"Then you'll have a flared ass." Reaveley moved off toward the tavern. His own weapon was strapped into his belt, gunslinger-style.

Overhead, the clouds darkened as the invisible sun slipped toward the mountains. Still wary, I said, "What's with all the guns?"

Danny's smile was instantaneous and nasty. "Oh. Melissa didn't tell you?"

"Look," I said, "this is stupid."

Slipping the cigarette from his ear, he took a drag so deep that the paper seemed to sag in his fingers. He didn't say anything.

"I have nothing against you, Danny."

"Well, I've got plenty against you, friend." He dropped the spent cigarette between his knees, then caressed the spinning chamber of his gun with a cupped palm.

"Melissa told me you were getting over this. Or at least getting used to it."

"Remember what I told you about how we like to hold our grudges around here?"

"But you're not from around here."

Danny whirled on me. "She told you about us?"

"She didn't have to."

"What do you mean?"

I allowed myself a faint, tired smile. "I work for the Federal Writers' Project."

Danny rolled his eyes and stood up. "Come on." We started walking toward the center of town.

They were all outside, now: farmers and millhands and shopkeepers. I didn't see any women or coloreds among them. Instead of talking, everyone was busy checking their guns.

"Danny," I said, "is someone about to get hurt?"

The door to Mr. Gene's swung open, and Melissa stepped out.

"Hey, now, Melissa Flynn," sang at least three different men in the crowd, not quite together.

"Well, hey," Melissa said, scanning the group. When she caught sight of Danny and me, a huge grin blossomed on her face.

"It's just a July 4th custom," Danny said. His smile faded as soon as she turned away. "A really old tradition. Like from before the Revolution. French, I think. Maybe Dutch. Maybe both. Except back then, it used to be done on New Year's. In a minute, a sort of parade of men will march to the front of every single house in Trampleton and shoot guns over the roofs. It's supposed to scare off devils or Indians or Yankees or whatever, and bring good luck. They do it in a lot of towns around here."

Melissa had her black bag slung down her back, and now she shouldered it to the ground. In addition to a frilly white blouse and black skirt, she'd donned white elbow-length gloves. Her hair looked even more yellow than usual under her kerchief. When she straightened, she had her knives in her hands.

"Ready?" I saw her say, though I couldn't tell if the question was directed toward anyone in particular.

The people closest to her edged back, and without any visible signal that the event had officially started, Melissa's knives leapt into the air. From my left, I heard a curse, then fumbling, followed by an ugly screeching sound as Tom Reaveley brought his fiddle to his neck. The sound took on rhythm and pitch, and became a sort of reel. The melody dipped and dove along with the flashing knives, whistling through the assembled crowd like wind through a tent. It was hypnotic, and a little eerie, watching Melissa glide forward like a majorette, twirling knives while the fiddle sawed away and the heat pressed down.

Then Danny whispered in my ear, "Want to know why you'll never have her?"

I shrugged him off just as my brother appeared.

He'd been lurking inside the tavern doorway, I guessed, and now he stepped out wearing a new tie and shirt with the sleeves rolled neatly to his elbows. Even from the back of the crowd, I could see the sweat streaming down his face. He caught sight of me and shot me a smirk, which I knew meant mostly that he was happy I was there to bear witness.

He parted the crowd as though wading through tall grass and fell in between Mr. Riley and a beaming Reverend Beagle. I saw him murmur something, smiling privately like a fellow priest preparing to officiate a wedding. Then he said something to Melissa, even as she twirled and threw. I stiffened—Danny did, too—and experienced a wave of dislocation more powerful than anything I'd felt in my whole, dislocated life.

Somehow, we'd formed ourselves into a rough, regimental formation, with Melissa and Tom Reaveley on point out front, then Reverend Beagle and Mr. Riley and my brother, followed by the rest of us in rows. Every time the front group took a few steps forward, we all did the same. When we reached the barber pole in front of Mr. Gene's Nice and Clean, my brother turned to face us and threw his arms in the air. Instantly, everyone stopped. The fiddle went silent, and Melissa swallowed her knives in her gloves.

"The spirit of God!" my brother shouted.

Fiddle lowered, Tom Reaveley smiled through his beard. The smile looked completely genuine, as though he was proud just to be near Lewis.

"The spirit of the nation!" Mr. Gene said from the doorway of his barbershop.

The muzzles of more than a dozen guns leapt to eye-level, pointing straight over his roof. Then they erupted.

I ducked. Danny laughed, and the crowd surged sideways a few feet, stopping in front of Riley's General Store.

"The spirit of God!" yelled my brother again.

"The spirit of the nation!" Riley replied.

Boom!

The fiddle kicked in again, and Melissa let fly, her knives nicking silver gashes in the overcast sky.

"Someone must like your brother a lot," Danny grumbled. "Being the crier for this is a big honor."

"Why?"

"He's calling out the evil spirits, that's why."

"Then shouldn't one of the reverends do it?"

Danny shrugged. "Beagle used to. Then the other one, Reverend Henry, convinced him the whole thing was sacrilegious or pagan or something, so now he just officiates. Then Riley did it for a few years, but some people aren't so wild about Riley, you know."

That tidbit was strangely reassuring.

"Some people aren't so wild about your brother, either, from what I've heard," Danny added.

I couldn't help but smile. "I bet they're quieter about it, though."

"I'm not so wild about either one of you, myself. I don't mind who knows it, either."

"Yeah," I said. "But that's for an entirely different reason."

After a moment, he nodded, his eyes slipping to his feet. He looked sad and tired.

Lewis's honorary duties lasted two more hours, while we traipsed from door to door down Sherman Street, then systematically up the side roads that spoked toward the hills. The only variation in the established routine was the "spirit of the nation" respondent, who was usually the owner or the person most responsible for the dwelling being shot over. Sometimes, our posse, or whatever it was, arrived outside a home to find women and old people and children picnicking on the front lawn. Some of them held out pieces of chicken or fruit for us after the firing.

"It's like Christmas caroling," I said.

That earned another sneer from Danny. "Not so much."

"A community celebration, anyway."

"More a show of force. Or an exorcism."

Of course he was right. There were guns being fired, after all. Knives being flung.

By the time we reached the trees that marked the perimeter of Trampleton proper, all the joy had seeped out of the ritual. Lewis and I had taken part in branding days on ranches a couple of times, and those, too, had a cruelly festive air to them that sometimes lasted whole mornings but rarely longer. By evening, when the last of the animals had given up their stamping and bleating—not because they'd become less terrified, but because their terror had exhausted them—the whole thing had become routine, and the knowledge that the next day marked the return of regular work made the final hours before knock-off even heavier than usual. Walking beside Danny, remembering those days and a radio speech I'd just heard Harry Hopkins, the WPA director, give on the redemptive, healing, character-affirming power of going to work, it seemed to me there was something fatally flawed about the travel guides, and indeed the whole concept of the Writers' Project. Something that missed the truth about the way most people spent the majority of their time, and what the work they did cost them. I was struggling toward naming it when I realized we'd all kept walking straight into the woods, and now we had stopped, and dozens of coloreds were facing us.

Every one of them was dressed more formally than anyone in our party except Lewis. I spotted Robert, who was standing next to Mitchell Johns beneath a skeletal hemlock, sweating in the clothes he'd worn on the night he took me to hear Teddy Anklebones. He hadn't seen me, and his face wore the same hard cast it had on the day Madame Duarte brought the news that his sister was dead.

Everyone else had settled into an uncomfortable silence. None of the coloreds were armed, or at least they didn't appear to be. Most kept close enough to the trees to dive behind them at a moment's notice. Even through the layers of slicked sweat, I felt the hairs lift along my neck and arms. Then, off to my left, someone muttered, "Fuck this." Immediately, a half-dozen members of our troupe split off and retreated the way we'd come.

Finally, Mr. Riley unslung his rifle from across his chest and, holding it low on the barrel and muzzle-to-the-sky, extended it toward the nearest colored. I recognized the man. His name was Warren; he was about my age and biked past Robert's to the mill every evening about the time I got home for supper.

For one crazy moment, everyone watched the gun. I half-thought Riley and Warren were about to play that sandlot game where you clamp alternating fists up the handle of a baseball bat to determine who gets first ups.

"Going to need that back, boy," Mr. Riley said. "First thing tomorrow morning, and I mean *first*. Hear?"

The rest of the transfer was accomplished quickly and quietly. Every remaining member of our posse handed his gun to a colored. The coloreds rarely met anyone's eyes. Some said, "Thanks," or, "Okay, boss," but most just nodded and said nothing at all. I didn't see where Robert got his gun. Like me, Lewis never had a weapon. The brothers Dent might have been the only completely unarmed people in the entire crowd. But just as the gathering broke up, I saw Lewis step into Robert's path, and a tiny twitch of misgiving shot up my spine. All Lewis did was offer a hand. Robert, looking bewildered shook it.

Then it was over. Within minutes, the forest cleared; the coloreds returned to their neighborhood, and everyone else dispersed home or to the tavern on Sherman Street to toast the country. Lewis caught my glance as he strolled off with Tom Reaveley. This time, he grinned.

Which left only Melissa Flynn and Danny and me.

In her wet, white blouse, with her kerchief slipping sideways and her skin shining, she reminded me of a lathered horse after a long gallop. She also looked happier than anyone I knew, or had ever known, for that matter.

"Hey, now, Melissa Flynn," I said, and smiled.

Her answering nod was slow and tired, and meant for both Danny and me.

I started to take her hand and hesitated, knowing that Danny would read it as claiming her. Then I wondered why I cared. While I was still thinking about it, Melissa kissed Danny on the cheek, then ran one sweaty, gloved hand over my face and through my hair.

"Good night, my boys," she said. "Thank you." And she left us.

I was too tired to chase her, and also content just to bask in her glow, and in the gift that Danny and I had apparently given her. She was already out of sight when I started out of the woods. At the first curb, I sat down, swatting flies off my neck. From the colored side of the woods, I heard a barrage of shots, then an eruption of laughter. With the sun down, the light leaked away fast, and night fell.

I waited for Danny to stalk past me. He sat down instead. "Now then, let's get back to why Paul will never have Melissa."

There was no question about it. Danny was the P.D. type, constantly burrowing under your feet, popping up to screech and chatter, then diving underground again.

"What say we call it a night?" I said.

"You aren't the only one who came here on a train, you know."

I glanced at him. "I guess she's been telling you about me."

"Don't look so pleased. It won't matter."

"Alright, Danny," I sighed. "Say it."

"Orphan Train."

Whatever I'd been expecting, it wasn't that. "You're an orphan?"

"She is."

I thought of the way Melissa had looked a few moments ago, and something turned over in my stomach. I wished she was the one telling me this.

Danny was watching my expression. "I guess she hasn't been letting *you* in on as much as you thought."

"Are you an orphan, too?"

I suspected he wouldn't answer, but he shrugged. "My dad's still alive somewhere. As far as I know. He just got sick of working double shifts at the mine, and really sick of West Virginia. So one day he decided he was sick of me, too. He woke me up bright and early a couple of weeks after I turned nine and walked me two towns down the road to the Pittsfield Children's Home in beautiful, slaggy downtown Charlottesville. I can still hear his parting words." He crossed his arms and puffed out his chest in obvious imitation. "'Ain't likely to make it back for ya. No point in your waiting.'"

He dropped his arms, and his voice fell into a rhythm. If nothing else, the Project had trained me to recognize the moment people slipped into the stories they told themselves.

"The thing is, I should never have gone inside. I should have waited until he was out of sight, then hitched a ride or hopped a train. But I was nine, what did I know? So I waltzed into this pathetic common room and told the stupid fat woman in there that my parents had burned to death. Then I asked for breakfast. I'd been there maybe fifteen minutes when these two wop brothers named Pandolfi strutted through the door, took one look at me and crowded around. I was a lot scrawnier, then. Kind of like you are now."

I looked at his gangly legs and the shoulder blades jutting through his shirt. But I didn't say anything.

"These were big kids. Really big, with black hair all over their arms and big wop noses and miner's eyes. You know what that means?" He narrowed his own eyes to slits. "To keep the coal dust out, see? Only these kids just inherited the look, or put it on because they thought it made them look nasty.

Which it did. The older one's name was Mario, and the younger one was Murder. I don't know why they singled me out for special attention, given all the other pitiful targets in that hellhole. But they did."

Actually, it wasn't hard to guess. Danny was scrawny, sure, but he was also idiot-stubborn, defiant, and resourceful as a raccoon. He was precisely the kind of kid someone like Lewis, for example, would have taken up as a challenge.

"The first time they really got hold of me was ten days after I got there. Until then, they just called me names, bounced my chin on the bathroom sink a few times, things like that. It was late October, freezing cold, the middle of the night. I waited until everyone was asleep, then unlatched a window, knotted up my bedsheet, and dropped down into the broken glass they used for a backyard. I headed straight for the fence. I hadn't taken a Goddamn thing; I was just leaving. All of a sudden, one of the Pandolfi brothers kicked my legs out from under me, and the other sat on my knees. Then they just kind of hung out and talked to each other for a while, without even looking at me. By that point, I figured I knew what was coming, and there was nothing in the world I could do about it. So I waited and hoped they'd just leave me out there when they were done. 'Cause unless my guts were pouring out of my mouth, I was going over that fence anyway. But instead of socking or kicking me or using me as a spit-rag, they let me get up.

"Mario, the older one, zipped a cig out of his pocket, lit a match, and said, 'Been watching you.'

"I didn't answer. So he said, 'Check this.'"

Twirling a cigarette I hadn't even seen him light, Danny tucked it behind his ear in one smooth motion and opened his arms wide.

"First time I'd seen anyone do that," he said. "I won't lie to you, I was pretty impressed. Murder was smiling, but not because he liked me or anything.

"'So. Practice,' he told me.

"The first few times, I didn't even get the cigarette through my hair. Every time I dropped it, Mario pinned my arms, and Murder grabbed the cig off the ground, checked to make sure it was still lit, then ground the tip right here." He pressed his index finger against his temple and left it there until I winced. "It's not just the pain. Or the smell of your hair burning, or the bubbles you can feel in your skin. It's the sound. Like—"

"I know what it sounds like," I said, remembering P.D.'s crazy, burnt-lipped smile.

For once, Danny let himself look surprised, and he even shut up a second. But he didn't ask. Eventually, he went on. "I could've run. I might even have made it. But I figured that's what they wanted. And it made me mad. Anyway, like I said, it was a good trick. In the end, Murder gave me his Chicago Cubs hat to cover the burns. It was the first hat I ever owned.

"'Same time tomorrow,' he told me, and they left me there.

"The next day, I showed up right on time. By the end of the second night, they had nothing left to teach me."

"Melissa." I tried to say it tough, though mostly I felt sad now, and also bone-weary and dislocated all over again.

"Melissa lived in Holy Hearts Afire, the girls' home across town. Every morning, the nuns would march her and the other so-called 'most promising young ladies' a mile and a half to our place so they could spend their entire day brushing rat turds out of the rug in our common room, washing our sheets, and doing our dishes. 'Learning skills necessary for work or marriage,' they said.

"She was heavier then." It was corny the way Danny's tone mellowed. "Honestly, she was downright hefty. Didn't matter, though. At lunch, we'd all get there early—even the littlest ones—and try to guess which corner of the room she'd be assigned to so we could be near her. She had this way of setting the table like she was dealing cards. Flick, flick, flick, perfect, done. She never exactly smiled, and she almost never spoke to us. I think it was forbidden. It didn't matter. The Pandolfis practically climbed out of their hairy skins when she went by. They'd start grunting and shoving each other like gorillas at the zoo.

"I don't know why she picked me. Or how."

After that, he stayed quiet a long time. The nighttime cloud cover thickened overhead like setting concrete. He flicked the cigarette off his ear into the street and stamped it out. He hadn't taken even one drag. "She looked into my eyes a lot. Which was pretty overwhelming for a kid like me. She probably looked into everyone's eyes. She wasn't flirting or anything. Just the way she is. But I looked back. One day, it was just too much, and when she leaned over to clear my plate, I slipped a note in her sweater pocket."

Danny stood up, his arms rigid as sawed-off two-by-fours at his sides. "I got a note back the very next day, stuck to the bottom of my plate. The day after that, the wardens arrived at the crack of dawn.

"All they told us was that the Pittsfield Children's Home was closing. Arrangements had been made. We each got one burlap bag for our belongings.

By the time we got downstairs, they'd already dragged the big wooden tables and benches out of the mess hall, and the rat-turd rug had been rolled up in the common room. I was just going along like everyone else until I remembered Melissa. Then I tried sneaking upstairs to hide. I guess I was thinking either the nuns would bring her or else I'd go find her. When the fat lady found me instead, I bit her. I just—"

"Son of a bitch!" I leapt to my feet, startling Danny badly. "I have to go."

Danny gaped at me.

"I'm sorry," I said.

He was waving one closed fist in front of him as if he were erasing a chalkboard, and it occurred to me that for half a moment, he'd forgotten why he was telling the story. The realization made me feel even worse.

"Danny, I'm really sorry. I forgot. I'm supposed to meet somebody. It's probably too late already." I started away fast, heading for the trail up the Back into the hills.

Danny followed, both fists lifted now. "She's exhausted."

I spun around and said, "I'm not meeting her."

I turned to leave again, and he grabbed my elbow.

"I said she's exhausted. Maybe you didn't notice. Or maybe you don't care."

I shook him off. He grabbed me again, and it all boiled out of me. "I said I'm not meeting her. Do you understand? Howsabout you go curl up on her doorstep like a good little lapdog. If you see me coming, you can bark."

"Fuck you."

That froze us both. Strangely, the person I thought of at that moment was Grace. In a horrible way, simply by demanding that I watch and listen so carefully, get everything down exactly the way it was, she'd taught me how to hurt someone with themselves. A flush flooded my face, and my clenched hands fell open at my sides.

"Danny, I'm sorry."

"Fuck you," he whispered.

But he didn't grab me again. This time, when I moved away, apologizing some more, he stayed stuck to the street as if I'd nailed him there. When I reached the base of the path and looked back, he was still in the same spot, arms hanging limp, head half-down, absolutely still in the windless air. Not for the first time, he reminded me of a scarecrow.

I started to run.

*****

Fourth of July. You want a real story?

It had to be close to midnight already. As I raced up the hill into the larger, darker woods, the hum of cicadas swelled. My lungs heaved. Vomit catapulted into the back of my throat but didn't spill out. I kept running. Despite months of inquiring, I still only had the vaguest notion of where I was going. My best advice had come from a guy who'd literally dragged me by the sleeve into the shadows outside Riley's General Store.

"You're the guy who wants to find Screwpine?" he said. He was wearing brown, checked knickerboxers, a bow-tie, and a beanie. In my notes, I named him Orville.

If I paid close enough attention, according to Orville, halfway up the Back I'd find an old wagon road branching off into the spruce woods. Follow the wagon road into the pines, and eventually I'd come to a fork. Bear left and stay on the trail, and I'd find Screwpine.

"You'll know it when you see it," he assured me.

I found the wagon road, all right, and I followed it deep into the gloom beneath the tightly bunched pines. Long, prickly vines and weeds had overrun the entire forest floor. I came to several places that might have been forks, bore left at each of them, but I never knew what I was looking for until I suddenly came across Cutter himself, waiting in an ankle-deep tangle of weeds, peg-leg planted in the dirt like the rooted stem of some petalless flower. His eyes looked even redder than they had during the train trip we'd shared. Despite the heat, he was wearing the same scruffy suit coat. He still looked like a hobo.

"There you are, Dent. I thought you weren't going to show," he said. "Thought maybe I was wrong about you."

As soon as I stopped moving, my lungs seized. I doubled over, unable to suck down any air. The sensation lasted long enough to send firefly-sparks shooting across my vision and panic coiling up my throat.

"You…" I started, breathing heavily. "You could have given me a little more to go on."

"You're here, aren't you? I gave you more than most around these parts, I bet."

He kicked his peg-leg high to avoid entangling it in the ground cover and left the path. I marveled at his agility, then remembered that he wasn't an old man. By the time we'd gone fifty feet, I could no longer distinguish where the trail had been when I looked behind me. The pines closed around us, their needles royal blue in the absence of moonlight. Their sweet-sharp smell pricked my nostrils.

"Is there really such a thing as a screwpine?" I asked.

"Depends who you ask," he grunted while gliding over roots and weeds. Not once did he so much as stumble.

Finally, we came to the top of a steep hill, and I realized it was true: I would have known the place as soon as I saw it. Assuming I'd found it, that is. But nothing Cutter or Orville or anyone else had said would have brought me anywhere near this spot.

Right on the summit sat a single, sawn-through tree stump so thick that my arms wouldn't have reached halfway around it. Hunched on the stump was an exquisitely carved owl roughly two feet tall, its head neatly tucked into folded wings. In the near-dark, I couldn't tell whether the thing was painted, but it was darker even than the pine shadows. Maybe that's what gave it its idol-like aura.

"Who did this?" I asked after a long time.

"*They* did. I mean, I assume they did. I never asked, and I never heard anyone say."

"Who's *they*?"

"The coloreds, of course. What do you think we're doing here?" Then he shivered, or maybe just shook himself.

I couldn't decide whether it was the sculpture itself or Cutter's attitude that was making me so uneasy. "Okay. What does it mean?"

"I don't know, Dent. National symbol? Screwpine mascot? This here's just the beginning of the story."

Pushing through the pine branches to the right of the stump, Cutter dropped out of sight down the other side of the hill. I moved to the edge of the slope. The gully was deep, its treelessness disconcerting given the density of the woods around it. If there'd been starlight, it would have blazed unobstructed all the way to the ground, which glowed an almost welcoming, grassy green. Instead, only a fingernail moon had scratched through the cloud cover, offering a single ray of light like a lantern shone down a well. The slope was covered in vines and pine needles, so that my feet slipped and scrabbled with each new step. Cutter waited at the bottom, looking up only when I dislodged a particularly audible stream of dirt. At the far end of the clearing I saw some kind of building with a peaked roof and a tall, square door-space that made it resemble a barn. A smaller, flat-roofed structure had been hitched to the back of it like a caboose.

I took my first step across the flat grass, and my shoes struck metal. Glinting dully out of the spectral green like a half-exposed fossil was a railroad track.

"Hey," I said. "What line was this?"

Looking up, I was startled to find Cutter with his head in his hands. I moved toward him, and he lifted his gaze. "You bring a notebook?"

"I...I usually just listen. And write later." I faltered under his glare. The woods remained silent.

"Then listen carefully." Scowling, he hopped away down the track toward the giant, looming shadows.

Ten steps away, I realized that it wasn't a barn. Through the gaping space where tall doors must have been, I could discern the skeletal shapes of sawhorses, giant metal bins, columns of black iron, and the dulled face of a circular saw-blade propped on a pile of dust and ash like a tousled head on a pillow. The walls had flaked to virtually nothing. Not a single structure or workbench remained intact. Some sort of rusted-through tractor was connected by filthy industrial cables to a pulley somewhere inside the smaller building. All the walls I could see were blistered and blackened; the one nearest me had tilted away from the sagging roof without completely collapsing.

"Must have been some fire," I said.

"The wind ought to have scattered the whole works by now. Don't you think?"

He was right. If I leaned on the doorframe, I could probably knock over the entire place.

"You'd think tramps might have found it after all these years. The scrap alone is worth more than a tinker's penny. But even the tramps won't touch it."

"Pretty remote," I said.

"Yeah, but everyone knows it's here."

Cutter stepped into the gloom. His shadow drifted among the bins and broken benches, burnt shingles and wood-shavings. I edged inside, staying close to the doorway.

"You wouldn't believe how many people they could tuck in here," Cutter said. "When this place was running full-bore, you couldn't see anything but bodies all over the place. Like bats packed on top of each other, flapping and yawing."

A shudder raced up my shoulders and along my arms. My breath still wouldn't go down right.

"See, they used to work the slave shift in town. All of them, together, all night. They had their own foremen, their own regulations, and no one messed with them. They got paid pretty fair, too. That phrase, 'slave shift,' it's just a name, you understand? It doesn't mean anything. They came up with it themselves."

"When was this?"

"Oh, 1919, I suppose. '20, for certain. '21. '22. I can't tell you how it got here, or exactly when, or who built it. It's like it grew here while we were gone, fighting the war. We came back, and there was this whole new world everyone knew about. Screwpine."

"*O, Old Screwpine*," I suddenly sang, the tune springing to my lips. "*Got what's mine.*" It was the longest and saddest Teddy Anklebones song I'd heard that night under the pear tree, outside the blue house.

"See?" said Cutter. "It even has its own songs, its own stories. That's the part I don't get. How'd they even find each other? How'd they figure out how or where the hell to go? Most of 'em can't read, let alone read a map."

He knelt in the dirt near the circular saw and touched the teeth.

"Still sharp. It's a damn good blade. Better than any they've got at the mill in Trampleton. So you tell me. Where'd it come from?"

"Mr. Cutter," I said, "could you start from the beginning?"

"I don't know the beginning. My family's been in these hills a hundred years, Dent. My grandfather helped build half of Trampleton, back when it was called Greentree, and my father lost all three of his older brothers fighting the Yankees."

"Greentree," I interrupted. "That was its original name?"

"Well, I think the Indians had a name for it. But that name meant something-tree, too. Point is, we've been here a long time. We know pretty much everything there is to know about this little region. And even after the War Between the States, not much changed. I went off to fight the Germans when I was twenty-four, and spent almost all of 1919 at a sanitarium in Cornwall, England. By the time I got home, there were two big differences: my father had died, and there wasn't a single colored still working at the Trampleton mill. Not a one."

My eyes kept flying around the space where we were standing. There were no birds or bats in those eaves, no spiders scuttling up the walls or lurking in the corners. The Screwpine mill was like a cargo container that had dropped off a train and tumbled into this clearing, scratched and beat to hell, but also right side up and sealed.

"As far as I could tell," Cutter said, "no one really minded when they stopped working at the mill in town. It just meant more jobs for the soldiers coming home. There were plenty of orders to fill in those days. Lots of people building things. Plenty of men wanting to earn their keep. Anyway, the coloreds didn't leave all at once. They kind of trickled off one by one.

"And I'll tell you a funny thing about that war. You see people doing things you just can't believe—sawing out each other's Adam's apples with bayonets, cutting each other in half with machine guns—and it makes you not care so much about what the coloreds are up to one way or the other, you know? Unless it makes you care more, I guess.

"The point is, no one even checked, see? We knew they were out here, all right. We saw the houses going up in their part of town. Fancier houses than they'd had before. And all we thought, if we thought anything, was…why not? We didn't realize…" He stroked his palm back and forth on the teeth of the sawblade. "The lumber boys were the ones who finally tipped us off. Like I said, there was so much business pouring in, even those guys began working night shifts. And that's when they started coming back to town all spooked, babbling about ghost trains in the forest, dark shapes in the trees, midnight dances at somewhere called Screwpine.

"It was only a matter of time before some of us came out here to get a good look at what was what. God knows, I'd seen enough dead people by then to believe a few of them might have set up camp in our woods, even built themselves a ghost railroad. But what we actually found…what those people made…" He was stirring the sawdust with his peg-leg as if revealing—or else erasing—some half-obscured message. I slumped to my haunches and put my hands in the dirt, which felt surprisingly soft, like down.

"The first thing we found was this mill. Better equipped than any within a hundred miles or more. Then we realized just how many people were working it. They were running day shifts, night shifts, weekends, every kind of shift. And these were workers who were peachy-happy to take home whatever the mill wanted to pay. They never made a fuss, and always showed up the next day whether they were sick or sad or what. Because it was theirs, see?

"And then we found the railroad. Miles and miles and miles of it. Tracks we'd never seen, had never even known were out here, stretching to Greenville, Abbeville, Mitchellville, Orangeburg, all the way to Savannah, then south to the Panhandle. Rosewood."

I'd heard of almost none of those places. But Cutter hardly seemed to be talking to me.

"It was like discovering a whole new country. A shadow-country operating right inside ours, but invisible. One with its own laws, its own by-ways and places of interest, hell, whole cities we knew nothing about. It was kind of thrilling, really. Kind of terrifying. A *real* Reconstruction. Only the places they made weren't recreations of what was there before. They were building brand new places."

Abruptly, his voice flattened. "For a while, the shock of it kept it safe. The sheer scope of what they'd done. Then, in '23, the news started filtering up the line. Whole towns burned to the ground in Florida. Lynchings like we've never had here, ever, no matter what you've heard, all through Georgia and South Carolina. Up here in the North State, we like to think of ourselves as more than a little different. Comfortable with our coloreds. Comfortable with ourselves. Civilized. Everyone knowing their place, working together to make a good life for everyone. So nothing happened here until well into '24. By then, what was left of these railroad tracks didn't run anywhere anymore. We could have just left it alone. It was already dying."

For a long time, then, he stopped talking. I half-thought he'd gone to sleep. "What happened here, Mr. Cutter?" I finally asked.

For the first time since we'd arrived here, he looked right at me. "July fourth, 1924. A hot, horrible night just like this one. We gathered with our rifles under the Sherman Street elms at dusk, same as always, and shot our way through town. But when we hit the edge of town, we reloaded our guns. And then we just kept going. I don't remember anyone suggesting it. There wasn't any big discussion. We just kept going straight through the woods. No one pointed a gun at anything but the ground."

For a moment, Cutter's voice went silent, but his mouth was still moving, as though the tale he was telling had slipped into a tunnel. Then it became audible again.

"We came upon a big group of them standing at the bottom of the path up the Back, out for an Independence Day picnic or something. Not a one said anything. It was like they'd been waiting for us. Like they were watching a parade. We marched straight up the mountain, down the same wagon trail you followed, through those trees, past the owl up there, and right down this hill."

Cutter rubbed his chin and squeezed his jaw a few times. "This part is almost funny. I mean, there we were, a good old-fashioned hating mob, the kind we'd heard about from our grandfathers but had never experienced or even seen. Carrying guns, no less. And for a good five minutes…maybe even longer…we couldn't even get the coloreds to notice we were there.

"See, they were all inside. In here. Dozens of them, humming, cussing, heads-down busy. Right to the end, holiday or not, they kept that sawdust flying and those shingles stacking, even though there couldn't have been many orders trickling in. Not a whole lot of the places they'd built were even standing anymore, from what we'd heard."

Peering through the burned-out holes where the windows must have been, I watched the grass turn even greener as the moon shouldered through the clouds. And all at once—as though I'd been here myself and witnessed it all—I could see Robert, limned in the moonlight, with his hands in his work-apron and that look in his eyes, more pride than defiance. He'd worked here, he must have, maybe as a foreman or something. For the first time since I'd joined the Writers' Project, I was fairly certain I had found an honest-to-God story, one that hadn't been told.

"Mr. Cutter," I said, my words tumbling out in a rush. "Could you please just tell me how many people died?"

Surprise flashed across his face. "I told you, Dent. This here's *North* Carolina." He stirred the dirt in front of him again with his wooden leg. "For the longest time, we just stood around. Eventually, someone got the bright idea of chucking wood chips at the building. We didn't even throw them at the windows, 'cause we didn't want to break any glass, see? It was almost like we were calling sweethearts out to dance.

"There was a lot of racket in there, obviously. So it took quite a while before they heard us. But when they finally saw us, it got real quiet in this clearing, man and boy. Quieter than now, if you can imagine, even with all those people packed down here. I never heard a woods so quiet. Not before a battle, anyway.

"The coloreds were all watching. Most of us were kind of shifting around, like we didn't want to see each other there. And still, not a single one of us raised the weapon he was carrying. You know, I think if they'd had guns and come out shooting, we would have gone down meek as mown hay.

"But whatever it was that had brought us here, Dent, it had them, too. I can't explain it. It was like being part of one of them mechanical clocks. You know what I mean? Where you just wind around your track, and at the right moment, you do the movement you've been made for, and the hour sounds, and you've marked it the only way you ever could."

I was nodding so fast that it felt as though my head might roll off my neck. Somehow, I really did think I understood. I'd spent the last few months advancing along my own track, oblivious to its existence, all the way to this moment. And now I was here. And my task was to record it.

"They didn't have guns," Cutter said. "So instead of shooting, or yelling, or fighting…they came out singing. I'll never forget that song. Ever. 'When my blood runs chilly and cold…'"

The second he started chanting the tune, I cried out. The melody buffeted against me like the wind that had battered Grace as she'd clung to the side of the boxcar the last time I'd heard it. I may have been oblivious to my own track, I realized, but Grace wasn't. God, had she conceived of this even then? It was why she'd sent me to Robert's. She wanted me—an outsider, with no foreknowledge or conceivable connection to any of these events—to make my way to these woods, discover this story, and bring it back.

I started singing right along. "'Do Lord. Do remember me.'"

That stopped Cutter. He looked alarmed. "You know it?"

"My friend does. I mean, I've heard it."

"Yeah, well, not like this you haven't. All of 'em singing together. There was no harmony, understand, none of that fancy church singing. But they were all doing it, real slow. Out they came. They didn't look at us, either. Most of them didn't. The ones whose faces I saw looked a little scared, a little sad. And tired. But there was this one big fella. Beady black eyes and forearms like clubs."

A violent shiver shot all the way down into my feet. Of course he meant Robert. It explained so much about the way people talked about him. The way everyone, not just the coloreds, knew him, or knew of him. *What had he done?*

"Dent, are you listening? The whole…evacuation, I guess you'd call it…couldn't have lasted more than two minutes. Then they were gone, and it got even quieter. Like they'd never been here at all."

Gliding past me, Cutter left the building. I followed on unsteady legs with that song still echoing in my ears. Outside, he looked at me, then up the hill, as though watching the ghost-parade of colored men all over again.

"I could be wrong. You never really know. But I think we'd maybe decided, somehow, that we weren't going to do anything else. It just seemed silly. We'd rousted them, proven we still could, and I guess that was pretty much the point. And the sight of this place, with all of them in there…well, I can't speak for the others. But it affected me different than I thought it would. I didn't like the look of it without them in it.

"I really thought we were just going to turn around. As a matter of fact, we'd already done it. We must have, because we were all looking up that way when the big, beady-eyed fella reappeared. Well, he just stared at us for a little while. Then he stepped over the ridge, like he was easing into a lake, and strolled right down. Alone."

With a last glance at the mill, Cutter started up the rise. Whether because of his leg or because he was tired, he kept slipping this time, though he never quite fell. I scrambled up behind him and put a steadying hand on the small of his back. We climbed the rest of the way together.

At the ridge, Cutter sighed and mopped his forehead. "As soon as we saw the big guy, every single one of us stopped. In those days, remember— hell, it's not so different now—most of us weren't used to coloreds coming unless we called them. And this one just kept coming. Still humming that damn fool song."

"Was his name Robert?"

Cutter's head swung around as if I'd shaken him. "Well, I didn't ask him, then."

"But you know it now."

"Same as you."

Dizzy with my own months-long obliviousness, I nodded.

"He reached the bottom of the hill and ambled into the clearing. He wasn't looking at any of us directly. But he wasn't looking away, either. He was muttering, too, like maybe he'd forgotten something. When he passed, we all stepped back, every one of us, as if he was some general come to inspect the troops.

"And then he stopped. Right beside us. And he kind of half-turned. He said to Old Man Riley, 'Mind if I borrow this?' And he put his big, black hand right on the petrol can that Riley had lugged out here. I was thinking maybe the man was plumb crazy. But not suicidal. If he'd touched a gun, someone would have shot him. Maybe even me. But the petrol can?

"Old Man Riley was too flummoxed to respond one way or the other. And the colored, he just took the can from him, easy as you please, uncapped it, and went back to muttering. Then he strolled right up to the mill and started dousing it, with these big sweeping tosses. He was kind of shouting as he did it, like he was throwing a child up in the air instead of splashing gasoline all over everything. He walked all the way around the building. When he came back, he dropped the empty can at Riley's feet, put his hands in his overalls and pulled out a match.

"Now I don't know why. You're the writer; maybe you can explain it. But here's the thing that's stuck in my mind, all these years. The colored just couldn't get the match lit. He'd put on all that show, but I could see that his hands were shaking, and he just couldn't get it lit.

"He was trying so hard, he finally snapped the match. That was the first time he actually looked up. And I couldn't believe it. The damn fool had this cockeyed grin on his face. The next match caught, and he flipped it. There was a little pop, and the place was ablaze. After that, we were all so busy watching the flames, none of us saw where the colored went. He didn't come back through us, so he must have crossed the railroad tracks and gone into the trees."

With that, Cutter lurched away toward the path.

"That's pretty much all," he said when I caught up to him. "We didn't stay long. We hurried back here, then split up. Nobody said anything. We just went home. It must have been months before the lumber boys started their damn-fool whispering again. Spooks in the trees. Lights. One night, I couldn't stand it, I marched right out of the tavern and came all the way up here by myself. I didn't see spooks or lights or anything else, just that empty shell of a building down there. Nothing remarkable about it at all, except that it was still standing. And there was no way it should have been.

"That was enough for me. I packed up my house and started building my cabin out here the very next day. Why? I don't even know, so don't go thinking you do. The only time I go back to Trampleton is to catch the train. And I've come to this clearing almost every night now for more than ten years. No matter what anyone else tells you, I've never seen lights or spooks or any other Goddamn thing other than what we saw tonight.

"But this is the point, Dent, and the reason I brought you here. I think about it all the time. That night, and what happened. So I just decided you might ought to put this place in your tourbook. Even if it's not really a place anymore. Just in case one day...I don't know. In case one of *them* takes a motor tour and wants to see *their* country. Come on, now. You've got a caller."

"A *caller*?" I was too mesmerized at that point to do anything but follow. A hazy whiteness seemed to be nosing along the ground between the tree trunks. Then I thought I heard music. And for a few wild seconds, I thought maybe the ghosts of Screwpine really were adrift in these trees. But the sound was emanating from ahead of us. Also, it had a peculiar, tinny quality to it. I could distinguish lightly strummed guitars, a lone clarinet murmuring over them, like a voice telling a story in some quiet restaurant.

To the lilt of the music, I followed Cutter onto a road and came in sight of a long, black car, just idling in the gravel. The hazy glow, I realized, was coming from its headlights. Cutter was bathed in it.

"Well come on, Dent," he said. "You can't keep a man like that waiting."

Both the passenger and side doors were open, but the only person I could see was leaning against the hood with his legs crossed at the ankles. He wore an elegant white suit coat that hugged his shoulders but dropped too loosely over his gaunt frame. His light brown hair looked mussed in a way that suggested he'd mussed it himself, and his face was as pale as the headlight beams. In his left hand, he held a cigarette poised girlishly between his second and third fingers. I froze.

Of course, I recognized him instantly from magazine photographs and the pictures shown during my Freshman literature seminar at Stillwater. I think I'd even been vaguely aware that he was holed up somewhere around here trying to nurse his wife back to health or sanity or something. My literature professor had devoted a whole, bitterly disappointed lecture to his failed third book, though I hadn't read it. The lecture included repeated allusions to the rumors about his Hollywood life and the reasons that none of his scripts got made into movies or even finished. Was he working for the Project now, too? Was this meeting Grace's doing? Or Cutter's? And where the hell had Cutter got to, anyway?

"Paul Dent," said Scott, his voice as musical as the clarinet's, his words clinking together like ice in a drink with an umbrella. "I've heard about you. I think it's time you learned just what it is your brother and Grace Lowie are doing with their Saturday nights."

From *The WPA Guide to the Old North State,* Tour 29B (deleted)

"*Right on this road* **400 yards** *to the Ashton Road. L. from this point* **3.2m.** *along the rim of Cutter Mountain, a granite slab marks the site of Cavendish Fairgrounds, once famous throughout the state for celebratory traditions such as firecrackers at daybreak and the often brutal Saturday evening "Interesting Exhibitions." It was here that the great Ashton fire broke out in August 1936. The fire consumed the grounds, the entire town of Ashton, thousands of acres of timberland, and most structures within a five-mile radius, and claimed the lives of more than 100 people (see Ashton and Bunk County, p. 269).*

Caleb Cavendish, one of the first settlers in this region of the Blue Ridge Mountains, originally claimed this spot for his homestead in the 1780s. He was kidnapped and murdered by the Cherokees. His son Bertram negotiated and supervised the removal of virtually all members of that tribe from the valley. Bertram's great-great grandson, Cuthbert, established the fairgrounds and later died on the Maine, but Cuthbert's brother, Bertram IV, maintained the family's prominent position in the region, eventually becoming mayor of Ashton and presiding over the township until the fire obliterated it. He was killed in the disaster along with his entire family.

At **8.8 m.** *is the junction with State 11, which leads between groves of blackened, skeletal horse chestnut trees, down the mountain into the ruined and abandoned townships of what was once Bunk County.*

PART THREE

Revolution

"The theory behind our tactics: The white man is always trying to know into somebody else's business. All right, I'll set something outside the door of my mind for him to play with and handle. He can read my writing, but he sho' can't read my mind. I'll put this play toy in his hand, and he will seize it and go away. Then I'll say my say and sing my song."

— Zora Neale Hurston, *Mules and Men*

1 — July 1936, Trampleton, North Carolina

On the Saturday after my visit to Screwpine, I conducted my last set of interviews in Trampleton and met Grace outside the Sherman Street train station to hand in my pages. The following week, she planned to dispatch me to Cherryville four miles or so up the mountain road.

"Can I keep staying at Robert's?" I asked. "Please?"

She was standing in the shade of the elms, sweating under her straw hat and long, checkered sleeves. She'd made me meet her there because she didn't want to have to hike through town in the heat, and also because, as she put it in the note she'd mailed, "The goddamn book I'm writing is eating me alive." I'd actually thought she meant the Project guide until I remembered the look she'd shot me upon finding me rifling through the pages of her writing case in the boxcar.

Now she looked up from my notes and said, "Suits me. I don't care. But the Project isn't going to give you a bicycle just because you feel like staying put. You better be in the mood for lots of walking."

I'm not sure what my expression might have been, but it made her laugh. "Don't worry, Paul. This place only feels like home because it's home to the people whose lives you've been living in. Occupational hazard. Nothing here is really yours."

It was the first time I ever heard her say anything cruel. Her casualness, more than the words themselves, made them seem that way. As if none of this could possibly matter to me.

"I'll see you later, Grace," I said, and went to find Melissa.

As usual, Melissa had half a dozen children buzzing around her at Mr. Gene's. I lingered by the door, watching her hands, the swell of her body under her apron, the smile opening on her mouth like butterfly wings over a flower.

"Mr. Dent," Mr. Gene said, nodding, as I made my way past his chair. The person he was hot-shaving startled under his towel as though scrambling to attention. Mr. Gene rested a hairy hand on the man's chest. "The *other* Mr. Dent."

Melissa glanced up and announced, "I'm taking five." A tow-headed boy leapt from her chair.

"Take two, you're busy," Mr. Gene said.

Then her hand was in mine and we were out back where it was quieter, though no cooler. As soon as the door closed, Melissa slumped against the bricks and closed her eyes. For at least one of our two minutes, she stayed like that, holding my hand. When I couldn't stand it any longer, I leaned in and kissed her.

She kissed back tiredly and opened her eyes. "Well, hey."

"Are you coming? Please tell me you've convinced Danny."

"I told him I was going," she said flatly. "That was enough."

"You don't sound especially happy about it."

"I wish I was going with just you."

Somehow, that made me even happier, and therefore more generous. "Me, too. But he'll come around. I like the kid. If we include him, make him understand that you're always going to be his friend, and I will, too, if he lets me—"

"Thank you," Melissa said, and kissed me on the mouth. But she was also crying, a little.

"Are you okay?" I murmured.

"What is this thing tonight, anyway, Paul?"

"I don't know. Something special, though. We'll find out together. I'll meet you both on Sherman Street at eight."

I got one more kiss, and a palm against my cheek. Then she was gone.

I went around the building rather than through it and headed toward Robert's. As I walked, I withdrew the elegantly folded piece of white linen stationery that Scott had handed me after leaving me at the edge of the woods on the Trampleton side of Lumberton Street. All the way into town, he'd chatted about driving. Motoring, as he called it. The seat of his car was littered with peanut shells.

"Do you like driving, Dent?"

"I've never had the pleasure," I told him.

"What *are* they teaching the children of Oklahoma these days?"

So he knew where I was from, as well as my name. But of course, he had to know Grace, and that probably meant he knew Lewis, too. It was strange, though. The longer he talked, the more certain I was that he was putting on airs. The shaking in his hands wasn't all vibration from the engine, for one thing. And there was a quietness to the way he watched the trees and houses passing, as if he were looking for someone.

"Can you tell me about these Saturday nights?" I asked.

Scott just sat a while, then shook his head. "I used to have a better idea of what they were for than I seem to now."

I waited for him to reveal more, but he didn't speak again until we'd reached Lumberton Street. Flicking his unlit cigarette into the night, he said, "You know, I came here for a vacation. A much-needed and oft-prescribed rest. But it turns out I don't like rest, Dent. It makes me nervous. What about you?"

Since my last sleep, I'd watched rifles fired over every single house in white Trampleton, had a brutal fight with Danny, and finally learned the story of Screwpine. Now I was driving in a car with perhaps the most celebrated author in the United States. Even the word "rest" caused my eyelids to droop.

"Sometimes," I said. "When I'm really tired."

For some reason, my answer delighted Scott. He tapped a shaky hand against the wheel. "Just so," he said. "You know, I think I'm going to like you. You say what you mean. Your friend Grace Lowie should pay attention." Then he pulled the car over to the curb, handed me the piece of linen stationery, and wheeled off into the night.

Even now, a week later, the paper gave off a calming odor of talcum powder. Scott's perfect cursive spooled across it like embroidery. Whereas months ago on the train, Cutter had provided me with a name but no address or directions, Scott offered an intersection. *The Corner of Mountain and Sourwood. 9 p.m. sharp, Saturday evenings. Dinner promptly at 9:30. Presentable attire, please.*

What Scott deemed presentable, I suspected, was nothing I could afford. But I spent almost half of the nineteen-dollar surplus I'd amassed since my arrival in North Carolina—the most I'd paid for clothing in any one year, let alone one afternoon—on a white dress shirt and simple, gray tie.

Back at Robert's, as the sun sank toward the foothills, I bounded upstairs and hustled into my new outfit. My pants didn't quite match the tie, and I had neither appropriate socks nor jacket. As far as I could tell, I looked like a prairie boy dressing up for Halloween. But it was the best I could do. I was already nervous as I ducked into the bathroom to scrub and shave my face, and was still rinsing the sweat out of my hair when Robert appeared in the doorway, causing me to bang my knee against the underside of the sink.

"Ow," I grunted, straightening and grabbing my knee. I dripped water all over my clothes, and tried readjusting the towel I had tucked around my shoulders.

Wherever Robert had just come from, he'd been exerting himself. Sweat and dust lay thick on his arms under his rolled-up sleeves, and his skin looked cracked, baked, and blacker than usual. His eyes were bloodshot beneath their sagging lids. In one hand he held a rag filthy with dirt, and I briefly entertained the notion that he was going to chloroform me.

"You never come up here," I said.

He just watched me in the mirror. "You think your sheets maybe wash themselves?"

"While I'm in the house, I mean."

Robert glanced at my shirt. "See, you're supposed to rinse *before* you get natty. Makes you look less wet."

I waited, the way Grace kept trying to teach me. But he was better at it.

"Robert, are you all right? I know it's none of my business, but—"

"Listen," he said, and his eyes found mine in the mirror. "Oklahoma, Paul. I want you to tell me about Oklahoma."

"What about it?" I said, instantly on guard.

"Were you with Grace when she found my sister?"

"No."

"You know the place?"

"Well, I've seen…" I started, and shut up fast. Robert was standing with the rag half-raised in one hand. The other was drumming distractedly against the doorframe.

"You were saying something, I believe," he said.

"Robert, listen." I glanced down at my tie and shirt. "Could we please do this tomorrow? We'll have an exchange."

"An exchange."

"I'll tell you about Oklahoma. You tell me about Screwpine."

If he was surprised to hear me say the word, he didn't show it. He just stood there with his red eyes boring into mine.

"I want to know it was like. Who worked there, and what you sang, who dreamed it up, and how it felt on the night when you—"

"What about your brother?" Robert said suddenly, and stopped drumming. "Was he with Grace?"

I met his eyes and held still. "Tomorrow," I said. "I promise."

"You can't avoid me, Paul." He'd taken a step back onto the landing, but now he jabbed his rag in my chest. "You can't outrun me. I'm slow to rise, maybe, always have been. Slow to latch on, sometimes. But once I know, I *know*.

And once I'm on to you, I *itch*. Like a rash, you listening? Like poison ivy, only you can't wash me off. Got it?"

"Avoid you? Outrun you? Robert, I've been trying to have just one regular conversation with you since the day I got here."

As quickly as it had flared, Robert's anger died, or banked itself, anyway. He put a hand against the tilting banister. His lips, which had been pressed flat, opened, and breath rushed through them. "Okay," he said. "Tomorrow, then."

"Right. I mean it. I'm sorry I can't right now. It's just hot as hell, and I've got maybe six miles to walk, and—"

"Closer to five miles," he said.

I stared at him. But he was looking down into the living room.

"Robert," I started, and with a grunt, he roused himself.

"It didn't, by the way."

"I'm sorry?"

"The Screwpine. It didn't burn down. Should have. But it didn't."

"I know." I edged past him. "I'll see you later, Robert."

"Indeed you will. Got to get myself washed and dressed, too."

Whirling, I saw the ghost of Robert's smile. Suddenly, I felt nine years old. "You, too?"

His smile hung there, and I knew it was true. He would also be at the dinner.

"Robert, what's this thing all about, anyway? What happens there?"

"Well, as usual," he said, bitterness seeping back into his voice, "you'd probably better ask Grace. She's the only one who really knows."

"What does that even mean?"

He seemed to think about it for a moment. "I'll tell you this much. The second you walk in there, you'll be someone else. Run along, now."

"You want me to wait for you?"

"Christ, no. We can't walk in there together. Man's got his reputation to consider. And I mean *my* reputation, in case you were confused."

"I wasn't," I said and left Robert's house to pick up Melissa and Danny.

They were waiting at the petrol station, Melissa in a long skirt and summer blouse, Danny squirming in a tie and suit coat he'd clearly never worn before.

"You ready for this?" I asked, careful to include both of them in the question, though I resented it.

"Come on," said Melissa, a little too brightly, and I noticed the red in her cheeks and realized they'd been fighting. Out of concern as much as anything else, I reached for Melissa's hand. Then I saw Danny's glare and stopped myself. Then I took her hand anyway.

Our route led north up Sourwood Road. For more than an hour and a half, mostly because Danny dawdled behind, we walked the Blue Ridge foothills, swatting mosquitoes the whole way. Dusk crawled down the mountainsides, softening the light but not the heat. Even the cicadas sounded sluggish, their screech pitched lower than usual. We hardly spoke, but if Danny was dragging his feet, he also left us alone. Melissa kept squeezing my hand, and occasionally she let it brush the hip of her skirt, though that could have been accidental. Eventually, we came upon a stand of oaks with a half-dozen bicycles arrayed around the trunks. A few were even tethered there like horses.

"Whatever tonight is, it's going to be good," I said, stopping to catch my breath.

"It's going to be different, that's for sure," said Melissa, and gave me her first full smile of the night.

"You have any idea where we are?"

"Nowhere we belong," Danny piped up suddenly. Melissa shushed him.

"I think it's just over this rise," I said.

Melissa took my hand again, and Danny's, too. "Then let's go see." We walked together up the hill and stopped. Before us lay the Belmont.

The entire spotless, white stucco building wavered in the late light, massive and unreal and incomprehensible as the Taj Mahal. I stared down the long lane of elm trees at the towering French windows, which were easily twice the size of me, all thrown open to the evening. It would have taken every able-bodied man in Blackcreek just to keep all that glass shining so that the reflection of the endless, green lawn could ripple in it like lakewater. How could any organization smaller than, say, a railroad afford to keep a place like this running, especially now when the number of paying guests had to be so limited?

"I think we found it," I murmured, then tugged Melissa and Danny into the lane, which turned out to be Mountain Road, though it hardly seemed a road to me, certainly not a public one. The elms arched over us like sculpture. I didn't dare set foot on that gently undulating grass. The second I did, I was sure I would sink.

Once we'd reached the building itself, the only action that seemed more dangerous than stepping through the centermost, double-set of French windows was loitering before them.

"We can't go in there," Danny said.

"Can we?" said Melissa.

Then a long, white curtain billowed gently outward and swept us inside. Crossing the threshold, I felt my filthy, sweating skin sloughing off me, as if by magic. Our footsteps ceased making sounds. We had gone somewhere else, all right. Become other people, imaginary things. Just like Robert had said we would.

"You've all but missed dinner," Scott said from above, his voice tumbling down like a perfectly pitched horseshoe.

Looking through a canopy of hanging bougainvillea, I located him against the banister of the grand, curving staircase, wearing the same clean but rumpled white suit in which I'd last seen him. His hair looked even messier.

"Long walk," I said, swaying to the currents of air created by fans I could neither see nor hear.

"There's some here who walk a lot longer. They don't miss dinner."

"Oh my God," Melissa whispered abruptly at my side. "Is that…?"

"Mr. Scott," I said, an absurd pride all but lifting me off to float among the hanging plants. "These are my friends. That's Danny, and this is Melissa Flynn."

"It *is* him," Melissa said.

"Is who?" Danny hissed, eyes everywhere, as if he expected to be dragged away.

"*The* Melissa Flynn?" Scott said, and Melissa's mouth opened as her fingers clutched mine. "I've heard your name, young lady. More than once. More than twice. Well, well. To be honest, I thought they'd made you up."

"They?" I said.

Scott gestured with his unlit cigarette toward a darkened ballroom across the lobby. "You'll find them in the Chestnut Garden. Her whole, eager team, primed for another night of breathless, world-shaking invention."

I'd heard the phrase "Chestnut Garden" before. But I couldn't think where.

"Mr. Scott?"

"Just Scott. Or, the Baron of the Belmont. Or Fritz."

"Fritz?"

"As in Crisler? The football coach? He's done a hell of a job with the Princeton boys. Are you a football man, Dent?"

"Scott, does Grace know I'm coming?"

The corners of his mouth twisted upward, giving me the impression— and not for the first time, though I'd seen him exactly once before—that everything he said was directed inward. And some of it was nasty. "You know," he halfway sang, "I really don't believe she does. Hurry, now."

Off we went, still expecting at every step to be blocked by a hotel guard and escorted off the premises. But we saw no one else. The ballroom floor glinted even in the dark, and my shoes set off sweet, round echoes. Out the other side, we came to a windowless corridor where soft electric lights glowed and made the tiles underfoot look liquid.

"That was really him," Melissa said to me.

"How'd you recognize him?"

"He's been in the papers around here. Doesn't he have a wife in some hospital nearby or something? She's sick, right? Crazy?"

I didn't know any more than she did, and was too charged up by the thrill in her voice to answer clearly, anyway. At the end of that hall, we pushed through another, less dramatic set of French windows, which finally admitted us to the Garden. A little riot of petals swirled around us like flung confetti in a chilly breeze.

Once again, I noticed the trees first. They were horse chestnuts, their leaves cascading over each other to within a few feet of the ground like long skirts. Bunched red flowers still floated amid the leaves like stitching. Beyond the trees, on a stretch of lawn that rolled away into the shadows, people in suit coats and dresses were clustered into small groups, their faces mostly hidden from me. Virtually all of them were holding white dinner plates or fluted champagne glasses or both, and conversing in low voices. The first person I recognized was Mr. Pierman. I'd never seen him anywhere but the shed where he showed scary movies. He was chatting with a woman in a gold-spangled evening gown who was smiling and rolling her eyes at the same time. His bald head shone in the gentle light. Just beyond him, I spotted Tom Reaveley, and then, off to the right, Riley from the General Store in a huddle of broad-shouldered mill-men I barely knew, all of them wearing starched and ironed work shirts.

"God, Danny," Melissa whispered, and I felt her hand tighten. Her other hand, which was holding his. "It's like home."

Danny was as startled as I was. "It's nothing like home," he said. But before either of us could ask what she meant, she'd strode out onto the patio. There were a few surprised glances. Then smiles broke out all around.

"Hey now, Melissa Flynn," someone called, and another someone, before a little circle of women at the back edge of the patio opened to admit her, and she slid in amongst them. One of them grabbed her elbow, and they all commenced whispering together. No one offered a "Well, hey" to Danny or me, so we stayed put.

The chestnut trees surrounded a parquet patio dotted with unoccupied wooden tables. Tall, standing torches flickered warmly between them.

"What is this?" Danny said.

I shook my head. For a while, we just stood, trying to figure it out. Not everyone was in formal wear, but they all looked scrubbed clean and wide awake.

"First time?" a voice stage-whispered at my elbow, and before I could answer I was whisked forward. "The pheasant is particularly fine this evening."

Unlike almost everyone else, this man was dressed exactly as he had been during our lone previous encounter in the shadows of the Sherman Street elms on the night he told me how to find the Screwpine mill: same checked brown knickerbockers, same bow tie. But in place of the beanie, he sported a tan trilby with a lilac in its band. He steered me to a long buffet table draped with crocheted white linen and laden with silver serving trays. Danny trailed behind us.

Even when he offered me and then Danny a plate, I remained too distracted to serve myself food. "Where are we?" I asked.

"You're in Bunk County, son," the man said, bow tie bobbing jauntily at his throat.

"Buncombe County? I've never heard it called Bunk."

He shook his head. "Buncombe's back down the hill. This is an entirely different place. You can call me Mayor, by the way. Mayor of Ashton."

"For a little longer," came my brother's unmistakable voice from somewhere in the shadows of a nearby tree.

The Mayor glanced that way and doffed his trilby. "For a little longer." Then he turned back to me and tapped my empty plate. "Tuck in now, young'un. We'll be commencing directly." He floated off across the patio, waving and smiling at anyone who cared to look.

Lewis stepped onto the decking and gestured at the last strawberry on the closest silver salver. "Either of you going to eat that?" he asked Danny and me. Without waiting for an answer, he popped it in his mouth.

"You're not surprised to see me here?" I asked.

"I figured you'd sniff this out in your own sweet time." His tone was almost affectionate. He took my plate and started ladling food onto it. When he'd loaded it, he returned it to me. The odor of pheasant wafted up to my nostrils, buttery and warm.

"Is this as good as it smells?" I speared an elegantly browned roasted potato and some cooked greens with a fork.

"Brother," said Lewis, "there is no taste or sensation in your past or mine to prepare you for how good that is." He glanced toward Danny. "I hope you're not waiting for me to serve you."

Glowering, Danny grabbed a plate and began scooping the last of the food onto it.

I ate slowly at first, then more quickly. A light breeze ruffled the skirts of the chestnut trees. Everyone seemed to be leaning together, laughing and whispering. Just as I was shoveling a final forkful into my mouth, Robert breezed past in a fancy white shirt and dark tie, spotted Lewis and me, and stopped. His face clouded over, and he seemed about to stalk over to us. At a loss for what else to do, I waved with my fork. He watched us for another long breath, then walked across the patio toward the back of the yard to join a small group of impeccably dressed coloreds I hadn't previously noticed.

Returning my attention to my brother, I was surprised to find his eyes still on Robert. "What are you doing?" I asked.

"Am I dreaming, or did your man Robert just throw down the gauntlet?"

His tone astonished me. It was absolutely flat, iced-over, the way it only ever got when something actually made him angry.

"What gauntlet?" I asked. "What the hell are you talking about Lewis?"

"Because if he wants to throw down the gauntlet with me, I'm more than ready to pick it up."

"Lewis," I started, but Danny interrupted.

"It won't work," he said.

I turned from my brother to Danny, and my annoyance overflowed. The two of them were spoiling everything. "What do you want, Danny?"

"It won't work."

Right then, I spotted Melissa. She was talking to the Mayor, gesturing with both hands, grinning. *It's already working*, I thought, and almost said it, but stopped myself. "Enjoying the food?"

"What, like it was yours to give?"

"I gave it to you."

He half-tossed his plate down on the banquet table. "It won't work," he said, and stomped off in Melissa's direction.

"Bit of a brat, that one," said Lewis, in his ordinary, taunting voice.

"Biggest pain in my ass since you," I said.

My brother smiled, closed-mouthed, and the atmosphere in that place settled over us once more. More than anything else, it reminded me of a barn dance, with the same giddy but deadly serious undercurrent to half-heard conversations, the constant, careful sizing up of anyone who happened to be near.

To my left, I spotted the young farm wife who'd sold me my first Trampleton pear, wearing a hand-sewn pink dress that cleaved to her hips and veed down from her shoulders to her breasts. She had her hair up, and I only recognized her from her mouth, which remained stitched into that familiar, determined tightness. Abruptly, I realized where I'd heard of the Chestnut Garden before. This woman had mentioned it during my first real Trampleton conversation.

Eventually, through a mouthful of the fatty lasts of the pheasant, I asked Lewis, "Should we sit down?"

For the most part, everyone seemed to be keeping to the grass or the shadows of the trees. Occasionally, I saw someone watching the patio the way people stare at a baseball diamond before a game.

Lewis shook his head. "No tables until the fun starts."

"This isn't the fun?"

He grinned with his mouth closed, and the Mayor reappeared in the center of the patio. "Citizens of Bunk County," he said, in an ordinary speaking voice, and everyone began dispersing toward different chairs around the tables. Lewis walked off to my right, nodding at everybody. The Mayor smiled serenely and waited, saying nothing more.

"Lewis," I called, "where do I go?"

"I've been trying to figure that out since the day you were born, Soft-Paul."

Hesitantly, I started toward Melissa. Lewis, to my astonishment, went to Danny, threw an arm around his shoulders, and half-dragged him away from Melissa's side toward a table near where the Mayor was standing. As if sensing that her shadow had somehow detached itself, Melissa turned in time to see my brother plant Danny in a chair. I took another step, and she looked up, a sly smile flickering across her mouth. Then she just strode straight across the patio toward where Robert was standing with the other coloreds.

I was too surprised to follow immediately, and I wasn't the only one. All around me, conversations wavered like candles in a draft, and whole tables full of startled faces swung to follow her movement.

Robert, for his part, looked positively alarmed. Beside him, Mitchell Johns took a careful step back. But not the pretty, silver-haired woman next to him. That was Mitchell's mother, Cordelia. I'd never actually spoken to her, but I knew she was a potter and sculptor, and that she had a degree from Fisk University in Tennessee. Even Robert professed to being intimidated by her.

Melissa just went straight up and extended her hand. After a slight pause, Robert took it and nodded once. Then, abruptly, the two of them were talking.

I would have gone there, too, but silence filled the Garden like water pouring into a canal lock, and I thought I'd better wait. I backed toward the buffet table, which sometime in the past minute or so had been emptied of trays, serving spoons, everything except the spotted and food-stained white tablecloths. I found myself alone, the last standing person other than the Mayor.

"Well, I'm just remembering," the Mayor said, and the whole space slowly quieted. "I've been doing that a lot lately, as I come to the end. I have enjoyed my run as Mayor, yes I have. But I'm old now. And I want to enjoy the other pleasures that this fine and rare county has to offer. Soon, friends, all too soon, we will hold our election. Next week, I believe. And even if enough of you write me onto the ballot—and I suspect there aren't enough this time, despite your kind protestations—I will not accept. We have eager new blood." He bowed toward the table closest to him, where my brother sat with his legs outstretched and his arms folded. "I'm right sure the new mayor—whoever he turns out to be—will do us proud."

Mayor of what? The man was a hobo, as far as I knew, or had been. Melissa, I saw, had taken up station just to the left of Robert. Lewis was leaning back to whisper something to Danny, then to Tom Reaveley. And Scott had materialized at the other end of the buffet table with a gold-colored drink in his hand. When he saw me looking at him, he raised it.

"Without further ado, then," the Mayor said, "and with the warmest of Bunk County welcomes to this week's newcomers—welcome home, y'all— I'll turn things over to the Power that Be. Miss Lowie, if you're ready…"

He was still settling into his seat at the centermost table when Grace emerged from the trees. She wore her hair bound up tight against her neck, a pen behind her left ear, a man's work shirt tucked into her trousers with the sleeves rolled to the elbows. In her arms, she held a dozen or more folded pamphlets of some kind and another stack of oversized paper.

"I have one late-breaking announcement for the whole county," she said as she made her way across the patio. "The rest you'll find in your *Gazette*." She waved the pamphlets once. "Out of consideration and concern for the needs of his family, I'm afraid Mr. Fuqua has abandoned his mayoral campaign."

All eyes swung toward the left side of the patio, where a Trampleton farmer whose name I *knew* was Hendricks sat with his arms crossed, his head on his chest. For a moment, there was silence. Then, from one of the colored tables, someone yelled out, "What family?"

"He said 'his family,' so shut your mouth," shouted Riley, who was seated at the same table as Hendricks, with a smug, satisfied grin on his face that I didn't understand at all. "Any of you have a problem with that?"

Grace banged her stack of *Gazette*s onto the Mayor's table. "Right," she said. "That's it. What are you waiting for?"

She might as well have fired a starter's pistol. Instantly, conversations broke out all over the Garden. At every table, faces swung toward one another, hands began waving, chairs were dragged closer to their neighbors'. Some people were laughing, while others—mostly around Riley's table—were arguing furiously. The farmer whose name definitely wasn't Fuqua just sat with his head down and ignored it all.

I went back to watching Grace. She'd dropped a *Gazette* and a short stack of what turned out to be blank foolscap onto the Mayor's table, and now she was leaning her hand on the Mayor's shoulder, answering a question from a woman across from her. Grace nodded twice, the woman laughed, and then everyone at the table pulled in their chairs as the Mayor took up the *Gazette* and began reading it aloud. Grace moved off toward the next table. Behind her, the buzz of voices and whirl of hand gestures intensified, as though the whole gathering were a propeller she'd just set spinning.

Twice more, I watched the process repeat itself. A couple of times, people popped up from their seats to intercept her. Mostly, she shooed them back. Someone at one table reading a *Gazette* whistled loudly and yelled, "Impossible!" Grace had just reached Lewis's group when the Mayor appeared once more at my elbow.

"You're going to make folks suspicious just standing there," he said. "We're not much for loiterers in Bunk County."

Steering gently but forcefully, the Mayor pulled me toward an empty seat right next to the farm wife who'd sold me my pears and across from an older couple in matching blue cotton shirts whom I did not know.

"Evening, Mayor," said the farm wife, her voice absurdly mannered, the words evenly spaced like pearls on a string. "Fine night."

"Evening, Mr. Hornshaw."

"*Mister?*" I blurted, and the Mayor yanked me down into the chair just as Grace came up beside him.

Her eyes grabbed mine. Across her forehead and the bridge of her nose, her freckles seemed to multiply even as I stared at them, like stars in the first moments of a clear night.

"About time," she said. "I was starting to wonder how long it would take you to show up here."

"You could have invited me," I said, unable to meet her gaze. The fragile confidence that had grown in me over the months of wandering, interviewing, learning, and writing was wobbling dangerously. Grace just shook her head, then glanced once around at each of us. Her smile was sudden, gentle, almost sweet. "Everyone's got to find their own way to the Garden."

She handed me a *Gazette,* which turned out to be a compendium of the week's Bunk County events, large and small. I tried asking again what Bunk County was, and the farm wife shushed me because Grace was still speaking. She placed particular emphasis on an upcoming wedding apparently involving a member of my group, the ongoing fallout from an altercation at a soap-box derby several months before, and the condition of Mr. Hornshaw's—that is, the farm wife's—1936 Nash.

By the time she left us for the next table and emphasized an entirely different part of the *Gazette* to that group, I'd given up trying to understand what was happening. But the otherworldliness of it all was unshakeable. Some of it had been generated simply by the food, which really was like a banquet out of a fairy-tale. And some of it probably sprang from that immaculate sea of grass across which we'd had to ferry ourselves just to get here. Then there was the hotel itself with its grand staircases and towering windows and hanging bougainvillea and horse chestnut trees.

But mostly, the magic was coming from Grace. Everyone else in the Garden appeared to be playing a role, being someone else. But Grace was playing herself. Her job was clearly to oversee and coordinate, rather than take part directly. In a way, she wasn't even there. By which I mean, I already suspected there would be no mention of any persona she'd adopted in any *Gazette.* Instead, Grace went from table to table, collecting tidbits of information handed to her on folded foolscap or whispered in her ear. Occasionally, she knelt by a chair or leaned over to make a suggestion.

Already, it was clear that she was the one cataloguing the various County stories in her head, knitting them into a nearly cohesive, all-inclusive imaginary history. Equal parts conductor, mentalist, and invisible woman.

In a daze, I watched her circle back to our table again. "Oh," she said, "I forgot to mention. There's been a fire at your house, Mr. Woodcock." She inclined her head sympathetically at the man in the cotton shirt, who looked taken aback. He had the dirtiest fingernails I'd ever seen. "It broke out late last night. You very nearly died."

"If he did, you'd be doing him a favor," said the pretty farm wife—Mr. Hornshaw—while the woman in the cotton shirt clapped her hands.

"And you," Grace said, whirling on me. "What's your name?"

"What?"

"Your name."

"Yes," said the cotton shirt man, and not pleasantly. He put his filthy hands on the table and half stood. "And while you're at it, maybe you can tell me what you were doing lurking in my orchard twenty minutes before the fire broke out."

"Wait," I said, holding up my own ink-spackled palms. "I'm Paul. Paul De—"

"No," Grace snapped. "Your name *here*. In Bunk County."

Okay, I thought. Everybody needed an alias and some sort of invented past. I needed one, too.

"Timmy," I said.

Grace yanked at one of her shirt-sleeves. "Timmy what?"

"Ank…" I started, and caught a barely perceptible shake of her head. "Funnybone," I finished, and she rolled her eyes. "I'm a traveling musician."

"Colored traveling musician," said Grace. "Might as well go all the way. You better think fast, Mr. Funny. You're in a pretty fix." She left for the next table. Staring after her, I saw Mr. Cutter glide up on his pegleg, lift some *Gazette*s from Grace's hands, and bow. He saw me watching and saluted.

"You know, come to think of it," the farm wife said, "I saw this man, too." Meaning me. "He was skulking around downtown." She tapped the table with her broken fingernails. "Talking to that Martha Brown outside the Red Pit."

"Martha Brown indeed." The cotton-shirt man hauled me to my feet and hustled me across the patio. All sorts of people glanced around, though few paused in the conversations they were having. My brother burst out laughing and waved.

"See this here?" said the man, waving at the overflow of branches from a chestnut at the very edge of the patio. "This is a cell. And you're locked in it." With a surprising grin, he turned on his heel and returned to his table.

And so, for over an hour, I stood there. At first, I watched Melissa. She was still deep in conversation with Robert. I tried to imagine what about, then decided that was a dangerous, anxiety-producing pastime. More than once, she smiled at me from across the patio, but she never got up to visit. Robert looked up more than once, too. Every time he did, he stared first at me, then at Lewis amidst his constantly swelling entourage at the center tables, his expression unreadable but far from blank.

Darkness deepened over the Garden. The torches turned everyone's faces whitish-red. Mostly, they just talked. Sometimes, someone would snatch up a pencil and scratch notes onto one of the pieces of foolscap that Grace had left on each table. Sometimes, someone else would grab away the paper and cross something out. Occasionally, someone would get up and fill a glass of water from the crystal decanter on the banquet table and drink it standing there before returning to his or her seat. And every now and then, I'd catch a solitary participant or even a whole group neither talking nor writing, simply sitting and looking at each other or into the trees, their faces flitting from anxious to blank to peaceful like sleepers between dreams.

"Amazing, isn't it?" Grace said at my elbow.

I'd lost track of her as she wove between groups and around the Garden, and then I'd forgotten I was looking for her. Sweat shone on her perpetually pale cheeks, and her hair had slipped free of its bun to lie like a half-unwound ball of yarn against her neck. Her eyes leapt continually from table to table.

"Bunk County," I said. "We're standing in it. Right? It's the Garden. You made it up."

"Look over there." She gestured toward the centermost table. "See the guy in the knickerbockers?"

"The Mayor of Ashton? Imaginary capital of this imaginary county?"

"Very good." Grace grinned at me. "I hear Scott himself was the one who finally invited you. I wish I could have seen the expression on your face. You do know who he is, yes? I told him about you."

That was a little disturbing. "What did you tell him?"

"That you were my new Trampleton spy. That I met you on a train. That you're Lewis's brother. That you just might be capable of producing something someday, if you ever decided to work at it."

"Work at it? I've been working hard for you every single day since you sent me here, Grace. I've never worked so hard in my—"

"Not the Project, Paul. Jesus, not the Project."

Even when she was only halfway paying attention, Grace always seemed to be bearing down on you like on an oncoming train. Except when she seemed to be hurtling away.

"So, he's your partner in this?" I asked. "Scott?"

She waved a dismissive hand. "He provides the money, and I'm grateful for that. Even though he's told me he only pays so he can be here when it all collapses. He's pretty sure that's going to happen soon."

"That seems unkind. Or strange. Or something."

"And there you have him. The Great Scott."

We stood silent. Except for the branches scratching at my elbows, it really did feel a little like jail: me doing a lot of looking, not a soul looking back.

"So you're the organizer, Grace. Right? You invite everyone. They pretend they're other people, with new names and made-up lives. And you set pretend fires to their pretend houses. It's a game."

That earned me a glare, which broke abruptly into the most naked smile I would ever see on Grace's face. "That's what Scott calls it. He's probably right."

"So after the dinner Scott provides, they become…"

"Whomever they want to be. Or whomever I tell them to be, when our collective story requires it. But they invent their own homes. Their deaths. Their new lives. Some of them have been here going on three generations."

"Grace, how long have you been doing this?"

She ignored me. "Every week, they turn in their proposed new developments. Just like you turn in your little Trampleton reports. And I go through them exactly the same way. Except with the Bunk County material, I'm mostly checking for continuity. Filling in gaps. Resolving contradictions. Inventing tornadoes. Whatever needs doing to sustain the momentum. Or cause a little trouble."

"And then you write all of it into the *Gazette*?"

"There. And elsewhere." Grace's smile was private, and too remote to be friendly.

"Elsewhere?" Understanding broke over me. "Like in the pages you send to Mother? For the *travel guides?*"

Grace went on smiling.

"Does Mother know? Does she come here?"

Grace looked at me as though I'd just drooled all over my chin. "Take a guess," she said, then changed the subject. "See the brunette? With the white gloves? She's the best figure skater ever to come out of the Carolinas. She would have been an Olympian if only her parents could have afforded the training."

"But Grace. Why—"

"That guy to her left? The one with the warts? Heads the County fire department. He lost two sons in the war, and claims, as a nine-year-old boy, to have trailed a cougar one hundred and thirty miles deep into the Tennessee hills over a six-day period just to shoot it. And that guy?"

This time, I was surprised to find her pointing at Rowlands, the day-laborer from the mill who'd had to bury his dog on the day I met him. He was seated next to the bright-eyed brunette, and both of them were laughing.

"Rowlands?" I asked.

"Is that his real name? Well, guess what? In Bunk County, he's his own brother."

Grace left, and not long after, Scott came up, still holding the same gold-colored drink, unless he'd refilled his glass. If the rumors about why he wasn't writing and what had happened to him in Hollywood were true, he couldn't have been nursing just one all night.

"Jail already, Dent?"

Somehow, here I was, standing in the Chestnut Garden of quite possibly the most exclusive hotel in North Carolina, having feasted on almost certainly the most exquisite dinner eaten by anyone within a hundred miles, talking to perhaps the most famous writer in the country.

Like Grace—but without the chatter—Scott stood and watched. But his interest seemed more incidental, as if he was focused on the relentless, myste-rious activity around an ant-hill. His cheeks looked scrubbed but sallow, his eyes clear but heavy-lidded. The hand that held his un-smoked cigarette didn't shake when he raised it, but I kept expecting it to.

"Say, Mr. Scott. Scott. Would you like to bail me out?"

He gave a close-lipped, distant smile. "I'm not here."

"You don't participate?"

"I make it possible." He lifted the cigarette to his mouth and dropped it to his side again.

"So you just do this as a favor to Grace?"

Scott coughed once, efficiently. "If I wanted to do Grace a favor, I'd have every one of you hauled back to Sourwood Road and dispersed, and then I'd have the doors to this hotel barred."

"How would that help her?"

"Because that way, she'd have no choice but to settle down and finish—really finish—the book she seems to think she's got." The chestnut leaves fanned around him like a peacock's tail.

"Mr. Scott, if that's how you feel, why do you help her do all this?"

"Because, my young and hopeful friend, the summer's always ending. And this…" His voice was mellifluous, halfway singing, as though he were commanding the moonlight. "This is the only party in town."

I spotted Grace moving toward the back of the patio in the company of a stunning colored woman with skin the deep blue-black of a locomotive, high, pronounced cheekbones, and cascading curly hair that flowed in a tightly contoured S down the middle of her back. The woman was wearing a white, laced dress that might have suited a Civil War plantation bride; she would have been the tallest person there even without her high-heeled boots. But the most amazing thing about her was the way so many of the white men she passed tipped their hats to her, or stopped her to converse briefly, or snuck glances as she swept by. More than a few women were looking at her, too. I saw Riley staring, but the expression on his face was different. When she passed his table, where he sat with a group of bearded, bulky men—and Danny, though I had no idea when that had happened—he crossed his arms and glared.

No matter what the reaction to this woman, Grace seemed to enjoy it. She kept making notes on her pad. Twice, she laughed outright. Once, she and the tall woman whispered together. Finally, they reached Robert's table, where Robert himself greeted them with some sort of diatribe. He stopped only long enough to introduce the tall woman to Melissa, who just stared her up and down, full-fledged Flynn smile beaming. Mitchell and Cordelia Johns chimed in with occasional supporting gestures. Cordelia touched Robert's shoulder once, tilted her head back on her long neck, and flashed her sparkling teeth. Robert nodded, glanced at her, then swept his gaze over the patio as though searching for someone. I started to wave, but he didn't see me.

Grace, meanwhile, was alternately shaking her head, making notes, and listening. Very occasionally, her writing hand flew off the pad to gesture in the air and then settle again like a spark popping off a fire.

Scott, I noted, was also watching Grace.

"She really seems to love this," I said.

"What's not to love? She's got her idyllic setting." He waved a hand at the Garden. "Food neither she nor anyone here could afford to look at, let alone eat. And the company, we mustn't forget that. All these shopkeepers, farmers, mill workers, housewives, wives-without-houses, at least three hoboes, and some children. All of whom arrive promptly every Saturday night to let Grace con them into thinking they're contributing actual ideas—most of which she has to discard the moment the session ends—to a fairy tale she's concocting entirely for her own private amusement." He seemed to consider what he'd just said, then nodded to himself. "You know, Dent, I take it all back."

There had been no heat whatsoever in his monologue. But the whole little speech unsettled me. "Take what back?"

"Maybe she's a real writer after all." Scott shrugged. "Don't stay in there all night, now. A writer's got to get out and experience things, don't you find? At least sometimes?" He took a tiny sip of his drink and walked away.

I couldn't stand watching Melissa smile like that from this far away anymore, especially not with Robert—I'd wanted to be the one to introduce them, someday—and started in their direction. But Lewis's hand clamped down on my shoulder and dragged me back.

"Is this a jailbreak?"

"Ha ha."

"Was I laughing, young buck? Young negro buck?" His smirk was the one I'd always dreamed of grinding off his face. "It's Mr. Funny, right? Funny Tim?"

"Timmy Funnybone."

"You're the talk of the town. Fiery entrance you've made."

"Can you get me out of here, Lewis?"

"Who's Lewis?"

At Riley's table, Danny had stood and was staring openly at Melissa. Riley was still sitting, but he kept looking that way, too.

"Know anyone who needs an arsonist?" I murmured.

Lewis' smirk cracked open into a grin. "Now you're getting it. I like that, Funnybones. I like it a lot. I'll ask around."

"How long has this been here, Lewis? How long have you and Grace been doing this?" I tried, and failed, to keep the jealousy out of my voice.

"Together? Since the Saturday after we arrived. But Grace and Scott started it a good month before that. I think she said she had fifteen people at the first meeting. The Mayor over there, and that one-legged guy, Cutter, and a couple of truckers and their wives from up in Cherryville, and a few share-croppers from up in the hills. And Riley, because she figured he'd make trouble fast."

It was all too much. I just watched some more. Lewis seemed content to stand with me.

"So you slick your hair, now?" I asked.

Actually, I was grudgingly impressed with my brother's appearance. His powder-blue dress shirt flowed smoothly over his ever-broadening shoulders. And his hair formed a neat, curling wave over his forehead instead of splaying out in all directions like kicked hay.

"It's called combing," Lewis said. "Try it sometime. Your little sword-swallower might like it."

"Sword-juggler. Knives, actually."

The conversations around us had cooled some, though there were still flares of argument or laughter from all corners. Somehow, the way Lewis watched them was completely different from Scott or Grace: as if they were trains he was about to jump. Or derail. Or rob. I tried following his gaze, and was surprised to see that he'd locked his eyes on Robert.

"You know him?" I asked.

"Oh, I know all about him," Lewis said quietly.

"You do?"

His shrug seemed more studied than usual, but I had no idea why. "Everyone knows him. Speaking of arsonists."

"You know he's Ruth's brother, right?"

His voice went utterly flat, and under the powder-blue shirt, his muscles tensed. "Since when do you know anything—anything whatsoever—about Ruth?"

"When do you think? I'm pretty sure I found out she killed herself before you did. I was with Grace when Mrs. Duarte—"

Lewis grabbed my shirt and the skin underneath it so hard, I thought he was going to rip out my collarbone. "Shut up," he said, and then made a noise I had never before heard from him. Half-gargle, and half-whimper?

"Lewis, what are you—"

"Don't talk about her, Paul. Not to me. And you better warn your friend not to talk about her, either."

"About his own sister?"

"His own sister. Right. Ask him how…you know what? Never mind. I think I'll ask him myself. I think I'll do that right now."

Shoving me hard into the branches of the chestnut, Lewis whirled and took several steps in the direction of Robert's table before Grace stepped into his path.

"Mr. Forsberg," she said, and Lewis's body twitched as though she'd dumped a bucket of freezing water on him.

"Stay out of this, Grace," he said. But even as I watched, his shoulders started to go down. And his voice was already modulating. Becoming his own again.

"Your constituents are watching," she said.

It was true. Riley's whole table was staring in our direction. Danny looked like he might leap up and start cheering.

But not Robert, I noticed, and not Melissa. They were too busy getting acquainted with each other. Lewis saw that, too. When he turned back to me, his expression was of the dump-Paul's-cake-in-the-dirt variety. "Well, I'd send you over to find out what on Earth those two have to discuss," he said. "But you can't go anywhere, can you? Unless you've already managed to tunnel under that cell door." He wiped some uncharacteristic sweat off his forehead.

"Okay now, Mr. Forsberg?" said Grace.

"Just fine, thanks," said Lewis, not even looking at her. Then he said "Thanks" again.

Tom Reaveley strode up, nodded briefly at me, and whispered something to Lewis.

"No kidding," my brother said, and Tom Reaveley left. Glancing around, I saw that Grace was gone, too.

"So who are you, Lewis?" I asked cautiously. "In Bunk County, I mean?"

He returned to my side. It was as though the last couple minutes hadn't even happened. "Well, let's see, Bonesy. I'm a war-hero. I'm much older, by the way. Going on fifty. I've been Sheriff. I also sculpted the memorial to the town's soldier boys killed in the Great War. It was just something I felt compelled to do."

"I didn't know you had sculpting in you."

"Oh, me either. But the inspiration…all that noble, wasted youth…" He grinned. "And now, if that small but swelling coalition by the buffet table has their way, when old Bertram Cavendish III steps down, I guess I'm going to be Mayor."

I snorted. "Lewis, why can't you pretend to be a hobo, for a change? Or a drunk? Someone who fails at things and has to struggle. Just for fun."

It was one of the few times that I could remember us smiling at the same moment. Cocking his head, he put a finger to his lips, as though genuinely considering what I'd said. Then he shook his head. "What would be fun about that? And who would believe it?"

A sudden, creeping suspicion flashed through my mind. "The other candidate for Mayor."

"Fuqua? What about him?"

"You drove him out of the election. Right?"

Lewis smiled even more broadly. "Let's put it this way, Funny Tim. I'm not sure Mr. Fuqua even knew he *had* a family until I told him what they'd done. You'll have to excuse me, now. I have favors to court—and dispense— at the Greater Ashton Business Association meeting." And off he went, straight to Riley and Danny's table.

I didn't even see Reverend Henry until he appeared at my side and mimed unlocking and swinging open my cell door. He was tricked out in cotton slacks and a blue work shirt and looked pretty credibly like a Trampleton millhand.

"Is Reverend Beagle here, too?" I asked.

Reverend Henry snorted. "That folksy, preening clown? He'd think of some reason it was blasphemous and have it shut down."

Yet again, I was surprised. I'd had Reverend Henry pegged as the holier roller.

"So in Bunk County, you're the jailer? Or are you an outlaw? Are we making a run for it?"

That made Reverend Henry smile. He patted my shoulder. "No, young Mr. Dent. I'm just a humble representative of the Widowers' League." He gestured toward a table near the back of the patio. I didn't know anyone else there, but Reverend Henry was apparently the only League member who still had hair. "We devote ourselves to providing aid and succor for the county's poorest and neediest. We'll see to it you get an attorney to help combat these trumped-up arson charges. And they are trumped up, aren't they, Timmy?"

"Oh, you bet," I said, shooting a glance toward Robert and Melissa's table. "Thank you, Reverend. *Are* you still a reverend?"

"Just a widower."

"Why a widower?"

Sighing, he slipped a handkerchief from his pocket and mopped his forehead. "Well, I wanted to be married again, Paul. But I didn't think anyone would stand for it."

Robert looked up, his gaze floating over Melissa and his friends, across the lawn and the tables toward me. Then he glanced at Lewis. There was no hostility in *his* face. Just bewilderment, or fascination. Melissa was chattering away next to him, and with one more thank you to Reverend Henry, I started in that direction. I *belonged* there anyway, after all. Where else in Bunk County could Timmy Funnybone possibly go?

I was skirting the edge of the patio, keeping to the trees, when Lewis reappeared, blocked my path. "Take them a message, would you?"

"Them?"

He waved a casual hand toward Robert's table without turning to look. "From the Greater Ashton Business Association. And from the presumptive new mayor."

"Meaning you."

His message involved possibilities for economic cooperation. De facto, if not overtly acknowledged, mutual growth. "In a Forsberg administration," my brother said, "even the coloreds prosper."

"Even them, huh?"

"You're right. Let me put that better." He stood with his head tilted back awhile. "A vote for Forsberg is a vote for Bunk County entire. Yes, that's catchy. Yes, I like that. Tell them, would you, Timmy-fun? Keep out of trouble, now." Off he went.

I'd reached the edge of the patio when I almost tripped over Grace, sitting alone in a corner table tucked under the overhanging branches of a chestnut tree. Spread before her was what I first took to be a massive pile of *Gazettes*. Then I saw the scratched-out sections all over the topmost page, the little notes slanting down the margins and scrawled everywhere.

"Hey," I said. "That's your book, isn't it? The one you were working on during the train ride."

Grace didn't look up, and gave no sign that she'd heard.

"You're carrying it around with you now? There've got to be quieter places to work."

"You're telling me," she said, still not looking up, still scribbling. "I can't help it. It just seems to want to come wherever I go, now."

"Is it almost finished?"

With uncharacteristic savagery, she scored through whatever she'd just written, and finally lifted her head. "It will never be finished, Paul. Not fucking ever."

Standing, she brushed twigs and leaves from her skirt. Then she bent over and scribbled some more before straightening again.

"So?" she said, and flashed a surprising smile. "What do you think they'll make of all this in Raleigh?"

"Grace. When you send these pages to Mother, you tell her it's a joke, right? I mean, she knows which parts are real?"

Her smile widened. "There are just so many things that would spoil."

"Why?"

She was watching the tables, tilting her ear toward first one conversation, then another. "I guess it seemed like fun at the time. It still does. I don't know, Paul. You can't waste too much time questioning inspiration."

I remembered something else she'd told me, that first morning at the Raleigh train station, about how Project work wasn't writing; she'd called it *humiliation*. "So what you're doing—putting a fake county in the travel guide—it's like a revenge thing?"

"You mean, because they'll only pay me to write motor tour guides, and not my own book which I can't seem to finish? Kind of. Maybe."

"You're taking revenge against the people who gave you a job that lets you keep writing, while lots of people don't have any job at all?"

"You're right. Can't be that; it wouldn't make sense." She started out from under the tree, then turned around. "How about because people have lost their sense of humor?"

"It disappeared along with the food, I guess." Even as I said that, I thought it sounded more like Grace than me. It might even have been something she'd said at some point.

"Okay. How about this one? Because the eleven or twelve people who ever open our guidebook—assuming it actually gets published someday—and then read it so thoroughly that they get to the two paragraphs, maximum, about Bunk County that I'll have managed to slip in there will thoroughly enjoy what they read?"

"Enjoy it. Sure. But then they'll come looking—"

"Which will give them something to seek, and a deliciously frustrating afternoon or two. And so a few more people will be entertained by our little side-project. But nope, that's wrong, too. And not the real reason I'm doing it. How's this for the real reason: every single resident of Bunk County wishes they really lived here. Every single one."

"Including you, Grace?"

Her eyes met mine. She pursed her lips, but stood still. "It's just another place to me. Tell Robert to go visit his damn nephew."

"I can't tell him anything anymore. He hardly talks to me."

"Why, what'd you do?"

The question was infuriating. "How do I know? Ever since he found out about his sister—"

"She was his last family, Paul. Except for the Patrol. I think he drove her out of his house for running wild, and now he feels horribly guilty as well as heartbroken. He's always been so stupid-proud. And lonely. Screwpine really messed him up. You know about that, right? Please tell me you know about that."

"Everyone knows about that."

"Get him to tell you more. He'll tell you. He likes you."

"I just told you he hardly ever talks to me."

"And I'm telling you he likes you."

The realization that it might be true flooded me with a new and uncomfortable sort of pride.

"Understand, Paul. Robert's been pretty much on his own. Ever since Screwpine, white people have feared or hated him for getting the last word. And the coloreds either fear or love him. Mostly they fear him, and love what he did. But he was alone even before Screwpine. God, has he told you about his brother?"

I shook my head.

"Completely crazy. Killed two people in a drunken bar-fight down in Savannah six or seven years ago. I think he's on some chain gang now. Wherever he is, he's never coming back, and I seriously doubt Robert would let him cross the doorstep if he did."

Grace put a hand on my shoulder and left it there. For that one moment, I think I had her entire attention.

Excusing myself, I made my way toward the lawn, and was maybe ten steps from Robert's group when I spotted Danny hustling between tables, moving fast to beat me there. I sped up, feeling five years old and also like it really might matter who arrived first. But there were chairs and bodies in my way, and Danny wriggled like an eel between some gossiping women and got to Melissa's side ahead of me.

She'd been too engrossed in whatever they were all talking about to notice us converging, and looked startled to find Danny at her elbow. Amazingly, he didn't stay or even speak. He just dropped a folded piece of paper in front of her, touched her shoulder, flashed a terrifying grin at me, and scurried off again. I reached her just as she unfolded the paper.

Then she crumpled it and closed her eyes.

"What is it?" I said, moving for her hand, not the paper, but she misunderstood and snatched away her closed fist. "Jesus, Melissa, what—"

"Goddamnit," she said. There were tears of frustration in her eyes.

"Let me guess. Bunk County Danny wants to marry Bunk County you. Melissa, please. You have to tell him no. Maybe this place is good practice. A good place to start. Tell him—"

"He's not proposing, Paul. He's reminding me to pick up penny candy on the way home. For our children."

Momentarily stupefied, I just stared at her. It took a while to remember that this was all play. That none of it was real. "It's okay. It's not true, I don't think. Until Grace puts it in the *Gazette*, I don't think it's actually happened."

But Melissa wasn't paying attention. "He's going to make me run," she said.

"Run?" The word burst from my mouth. Robert and the Johnses and the rest of the table had studiously ignored me, but now they glanced around. I leaned over and made myself whisper, "Melissa, why don't you just tell him? I know it's hard. But you'll have to, sooner or later."

Slowly, her teary eyes lifted to mine. "I meant I'd have to run here. Not in actual life."

After that, she barely acknowledged me for a while. I stayed next to her anyway, and I watched the Garden, and I listened.

There, as elsewhere, the coloreds' world was almost entirely separate. No one from the rest of Bunk County came over to check on them. No one from the colored tables got up to go anywhere. Aside from the Johnses, the only other person in this group that I recognized was a worker from the mill named Baldwin who often lingered on the front porch of the boarding house while Robert swept in the late afternoons. Robert's sole accommodation for the purposes of Grace's game was to drop the "tuh" from the pronunciation of his first name and change his last name to Gill. But I quickly learned that here, too, he ran the preeminent boarding house in the region, served legendary food, and seemed friendly with every man, woman, and child at every table off the patio.

The one notable exception to the coloreds' isolation was Martha Brown, the towering woman in the boots, who apparently ran the most successful business establishment in the entire county, with a clientele that drew from every constituency. She took long, regular strolls around the Garden and across the patio, stopping to exchange seemingly polite words with some millhand or farmer who always wound up blushing, and returning to the lawn only occasionally, but always to the raucous laughter and respectful, silent clapping of almost any colored she acknowledged.

"I have a message," I finally said, interrupting several conversations at the same time. It took a few seconds, but all of them slowly turned their heads to me. "It's from the Greater Ashton Business Association. Lewis—Mr. Forsberg—he said to tell you that in a Forsberg administration—"

Robert cut me off. "Who does he think he is? In fact, who do *you* think you are?"

"Hey," I said, "don't shoot the messenger. I just—"

Robert pointed a long finger at me, but he was angry at Lewis. At least, I thought so. "What does your brother think he's doing?"

"Taking over," I said. "The way he always does."

"That right? Is that how it was in Oklahoma?"

Now I was baffled. "Mr. Forsberg's from Oklahoma?"

To his side, Cordelia Johns laughed. She patted Robert's arm, but he didn't release my gaze, and his shoulders slumped some.

"That man has a comeuppance coming," Robert said. "You messenger him that."

Cordelia was still laughing as she tugged him back around. Swinging away from me, they resumed where they'd left off.

For a good while, I just stood there. Eventually, Melissa gestured me down beside her, and I knelt since there were no more chairs. I thought I might ask if Robert's Bunk County house had a spare cot for me. I could wash dishes, cut wood, maybe perform a concert or two, since I suspected Timmy Funnybone wasn't carrying a money-belt stuffed with cash when he fell out of the sky into Mr. Woodcock's orchard. Then Mitchell Johns leaned Robert's way and said, "We need to check on that Orangeburg shipment. They say it's still missing." And only then did I understand what everyone in this part of the Garden was talking about.

"Oh my God," I said. "You're recreating it."

For the first time since pointing his finger at me, Robert turned his full attention my way. "You say something? Whoever you are?"

"Orangeburg. Roseville. Screwpine. You're rebuilding them."

Robert shrugged. "We're *imagining* rebuilding them, yes. Most of them never got all the way built in the first place."

After that, I listened, astonished and admiring and maybe just a little nervous. There, in the shadows of the chestnut trees, on the lawn off the edge of the patio in the Belmont Hotel garden, Robert and his friends were resurrecting the nascent Negro nation right under everyone's noses—yet again.

Somehow, Melissa had already insinuated herself among them, become a functioning and essential community member. She was now a central dispatcher/bookkeeper, though whether for a rail line or a construction concern or the county hub, I couldn't tell.

"Melissa," I finally said.

"Sonja," she corrected. "A quadroon from Louisiana. My grandmother escaped off a plantation and raised me in the swamps."

Her irritation over Danny's note—not to mention my simultaneous arrival and jealous badgering—seemed largely to have left her. She even gave me a smile and touched my hand under the table with her fingertips. Then she leaned over, and her voice tickled my ear.

"I knew you'd take me somewhere different, Paul. Somewhere new. I knew it the very first time you sat down in my chair."

That got me so excited that I stood up, leaned right into the startled lot of them, and blurted, "I've got an idea."

They all looked at me and stopped talking.

"This here's a private conversation, Mr. Bone," said Robert, in that old, iced-over tone I'd somehow convinced myself I'd chipped my way through.

"I know," I said. "I'm sorry. But it's a good idea. You're going to like it."

"Idea for what?" said Cordelia, her voice neutral, but unlike Robert, she and her son actually looked interested. When I nodded at them, Mitchell even reciprocated.

"A bit of apple-cart tipping."

"Apple cart," repeated Robert.

"Maybe a little balance redressing."

"Who's he undressing?" said Robert's friend Baldwin.

"Stopping my brother," I said.

That shut them up. Even Robert.

2 – June, 1938, Washington DC

It had been a while since any of the senators had interrupted me. I'd been asked to tell this story from the beginning, and it was affecting me in ways I'd never expected. Just by saying the names out loud, I'd catapulted myself back there. I could smell the torches and the green grass and the chestnut blossoms, and I could see everyone's faces, and I could hear their voices. For two years, I'd dreaded this experience every time I closed my eyes, and also longed for it.

So I wasn't paying the slightest attention when Senator Cain pushed back from the table on the dais and stood.

"Norman," Senator Froad said, rocking me out of my reverie and back to my present circumstances. "You have a more pressing engagement? I certainly have some. If you and your friend Representative Dies would just let go of this little crusade and—"

"Froad," said Senator Cain, in a tone entirely different than the skeptical, badgering one he'd employed the entire morning, "clear the room."

"What?"

"The reporters. Get them out. Now."

From what I'd seen, the reporters had spent most of my testimony sleeping, or trying to. But that woke them up.

"Hey, just a minute," one of them said.

Senator Froad just studied his notes. When he looked up, his amphibious eyes were deadly cold.

"Gentlemen," he said to the reporters. "If you'll excuse us."

"This is an open hearing," another one protested, his voice rising.

"Yeah, you can't just—"

"Whichever of you does *not* want a full briefing outside my office at the end of this day's testimony should speak next," said Senator Froad.

None of the reporters liked it. But all of them left. The moment they were gone, Senator Froad turned to Senator Cain, who was still standing at his place, staring down at me.

"Now, Norman," Froad said. "What is it?"

Senator Cain cleared his throat, then shook his head. "You can't tell me you don't see it. You can't defend this. My God, Martin was right."

"What?" This came from my brother, and Senator Froad glanced over his shoulder.

"The junior senator speaks?"

But for once, my brother looked completely unsure what to say. The sight shook me more than anything else that had happened in the room to that point.

Lewis started to lift a swollen hand, then put it back on the tabletop. "I'm just not sure what has gotten the good senator from Missouri so excited."

Senator Cain was shaking his head again, leaning over his hands across the table. "How can you not see? How can any of you? Martin was right. It's so much worse than even Martin dreamed. They're not just here."

"Who?" said Senator Froad, but he, too, was agitated now. He pulled his cigar stump from a pocket of his jacket and began jabbing with it as though trying to poke a hole in the air.

"Who do you think? We're not just talking about subversion anymore. You do understand, don't you? This isn't a handful of radical crackpots seizing control of government works for their own political ends. You do understand, don't you?"

I couldn't do anything but gape. The man was insane. Any moment, I expected Senator Froad to let loose with one of his icy epithets and silence him. Instead, Froad stuck the cigar in his mouth, leaned back in his chair, folded his arms, and blew out a breath through his nose. When he spoke, he sounded sad. And just a little frightened.

"Supposed you tell us what it is, then, Norman?"

"Froad," said Senator Cain, collapsing into his seat to stare at his colleague. "Jesus. It's the Goddamn revolution."

"That's *ridiculous*!" Lewis barked, quickly standing as though he were about to challenge Senator Cain to a brawl. Then he remembered where and who he was pretending to be—who he actually was, I guess—and sat down. "It's absurd. You don't know what you're talking about. Froad, can we wrap this up and go on to the more serious business I'm sure each of us needs to conduct before the day is over?"

But this time, Senator Froad didn't even bother looking at him. "Explain precisely what you mean, Norman."

"What I mean? They're holding elections, Froad. *Elections*. Farmers. Mill hands. Local business owners. Layabouts. All of them being guided by these so-called writers. They're holding elections in imaginary counties, and then they're slipping these counties into our guide books. How many other imaginary counties are there in the guide book manuscripts, Froad? In how many more states? How many are already on their way to becoming legitimate places? How far has this movement already spread? Sweet God, you heard it yourself. Negro infrastructure. A whole separate commerce. Railway lines all over the South. Their own mills. Their own economy. Did the Negro railway run through my state? Through yours? Is it still happening right under your fat, warty nose, and you don't even see it? They're taking it all, Froad. The people. The roads. The railways. What is it Grace Lowie said about Bunk County? *'Every single resident of Bunk County wishes they really lived there. Every single one.'* This is a Writers' Project, all right. And what they've written is the Manifesto. "

I still couldn't get my mouth to work. Neither Senator Froad nor Senator Cain were paying the slightest attention to me anymore, anyway. But Lewis caught my gaze. In his eyes was something brand new. It looked a whole hell of a lot like panic.

"Froad, we've got to get Martin Dies in here right now. We should get the whole HUAC in here. We need to do this together. We need to do it today. We should call those reporters right back in, and we should—"

"You're wrong," I said, and Senator Cain rocked back in his chair as though I'd shot him.

"Paul," said Lewis, but I didn't care. I stood up.

"You've got it wrong."

"Wrong?" Senator Cain had recovered himself now, and he banged the table with his fist. "Froad, get this duped, deluded impostor out of our sight. We've got to start right now. Lord only knows how far—"

"Wrong, you say?" said Senator Froad. I was almost happy to hear his savage undertone.

"Yes. Completely. Listen. Please. What happened in Bunk County...it went so badly, and it happened so fast. It hurt so many people. But it wasn't this. It wasn't ever this."

"Froad. Enough. We need to act. Right now. We need to—"

"Adjourn," Froad snapped, and banged his gavel. "We need to adjourn for forty-five minutes to let the excitement you've stirred up boil off, just a little. Forty-five minutes, Senator Cain. Then we're going to come right back in here. And you're going to sit down in your chair and stay seated and shut up. And Senator Asbury and I are going to sit down in ours and do the same. And Mr. Dent down there is going to tell us, at long last, just what did happen in Bunk County."

Banging the gavel again, Froad shoved back from the table and, without waiting for either of his colleagues, stalked from the chamber.

*****

I was staring at my own haggard reflection in the gilded mirror over the bathroom sink when Lewis slipped through the door. I didn't turn around, but I pushed out a breath and met his reflected gaze.

"Did you try the towels?" he asked, and for the first time all day, his accent was his own. Our own. He brushed absently at lint I couldn't see on the sleeve of his suit coat.

My sudden lunge pinned him against the tiled wall. I pressed down hard with my forearms, waiting for the kick to the groin, the lightning punch that would drop me to my knees.

"What are you doing, Lewis? Why are you doing this? Haven't you done enough? Haven't we? Isn't it ever going to be—"

"You're faster than you used to be," Lewis said, and broke into his grin. "Want to see my office?"

Slipping deftly from under my arms, he pushed out into the empty, echoing hallway. I stumbled after him. He was already ten feet away, whistling as he strolled between portraits of men I probably should have been able to identify. Congressmen. Like my brother.

No matter how lightly I stepped, my footsteps made smacking sounds on the marble floor. Only a handful of people—pages, mostly, with piles of government papers clutched to their chests—passed as we moved down the corridor. Most of them nodded deferentially toward Lewis, or murmured, "Afternoon, Senator." Sunshine poured through the towering, rectangular windows. I'd half-forgotten the hour, the city, the late summer daylight.

Turning down a much smaller corridor, Lewis stopped before a plain, wood-paneled door. He gestured at the nameplate nailed there. It read, *Hon. Sen. L. Bertram Asbury. South Carolina. Elected 1938.*

"Shall we see if he's in?" Lewis said. Grinning wider still, he twisted the knob and passed through.

"Darlene, honey, you know what I need," my brother said in perfect, gliding South Carolinese to his receptionist. She stood immediately and bustled off down the corridor.

The office was smaller than I expected, and reminded me of Mother's Writers' Project bureau in Raleigh. There were two equal-sized rooms, one a waiting chamber with the receptionist's desk and large gray filing cabinets and a hat-stand, the other Lewis's inner sanctum. Two decorative landscape paintings of what I assumed were South Carolina rolling hills hung on the wall opposite his desk, which was buried in jacket folders overflowing with papers. An upholstered armchair was tucked beneath a tall window so that light could stream through the gauzy curtains and over the shoulder of anyone who was sitting there.

Lewis fumbled through his top desk drawer and came up with a cone of butcher's paper filled with tiny chocolate-chip cookies. He extracted one, popped it into his mouth, then waved the cone at me.

"Want one?" His accent was ours again. "There's a little Greek place around the corner that makes 'em fresh every six hours, eighteen hours a day. They say the secret's in the poppy seeds."

"Don't you ever get confused?"

"About what?" He ate two more cookies. Then he dropped into his everyday cherry-wood work chair and propped his feet on the smallest stack of papers.

There was nowhere else to sit except the armchair. I hesitated a moment before sitting down. The chair smelled of sunlight, new leather, and cookies. I could have punched the armrests, or burst out crying.

"Lewis, what are you doing?"

"Learning," he said. He was no longer smiling.

"Lewis, they're not playing. I know you think you are, but this is Grace's life. And mine. And yours, because if you really think I'm going to sit quietly while—"

"It wasn't her life's work," he interrupted. "You knew her well enough to know that. Grace certainly wouldn't call it that."

"She's going to wind up in jail. Is that really what you want?"

"I didn't want any of this, Paul. But as soon as I heard they were going to start full-scale investigations into every conceivable gaffe and misdeed perpetrated by the Theater and Writers' Projects, well, I thought maybe I'd better get myself on that bus. Just so I could keep a hand on the wheel."

"It doesn't look like you're driving, to me."

"Not yet, Paul. Not yet. And you haven't thanked me, by the way."

I managed to keep from hurling myself across the desk. Barely. "For what, exactly?"

"Saving your life," he said.

"After wrecking it. After being so hell-bent on making your own mark, playing out your endless power games, that you managed to trample everyone else. Even the ones you supposedly loved."

Lewis ate another cookie. After a while, he nodded. "I suppose you could see it that way. So that also means you aren't going to thank me?"

There was nothing to say.

"You don't look so soft anymore, Soft-Paul. Dockwork's been good to you."

"You sound almost disappointed."

"Maybe I am. I can't help thinking dockwork isn't quite what you were made for."

"Hold on, Lewis. Are you being my brother now? I'm just trying to keep the identities straight. Oh, wait, you can't be my brother. He wouldn't care what I was doing."

Lewis popped another cookie in his mouth, then grinned again. "I'd pay good money to watch you do dockwork, though."

All the questions I hadn't been able to ask finally began boiling out. "Where are they, Lewis? Is Grace here? Where's Robert?"

The question seemed to amuse him. "What, you think I have them hiding under my desk?"

"Just answer. For once."

"You think I'm waiting for the right moment to spring them on you?"

"Okay. I give up. Let's try, how the fuck did you get here, Lewis?"

"To this room? Why, Paul, I was elected."

"Lewis, please."

He laid the empty cookie cone on the desk and dropped his feet to the floor. "Now, see? All you had to do was ask nicely." He leaned forward, hands lifting as he warmed to the conversation, and I realized there were things he'd been eager to tell me, too. "You know, I had to get out of there. I knew Grace would take care of you."

"Yeah, well, I'm not likely to argue much about that, am I?"

"Do you want to know what I can tell you, or not?"

Twisting sideways in the chair, I made myself shut up.

"We hid out in the woods up the Back awhile," he continued.

"Both of you?"

"At first. Then I crept down to Tom Reaveley's house. He turned out to be a pretty good friend, to a whole bunch of people. Also generous. He gave me food, then told me I should light out for Columbia, South Carolina, and stay with his father. He also assured me he'd look in on you."

"He did. A couple of times."

Lewis nodded. "What he didn't tell me was that his father was a state congressman, and a force to be reckoned with in the legislature down there. I went to work in his office. Pretty soon, I was running it."

"There's a shock."

Lewis ignored me. "I did that for a while. Then he wanted me to leave his office and run the election campaign for his old-money, broken-down, ex-whiskey-running college professor, whom the party fellows, in their infinite wisdom, had selected to run for the national Senate seat that was there for the taking in the fall. So I went to work for him, and I took over *his* office. The guy didn't have a chance, so he did the best thing he could have done for the party."

"Let me guess." I meant to sound cutting and sarcastic, but it didn't come out that way. "He stepped aside and anointed you, because as a wanted ex-hobo and town thug from Oklahoma, you were clearly a much more appropriate candidate than he was."

"He did better than that," said Lewis. "He adopted me. He helped me fabricate a history. The prodigal orphan, returned from making something of myself out in the wilds of Oklahoma, home now and ready to give back to the man and the state that had given me so much. Then he died."

I shut up again.

"So the party fellows had a weekend-long shouting match on Thomas Reaveley Sr.'s colonnaded veranda, over mint julep after mint julep. I was there as Old Tom's right hand and associate, and as the late Colonel Asbury's adopted son. I worked myself right smack into the middle of the argument, quietly pointing out the Achilles heel of each new potential replacement candidate.

"The funny part is, for once, I really wasn't up to anything, Paul. At least, I wasn't up to that. It never occurred to me that the nomination discussion would veer around toward me."

"Sure."

"Not then. I figured I had at least another five years of work to put in, first. Establishing my new identity and all. But Old Tom just up and suggested it, out of nowhere. And the others, well, they suddenly stopped talking and agreed. They liked the youthful vigor angle, I think."

It wasn't hard to imagine three or four white-haired, tie-wearing South Carolina Democrats sipping drinks and mopping at their own sweat, startled into abrupt action by the magpie in their midst.

"But Lewis," I said after a while. "Really. I mean, I get that they thought you could do the job. Hell, I'm not surprised you can do the job. I just don't understand how you pulled it off. You're not an orphan, and all you made of yourself in Blackcreek was a burn victim."

"Cute," Lewis said.

"You have no education to speak of. Even less than me. This is the United States Senate. Didn't anyone check these things?"

"This is still the Depression, little brother. There are all kinds of people appearing out of nowhere and reestablishing themselves. No one's doing much checking. And who would they find in Oklahoma to check on me, anyway? And who has the resources, as your own experience as a federal employee should tell you? Anyway, Grace gave me pretty good practice in the art of reinvention."

Which meant, ironically, Bunk County had wound up serving a useful federal government purpose after all.

"The rest was hard work, plain and simple. Plus some luck. The South Carolina Democratic Party desperately needed stirring. I'm good at stirring. They needed someone new who could take the punches that the clever and rather vicious Republican gentleman I unseated tended to level at his electoral opponents. And I needed a job. So. See?"

Lewis sat back, folded his hands on his chest, and looked out the window. The sunlight felt hot on my back. We sat in silence. Eventually, he laughed. "Want to hear something strange? If Dad were here, I'm pretty sure he'd be more proud of what you've been doing than what I have, considering how he felt about government work."

As always, it was his smugness, more than anything else, that set me off. "You're not even the slightest bit worried?" I snapped.

"About what?"

"I have the ace. I can reveal who you really are to these people."

Leaning on one elbow, Lewis checked the clock on the corner of his desk before dropping his feet to the floor and standing up. "Maybe you have the ace because I want you to have it. Maybe I want to see what you'll do with it. And maybe your ace is no ace at all, Paul, since playing it won't stop anything from happening to you or Grace. It will only make whatever it is happen quicker. I want you to do me a favor."

"You're joking."

Lewis cocked his head. "I have a plan forming, Soft-Paul. I want you to write all of this down. Write it just like you're telling it today."

"But keep you out of it."

"No, keep me in it. Just be fair."

"You trust me to be fair to you? After everything you've done?"

"Well. We'll see, won't we?"

Lewis's receptionist Darlene returned, frowning.

"What?" said Lewis, coming around the desk. "What's that frown for? Don't tell me they were out, they're never out. They know to save me—"

Visibly delighted, she withdrew a fresh cone of cookies from inside her coat. "You're so much fun to tease."

Lewis chuckled and took a couple of cookies. "Take the rest home to your daughter," he said as he strolled from the office.

"Thank you, Senator," said Darlene.

"Hey," I called, trailing after him. The tremor in my voice was mostly exhaustion. "Lewis. What do you want me to do in there now?"

"Tell the truth, Paul," he said over his shoulder. "In as much excruciating, overwhelming, complicated detail as possible. I have confidence you can do it. You may just be the only one."

"Lewis, Goddamnit. Have you heard from him?"

He stopped and turned around. "What, you think maybe Scott drops in for a drink?"

"You know who I mean." For a second, I thought he was toying with me again. I enjoyed a moment's unexpected hope.

But all Lewis said was, "Actually, I was hoping you had. His aunt hasn't either, I'm afraid."

"You destroyed him," I snarled, angry tears leaping to my eyes, and for the second time that morning, Lewis flinched. The sight amazed and also encouraged me. "And you never loved Grace. Or anyone." I was whispering, but the walls caught my words and tossed them back and forth.

"I loved you both," Lewis said. "I still do."

Then he strolled towards the senators' entrance, leaving me to find my own way back to the chamber floor.

3 — November 1953, St. Louis, Missouri

I think of it now, and it makes me want to weep. Which seems ridiculous given that I experienced Bunk County—the way it must have been, during most if not all of that spring and summer—for maybe four hours, less than one complete evening. By the end of that night, when Martha Brown delivered the announcement that we'd helped her craft and Robert and Melissa made their choices and Danny made his, everything had changed. I don't think a single one of us knew how drastically, though. Not Bryant Cutter, or the Mayor, or Scott, or me, or even Grace, though I don't know how she missed it.

Maybe Lewis. Just maybe.

Even now, after all this time, I'm not sure I can explain it. Certainly, I couldn't to Senator Archibald Froad in 1938. I've been to airplane races and county fairs and ballgames and weddings and family picnics, sometimes even with people who felt like they were my family. I was at a blocks-long V.E. Day celebration in Chicago that lasted ninety-six hours, and I was awake and dancing in the streets for eighty of them. I have seen my wife's face with our newborn daughter on her breast.

At all of those occasions, I saw people who looked happier than the inhabitants of Bunk County. In fact, there were plenty of people in the Chestnut Garden that night—and, I suspect, on any of the preceding Bunk County nights— who looked unhappy, even angry. And no one felt at home there. Not even Scott, I sometimes think.

But there was an expression that alighted on every single face at least once. As though it were a living thing, a djinn loosed by all that fevered scratching of pen against paper, spinning in the wind of a thousand simultaneous wishes it could never have sorted, let alone granted. It always looked different, and yet it was instantly recognizable on each new countenance. Usually, but not always, it came just as the participant sat back in his or her chair, having just grabbed at the foolscap in the center of a table or whispered furiously to a group-mate. Sometimes it came in the middle of writing, occasionally in mid-word, as the whisperings all around swept unexpectedly through the room like a tide rolling in. But it never stayed long. It took me years to understand what that expression was, because I'm not sure I'd seen it before on anyone's face, ever. Certainly not on any group of faces. And certainly not on mine.

They looked free.

4 — July 1936, Trampleton, North Carolina

When I'd finished telling them my idea, Robert, who'd started out on the edge of his chair, prepared to shut me down and cast me out at a moment's notice, leaned back. His friend Baldwin was simply staring at me with his mouth wide open. I don't think I'd ever had a more gratifying reaction from anyone to anything I'd ever said.

"That," Robert said, "might actually be dumb enough to work."

Cordelia Johns nodded her silvery head and laughed. "It's crazy enough."

Her son nodded. "It's the kind of thing Miss Grace always likes."

"Who's Martha Brown?" asked Melissa.

It took a matter of seconds to locate her across the patio near the banquet table, towering over a huddle of white men in full evening clothes, all of them laughing. "The most successful businesswoman in the county," I said. "Right?"

"She is that," Robert murmured.

Cordelia leaned forward and grabbed some paper. "All right, let's think this through, now. Let's test this. There are definitely votes she could get."

"Like all of ours," said Baldwin, and Cordelia nodded.

"There are some reluctant others she could probably sway. A little black-mail. Maybe just the unspoken possibility of blackmail."

"I'm not even sure they'd be so reluctant," Robert said, sounding more enthusiastic, suddenly, than he had since the night he took me to hear Teddy Anklebones.

"No, no, I think you're right," said Cordelia. "She's local, after all, mighty and feared and well-respected. She's one of us. Given the choice between an interloper and a colored woman…"

Those last two words seemed to float above the tabletop. We all sat there a few seconds and watched them spin.

"Think I'll go track down Grace," Robert said.

"Think maybe you should track down Martha first?" said Cordelia, eyes twinkling, and Robert gave her a look of obvious and genuine affection.

"We need ourselves an organization," said Baldwin Shell. "The Colored Electors."

"Sounds like a model train set," Robert snapped.

"The Colored Vote," said Cordelia, then shook her head. "The Alliance. The Colored Voters' Alliance."

"You'll need flyers," Melissa said abruptly. "Lots of them." And she grabbed paper and started sketching.

We spent most of the next hour making lists. There were potential donors, likely petition signers, members of the Bunk County press. We also brainstormed last-minute promotional events. Atop that list sat a benefit concert—the first live appearance in seven years—by the legendary guitarist and suspected arsonist Timmy Funnybone. Robert rejoined us periodically, but he spent much of the time in quiet conference near the trees, first with Grace, then Martha Brown, then with both of them. Once, Grace glanced our way and caught me looking. Her grin was positively Melissa-like; it lit up her face.

Not until I left the coloreds' table to disseminate flyers and see if I could glean the tone of whispered conversations as news of our little planned coup spread through Bunk County did I realize that everyone was watching. But they weren't ruminating on our little secret, because they had no inkling of it yet. Instead, they were watching all the county's colored citizens chattering away with Melissa.

By strategy, but also by long-honed instinct, I wanted to keep news of our plan away from Lewis, give him as little warning as possible. So I started cautiously with the flyers, giving them first to the people I knew when they were either away from their tables or temporarily outside whatever discussion was happening there. I gave one to Reverend Henry, and he whistled. I gave one to Mr. Pierman, and he just stood there, staring at the paper, until I said, "After all, sir. You're from Chicago." Then he laughed and clapped me on the back.

Meanwhile, Martha Brown had returned to the patio. I watched her move from table to table. All around her, heads bent back, bodies leaned, as if she were a wind blowing through them. Her eyes never quite lowered to those of the persons in her path. Maybe it was that—along with the way she kept moving, slowing to speak at almost every table but staying at none—which made her seem so strangely removed from the proceedings. Almost like Scott. Or the Mayor, I thought, smiling to myself, and then I bumped right into Lewis.

He hadn't been looking for me either, for once. He was too busy watching Martha Brown. The expression on his face was almost pensive.

I couldn't resist. "She's pretty impressive, isn't she?" I did manage to keep any trace of taunting out of my voice. At least, I thought I had.

"Martha Brown?" said my brother. "That's one word for it." After watching a few more seconds, he shook his head. "You know, it's funny, now that you mention it. There are at least four white people in the Garden pretending to be coloreds. Or, *being* coloreds, which is how Grace would put it."

"Are you counting me?"

"Five. Sorry, Mr. Funny."

"And Melissa?"

"She's colored, too? Quite a stir she's creating, you know."

"She's only part-colored. A quadroon."

"That'll comfort 'em," Lewis said flatly. Once again, he went uncharacteristically still.

"What's your point?" I prodded.

"Huh? Oh. Only that I'm pretty certain Martha Brown is the one and only colored pretending to be white. You'd imagine it would be the other way around."

I thought about Robert's house, and everyone I'd met there. "You think so?"

"You don't?"

"Does Martha Brown—or whoever she is, really—always dress that way, do you think? In real life?"

"Real life? I know what Grace would say to that."

"What?"

"'Real life, as in where most people spend the most meaningful, memorable moments of their lives? In their dreams, in other words? Because that would be this life.'"

I grinned. He sounded exactly like her. "Okay. But you've got to admit. Whichever life you think is the real one, what she's done is kind of amazing. Seriously. A colored woman—a single colored woman, by herself—dreams up an establishment so appealing and so successful that it draws white *and* colored clientele—"

"'Establishment'?"

"I mean it, Lewis. Look at the way people treat her. She's the richest, most respected business owner in this—"

"Madam," Lewis said, and the rest of my words dried up on my tongue. When I didn't answer, he looked over, and that hateful, triumphant grin burst out on his face. "What, you didn't know, Paul? Timmy-Paul? About the busiest, most scandalous brothel in the history of our Old North State? Maybe you should drop by her place some night. There really ought to be a first time for…whichever one you currently are." He returned his gaze to the patio.

My eyes, meanwhile, flew toward Martha Brown as new and deep misgivings crawled through me. Did Robert and the Johns and Baldwin know? Of course they knew, only I had somehow managed to miss it. But then, how could they think this would work? I looked toward the lawn, where Mitchell and Cordelia and Baldwin had formed a protective hive around Melissa and Robert, both of whom were talking and gesturing animatedly. Robert pointed once in Martha Brown's direction, and Melissa shook her head, whacked the tabletop with her palm, smiled, and started writing furiously again. I wished desperately that I was over there with them. But I was reluctant simply to walk away from Lewis just yet. I wanted to know if he knew.

So I waited, and I watched. I saw Bryant Cutter chatting with the farmer—Woodcock, at least in the Garden—whose house I'd been accused of razing. The farmer's fingernails looked filthy even from across the patio, and the blisters and calluses all over his hands reminded me of snail shells. I suddenly wondered what every other waking second of that man's life was like. Probably pretty much the same as almost everyone else's in this place. The same as my father's had been.

"Interesting boy you've brought me, by the way," Lewis said. When he knew he had my attention, he nodded toward the table where Danny was huddling with Tom Reaveley and two other men I recognized from the Trampleton mill. Danny was doing most of the talking. "Eager," Lewis said. "Especially if I can arrange it so he's married to your girl."

"Leave that alone, Lewis," I said. "I mean it."

"Well, well. Hello, little hornet. Do you sting?"

Say nothing, I snarled at myself. My whole life's training had taught me this. And for once, I kept quiet.

Martha Brown had been talking to Grace, and Grace was nodding and writing down note after note. Now the two of them were smiling at each other, and Martha moved off on her high boots.

"Hmm," Lewis murmured, "I'm not sure I like that."

"What is it you think's going on?" I asked, trying hard to sound casual, and not like I wanted to stick a butter knife in his spine.

"I don't think even he knows. I don't think he's ever known. And that's really making me start to wonder."

Surprised, I followed his eyes and realized he wasn't looking at Martha but at Scott, who had returned to the shadows behind the banquet table. The great man, too, had been watching Martha and Grace. The hand that wasn't clutching the gold-colored drink was tucked into the pocket of his sport-coat.

"Scott?" I asked. "What about him?"

"I don't know," Lewis said, in an oddly ruminative new tone. "It's just strange. He's spending so much money."

"It seems like he's got plenty to burn, Lewis."

"He might. But what's he buying? It's not just the food he pays for. I've met the people he bribes to let us in here and also serve us. He makes sure everything goes off as smoothly as a society wedding. And then he never so much as takes up a pencil or says a word to almost anyone, except maybe in passing to Grace."

"Maybe he likes the company."

"He says he doesn't 'feel comfortable with a colored.' He doesn't feel comfortable with anybody, as far as I've seen. He certainly doesn't think anything useful is happening here."

"The summer's always ending," I repeated, doing my best approximation of Scott's voice. "And this is the only party—"

"I think he does it for Grace. And the thing is, Paul, I don't even think he likes her."

With that, my brother left me, weaving between tables toward his lover. He barely acknowledged respectful hellos from the people he passed, and he didn't interrupt when he got to Grace's side. He just stood behind her until she glanced around, smiling, and shooed him away.

It took me another twenty minutes of circling the patio to dispense the rest of Melissa's flyers. By the time I got back to Robert's table, everyone at it was standing, sweating as though they'd just completed a bicycle race together. I took my spot by Melissa's side. Robert and his friends were still talking.

Melissa swept at her hair, which had gone limp in the humidity. "Your plan needed fixing."

"I'll say it did. God, Robert didn't tell me—"

"So. I fixed it," Melissa said, and leaned into my arm, and I forgot to speak.

The evening was winding down. I caught sight of my brother seated at the center table beside the current Mayor. Various County residents paraded before him like lesser lords paying tithes. As always, he seemed to sense me looking, glanced toward the trees where Martha Brown was standing, and winked. I remembered what I'd meant to ask and interrupted Robert.

"Hey," I whispered. "You do know what Martha Brown does here?"

For a moment, he seemed confused. He looked at Cordelia. Then he burst out laughing. "You mean you didn't?"

"I just thought…"

"Thought what? What other means would that person have to achieve such a *unique* status here? Man, Paul, for once, I overestimated you. That's what made your whole idea so ingenious. Downright wicked."

"Wicked?"

"Well, what did you think we meant when we suggested the blackmail options? What do you think she's been doing all night since we suggested this to her?"

At that very moment, Martha was leaning over the shoulder of the farmer who'd jailed me. His filthy fingernails had gone still, and his wife's smile looked too wide. Her cheeks were blazing.

"Campaigning?" I said weakly.

Baldwin snorted, and the rest of Robert's party laughed.

"Well don't look so shame-faced about it, Paul. After all, why should a Bunk County election be any different from any other white man's election?"

I hadn't seen Grace approach, but I was relieved when she materialized over Robert's shoulder and diverted his attention.

"Well, well," she said. "This really might be something." She shot me a sidelong look. "Troublemaker."

"Does Lewis know yet?" I asked.

"I can't tell. I don't think so. He's too busy anointing himself."

Robert took her elbow and led her off to the trees. Melissa rested her head on my shoulder, and I twined my fingers through hers and held on.

By now, it was well past midnight, and most of the conversations at most of the tables had stopped. Just as a black-jacketed official from the hotel came out to confer with Scott, Grace returned to the patio and signaled the Mayor. His voice pealed over the gathering as the black-jacketed man nodded and went back inside.

"Friends." The Mayor was standing with one arm on the back of Lewis's chair and the other waving in front of him. "My dear friends."

Martha Brown slipped from the shadows of the trees and perched on the edge of a nearly empty table amid a small circle of gawking mill-hands. She aimed a single, triumphant smile toward Robert.

Robert, to my surprise, looked away as if he hadn't seen her, except that I was sure he had. Both Cordelia and her son were staring determinedly down at their hands. Only Melissa was looking back at Martha, and she was very subtly shaking her head.

"Melissa?" I whispered. "What's going on?"

"Sonja," she said. "Ssh."

"Citizens of Bunk County," Grace said. "It's been an eventful week. It's late, and all of our respectable citizens should be home abed. But I do have an announcement. If you could all be seated just a few moments longer."

Robert sat ramrod-straight, with his clean, work-scarred hands on his knees, looking for all the world like the photos I'd seen of the new Lincoln Memorial.

"As you know, we have an election next week. And with the withdrawal of Mr. Fuqua and the surging popularity of Mr. Forsberg, we appeared poised for yet another unopposed run for office. But now I am duty-bound to report that a credible rival has emerged. A significantly bankrolled and well-supported one."

I watched my brother. He'd gone as still as Robert. But unlike Robert, he was leaning back, legs crossed, one fist tucked under his chin.

"Ladies and gentlemen," Grace said, "Miss Martha Brown."

I'd been expecting the eruption ever since Lewis's revelation, but not the violence of it. "That *harlot*," shrieked a woman at a table across the patio, and Mr. Riley and a group of farmers—in Bunk County they were farmers, I have no idea who they really were—leapt to their feet, waving a black book which I immediately understood to be a Bible.

Grace let the shouts echo back and forth across the lawn until the hotel doors opened and the man in the black jacket stalked out. He made straight for Scott, who was lingering by the buffet table. Scott waved a cigarette casually at Grace. She climbed onto a chair and gestured everybody to silence. Mr. Riley grabbed the book out of the nearest farmer's hands and waved it, but the rest of his party sat back down.

"I have a question," my brother said, just as quiet settled back over the Garden.

"Mr. Forsberg." Grace gazed down neutrally.

Lewis stood. I got one sidelong glimpse of his face and got nervous all over again.

"None of us here have any doubt about Miss Brown's financial viability." Lewis paused here, his smile slow and sly, at once including and implicating the entire gathering. "After all, how could we?"

Then his voice hardened, but not too much. Mr. Forsberg wasn't offended. He was simply doing what was necessary. "However, in the interest of protecting my community, my lifelong companions, my brothers-in-arms, and my friends," and on this last, he unbuckled his arms from across his chest and opened them to all of us, "I need to ask. And I mean no disrespect to Miss Brown." He gazed at the tall woman, who offered no response. "You used the words 'significantly bankrolled,' I believe," Lewis continued. "And also, 'well-supported.' Given the circumstances, I have a right to ask. Is the source of this bankrolling public? Is this support a verifiable reflection of the people's faith? Or is there something more shady, perhaps more dubious at work? Because I have doubts, friends. I have severe doubts. And if the politics of Bunk County have been tainted by extortion or blackmail of any kind, why then, I'll—"

Martha Brown was on her feet now, starting toward my brother with a long finger raised, but before she so much as opened her mouth, Grace overrode her.

"Among a number of other groups, Miss Brown has won the unconditional and unanimous support of the newly formed CVA."

Around me, the members of my table exchanged satisfied grins. But Lewis's attention stayed riveted to Grace. So mine stayed on him.

"CVA?" he said.

"Colored Voters' Alliance."

For the first time all night, Lewis's new, more stately cadence slipped. He was seething. For real. "No. No! Not fair. No way."

"Fair?" hissed Martha Brown, and she started forward again, glancing at our table for support. I dutifully began waving my hands, expecting Robert and Baldwin and the Johns to shout out, stand with me, raise a ruckus. Instead, they sat silent, looking mostly at the trees or the grass. Except for Robert, who was watching Lewis, and Melissa, who was looking at me.

"Is there anything about you that's fair, Mr. Forsberg or whoever you are?" said Martha. "Waltzing in here. Acting like you own—"

"Give me a reason," Lewis said, still speaking only to Grace.

"Mr. Forsberg—" Grace started.

Lewis shouted her down. "I mean it. Give me one."

"I'll give you one. I'll give you ten," Martha Brown said. By now, she was right next to Lewis, finger waving like an open jackknife.

"Citizens," Grace said.

"It makes no sense," Lewis snapped, so viciously that Martha seemed to teeter on her boot-heels. She took a full step back.

"Just what about it doesn't make sense, Mr. Forsberg?" she said. But her bravado was wavering.

"Why anyone in any so-called CVA would even vote for you, let alone support or bankroll you, that's what. Think about it, Grace. I have given forty years of service to this community. I have offered specific plans to improve our three fine Negro schools. I have laid the groundwork for a yearly County Business Fair where colored and white shop owners will have the chance to spread wares together and exchange goods, ideas, even customers. I—"

"Lewis," Grace said. Even from across the patio, I could see how angry she was getting.

But Lewis was in full fighting mode. "In spite of all that, and in spite of anything in the historical record, Mr. Robert over there," and he swung as he said the name, spitting the final 'tuh' like a seed, "has seen fit to use his considerable and well-earned—hear me, I give him well-earned—influence and support to form a bogus organization to back a community cancer. A keeper of whores."

Even Riley started at that, and around the patio, murmurs broke out again, but Lewis wasn't through.

"A woman who has done not one thing to better the lives of Bunk County's numerous and valued colored citizens. A keeper of whores, I say. And a white one at that, just in case anyone's forgotten. Go ahead, CVA, whoever you are. Explain it to me."

By now, the trees themselves seemed to be buzzing. Even the bald hotel man had retreated a few steps toward the doors. Amid all the movement and heated exchanges, there were precisely two islands of calm: the dead center of the patio, where Lewis stood with his arms folded, staring up at Grace; and my own table, where I remained the only one standing.

"No?" Lewis said, at just the right moment, and the whole space burbled and then went quiet. I held my breath. So, I noticed, did Robert. "Then how about I explain it to you."

Grace was furious. "Okay. How about you do that?"

"It's very simple. Not one person who has aligned themselves with Martha Brown—least of all Mr. Robert 'Gill,' or the CVA—is playing the game. Nothing that's happening here has anything whatsoever to do with Bunk County."

"You bastard," said Martha Brown, and the room erupted again. From all corners, people were shouting, now. Really shouting. At least, it seemed real. Tom Reaveley stood up at Lewis' side and began yelling at the Bible-waving farmers, who were also back on their feet. The farmers were chanting, though I couldn't quite understand the chant. And Riley was taking slow, steady steps toward Martha Brown. Pretend-white woman or not, I realized, she might well have just risked her life speaking publicly that way to an actual white man, even an out-of-towner, and now she'd realized it. She was backing toward the trees, waving her hands in multiple directions. Baldwin and Cordelia had stood, too, though they didn't seem sure of what to do.

On her chair, Grace had dropped her hands to her sides, and she was swaying like a scarecrow in a field on fire.

"I'll say it again," Lewis shouted, and not everyone quieted this time. But we were all listening, just the same. At least Riley stopped closing in on Martha. "And I'll say it clear. The people supporting Martha Brown—especially the Colored Voters' Alliance—aren't doing so for any justifiable Bunk County reasons. They're doing it because Robert over there has decided he doesn't like me, and because Martha Brown is nothing like me, and because in real life, Martha Brown is a colored woman. Period."

That last was like a twist of a tap. All the voices in the Garden choked off at once. Robert had finally gotten out of his chair and started around our table. Melissa, to my amazement, freed her fingers from mine and followed. She put a hand on Robert's arm to restrain him.

Taking a long breath, Grace folded her right shirtsleeve high and hard above her elbow as though tightening a tourniquet. Then she exhaled, staring at Lewis.

"Can I finish now?" she said.

Instead, Martha Brown lunged forward yet again. She really did radiate a regal bearing that was equal parts skin coloration, height, and style. She was also shaking, and in tears. "Are you saying support from the coloreds' alliance is going to help me? It's going to make me win? Is that how it works in whatever Bunk County you live in?"

Riley had turned on her again, but my brother pushed him aside. "What I think is—"

But we never got to find out.

"He's right," Robert boomed, and for once even Lewis pulled up short. Gently removing Melissa's hand, he stepped fully onto the patio. His arms swung open as though he were embracing a congregation. "And so are you, Martha. You have been cruelly used for so long by so many people here.

And when I'm Mayor…" And with that, he paused, held the silence, and even Lewis dropped his arms and ducked his head, ceding the moment. "When I'm Mayor—that's right, a colored man, right here in Bunk County, where opportunity really may exist and almost anything just might be possible, at least for some—I'll do my level best to make it up to you. The CVA is hereby withdrawing its support, Martha, because you can't win. But I can. You all sleep on it, now."

He'd never stopped advancing; he was all the way across the patio. Melissa turned and gave me one last look. Then she hurried after Robert, caught up to him at the buffet tables, and the two of them strolled together right past Scott, past the bald hotel man, and out of the Garden.

Everyone broke into motion. Danny, who'd been hunkered beside Tom Reaveley at the table next to my brother's, didn't even look around or wave goodbye to anyone. He just took off through the doors after Melissa. I started in that direction, too, then had my route blocked by the citizens crowding to their feet, pushing toward the center of the patio, arguing and sometimes shoving at each other, though the ferocity—or the danger, anyway (if that had been real; I honestly wasn't sure)—seemed to have drained away.

By the time I got clear, a new tableau had formed. The Bible farmers were still shouting as they disappeared through the hotel doors, Riley among them. Scott was lounging by the banquet table, unlit cigarette in his mouth, eyes aimed over the patio at no one in particular. And off to the right, near the jailhouse tree where I'd spent the first hour of my Bunk County life, Martha Brown had dropped into a chair, shaking and sobbing. Kneeling beside her, one by either arm, were Grace and my brother. Grace was doing the talking. But Lewis was holding her hand.

What I wanted to do was launch myself through them all, out the nearest French window, and across the sea of grass in front of the Belmont so I could chase down Melissa and Robert. But even if I caught them, I'd only wind up arguing with Danny or getting pummeled by him, which would agitate or—worse—hurt Melissa. But I couldn't think what else to do.

Finally, in sheer frustration, I grabbed a chair and dropped myself into it. When I next lifted my head, Martha Brown was gone. Grace was at the center table, gathering her piles of paper as Scott drifted toward her. Lewis was still kneeling where he'd held Martha's hand.

He turned. I thought he might come over and punch me for the trouble I'd started, or stalk away, or say something devastating.

Instead, he grinned.

For the longest time, Grace kept her head down and collected her papers. Every now and then she took a pen and scratched savagely at a notepad. My brother stood up and made a grand show of straightening chairs and loosening his tie, and I realized he was hoping Grace would acknowledge him. Scott had seated himself at what had been the Mayor's table and was sipping water from a shot glass.

I was nodding dangerously close to sleep when Grace dropped her pen and turned on Lewis.

"Thank you," she said, her fists curling at her sides. Lewis stopped whatever he'd been doing. I sat up. Scott did, too. "Thank you for nearly destroying a year's work in a matter of minutes, Lewis. A year's work on something I care deeply about."

"For saving it, you mean," Lewis said.

She was less than a foot from him, now. Her shoulders were shaking. "What do you mean, saving it?"

"From you, Grace. All I did tonight was keep you from weakening your precious boundaries between *out there* and *in here*—between Buncombe County and Bunk County, those are your words, darling—so severely that no one would ever again be able to tell—"

"That poor woman," Grace choked, arms twitching against her ribs as though struggling with bound ropes. She glanced toward the chair where Martha had broken down. "My God. Do you even realize how you made her—"

"Not me."

Even more alarming than the fury radiating from Grace was the aura it had lit around my brother. Lewis wasn't shaking, and his fists weren't curled, and except for the set of his shoulders, I'd have taken his pose for one I'd seen a thousand times at Town Couch, beside the Hooverville bonfire, at the Trampleton mill. Only his lips kept working, even when he wasn't speaking, as though he couldn't catch up to his own words.

For the first time in my life, I thought my brother might actually mean everything he was saying.

"Try Paul over there. That was a typically imaginative and completely impractical idea, there, little brother. Too bad about the havoc and all."

"Leave Paul alone," Grace said icily. "Unlike you, he was just playing along. Dreaming crazily. Doing what people are supposed to do in Bunk County—"

"Or Robert," Lewis interrupted. "Smooth double-cross he pulled on poor Martha, how about you yell at him? Or Paul's little sword-swallower, what the hell is she trying to prove? They're the ones who—"

"You created the conflict, Lewis. You forced the confrontation. If you'd kept your mouth shut for one blessed minute—let Robert have his moment, let someone else carry the honors for just one Godamn night—I would have taken it all under consideration and found a solution. You know I would have. For all of us. One that kept the boundaries you say you hold so dear—"

"I said you do, Grace." He reached abruptly for her, and she swatted his hand away.

"—that kept the boundaries sound, allowed you the fair fight I'm sure you'll claim is all you wanted, and protected the real-world dignity of someone who isn't allowed to have any in the real world. That's the piece you keep forgetting isn't it? I mean, my God, that woman."

"This is only about Martha. Right?"

Grace stopped. Even in profile, her gaze was hard to hold for more than a moment.

Lewis stared right back, though. "This is only about what happened to Martha. Not what I said. Because what I said was the truth. And you know it."

After a long time, Grace nodded. "It's just…that should never happen here. Someone getting hurt like that. Humiliated like that. This is supposed to be a different kind of place, Lewis. The kind of place almost everyone who isn't you would rather be."

For the second time, my brother reached for her. This time, she let him touch her hip before shaking free.

"Grace," Lewis said, his voice modulating ever so slightly, "I'm sorry I hurt her. But I didn't put her in that position. I didn't make her play white, or accept a hopeless nomination for Mayor. So how about you and I concentrate our efforts on figuring a way to get her out of the situation. And me along with her, now that I've stuck my neck out."

Grace's renewed vehemence shook him visibly, "I know you think you've suffered, Lewis. Grew up hard. Lived rough. I know you think the world has thrown you the same punches it throws everyone else. Which just goes to show that you really don't understand anything at all. The world can't hurt you. It can't even touch you. It'll kill you one day, but it'll never reach you. Because it can't. You are not reachable. Just like me."

Amazingly, instead of fighting back, Lewis got gentler. That was when I realized the two of them really might love each other.

"You're seriously saying I haven't reached you, Grace?" There was just a momentary trace of his grin, now. "You're wrong about that."

"You're probably right," Grace snapped. "Martha Brown was never going to be Mayor. Even here. But at least here, just for a couple of hours, people like her get to define their own limits. Or redefine them. At least here, the fights people lose are fights they choose themselves."

"Wait," Lewis said, in a voice I knew much more intimately. "You actually think—really, you think this?—that Martha Brown left here shattered because she can't be Mayor? Because some pretend-farmers called her a pretend-whore in front of a few dozen pretend locals? Grace, she was crying because she got suckered. Badly. And not by me. She was crying because she let herself believe that most of the county would welcome her. And let's face it, given her situation and her choices here, that is either five year-old naïveté or jaw-dropping stupidity. She was crying because she's spent the last six months of her Bunk County life dreaming that she was better at dealing with other people than she actually is. Which is pretty much the only thing most of us who aren't you spend our time dreaming, Grace."

With every word Lewis spoke, Grace seemed to crouch deeper into herself. "Lewis. My God. If you were any better at dealing with other people, someone would have to kill you."

She wasn't joking, and neither of them smiled. But even I understood that she was asking Lewis a question.

"It's your only mistake, Grace. You think we all tell ourselves these grand tales. That our imaginings are full of better worlds and richer lives. But the only thing most of us dream about is what we wished we'd said. Or hadn't said. Or could say, just once. The real pleasure of Bunk County, and the reason real people spend their precious Saturday nights here, is that sometimes, when events fall out just right or you create the perfect opportunity, and we have enough time beforehand to think about it, we actually get to say them."

Then he took Grace's hand. Tears snuck down her cheeks. I watched in wonder. How any of us were paying enough attention to note the rain-whisper rustle of a page being turned, I'll never know. But all three of us did.

Turning, Grace looked at Scott. Her mouth fell open. "What are you doing?"

Scott glanced up from the manuscript pages he was holding. "I'm sorry," he said airily. "I was under the impression that you actually wanted someone to read this sometime."

"Sometime." Grace's voice had a quiver in it again. She wasn't angry now, though. She was scared. I'd never even imagined Grace scared. "But not you. Not yet. It's not ready."

"I can see that."

"Just…" She started forward, hands outstretched. Her voice steadied. "What, you're Mozart, I suppose? Your manuscripts come out perfectly on the first try? You never cross things out or scribble all over everything you've done."

"All the time," said Scott, in his summer's-always-ending lilt. "Every day."

Grace took the pages out of his hands.

"You're really not going to let me read it?"

"It wouldn't make sense. You wouldn't even be able to follow which sentence is supposed to go where."

"Then read it to me." He sat back in his chair, arms folded, his cryptic smile floating over his face.

For one more breath, Grace wavered. Even then, there was a stillness to her, as if she were some sunken river stone the world was rushing over, reshaping itself but never dislodging her.

"Okay," she said, and sat down with the manuscript in her lap. Immediately, Lewis came over and stood beside her.

This is the moment, for me, where the timing goes wrong, and the dam that separates what actually happened from what Grace got all of us to dream begins to crack. Lewis was Lewis from the moment he was born. That night in the Chestnut Garden, he seemed a little more polished, maybe, but he was still my brother through and through.

And Roth, the limping, whistling gadabout at the heart of Grace's novel, was the same character I'd first encountered when I stole a peek at her notebooks during our train ride east, which meant he'd been conjured months or even years before Grace ever met Lewis. And Roth's slow, ruthless, terrifyingly guileless takeover of his step-father's farm, family and fortune had no obvious echo in our lives. So Roth was no one my brother had inspired, and Lewis was no one Grace had created. And yet…

She read us the book's most famous scene, what Mencken called the American Moment, when Roth realizes just how much it's possible to take. How giving might get you love, but taking makes you matter. Grace told me later that she'd finally gotten it down that very afternoon after avoiding it for weeks and dreading it much longer. For most people, the scene reverberates because it centers on Roth's lone moment of self-revelation, which should have been devastating and winds up something else. But what always haunts me is the sister.

I think it's the fact that Roth leaves the front door wide open. At any moment, all the sister has to do is get up off her threadbare rug and walk out. The way Grace wrote it, or at least the way she read it, Roth wouldn't have stopped her, and in fact can only follow through with killing her because she lies still and lets him, having resigned herself, finally, to her fate.

My chair felt cold where my fingers clutched the edges of it. My brother kept lifting his hand to touch the back of Grace's neck and then deciding not to. He finally just sat down and listened in a sort of daze.

Scott, meanwhile, sat motionless, right up to the end of the scene, where Roth stares down into his sister's face and makes his observation about how death is really the natural state forever flooding in, and life the aberration.

When she'd finished, we all stayed quiet a long time. I was watching Grace, who was staring at the page she'd just read as though it were a telegram full of the most marvelous and terrible news.

Then Scott dropped his shot glass to the tabletop, left it there a moment, and with a nod, tipped it over as though conceding a chess game. Without so much as a glance, he stood up and strode from the garden.

*****

Most of the next day, there were thunderstorms. I slept late and came downstairs to find a cold breakfast laid on the table for me but no one else in the house. During a break in the weather, I jogged into town, but Sherman Street was all but empty. I wanted to see Melissa without Danny, so I didn't go knock at the boarding house where they lived. A cloudburst trapped me under the eaves of Riley's General Store, and I stood there missing Melissa and sorting through the kaleidoscope of the previous evening and the county Grace had made. I wondered whether there was anyone alive who didn't dream of escaping who they were and becoming someone else. Or being the same someone, but known or loved for something different than they actually were. The only person I could think of was Grace; she spent her time dreaming that everyone else was different, while she stayed the same.

By the time I got back to Robert's, drenched and bored, it was already dark again. I found him hunched on the couch with a single, tapered candle flickering in the drafts on the table before him. He looked so peaceful there, and I'd so rarely seen him that way, that I hovered for some time without entering.

When he saw me, he grunted and ran a tired, shaky hand over his head. In his other hand, I noticed, was a photograph.

"About time," he said. "I've been waiting for you."

"You have?"

"I thought you and me were going to have ourselves a chat. A trade, I think you called it."

"Now? Great. Right." I moved toward the couch to sit, but stopped when I realized he was staring at my pants, which were squelching.

"You don't really think those are going to touch my couch?"

"Your wish is my command," I said. Then I smiled. "Mr. Mayor."

Robert didn't drop his scowl. But he settled back in his lopsided cushions with a muttered "Damn right." His shadow loomed huge on the curtains behind him.

"Power's out," he said.

Rain thundered on the roof. My thoughts were still whirling with the previous night, and I couldn't even imagine what Robert was thinking. But sitting at his feet in the candlelight, I felt almost like a nephew clamoring for war stories. In the end, I just up and asked.

"Robert, what was it like?"

Right away, as though he'd been waiting, he responded. "You want to know about Screwpine. The night it burned down."

I shook my head. "I already know about that. I want to know about before."

He looked confused.

"When it was up and running, I mean. When it was going full-tilt. What was that like?"

For a while, he seemed at a loss for words. Finally, he shrugged. "It was a mill."

"Okay. Yeah, but—"

"Just a mill, Paul. That was the beauty of it. That was its magic. Punch in, same as Trampleton. Work hard, no breaks. Uppity-ass foremen breathing down your neck all day. Twenty-minute lunch breaks with the mosquitoes and wasps in the woods. Logs tumbling everywhere, sawdust flying, sweat sticking everything to you like you were walking glue. Loading up all those trains bound for all those mysterious places. Mitchellville. Anderwood. We never saw them either, you know. But we used to sing their names, preacher-and-congregation style, when the trains left. *'Mitchelll*ville. Mitchelville. *Orange*burg. Orangeburg. *Alll aboard.'"

He was gazing away over my head, and in his lap, the fingers holding the photograph had come open a little.

"You were one of those uppity-ass foremen, I presume?"

"No. See, I done told you. Some of us *like* to work."

"Uppity-ass workman, then."

"There you go." He even smiled briefly. "You know, that was probably the best thing about your typical Screwpine day. And also the worst thing."

"What?"

"The singing. You've been out to the Trampleton mill. You hear a lot of singing there?"

"None," I answered. And then, after a moment's thought, "As a matter of fact, I don't hear much singing anywhere in Trampleton. Except in Reverend Henry's church."

"That's not singing. That's honking. Bunch of penned-up summer geese."

I laughed.

"I'm not claiming we were a mill full of Teddy Anklebones or anything. But man, when we got going, that sound would get up in your rib cage like air in a balloon. Fill you out. Lift you right out of your socks."

"That must have been something."

"It was."

"I wish I'd heard it."

"Which brings us to the worst part. We always sang the same song. Always. All day, every day, for going on three years. Why did we do that?" And then he sang it. *"When my blood runs chilly and cold…"*

"I got to go," I sang, so tunelessly that he didn't realize I was accompanying him at first. I made myself slow, tried to hit the notes. *"Do, Lord. Do, Lord. Do remember me."*

Robert slapped a palm against his thigh. "See?" He sounded at once delighted and bemused. "Even now, the damn thing won't die. We used to try to chase it out. We'd start off every damn day singing anything else, as loud as we could. Didn't matter. Within a few hours, we always wound up back at *Do, Lord.*"

"Grace sang it to me. On the train, before I even knew I was coming here."

Right then, for the first time, I understood the genius of the Federal Writers' Project. I'd just saved something. Pulled a tune and a bit of real, lived life out of the oblivion to which even the people who'd been there had consigned it.

"Which brings us neatly around to your side of the bargain, Dent." All trace of wistfulness had drained from Robert's voice.

I'd been too busy mulling my Bunk County experience, and also the plans I'd just realized I was making for Melissa and me, to consider what I would say now. As much to buy time as anything else, I gestured at the photograph in his lap. "That's your sister, isn't it? That's Ruth."

Instead of showing me the picture, he looked down at it. "That's her."

"What was she like?"

"Fierce. Beautiful. Headstrong. Reckless. Looking for trouble. She found plenty."

"So she was more like your brother?"

"Well, I wouldn't quite…" Slowly, terribly, his head came up, and his gaze swung to me. He was staring at me so hard, it felt like I might ignite. The sound he eventually emitted wasn't a laugh. But it wasn't exactly angry, either.

"Who told you about Frank?"

"Who's Frank?"

"My brother, damn him."

"Oh. Grace."

"Naturally." He picked up one of the empty beer bottles from the table, blew breath across the lip, then let it fall into the pillows beside him. "Ruth was nothing like Frank. Frank isn't like Frank, either, except when he's drinking. When he's drinking, there's not a man alive who can control him. And after Screwpine… After I did what I did, Frank and I decided it might be best if we all scattered for a while."

"Where'd you go?"

"Ruth and I went to stay with my aunt."

"Mrs. Duarte."

He nodded. "But she wouldn't have Frank. So he went to Georgia. By the time we thought things were quiet enough for us to come back, our mother had died. Frank came home an even drunker fool than he'd been before. And Ruth decided it was all my fault Ma had died alone. Ruth started stepping out nights with Frank, knowing full well he'd gone over the edge. For seven years, I fed them. I bailed Frank out of jail or scooped him out of whatever ditches he drank himself into. I chased Ruth down when she stayed out too late, and I made her stay in school. But they kept sneaking out the windows, and slamming the front door in my face. In the end, I saw so little of them, I didn't even know she was gone for a couple of weeks. Got me a postcard. This was right after Frank up and vanished for good. The postcard was from Oklahoma.

"I didn't hear from her again for two years. By which time she'd had her kid. It was just that one thing too many, you know? I was still so angry at both of them. I wrote her right back and told her exactly how stupid I thought she was. And that was the last letter she sent me, until the one begging me to come West and get my nephew. Just last winter."

"And your brother? Grace said he was in prison."

"Yet another family member I'm sure she thinks I owe a visit."

Robert dropped his head into his hands. Through his fingers, he said, "I don't want to talk about Frank anymore. I want to talk about Oklahoma. I want to talk about the brothers Dent and my sister and Oklahoma."

"Why?"

"Why? *Why?* Because she's dead, Paul. Because she killed herself. Because she was all I had. All there was. And I didn't do right by her. I could have, and I didn't, and I'm never going to forgive myself for that, but I'm damn well going to know what happened after she left." Abruptly, he stood up.

"Robert," I tried, but he didn't stop.

"Because she deserved better. We all did. And I failed us. Now it's too late, and all I've got left of my family is a pathetic bastard kid who can't even look at me or know my name. And I've got to figure out some way to stand the thought of being with him, and I can't do it, because it's just a little too much to imagine looking into his face. Every time I do, I'm going to see her."

Several seconds passed before I realized he was holding out the photograph. I took it, tilted it toward the candlelight while Robert stood nearby and shuddered.

"She was prettier in person," I whispered.

"*What?*"

I got halfway to my feet before Robert shoved me down. Dropping his hands to the back of the couch on either side of me, he lowered his face to within inches of mine. But he was also tilting to his right like a tree in a gale, as though he might tip over at any second. "Start talking, Dent. Right now."

"I saw her. Once," I said fast. "One time. For maybe two minutes." Robert's face dipped closer still. "Right before I met Grace. They lived in a Hooverville. A hobo camp—a huge one—a few miles outside of Blackcreek. Where we're from."

"'They'," said Robert, staring right into my eyes. "Who is 'they'?"

Understanding finally broke over me. "No. No, not like that. Lewis was trying to help her, Robert. I think they were friends. God, she was so sad. Beautiful, and fierce, like you said. But really sad."

With a swat I first thought was meant for my face, Robert snatched the photograph out of my hands. When I dared to look up, his eyes were full of tears.

"A Hooverville," he said. "She died in a Goddamn Hooverville."

"Robert…"

Clutching the photograph to his chest, staggering some, he went straight out the front door and disappeared into the rain.

He didn't say another word to me for the rest of the week. In fact, I almost never saw him. My breakfast was always waiting at the table no matter when I came down, and he never emerged from the kitchen or the garden or wherever he'd tucked himself away until I got up and left.

On Tuesday morning, instead of working, I hitched a ride into Asheville and found the jeweler's shop that Mr. Cutter had suggested when I spotted him picking up groceries in town the previous day. It was run by a seventy-year-old man with palsied hands and his silent, hare-lipped son. I spent two hours choosing the ring and negotiating a payment plan. The next day, in the middle of a broiling afternoon, I hurried into Mr. Gene's, waited for Melissa to finish with a customer. Then I hurried her out back. She allowed me a single, distracted kiss. I saw the worry in her eyes, the circles under them, and the unaccustomed pallor of her cheeks. But I had the box half out of my pocket anyway when she said, "Paul. You need to stay away for a couple of days."

"Stay away? *Stay away*?" I was stunned stupid. I stood with her hand in one of my own that wasn't holding our engagement ring.

"Please? Please, please, please. Don't be like him."

"Like him? Like *Danny*? How the hell am I like—"

"Paul. Please just understand. He needs time. He's not stupid. He sees what's happening between us."

"Seeing isn't enough, Melissa. He has to hear it straight from you. It's the only way. You have to tell him."

"I told him," she said, and I shut up and held on as she tipped her honeyed head back against the filthy bricks and didn't cry. But only because she'd clearly cried so much already.

Settling against the wall beside her, I squeezed her hand but otherwise kept still. She didn't lean into me, but she didn't ask me to go away again. At least, not yet.

"It was that bad?" I finally asked. "Really?"

She passed a hand over her dry cheeks. The look on her face was brand new, or rather, new on her. "Yes, Paul," she said, and made to go inside. But I held her back.

"Melissa. When you first saw Bunk County, you told Danny it was just like home. What did you mean?"

"What? Paul, I have to work."

"I know. I'm sorry. I don't know why I'm asking now. But I need to know. Danny told me you were an orphan. I know it must have been grim."

"Grim?" All at once, as though peeking from behind a curtain, Melissa's smile crept over her face. "Grim? Let me tell you about Holy Hearts Afire. Where I grew up."

She returned to her perch beside me, head tilted to catch the light. "Every minute of every day, all day, we had to do spelling worksheets or clean or pray. But as soon as the dinner table was cleared and the dishes were done, we got to go to the Submarine Room. That's what we called the basement. There wasn't any electricity in the house, and the Sisters were thrifty about conserving candles and lantern oil. So we played games down there like Wishing Well.

"One of the sisters would stand on the steps and roll a single penny into the pitch black. Then we'd all get on our hands and knees and crawl around until we found it. Winner got to make a wish, which was usually to play another round. There were these three younger Sisters who were maybe five years older than most of us. Sometimes they'd act like owls and swoop down off the walls and snatch us and make us scream.

"Some nights, they let us light a candle, and we'd sing songs down there or gossip about the boys we'd seen but weren't aloud to talk to at Pittsfield Children's."

"Where Danny lived."

"Right. Half the nights I spent in that place, we never even came up out of the basement. We just tucked ourselves on these pathetic little rugs around the woodstove. I don't know where the Sisters slept, but so many times, I remember waking up and seeing one of them outlined in the light from the stove door, shoveling coal in tiny little loads to keep the clatter to a minimum so the rest of us could sleep. The Mother Superior wouldn't even let us call her that. She preferred Superior Mother."

Melissa went quiet for a while. I was quiet, too. Hers was the first genuinely happy childhood I think I'd ever heard of. Eventually, I said, "It must have been horrible to leave."

The smile never left her face, though it turned rueful. "It shouldn't have been. It was my fault. Understand, Paul, I was plenty old enough to know the nuns were right when they decided to close the place down. I knew they couldn't afford to keep us anymore. I also knew the Superior Mother would never have agreed to put us on the Orphan Train unless there were already families arranged and waiting for us at the other end. Sometimes—lots of times—I wonder how different my life would have been if I had gone. What my new family would have been like. But I just wasn't ready to leave the home I had. So I figured I'd show them.

"I waited until we were on the train platform in the drizzle, waiting for the train. And then I just slipped away. I was such a little fool. I was practically skipping when I heard them calling my name and getting panicky. I just wandered around that empty downtown for hours. I didn't know what I was going to do. I started to get really scared. I went back to Holy Hearts Afire, but no one was there. Somehow, in the end, I wound up outside Pittsfield Children's. And there was Danny, waiting for me.

"We spent that whole winter and spring begging and wandering, living mostly outside. In one hobo camp, I met a tramp who taught me to juggle. One night, Danny and I snuck in to see the Tiger Moth Man at the Circus of Flying Wonder, and later that same night, we joined it. Danny worked as a stable boy. I sold peanuts at first, then got sick of that and tried to convince them I had an act, since I was already pretty good at juggling. But they didn't even consider me until I tried it with knives.

"We'd probably still be there if the whole operation hadn't been a front for a pickpocket operation. Down in Carrboro, the police poured in and seized two giant traveling trunks worth of stolen wallets and pocket watches. The circus disbanded. Danny and I fled and somehow wound up here.

"You know, I think maybe if I'd never met Danny…but then I would never have found the Flying Wonder. And we'd never have come to Trampleton. And I wouldn't know you. Makes you dizzy to think about, doesn't it?"

Pushing off the wall, she gave me one more kiss and turned to go. "Just give it a few more days, Paul. He's hurting so badly. You have to remember. I'm all he has. I'm all he's ever had. He's been all I've had, too. For a really long time. Right up until you. Let me help him—"

"Melissa Flynn, marry me," I said.

If I'd strangled her, I couldn't have shut her down any faster. The sunlight slanted sideways across her face and honeyed the yellow in her hair. I knew, even then, that this was the way I would always see her. She was one of those people brightness shines from, and darkness stalks. Or maybe it stalks everyone, but on the shining people, you can see its shadow.

After a long, silent time, she said, "Oh, Paul." She brushed my cheeks with her fingertips. Then she went inside.

I remember almost nothing about those next lonely days, and now I can't imagine how I made the time pass. Not with work, because I couldn't think about work. Somehow, I kept to my word and stayed away from Melissa. At some point, as I was walking by Reverend Henry's church, Mr. Pierman appeared and stopped me with a raised hand.

"Mr. Dent," he said without preamble, "you might want to have a word with your friend."

I mopped the sweat out of my eyes. "What?"

"About her *associations*. People in the county are talking."

"In the county?" Comprehension came slowly. "In Bunk County?"

The bald man wiped at his own sweat and shifted his feet.

"Did I miss a meeting somewhere, Mr. Pierman?" I said, my blood beginning to boil. "Did someone slip in a Saturday when I wasn't looking? Which people are talking?"

"It's not me," he said, and walked away.

On my way home, I passed Riley's General Store and spotted a poster in the window with a sketch of some futuristic looking train and the words *A Vote for Forsberg: A Vote for Progress*. How many passersby who'd seen that poster would have any idea what it meant? The air had acquired a wavering quality, as though the whole town were melting into Grace's story. Or vice versa.

At long last, Saturday came. There'd been no guests all week at the boarding house, and Robert was gone by sunup. Even the Still Standing had stayed home. Sometime after lunch I got my notebook, though I had nothing whatsoever to write. But I wrote anyway. I'd never done that before. Nothing I jotted down made much sense. Most of it was just names. Eventually, I ripped the afternoon's pages out of my notebook and crumpled them and threw them across the porch. So many names.

Ginny.

Dad.

Dust Cow.
Lewis.
Patrol.
Grace.
Danny.
Robert.
Scott.
Melissa.
Robert.
Lewis.
Melissa.
Grace.
Lewis.
Melissa.
Lewis.

Fireflies rose from the ground, and dusk fell. Hurrying upstairs, I dressed fast, then pushed myself as fast as I could possibly go up the road out of Trampleton toward Bunk County.

By 8:00, I'd ensconced myself in the shadows of the elms at the corner of Mountain and Sourwood. Barely thirty minutes later—a good hour before the traditional start time—the first county residents started appearing in furtive groups of three or four. Almost no one was speaking as they moved warily down the lane toward the Belmont. None of them saw me, even though they were glancing all about. Lewis passed with an entourage that included Tom Reaveley and Mr. Pierman. His was the first voice I heard all night. If anything, he sounded slightly louder than usual. He was praising Myrna Loy.

Fifteen minutes later, Robert showed up alone, tie knotted at his throat, his dark suit brushed to such a sheen that it reflected the moonlight. He strolled down the lane with his hands in his pockets. The silent throng that had gathered outside the hotel turned as one to watch him. I was so busy staring after him that Melissa and Danny got several steps past me before I realized they were there.

What we needed, I realized, was a secret signal. An owl hoot. Something Melissa would notice, and Danny wouldn't.

I stepped into the lane. They didn't turn around. They were walking several feet apart, and not talking to or even looking at each other. I almost called out, but made myself wait. The French windows at the front of the hotel swung open, and the residents of Bunk County streamed silently through it.

By the time we'd all passed through the foyer, under the chandeliers and down the corridor to the Chestnut Garden, Lewis had somehow gotten hold of Danny and pulled him forward. That provided me with my opening. I caught up with Melissa just as we reached the doors that led out to the trees, grabbed her elbow, and pulled her silently away.

"Ssh," I said, and she burst into tears.

"Paul, he's—"

"Ssh."

I drew her back down the corridor, then through the first side door into another garden. This one was small and enclosed and surrounded by rose bushes. The bushes were full of bluejays. We sat on the Garden's lone bench, next to a circular stone fountain that wasn't running.

"Thank you for staying away," Melissa said. "Thank you for giving him time."

"It was hard," I told her. "I missed you."

"I missed you, too."

"Did it help?"

Folding her hands in her lap, Melissa took a long breath and watched the jays. "He sat in the street outside my house the whole night last night. The entire night. Weeping. He'd stopped screaming, and when I came out to go to work, he didn't plead or anything. He just sat there and wept."

"Melissa," I said, "he's bullying you."

Her slap landed before I could even register what was happening, let alone duck back. Then she laid her head against my chest and left it there. I didn't try holding it or even touching her hair. I just closed my eyes and breathed her in.

"I'm sorry," I said.

"You have no reason to be."

"Then here."

I took the jeweler's shop box from my shirt pocket and handed it to her. She lifted her head, took the box, and stared at it.

"It's just pewter," I said. "It's all I can afford. But if you'll have me, Melissa…"

She put the ring on her finger and left it there a moment. Then she slid it off and put it in her pocket.

"Is that a yes?" I asked.

The first, thundering *bang* sent the bluejays screaming from the rose bushes. Then came the shouting that seemed to saw straight through the hedge separating our little sanctuary from the Chestnut Garden.

"Jesus Christ, kid!" someone howled, and then Melissa was off the bench, flying through the door and down the corridor. I raced after her, and we reached the Garden simultaneously.

In the center of the patio, amid a sprawl of shattered glasses and scattered salvers, lay Danny, his face red and contorted. He wasn't actually making any sound, because Lewis was kneeling on both his arms and sitting on his chest.

"All right?" he was yelling. "Alright? She's right there." He nodded toward the doorway. "Can I let you up?"

I didn't see Danny answer, and his face didn't relax much. But he must have communicated something to Lewis, because Lewis got off him and stood up. Then he offered Danny a hand. There were hotel people everywhere, buzzing around Scott and Grace, who were standing together by the chestnut trees on the right hand edge of the patio. Grace looked either horrified or furious, probably both. Scott's face bore no expression whatsoever.

"Come on, let's get this cleaned up," Lewis said, though it wasn't clear to whom he was speaking. "We've got an election to hold." With a shove, he directed Danny into the arms of Tom Reaveley, who led him away toward a group that included Lewis's entourage and at least a few of Riley's Bible-thumping farmers. Danny glanced our way just once. He was looking at me, not Melissa, and I realized I'd mistaken his expression. That was no snarl on his face. It wasn't even hatred. It was panic, plain and simple.

"Shit, shit, shit," Melissa said, swiping angrily at the fresh tears streaming down her face. Her eyelids looked puffy, her skin drawn and waxy.

"I really am sorry," I murmured. "I never meant to put you through this. Or him either, for that matter."

My brother sauntered up. He wasn't quite grinning. That is, you'd have to know him like I did to realize he was. "Evening's barely started, and you two are the new stars of the show."

"Lewis," I began, but Melissa cut me off.

"What happened?"

"What happened? Little Lovelorn over there noticed you weren't in the Garden, that's what happened. It was like an alarm clock that just went off. Like a bee stung him. There I was informing him of my last, boldly brilliant pre-election plan, when he looked around and went flat crazy."

Melissa wasn't even bothering to wipe the tears anymore. I did it for her, cautiously, and was relieved when she let me.

"He almost killed the Mayor. The outgoing Mayor, I mean. He flipped over that table on him, then started throwing plates and food everywhere. Running around the Garden, shouting. It took four guys of us to bring him down. Until you showed up, I thought I was going to have to knock him out."

By the chestnut trees, the hotel officials seemed to be having a quiet but furious argument with Scott. He was saying little, and nodding occasionally. Eventually, he shook hands with each of them and then slipped from between them. To my amazement, he went straight over to Lewis's group, leaned over the table, and came away with Danny. The two of them disappeared into the shadows. I had no idea why that sight, as opposed to everything else that had happened in the past few minutes, unnerved me as much as it did.

In a remarkably short period of time, the patio was cleared of debris. In place of the rough circle of round tables, a single, rectangular table had been set up in the center, and Mr. Cutter and the outgoing Mayor had taken up seats behind it. Grace was standing beside them with her arms folded. Everyone else had moved to the lawn.

"Right," she said, still seething. "We are going to do this in an orderly fashion. With no further interruptions. And no further electioneering. This is now a polling place. We're going to keep quiet, citizens, and we're going to do this correctly."

Close to the hotel, where the banquet tables usually were, Danny had returned to Lewis's group. He was whispering to some of them, his head bobbing and his hands waving like Tom Sawyer at a treehouse meeting.

"Two minutes," Grace snapped, and leaned over to help Mr. Cutter and the Mayor organize ballots.

Glancing sideways, I saw Scott slipping through the Garden doors into the hotel. The impulse to follow was sudden, inexplicable, and irresistible.

"I'll be right back," I murmured to Melissa, and squeezed her hand. She squeezed me, too, and let go.

Scott wasn't in the corridor. I hurried through the empty halls toward the lobby, just in time to see him stepping through the front windows into the new, brilliant moonlight. A bellhop followed, wheeling a traveling trunk and a single leather valise on a cart. The bellhop loaded the bags into Scott's waiting car, and then Scott himself settled into it.

I charged across the lobby. Scott's car was already rolling, and he'd reached the lane before he saw me run outside and stopped. He rolled down the window, and the breeze caught the sleeves of his blousy summer shirt.

"Better get back in there," he said. His voice was different than usual, less musical but more animated. "You're going to miss the fireworks."

"Where are you going?"

He gestured toward the road, and his perfect teeth glinted in the light. "Away. To work. I've been so long away."

His hand had no cigarette in it. His smile was blinding. He started to push the accelerator down, and I grabbed hold of him through the window. "Wait. What have you done? What did you say to Danny?"

The car had already dragged me several steps before he put on the brakes. My fingers were twisted in the silky sleeves of the great man's shirt. Then he shut off the engine, brushing away my fingers as though they were bread crumbs.

"Listen, Dent," he said, in his hard, bright new voice. "You tell that woman, okay? Tell her I only went along with any of this because it amused me. Really, it astonished me. Of all the ruses people who think they're writers come up with *not* to write, this was the most elaborate. Only I was wrong. And she is an idiot. She has no idea how short the time is."

And then he was gone. And I became aware, suddenly, that there were uniformed people everywhere. Surely, there'd been personnel around during each of my previous visits, but I hardly remembered seeing them. Behind the reservation counter, two men in suits looked up, scowling either at my sweaty clothes or the commotion I'd just caused racing back and forth across the marble floor. Near the fireplace, two bellhops were dusting the chairs and the little wooden drink tables while a third was on his knees, picking lint out of the Persian rugs. On the staircase, a red-headed girl no older than fifteen was polishing the balustrade, while a much older woman in a black maid's uniform crouched on all fours to buff each marble step. It was as if a stage were being struck, all traces of the former production erased.

Racing all the way back to the Garden, I threw open the doors. This time, what halted me was the sheer expanse. Without the giant buffet table and its silver salvers, without the circular wooden tables and their candles and notepads and surrounding chairs, the Garden fell away into its own shadows like a harbor emptied of boats. The only light that wasn't moon came from the row of standing torches, which seemed to bob in the almost-dark like buoys.

I registered the twin lines of people, one on either side, both curling toward the lone table in the center of the patio manned by Mr. Cutter and the Mayor. One by one, they handed over folded squares of white paper and retreated to the grass. I saw Riley and his farmers—there were more of them, tonight, at least ten—hovering and moving around each other at the very right-hand edge of the patio. A little farther back, out on the lawn, I saw Cordelia and Mitchell Johns and Baldwin Shell and a few other coloreds I didn't know. Their eyes kept flicking toward Riley's gang.

Lewis had been lurking not far from the voting table, but he came over when he saw me.

"Better get in line, Soft-Paul. Your vote may matter."

Only then did I notice his suit: creamy white, dropping in an elegant line off his boxer's shoulders and down his chest, yellow tie with a matching yellow flower buttonholed to his perfectly creased lapel.

"Is that *Scott's*?" I stared him up and down.

He studied me right back, taking in my muddy shoes, the sweat soaking through my rumpled shirt. "Is that Robert's?"

"Funny," I said, and spotted Robert. He was close, too, maybe fifteen feet away. Unlike my brother, he was paying no attention to the lines of voters. He was watching us.

"Go on, Paul. Polls close in…" Lewis made an elaborate show of sliding back his linen sleeve so that it whispered against his skin. The watch there was brand new, too. "Less than ten minutes."

Melissa was standing near Cordelia. I was immensely relieved to see that she was smiling. When I caught her eye, she glanced quickly around the Garden, then blew me a kiss.

Meanwhile, Robert had taken several steps in our direction. "What did you do?" he hissed.

"What?" I said. "When? What are you—"

"What did you do to her?"

Whatever Robert was talking about, Lewis already understood him. His voice got quieter. More deadly. "You mean, when you were done destroying her?"

Of course he'd already intuited more from the situation—Robert closing in on the two of us, Bunk County mayoral mask pushed aside by the fury contorting his features, his hand clenched hard over his shirt-pocket—than I had.

"I'll be right back," I said to Robert, backing away. "I have a vote to cast. For you, by the way."

That held him up, momentarily, or at least seemed to remind him where we were. I nodded at him, then turned for the voting lines. I was even with the center tables, having collected a blank square of white paper from Mr. Cutter as I went by, when Grace stepped out of the trees. It was the way she walked that froze me.

In her hands, she held open the notebook where she made her notations for the weekly *Gazette*. Even as she moved—haltingly, a little crookedly, as though someone had just delivered a blow to her head—she kept her eyes directed downward, reading and rereading whatever was written there. Which only she could have written. Grace never let that notebook out of her hands.

Her hair had come down in the back, or she'd never put it up, and it stuck to her neck. She came to a stop. It was like watching the jaws of a trap quiver. She looked up.

"Polls are closed," she said.

At the center table, the Mayor and Mr. Cutter stopped collecting ballots. Everyone lurking at the edges of the patio took several steps forward, and Mr. Riley's whole gang stopped murmuring or stealing glances at Melissa and the coloreds and moved as one off the grass onto the decking. Danny appeared out of the same trees from which Grace had emerged. When he saw me, he grinned so hard that I thought he might break into a dance.

"What?" barked Robert, and instantly, lots of people were shouting.

I couldn't even make out most of the words, and I had no idea what the issue was, anyway. From what I could see, there were maybe ten citizens of the county left, including me, who hadn't cast ballots. Riley and his farmers had lurched right into the path of Cordelia, and now the farmers and coloreds were snarling and gesturing at each other. With surprising alacrity, the Mayor climbed on top of the voting table and began waving for calm. Robert, meanwhile, went straight for Grace.

"You rigged it!" he was shouting. "You couldn't stand it. Couldn't face it. None of you could."

"Robert," I said, hurrying to position myself between him and Grace. None of it made sense. How did he even know the closing would hurt him? I held up my hands, and Robert yelled over my head, ignoring me completely.

Other than me, there were only four people I could see who weren't screaming at someone: Melissa was just standing, open-mouthed, not ten feet away; Lewis was watching from over by the door with that cryptic, perpetually satisfied smile on his face; Danny was hopping back and forth from foot to foot, still grinning wildly, looking right at me; and Grace now stood motionless.

"Shut up," I heard myself say, though I hadn't meant to say anything. "Everyone shut up."

Then the Mayor was saying it, too, and Mr. Cutter was on the table beside him, banging his peg-leg off the top like a gavel and shouting more loudly than his gas-ravaged lungs should have let him. Eventually, the racket seemed to reach Robert's ears, or he realized that haranguing Grace at that moment was useless, and he did shut up. By the time the rest of them went quiet, the circle around us had drawn even tighter, so that the entire population of Bunk County stood jammed together.

Grace looked straight into my eyes and opened her mouth to speak.

"Don't," I said. "You don't have to."

I didn't really know what I was saying. I had no idea what was written in her notebook. What I did know was that Grace didn't want it to be there. "It's your story." I was speaking fast and low. "You get to decide, right? That's how it works. Until you make it official, it hasn't actually—"

"But that isn't how it works, Paul." She tilted her head back, and her sigh shook her. "All I do is make it make sense. Put it in order. I can't change it, that wouldn't be fair."

"They're your rules, Grace."

She nodded. "So not playing by them wouldn't be true to the story. Once something that's actually possible happens, all that's left for me is to hope it—"

"Why are the polls closed, Grace?" Robert's voice had gone utterly inflectionless. "There's still time. Or there was."

Grace raised her eyes to his. "Because the election is over."

"Who the hell are you, exactly, to say so? And why is that? You tell me one good reason."

"Because you're dead." With an exhausted nod of her chin, she gestured toward Danny. "He killed you."

*****

Bunk County shattered so fast it was as though a bomb had dropped on it. Even before Grace finished her sentence, someone in Riley's gang whooped, and then all of them were laughing and cheering.

Cordelia spun toward my brother and bared her astonishing teeth at him as she advanced. "Why?" she was yelling. "Why? Why bother? You really couldn't stand it, even pretending? Even for one night? It meant that much to you?" She was halfway across the patio, now, and Riley himself had moved into her path. Everyone else was still hovering, shocked, when it finally occurred to me to look at Lewis.

His arms were folded, his eyebrows raised. A calm and genuinely quizzical half-smile had settled over his face. Whatever had happened, Lewis hadn't been behind it. Cordelia was right, in a way. He wouldn't have bothered. Partly because he never would have believed he could have lost. And even if he had believed it—I only understood this for the first time right then—he still wouldn't have bothered. Winning that way just wouldn't have been satisfying enough to feed his hunger.

"Is one of you going to shut this woman up?" Riley was shouting toward the rest of the coloreds. "Is someone going to come get her? Or do I have to do it for you?"

One more time, Melissa almost saved everything, in the same way she'd almost saved so many things in her life: she laughed. It wasn't a happy sound, more of a half-sob, but it had the effect of halting everybody, just for a second. It also seemed to remind at least a few people on the patio who they were. Or who they'd imagined they were.

"Oh, God," Melissa said. "What?"

Danny finally jerked his eyes away from me. His grin slipped, and his clenched jaw slackened. All at once, there he was: a little boy bursting out of himself. A *de facto* orphan drowning in a love he could neither let go of nor manage.

"Well, Goddamn," said Mr. Cutter up on the tabletop, and he put his hand on the Mayor's shoulder. "Looks like your term might not be up quite yet, Bertram."

"Yes, sir," said the Mayor, shaking his head.

"Looks like that well-earned retirement might have to wait."

"Yes, it does."

Then Robert whirled on my brother. Just as his hand flew to his shirt pocket—way too late, when there was no hope of stopping or even slowing anything—I finally understood the separate stories they'd all constructed for themselves. And even as I opened my mouth, shouting, "Robert, no!" I realized there really was something grotesquely, desperately funny here. Because every single one of them had got it wrong.

Grace really did think Bunk County was a joke without butt, history with no bloodshed, a story that required no ending.

Scott had decided that dreaming and organizing this place could actually stop Grace from finishing her novel.

In his roiling, all-consuming panic, Danny had convinced himself that Melissa was going to say yes to me even if it meant leaving him.

And Robert genuinely believed—it must have felt so viciously good, after everything that had happened to his life and his family and everyone he'd known or loved—that Lewis had somehow caused his sister's death.

"You killed her," he hissed.

"Actually, that would be you. Brother."

"You left her. At the moment she needed you the most. On the night she gave away her son. You up and left her in that camp to die."

"You mean the Hooverville she ended up in after you chased her out of your life and away from her family?"

"It's not his fault," I tried to interrupt. "In a way, it's mine. Our father…"

Robert's roar took time to shape itself into words. "I *NEVER* would have left her."

"No. You got her to leave you. In terror. She and your soused, useless, raging rapist of an older brother. Because they knew what you'd do when you realized who the father of her baby really was. But then, you've always known, haven't you? Deep down, you've always known."

My jaw dropped. It wasn't the revelation, though. It was the quiver in Lewis's voice. The fact that he wasn't glancing around to make sure everyone was watching, me in particular. The fury boiling out of him at that moment was as genuine as Robert's and had been building almost as long.

"You knew, all right," he said. "You knew, and because you couldn't face what you knew, you never came to find her. You never told her to come home. To this day, you've never seen her son. You're not just an overheated, barking, black bastard. You're a coward."

Robert decked him.

Lewis came up bloody, coiled, and grinning. "That's right," he said.

Robert socked him again, but this time Lewis turned his shoulder into the blow and blunted it.

"Lewis, don't," I said, breaking out of the paralysis that seemed to have gripped us all as Robert reared back for another assault. My brother grabbed his hand and yanked him forward until they were forehead to forehead, inches apart.

"You ruined my sister," Robert snarled.

"I saved her," said Lewis. "I almost saved her. If she'd waited one more week…one more…I would have. And you know how? I would have come across the country and found you and dragged your sniveling, whining ass all the way to Oklahoma."

Robert doubled over as though Lewis had stuck a sword through him. He shook wildly but couldn't free his wrist from my brother's grasp. Yanking and twisting, Lewis spun Robert around so that he was holding him from behind. His mouth was right at Robert's ear.

"Ruth knew she had to run from you. But she had one weakness. She really believed, someday, that you'd finally admit to yourself what had happened and then figure out how to forgive her. Only you never did."

With a cry, Robert ripped free and whirled. Dropping his head, he drove straight into Lewis's belly, driving him savagely to the ground.

Riley's Bible farmers went insane. In seconds, they'd completely encircled the rest of the coloreds and herded them sideways off the patio onto the lawn. I saw Mitchell Johns in the center of the group, spinning helplessly around, eyes everywhere, and when the torchlight caught his gentle, scholar's face, his expression had frozen at that exact halfway point between disbelief and terror.

Grace had moved first for Lewis and Robert, and she'd actually gotten a hand on Robert's shoulder just before he'd thrown himself at my brother. When the pain from the blows that Robert kept driving into his ribs rattled him out of his momentary daze, Lewis bucked hard and somehow kicked Robert just far enough back so he could stagger to his feet. Grace saw the look on his face at the same moment I did. She recognized it, too.

"Oh, fuck you both!" she yelled. Then she was hurrying away from them and around the table, waving for me to help, screaming at the Mayor and Mr. Cutter, "Get down off there and do something!"

I have no idea who grabbed the first torch. In fact, the one I saw was already pinwheeling into the great, sweeping skirts of a chestnut tree, which swallowed it whole. For one wondrous second, the whole place seemed not to be burning but glowing. Then the branches bloomed fire.

By now, hotel personnel had poured screaming into the garden, adding to the clamor. The fire gathered itself along the easternmost edge of the patio, then rushed the hotel and hurled itself up the walls. I saw Cordelia on Riley's back as she frantically tried to drag him away from her son, and Robert's other friend Baldwin being ripped off his feet by two of the farmers. Robert and Lewis were clinched together and rolling across the one table that hadn't tipped over yet. I didn't even feel the knife go into my side. At least, not until Danny twisted it.

I went down so fast I almost knocked myself out on the edge of a tabletop. Shock paralyzed my hands, or maybe that was Danny stepping on them. A gurgling rush filled my ears, not so much obliterating the shouting and crackling and thudding all around as swelling beneath it, lifting it up, like the thundering of a waterfall as you approach it.

All I could do was lie there and look at Danny's face while everything inside me rushed for the new hole in my ribs. Unraveling spools of smoke streamed into my mouth and rose in clouds over Danny's head.

He was weeping. Staring at his hands, then at my chest. Out of the corner of my eye, between half a dozen scurrying legs, I saw the bottom of Melissa's skirt at least twenty feet away, turned in some other direction. The skirt swirled, and I thought I glimpsed an ankle under there. My vision didn't so much waver as skip, and all that sound winked out and then came back and then winked out again like a fading radio signal.

Then she was beside us, and she was screaming.

I have no idea how Robert even looked up long enough to see what had happened. But I did see Danny. And I really do think that at the moment he saw Melissa, reached a bloody hand toward her, then abruptly dropped to his knees and clutched at the handle of the knife he'd stuck in me—the last moment of his life—he was trying to help me.

I'm pretty sure Robert hit him with a chair. Whatever it was snapped Danny's head back so far on his neck that I swear I saw the tendons tear like the stem on a decapitated flower.

"Oh, Robert, no," Melissa yelled.

Danny went down backward on my legs, and all sound drained out of the world. The whole Garden—even the fire—had gone silent one last time.

In my memory, which can't be right, the flames had already penetrated the hotel. I could see them hurtling down hallways, roaring through those elegant ballrooms, leaping from hanging bougainvillea to chandelier to hanging bougainvillea to stairway banister. Everyone not in the process of threatening or fighting or shouting at somebody else was already fleeing across the lawn onto the paths that led around the Belmont and back to Mountain Road.

But somehow, the snap of Danny's neck had reverberated through the space. I couldn't possibly have heard Grace's sucking intake of breath that seemed to go on for several seconds, or Melissa's crushed, whispered, "No. Not both."

But when I dream that moment—which I still do, every single night of my life—I hear each of them.

Then comes Melissa's wail. I suspect it was actually that, and not what Robert had done to Danny, that triggered Riley's men.

Across the patio they came. They weren't shouting anymore. Smoke seemed to have infiltrated their skins, turned them gray-orange, like the rekindled embers of a blaze we'd all suckered ourselves into believing had burned itself out.

"Now look what you've done, boy," Riley said as he reached Robert. "You've done given us an excuse."

I was fighting for consciousness as Lewis stepped over me from behind. Not toward Robert, but into line beside him, facing Riley. He was still smiling, fists raised. I saw the slab of wood in Riley's hand. Watched him raise it.

And then I saw Melissa. She was just gazing down at Danny and me, with the most incomprehensible look on her face. There were tears pouring down it, pooling in the corners of an eerie, disconnected echo of her smile that looked hung on her lips like a hat on a peg, something pasted over rather than part of her. I watched her glance up at Robert and Riley just as Riley launched into his swing. How much of her decision was conscious? Obviously, I'll never know.

All I know is that she stepped between them, right into the path of the blow. I tried to scream, and the smoke in my own brain rose up and swallowed everything.

*****

I slept the better part of a week. The first time I opened my eyes, flames leapt off the white walls and flew at me. I tried to scream, got no air, panicked, and passed out again. The second time—more than a day later, so I'm told—I stayed conscious long enough for a nurse to tell me that I was at the Biltmore Hospital in Asheville, and I needed to eat. I got down two mouthfuls of water and one of transparent soup that tasted like smoke before I vomited and blanked out again. The third time, Grace was there.

I had no idea what day it was, let alone what time, but it seemed like night; there was no one else around, and most of the lights were off.

"Melissa?" was all I could say.

Grace put her hand to my mouth. From between her compressed lips came a strangled yelp. Her thin shoulders began to shake.

Then she said, "Paul," in a new, crackly version of her voice. Her eyes seemed to have sunk into their sockets, and her hair hung limp across her forehead. "Paul, Melissa's dead."

Everything disintegrated. Grace slumped to her knees beside my bed and put her head in the sheets and sobbed.

"I can't believe it," she kept saying. Along with, "What have I done?"

I couldn't sob. I couldn't even breathe. "You mean Danny," I finally managed to whisper. I had to say it again before Grace heard and made herself look up.

"Him, too," she said. "It's my fault. I didn't understand, Paul. I got it all wrong."

Struggling to sit up, I knocked the bedpan and pitcher of water off the table, and the pitcher shattered all over the floor. The room spun, and my lungs heaved. I held on. Tears exploded onto my face.

"Paul, sssh. Stop." My sudden movement had brought her back to her feet, back to herself, and now she was pushing me down onto the bed. I had the momentary, insane notion that she was going to drag a pillow over my head and suffocate me.

Then the fog in my head cleared, at least a little. Grace had stopped sobbing, too. She was standing over me. Her gaze was almost gentle, but also icy-clear.

"I think she was trying to save Robert. Which is exactly what she did."

Something inside me broke. I felt myself curl like a piece of paper burning from the edges, and I stayed balled that way for a long time. Grace didn't touch me again. She also didn't leave my side.

"The second Melissa went down, everything stopped. Everything. Riley…well, it was like someone had sucked all the bones out of him. He went completely blank. He just stood there. And God, you should have seen the rest of them. A dozen stupid, murderous men all collapsing to their knees. Robert was ready to throw himself on the whole group and start flailing away. But your brother…your freakish brother…he grabbed him and dragged him off. He looked back exactly one time, and blew me a kiss. The bastard actually blew me a kiss. And then they vanished. Both of them.

"After that, it was mostly trees burning and people running. Half the hotel burned down."

I don't know how long Grace stood there. I'm not even sure I was conscious the whole time. Her words poured into me in one liquid rush, like fluid through a needle, and I could feel them slipping down my bloodstream, working toward my brain and my heart. Once they reached there, I knew I'd never be the same. Ever.

Eventually, from the hall, I heard stirring. Then voices. Grace was leaning over me again. "I have to go, Paul. But I need you to do something for me. I need you to talk to Mother. I have to figure out how to…I mean, there isn't any way. I can't ever make this right. But she won't even talk to me."

"You haven't talked to Mother?" I croaked.

"I tried. I've kept trying, and I'll keep trying. She says she can't bear to look at me. She fired me. She says I should get the hell out so she can clean up the mess. She says I've hurt more people than I can even dream of, and of course she's right. I sent her a telegram today and told her you'd help."

With her hand on the doorknob, she turned to me one last time. She was crying again. "Tell Mother I'm sorry. Tell her I wasn't doing…I didn't mean for it to be anything, it just…"

Her knitted brows relaxed, and she leaned her forehead against the doorframe. "Get well, Paul," she said. "I'll miss you." She slipped out the door.

A few hours later—or maybe it was the next day—a policeman came. I was barely awake when he entered and stood gazing down at me. He asked if I knew the whereabouts of Robert Couvier or Lewis Dent. I shook my head, exploded into coughs, and he slapped his palm against the wall over my bed.

"Why can't I get one single person to just tell me what in blazes happened out there?" he said.

*****

Maybe a week after that, in the middle of a humid, heavy afternoon, I convinced the nurses to let me make my way to a bench in the hospital's flowering back garden. Once there, I just sat with my head thrown back, feeling the heat on my face. Birds trilled and squawked, and bees buzzed through the tired branches and over the brittle grass. No one except Tom Reaveley had been to see me in days, and I'd been too exhausted and in too much pain to speak to him. When I had thoughts, they were of Melissa.

Worse, they were of the last few minutes of her life.

I was considering returning to my bed when I heard a bustling sound from the building behind me, followed by jangling, as though some otherwise undetectable breeze had stirred the wind-chimes suspended from the hospital gutters. My bench squeaked as Henrietta Klein dropped down next to me.

Her hair had gone even wilder than the first time I'd seen it, sprouting in all directions like an untended hedge. Except for the bracelets running up both wrists, her clothes were careful, businesslike. Under her arm she held a bouquet of purple geraniums.

"You know who I am?" she said.

Although I'd met her once, for all of ten minutes, the question was rhetorical, and I didn't answer. Instead, I asked, "Are those for me?"

Mother slapped down the geraniums on the bench. "I just brought them in case I had to pretend we were friends so I could get in here and speak to you."

She meant, I'm sure, to be intimidating. She was still seething. But I was too weak, too tired, and most of all too sad to care.

"I don't know where Grace is," I told her.

"I don't care where Grace is. I hope never to know where that woman is again. But she said you would help me."

"Help you?"

"To undo at least a little of what you all have done. You realize people died, right? You realize people are dead because—"

"I realize," I said, and something in my voice stopped her. She looked at me fully for the first time since her arrival. Abruptly, she handed me the flowers.

"Look, I'm sorry. But this could affect a lot of people besides the ones who got killed. A lot of people who have nowhere else to go and nothing else to do if they lose their jobs. If Washington gets wind of this…" She stopped again, looked me up and down. "Are you all right?"

There was no answer to that question. And for the first time, I began to realize just how alone I was.

"I'll help in any way I can," I said.

"Come to Raleigh, as soon as you're able. Help me sort through every single paper Grace Lowie turned in during her tenure with the project. Help me find what's real."

"Okay."

She got up.

"Mother," I said, "Grace wanted me to tell you—"

"I don't want to hear it."

"What she did…it wasn't because of the Project. She wasn't doing it to you. Or anyone. She was doing it *for* people. Really. You should have seen it. It gave people something to think about. Other than food or money. I think it gave them—"

"I'll see you in Raleigh," she said, and started across the garden, then turned back, glaring. "You want to know what the Federal Writers' Project is, Mr. Dent? Did Grace ever tell you? I'm betting she didn't, because I'm not sure she ever knew. The Federal Writers' Project is a bunch of pathetic career do-gooders like me bribing and cajoling a government full of deeply doubtful officials into giving money to a whole bunch of writers who resent the work, and somehow from all of that producing the best picture this country will ever have of what it really looks like. Not what anyone imagines it looks like. But what it *is*."

She watched me for a few more seconds, and left.

Upon my discharge two days later, I went straight to the Asheville train station. I took the train to Raleigh and stayed in the flophouse where Grace had first ensconced me. Every morning, I went to Mother's office, and she piled stack after stack of typed pages in front of me, and I read them all. The pages overflowed with places I'd never heard of, sights I would never see: Jumpoff Mountain, and the skeleton of the unfinished and uninhabited Fleetwood Hotel; the roadside spot off US 25 where duels were held prior to the Civil War, including the one where a Major fired his pistol into the ground, only to have the ricocheting bullet wound his opponent anyway; the deep hollers of the mountain country, where hogs are killed and rails split only when the moon is right; the Buncombe Turnpike.

Very occasionally—maybe five times, in total—I found references that had been culled from the Bunk County Gazette. Even then, though, I wasn't certain whether the events in question were untrue, or just displaced. I made notes in the margins and moved on.

It took me the better part of a week to finish scouring Grace's submissions. When I brought the last of them to Mother's desk, she said, "You still don't look good, Dent," then gave me five dollars. "Okay. You're fired. Goodbye."

By evening, I was crouching in the woods across the tracks from the Raleigh train yard. I was waiting for a freight, but it was after midnight before one came. This time, though, when I slipped from the trees, no one grabbed me and threw me to the ground. And when I swung myself into the first open boxcar, there was no one inside it.

From *The WPA Guide to the Old North State, Tour 25*

"Trampleton (224.6 mi.), burned to the ground by General William Tecumseh Sherman during the Civil War, was rebuilt by a lumber company to serve several large band mills. The train station, nestled among the elms that line the town's primary thoroughfare, is remarkable for its woodwork and dollhouse filigrees."

PART FOUR

Nation

"So perhaps I am destined to return some day and find in the city new experiences that so far I have only read about. For the moment, I can only cry out that I have lost my splendid mirage. Come back, come back..."
— F. Scott Fitzgerald, "My Lost City"

November 1953, Trampleton, North Carolina

Snow flurries swirl through the gray twilight as I follow the tour directions in my battered copy of *The WPA Guide to the Old North State* and turn my Ford onto Sherman Street. The drive from my St. Louis home has been long and icy and slow. I have had plenty of time to think but have thought little. Now I let the car drift to the side of the all but empty road and look through the windshield down the little blocks that I've long imagined as the heart of my life.

The trees are gone. They were cut down not long after I left in a desperate and ultimately futile attempt to halt the rampant spread of Dutch elm disease. Then the chestnut blight wiped out the remaining trees, too. Now there are a few scraggly oaks, some evergreens, and in their shadows a handful of businesses already shuttered for the night. There's still a barbershop where Mr. Gene's used to be, but it's just called *Barbershop*, as far as I can tell.

The Methodist Church is still there, and the new, young Reverend lets me through the locked back gate into the cemetery without so much as a raised eyebrow, despite the hour. The graves are grouped roughly by decade, and the cemetery isn't large, anyway. Against the wooden back fence, along a tiny, grassy rise, I find Melissa's grave. The tombstone is gray but well-kept, maybe even recently polished. The epitaph is simple, in plain lettering:

MELISSA FLYNN 1912(?)-1936
WE LOVED HER

Kneeling beside it, I put my hands in the dirt, which is hard and cold. The inevitable tears come, but in a trickle, and only after a long time. Glancing to the right, I find Danny's grave. The tombstone is smaller, unpolished, and bears only his name. I'd feared that the sight of it would drive me wild, make me want to dig him up and drag his body over the fence and dump it somewhere else, where he could hound Melissa no more.

But she never considered it hounding. And it all seems to have happened so long ago, even longer than it was, in a place that seems as imaginary as the invented county we all dreamed up together. Our own little Brigadoon.

I'd meant to stay in some motel or boarding house as close to Sherman Street as possible, but it's fully dark by the time I leave the cemetery, and I am due in Washington, D.C., to face the second Congressional committee of my life first thing in the morning. I buy a cup of coffee at the petrol station where Danny once worked, then I get back in my car and start down the mountains toward the interstate.

I have one more stop to make before I head north, and even though it's midnight when I arrive, I get out of my car and walk straight up the little path to the squat, stone porch and knock. I'm surprised, but only because of the hour, to hear children's laughter. Mrs. Duarte herself answers the door.

Scoliosis has shrunk and twisted her. But she is barefoot, wearing a spangled green nightgown and robe, and carrying a tambourine.

"Well, well," she says after staring at my face for a long minute. "You look old."

"You don't," I tell her.

"Bent, though." I smile. "What do you want here, Mr. Dent?"

"Mrs. Duarte, I just wondered if you'd heard from Robert."

Her eyebrows rise in obvious and genuine surprise. "Robert? Why no, I haven't seen Robert since he came to pick up his nephew. Eight…nine years ago now."

"I thought his nephew lived at South Roanoke."

"South Roanoke doesn't exist anymore. The last of those kids got sent here. I wrote Robert and told him, just in case he ever wanted to visit. He showed up two days later and took his nephew with him. I haven't seen hide nor hair of either one of them since, and they haven't sent any forwarding address. They done vanished. Anything else?" Mrs. Duarte says. Her tone is as brusque as ever. But her eyes are sadder.

"You've still got my address?" I ask.

"I've got it."

"If he ever writes or calls and wants to speak to me, or anything…"

"Do you really imagine that happening, Mr. Dent?"

"I guess not."

She doesn't shut the door until I'm gone.

There is a moment, just as I cross the Virginia state line, when I find myself almost smiling as I remember my first Congressional hearing. That, too, seems almost like something I dreamed. Somehow, as that 1938 afternoon wore on and a suddenly confident Lewis led me down ever more convoluted paths of detailed, specific questioning, the Senators Froad and

Cain became first baffled, then frustrated, and finally furious. At the first adjournment, even Froad had seemed convinced that Bunk County really might be part of some massive Socialist/Negro conspiracy to undermine the government or trigger the revolution. But by the end of the day, it was all either of them could do even to remember what state we were talking about.

Froad ordered me to remain in Washington pending further questions. But the next morning, the very real radicals at the New York office of the Federal Writers' Project staged their latest sit-in, demanding loosening of censorship rules and substantially increased pay for every writer on the Project, and the attention both of the Senate and Martin Dies' House Un-American Activities Committee swung decisively toward less elusive, more celebrated targets. They forgot about us completely. And by the time those hearings were finished, the Federal Theater Project had been dismantled and the Writers' Project director dismissed, though enough funding was found from individual states to allow completion of the Guides. In 1943, in the midst of the war and the country's economic resurgence, the entire WPA quietly evaporated into history.

But now, given everything the papers are saying about Senator McCarthy, it seems unlikely that they will forget Grace Lowie this time.

Crossing the Potomac not long after dawn, I find a truck-stop diner and call the private number Lewis gave me, expecting to get his answering service. But Lewis himself picks up.

"I'll be there at nine," I tell him.

"Come early," Lewis says. "Are you here? Come right now. Meet me at the corner of fifth. We'll go in together."

I call home first. My wife puts our daughter on the line, and she gurgles and then whimpers because her blankets have come off.

"It's about to be over, Paul," my wife says.

"Yes," I tell her, because she needs that to be true more than I do. Then she sighs, and I can visualize her dark hair on the crocheted pillowcase that leaves faint crisscrosses like little drafting marks on her cheeks, and I can feel her lips against my shoulder, moving toward my mouth.

In the diner's bathroom, I wash and shave and change into my one and only suit and pull on my overcoat against the cold. The drive into the city seems to take no time at all, and I park not far from Lewis's meeting place.

Then I'm out in the November slush, and even this close to the nation's Capitol, there are only solitary walkers picking their way down the block with newspapers over their heads. Occasional cabs with their lights on burrow through the streets.

Less than a block from Lewis's rendezvous point, I pass a newspaper stand where the agent kneels in the gray, sloppy wet, cutting twine off a stack of papers. I get a glimpse of the headline and the picture beneath it. Grace Lowie's face is folded in half on the front of the morning *Post*.

With unsteady hands, I buy a paper and unfold it on the spot in the freezing rain. Grace looks older. Her hair is still red, her cheekbones if anything more pronounced. But the hardness around her mouth has set now; it's impossible to imagine the smile I sometimes remember there. By comparison, Senator McCarthy's face, in the directly adjacent photograph, looks almost cuddly with its hint of jowls and floppy ears.

Along with the schedule for the morning's hearings, the article includes comments from a Yale professor of literature about Grace's most infamous, celebrated novel. Clearly an admirer, the professor ruminates on why Grace's "limping, marauding Kansan," though almost as well known and widely taught, is never regarded with the same affection as Scott's "brooding, naive Minnesotan."

"Maybe it's that Roth isn't haunted and doesn't lose," the professor is quoted as saying. "Maybe we're still not ready for what that sort of American really looks like. Or maybe it's simply that Grace Lowie didn't die young, in the midst of her own resurrection."

Near the bottom, there is a brief paragraph noting Grace's participation in and dishonorable dismissal from the Federal Writers' Project. The Project, the article notes, most notably produced the American Guide Series, covering all 48 states and every major region as they then existed. Nevertheless, the FWP and its sister arts projects "were always among the most controversial and least-understood of WPA undertakings," organizations that in most instances "paid artists *not* to create." Even writers such as John Steinbeck questioned its worth. "Are we feeding artists or creating artistic expression?" he asked. The half-hearted riposte came from Florence Kerr, the former Assistant Administrator of the WPA: "You must admit, it was one of the higher forms of hypocrisy."

But the most amazing thing, to me, is how arcane and unfamiliar the whole thing sounds. From this side of the Second World War, standing in the rain in the capital city of the most prosperous nation on Earth, the entire enterprise already seems an obscure, largely forgotten, incomprehensible footnote in the history of a completely different country.

The rain has intensified. I start to cover my head with the paper, then tuck it into my coat instead. Before I've reached the end of the block, icy water is streaming down my face and neck into my shirt collar. By the time I spot Lewis perched smartly near a lamppost under a black umbrella with his hair combed back and his face already breaking into that calculated grin, I feel sick.

"At least tell me you didn't sell her out," I say as I approach him. Lewis is still lifting a hand out of his trenchcoat pocket to wave when he hears me and puts the hand back and smiles wider.

"Well, hello, Paul. What's it been, seven years?"

"Didn't you put her livelihood in enough danger the last time you let her name get dragged into Congressional hearings? How much capital is this trade earning you, Lewis? Is Senator McCarthy going to buy you a steak dinner after you help him crucify Grace? Or wait, let me guess, you're buying him one. Then you're going to take *his* job."

Lewis laughs outright and lowers his umbrella. The rain pours down his face, too. "Your limp looks better," he says. "It's hardly noticeable, now."

Which almost draws a nasty grin of my own. I know it rankles him that my war injury proved so much more serious than his, even if I didn't qualify for the actual army and got my wound falling off a ladder during a freak shelling barrage at my newspaper's Berlin office after the fighting was mostly over. Lewis got shot twice in the shoulder on a Normandy beach and returned home even more of a hero than when he left, the only sitting senator to vacate his seat and join the infantry. No one even bothered to oppose his reelection bid.

"You know, I really do want to thank you, Paul," he says as the great Capitol dome looms into view. "Yours was the key piece, as I knew it would be. It's why I asked you to write it all down in such detail and send it to me ahead of time. I knew sooner or later you'd give me what I needed."

It's the coolness in his voice, more than anything he says, that makes me grab him by the arm.

"Goddamn you, Lewis. Nothing I wrote down is any different than what I testified to fifteen years ago. Have you really been planning today's little witch-burning since the moment this whole Communist thing started up again?"

So artfully does he slip from my grasp that I hardly notice he's escaped. "Since the day I got myself appointed to the committee. You bet."

I take a deep breath, trying to fight back the return of every doubt I've ever had about my brother. "Why, Lewis?"

"*He'd* been planning it, Paul. Ever since the Wheeling speech. Grace was on his very first list. I've seen it. That's part of why I joined the committee in the first place."

I thought about that, then shook my head. "I still don't understand."

Lewis ducks under an awning and props himself in a doorway. Across the way, even at this hour, literally dozens of vans have packed themselves into the tiny turnaround there, and reporters and cameramen are scurrying in all directions, positioning microphones under protective tenting, scribbling on notepads, setting up miniature camps halfway up the Capitol steps.

"It was inevitable, when you think about it." Lewis sounds more cheerful than ever, though his face has taken on an uncharacteristic, pensive air.

"That you would sell her out? Who's next? Me? Not that anyone would care."

"Let's face it, Paul. That book she wrote earned her a whole world of admirers but not so many friends. Also, she attached herself, especially in her younger years, to all kinds of faintly and not so faintly pink projects like your beloved FWP. Plus, as you so thoughtfully point out on, let me see…" he makes a positively Froad-ian show of rustling around in a pants pocket now and withdrawing a little notepad. "…Yes. On page 195 of the impressively exhaustive report I knew you'd provide me, you indicate that she really did attend Party meetings. That she did meet and associate with known Communists. And then, of course, she was the lynchpin, the originator, for God's sake, of the Bunk County fiasco, which did so much damage to so many lives and helped destroy the very government project that furnished her with a living and—"

"Never mind that you were there, too," I mutter. I hate how bitter I sound, for the satisfaction it will give my brother. "Never mind that you also associated with such a threat to the very fabric of our country. Never mind that you also attended Communist meetings. She told me you did. Do you imagine she won't say so just because I stupidly kept my mouth shut when you dragged me in front of a committee? Never mind that by McCarthy logic, you're practically as implicated in all of this as—"

"Never mind?" Lewis says, and he straightens now, brushes at his shirt cuffs and settles his tie tightly at the button of his collar. "Why never mind? The information about me is in your report, too, isn't it? Also on page 195, I believe."

"But carefully excised in the version you provided Senator McCarthy."

"Now, Paul. That would have defeated the whole purpose." Lewis steps forward and throws an arm around my shoulders. Neither the bulky coat nor the suit underneath it nor the years of Washington wining and dining have softened that arm any. "Look around. Open your eyes. See what's in front of you."

"The lynch mob, you mean?"

"These hearings have dragged on for more than three years already, Paul. Three years. And with all due respect, Grace's considerable notoriety is based on one thirteen-year-old novel, not on anything she's written or done or said since. Do you really think all these people are here for her?"

The realization doesn't land, not right away. Not even when I note the still-familiar fighting smile on my brother's face.

"You gave him the whole thing," I say.

"At 7:45 last night. Just as he stood up from our strategy session to head home for the evening."

When Lewis removes his arm from my neck, I think I might just slide down in the slush.

"But he'll know I'm talking about you."

"I marked the pages for him, just to make sure."

"Lewis. Why would you pick this fight? You can't win it."

"I don't want to." He shrugs. "But someone has to. Mr. McCarthy has gone quite far enough, don't you think? It's far past time."

"Time for what?"

"The Committee is a black spot. Always has been. And I, my dear Paul, am a very popular senator."

"You'll go to jail."

"I will resign—in front of the full press corps, with McCarthy raising his fist and your report in triumph behind me—and I will vanish from public life. That is the deal I brokered last night. I had to hint at naming people to buy myself a little time. But Mr. McCarthy won't have that time."

Despite his typical bravado, his lips have tightened. In our entire lives, I think this may be the first time I've seen Lewis nervous. The rain streams down his face, barely mussing his hair and leaving only artful droplets on the shoulders of his coat.

"You're going to try and bring them down. For what? For the country? You don't care about the country."

"I went to war for it, didn't I?"

"You're doing it for Grace."

Lewis laughs. It may be the easiest, most genuine-sounding laugh I've ever heard from him.

"You're not doing it for her?"

Straightening his perfectly straight tie once more, Lewis pats me on the arm, steps to the corner, and glances back.

"Maybe I'm doing it for you."

I'm just staring now. He laughs again.

"What are you talking about, Lewis?"

He waves a senatorial hand in the air. "I finally got you to write the whole thing down, didn't I? You really should have done that a long time ago."

The moment he reaches the opposite side of the street, the crowd at the base of the Capitol seems to turn like a single, giant bird. The reporters swoop down, bulbs flashing, voices squawking. Lewis strides straight through them. They hop from his path, sweep back over it in his wake.

And I find myself plunged, yet again, into the maelstrom of feelings I have always had about my brother: disgust not so much at his ruthlessness as at the arbitrary way he wields it; fury at his ability to manipulate virtually everyone he meets; amazement at his dispassion; admiration for his savvy and his strength; longing, because there was never any chance of befriending or even really knowing my father, but sometimes—just occasionally—there really might have been a chance with Lewis.

He has reached the first bank of microphones now, and he turns around. I can't hear what he's saying, but his head is up, shoulders squared, hands gesturing as he orchestrates his own downfall. Behind him, Senator McCarthy himself has appeared in a dark coat, looking every bit the hangman. But for once, no one seems to be paying much attention to him.

Why have I always assumed the worst of my brother? Maybe because I am his brother, have seen the worst, and know it's there.

But right now, the reporters who came to tar and feather him have gone so respectful and orderly that they're actually raising their hands and waiting to be called upon.

My gaze wanders away, and that's when I spot Grace. She has just emerged from a cab, and she's staring up at the teeming crowd of reporters and congressmen. I can tell it's her by the set of her thin shoulders, and I start to call out, take a step in her direction, and then stop on the curb.

There really was something in the way we talked to each other back then.

When we were a nation of dreamers, not a dream of a nation. When the idea of a permanent, private home was barely conceivable, let alone affordable. When even the country's leaders were so unsure of who and what America was that they dispatched an army of reluctant artists and writers and folklorists to identify characteristics that distinguished each individual place within it, even as a different arm of the same Project began orchestrating the highway system that obliterated most of those distinctions and more than a few of those places.

Grace is riveted by Lewis now. She has taken a notebook from her coat pocket. She has always known what I have sorted out only today: that Lewis manages to take care of and uplift a startlingly wide circle of people on his way to taking care of Lewis. Of course, broad as it is, the circle is never broad enough. There is no room in the country my brother has helped create for the sullen or the dispossessed or the disappointed or the weak. No P.D.s allowed. No Lamplighters. No Danny.

How, amid all that tumult and chaos, does Grace notice me? It's her nature. She just does. She lifts a hand. I immediately do the same.

Then, as though drawn by something in the air or the earth, she turns away. And I stay where I am, doing what she taught me—what my body and brain were apparently issued to do, what my brother always wanted: I watch.

THE END